I0778771

The Lost Inca Gold

AI Meets Space Archaeology

by

William R Wood Jr

Mainiac Press

Published by Mainiac Press (www.MainiacPress.com).

ISBN: 979-8-9907011-0-6

First edition
Printed in the United States of America

Cover design by Hampton Lamoureux.

For Bunkie

Acknowledgements

I first want to thank my wife, who helped me push through the Brownian motion, leading me subtly, and often not-so-subtly, in a forward direction. None of this would have been possible without her support.

Bill, my son, put his MFA to good use by providing valuable feedback early on.

Mary Pryblo also provided much appreciated encouragement, including introducing me to Vijayanta Jain, who helped verify the components of artificial intelligence.

Others who helped shape the manuscript included Joe and Lynda, Mike, Doug and Ferolyn, Ann, and Hans, all original members of the crew.

Bill Gartley was my actual math teacher in high school and is the real deal. His lessons from years ago kept me grounded while allowing me to dream.

My editor, Stephanie Harp, worked tirelessly and patiently, and made me a better writer. Any lingering errors, however, are solely my responsibility.

It was a pleasure working with Hampton Lamoureux on the cover design. He understood and articulated my vision.

Finally, the concept of this novel rests upon the groundbreaking work of two true pioneers in their fields of endeavors.

Dr. Sarah Parcak, who won the 2016 TED Prize award, has brought Space Archaeology into the mainstream with her GlobalXplorer project searching the mountains of Peru. She is currently a tenured professor and the founding director of the Laboratory for Global Observation at the University of Alabama at Birmingham.

Dr. Ved Chirayath is a research scientist who developed FluidCam, a unique combination of camera and software to peer up to ten meters underwater. He is the inaugural director of the Aircraft Center for Earth Studies (ACES) at the University of Miami's Rosenstiel School.

Thank you all.

www.TheLostIncaGold.com

You will find more about the Incas, space archaeology, Dr. Sarah Parcak, FluidCam, and Dr. Ved Chirayath, along with full-color maps of the lakes in Maine and the Llanganatis at www.TheLostIncaGold.com. They are there for those who want to learn more about the background technology or who may want to mount their own expedition into the Llanganatis.

Powell's radio voice was tense in Donovan's ear: "Now, look, let's start with the three fundamental Rules of Robotics — the three rules that are built most deeply into a robot's positronic brain." In the darkness, his gloved fingers ticked off each point.

"We have: One, a robot may not injure a human being under any conditions — and, as a corollary, must not permit a human being to be injured because of inaction on his part."

"Right!"

"Two," continued Powell, "a robot must follow all orders given by qualified human beings as long as they do not conflict with Rule 1."

"Right!"

"Three: a robot must protect his own existence, as long as that does not conflict with Rules 1 and 2."

"Right! Now where are we?"

From Runaround by Isaac Asimov © 1945

Table of Contents

The Legend

About five hundred years ago, the Incas hid hundreds of millions of dollars of gold and silver from the invading Spanish conquistadors in the Llanganatis, a remote mountain chain in Ecuador. Gold and silver had no intrinsic monetary value to the Incas. Rather, the precious metals were a tangible way to worship their gods, the sun and the moon.

The Incas, the largest pre-Colombian civilization in South America, amassed this fortune in only one hundred years, expanding an empire along the Andes with over ten million people, spanning one thousand miles including portions of modern-day Colombia, Ecuador, Peru, Bolivia, Chile, and Argentina.

Yet everything collapsed when the Spanish arrived in 1532.

The Inca empire was notable for its architecture. Machu Picchu, discovered on a mountaintop in 1911, is a stunning example. Their ability to work with gold and silver was equally remarkable, although they did not have a practical knowledge of advanced metallurgy.

The Incas also lacked a written language. Everything we know is through the prism of the Spanish, typically the religious. The Incas, however, kept meticulous records with *quipu*, a complex counting device of colored ropes and knots, but few quipus have survived, and scholars still struggle to interpret their meaning.

Historians debate the cause of the abrupt collapse of the Incas when Francisco Pizarro, the leader of the Spanish conquistadors, arrived in Cajamarca, Ecuador. Many believe the Inca defeat was the combination of a civil war between two brothers battling to assume leadership of the empire, the scourge of smallpox brought to the New World by the Spanish that decimated the Inca population, and the superior weaponry of the Spanish. Other scholars suggest "defeat" is a misnomer. They suggest the Inca commoner may have viewed the Spanish as liberators from the Inca empire cobbled together by vanquished tribes.

Despite no written language, one story has persisted— the legend of the lost Inca gold hidden in the Llanganatis. In 1532, Francisco Pizarro captured Atahualpa, the Inca King in Cajamarca. Atahualpa, understanding the Spanish obsession with gold and silver, offered Pizarro a ransom of the precious metals for his freedom. Atahualpa promised to fill one room with gold and two other rooms with silver. Pizarro accepted the deal.

In late 1532, the gold and silver trickled into Cajamarca. But Pizarro, becoming increasingly impatient with the slow flow of the precious metals and concerned the Inca were planning an attack, executed the Inca King the following summer in 1533.

At the time of the execution, General Rumiñahui, a half-brother of Atahualpa, along with 40,000 Inca soldiers were en route to Cajamarca with the rest of the ransom. Upon hearing of the execution of their King, General Rumiñahui turned his troops back into the Llanganatis, where, according to legend, he hid the rest of the ransom in the mountains. Today, the Llanganatis is a national park. Yet it remains one of the most remote regions in the world, with much of the eastern park still unmapped.

Over the last five hundred years, many have searched for the gold. Some have perished, but no one has found it. There have been clues, maps, guides, expeditions, and books written about the treasure. A few have claimed to have found a portion of the gold, which has only intensified the search for the rest.

The story is now a cliché. We already know the outcome before the adventure even begins. The only mystery is how badly it will end.

It is the way of the Llanganatis.

Perhaps the time has come for a new ending, a new outcome.

This is the story of how a Middle Eastern arms dealer dupes an unlikely trio of a dealer in Inca antiquities, a gifted undergraduate, and an archaeology professor to virtually search with artificial intelligence and state-of-the-art satellite imagery for the lost Inca gold.

But remember, those on the cutting edge, bleed.

The Tutor

Thursday, October 11, 2018
Computer Lab
The University of Maine
Orono, Maine

Tom was passing time in the computer lab, waiting for yet another student who needed his help. He was already tutoring about a dozen students who had panicked at this point in the semester, realizing they were in over their heads.

He was a senior in the Honors College with dual majors in anthropology and computer science, tutoring in both. Most thought it an odd combination, but he had a singular purpose in choosing these two.

Tutoring was decent money, and he was good at it. But the students he tutored were often failing, just going through the motions, not putting in the effort. He got little satisfaction helping a laggard elevate their grade to a C, but he needed the money.

Tonight, he was meeting a new student who needed some help with COS 140 - Foundations of Computer Science, a popular course for computer science majors.

The computer lab was in the basement of the Memorial Union, a sprawling building in the middle of campus. At night, the open room with five long wooden tables, each with a complement of four computers, was usually empty. The blurry-eyed students had shut down the computers hours ago. Without the constant whirling of cooling fans and hard drives, the lab was quiet, and he often studied or tutored here.

But tonight, he was reading a book for fun, *Valverde's Gold*, about the search for the lost Inca gold in the mountains of the Llanganatis in Ecuador. Tom always enjoyed a treasure hunt ever since he was a kid. Maine had plenty of stories about pirates like Captain Kidd or Blackbeard, but nothing matched the legend of the lost Inca gold.

Tom was deep in the Llanganatis when the lab door opened. Her soft footsteps gradually brought him back.

As she approached, her blond hair swayed. She wore a light green blouse and jeans. He stood up and looked down to meet her blue eyes. Even in the harsh overhead LED light, she had a softness. He wished he'd taken a few minutes to comb his hair and wear a clean T-shirt and maybe real pants instead of cargo shorts.

As she extended her right hand, his throat tightened. What was her name? His mind was blank. He couldn't remember her name.

"I'm Jenny, Jenny Kellogg. Are you Tom Kirkpatrick?"

Tom extended his right hand. With his left hand, he swept back his light brown hair, catching his fingers in a knot. He needed a haircut.

Clearing his throat, "Ayuh, I mean yes. Nice to meet you, Jenny."

Tom just stared. She released his hand.

"Nice T-shirt. I was thinking of joining Sub-5. Do you run a lot?" asked Jenny. Sub-5 was a local running club.

"Yeah, but not too many races anymore."

"I like running too. Thanks for helping me out. I'm a little overwhelmed. The course description said no prerequisites or mathematical skills, and now it's too late for add-drop. Dr. Wade recommended you. He said you were the best, so here I am."

His mouth was dry. Swallowing didn't help. Was the slight tremor from too much coffee? He cleared his throat again.

"Okay—no problem—ah, let's get to work. Is there something in particular you want to work on? Dr. Wade didn't give me a lot of direction."

"Well, I'm struggling with what he covered this week. How about we start there?" she said, pulling her shoulders back to slide off her backpack.

He closed his book and scuffed-up laptop and stuffed them into his backpack. He led her to a smaller room off the front of the computer lab. The ten-by-twelve foot room had a large, worn oak table at the far end by a whiteboard. Centered on the table was a well-used desktop computer and keyboard with one monitor and another monitor askew, which Tom used to watch the student work.

Tonight, however, he pulled his heavy oak chair, screeching across the linoleum, to just behind her. He booted the computer as she settled in front of the keyboard.

Her shoulder length hair smelled fresh.

She also seemed a little uneasy, which oddly helped him relax, unless it was because he was too close. He backed off a bit while the Acer did its BIOS check.

"Okay," said Tom, as the home screen flickered on. "This week was the introduction to higher-level programming languages. Let's start there."

He often found these tutoring gigs hopeless, but after a few minutes, he realized Jenny understood most of the core principles. She was not one of his typical tutoring students.

At the end of the hour, Jenny pushed her chair back from the table, just missing Tom's knee. "That was helpful, Tom. Thanks for getting me back on track."

Oh no, thought Tom, is this just a one-off?

"Does this time work for you next week?" she asked.

Tom cleared his throat. "Yeah, this is probably the best time to meet."

Jenny stood up and slipped on her backpack. His throat tightened again. He put his hands on his knees to hide his tremor. He had never done anything like this before with the dozens of students he'd tutored.

As he stood up and hoisted his backpack, he said, "I know it's getting late, but do you want to grab a bite at the Bear's Den?" The popular café was one floor up from the Computer Lab.

"How about a rain check? I have a quiz every Friday in my English class, and I haven't cracked the book yet." As Jenny got up, she simply said, "Same time next week?"

"Sounds good. Oh, we should exchange phone numbers in case one of us needs to reschedule," suggested Tom. "What's your number and I'll text you my contact info?"

∽∾∾

It was about a five-minute drive back to the "Pizza Palace" in downtown Orono, the apartment Tom shared with Dave, who had just finished his shift downstairs at Pat's Pizza. Dave was stretched out on the small, tattered couch, still wearing his white apron dabbed with red sauce. Although Pat's was a full-service restaurant, Dave spent most of his time making and baking pizzas.

Dave had been Tom's roommate since they had started college, first in Gannett Hall and then at the Pizza Palace. Dave was already working at Pat's Pizza when the Pizza Palace upstairs became vacant before their sophomore year. They'd been in the apartment ever since.

"Hey, how did it go?" Dave asked without looking up from his book.

Tom usually just grunted. But not this time. "Great."

His roommate looked up. "What did she look like?"

Tom smiled as he remembered the scent of her hair. And what else he remembered, he did not want to share.

"Nice."

"Nice? What's that?"

"She was blond with shoulder-length hair, a little shorter than me, and she likes to run. I've never tutored anyone who picked up material so quickly."

"Blond, tall, skinny, nice, whatever that means, and probably a nerd. She sounds like a real gestalt and is perfect for you."

He wasn't sure what gestalt meant, but Dave said it with a knowing nod, so Tom agreed.

~∞~

When Jenny entered her dorm room in Somerset Hall, her roommate, Robin, was lying on her bed, tapping away on her iPhone. She lifted herself up on her elbows. "How did it go? Are you any smarter now?"

"Yeah. It went really well."

"Was he a nerd?"

"He was smart and nice. And he likes to run, too."

"So, he was a nerd."

"Yeah, a really nice nerd. I felt really comfortable with him. He wasn't what I was expecting."

~∞~

Wednesday, October 17, 2018
Orono, Maine

The next Wednesday, Tom sent Jenny a quick text message. He hoped if they met earlier, maybe this would give them a few minutes at the Bear's Den after tutoring.

< Hey Jenny. Tom here. Any chance we could meet at 7 instead of 8 tomorrow? >

< Sure. See you then. >

The Arab

123 REPORTED DEAD, 550 INJURED AS ISRAELIS BOMB P.L.O. TARGETS IN BEIRUT AND SOUTH LEBANON

New York Times - Saturday, July 18,1981 - Front Page

Friday, July 17, 1981
Beirut, Lebanon

He spent hours swinging on the rusty play set in a scruffy neighborhood park near his gray apartment building. Swinging cooled him off. When he leaned way back and touched the clouds with his toes, the swing squeaked. Only a few of his friends dared to swing high enough to hear it squeak.

Today, he was alone on the play set. Most of his friends had left the city with their families, worried about the escalating Israeli attacks on Beirut.

He saw it before he heard it. A bright light silhouetted his apartment building, followed by a blast that almost shook him from the swing. Then the heat and sand hit his face. Staggering off the swing, shielding his eyes, he watched his home slowly wrench to the ground.

He ran away, but no matter how fast he ran, he could not shake off the fine gray dust that covered him from head to toe.

He ran until he heard the siren from a fire truck careening down Rue Baghdadi.

Then he turned and ran back, following the siren.

Omar Al Tajir was twelve years old when the Israeli airstrike killed his parents in the Fakehani neighborhood in Beirut.

His uncle arrived the next day and took him away to his vineyard in Zahlé.

He still cannot remember the twenty-four hours until his uncle arrived, as he searched the rubble for his parents, squeezing into places only big enough for a child. All he remembers is how alone he felt, a feeling he would never truly escape for the rest of his life.

Years later, his uncle told him he'd found a few survivors in the rubble, but not a trace of his parents. He does not remember. He wonders if it was true.

☙❧

Despite the constant turmoil while growing up in Lebanon, Omar did well in school and returned to Beirut to attend the American University. He graduated with a degree in business administration and a minor in archaeology, planning to enter the antiquities business.

His junior year was his most formative year, studying archaeology at Birzeit University in Palestine, as part of an exchange program with the American University. At Birzeit, he experienced firsthand the impact of Israeli policies on Palestinians.

During his year there, he met another student, Yahya Ayyash, whom Hamas would later nickname the "Engineer" for his skills making bombs out of ordinary household items. Ayyash was brilliant and passionate, sometimes a troublesome combination. In spite of their different backgrounds, they shared an interest in archaeology, and the young Omar admired Ayyash's dedication to Palestine. He wished he felt this passionate about something—anything.

Ayyash introduced Omar to Hamas. Soon thereafter, Ayyash asked him to help smuggle essentials like medicines and other necessities into Palestine. With Omar's travel visa, smuggling was much easier for him than for a Palestinian. Although risky, it was an easy decision for Omar. It was only years later that Omar appreciated Ayyash had essentially recruited him to Hamas.

Ayyash also introduced him to the underbelly of Middle Eastern antiquities, from looting to buying to selling.

After graduation, Omar traveled throughout the Middle East networking and building his burgeoning antiquities business. There was a relative glut of undocumented treasures that were difficult to move. He took advantage of this opportunity with his talent for fabricating documentation and provenances. With his comfort in skirting the law, his business and connections expanded throughout the Middle East.

July 1993
Abu Dhabi, United Arab Emirates

Omar was twenty-four when another Israeli bomb killed his uncle who was visiting a refugee camp during the Seven Day War in late July 1993. Omar was living in Abu Dhabi by then, partly to escape the chaos, and partly for his business.

After he lost his uncle, he became more involved in supporting Hamas.

Omar learned to insulate himself with intermediaries. While he procured the weapons, his agents made the actual deliveries. This model would also serve him well in his antiquities business.

Hamas was also a supplier of antiquities. They would acquire the artifacts and then sell them on the black market, which is where Omar typically transacted business. Hamas would then use this revenue to buy arms from him. The circle of life.

Even though they were codependent, Omar carefully used different intermediaries to keep his arms and antiquities dealings separate.

✌

Hamas slowly changed their tactics and became more political. In 2006, they won a majority of the seats in a legislative election in Palestine. For Omar, this meant more foreign aid flowing into Hamas, which meant more money for Hamas to buy more weapons from him.

By then, Omar was an established dealer in Middle Eastern antiquities to the world market. He had amassed a huge inventory. Anyone looking to buy a significant volume would deal either directly or indirectly with him.

His arms trading was also thriving. He ultimately became a major wholesaler of arms and weapons to Hamas. He was also the middleman for various other countries in the region. Unlike many of his contemporaries, Omar preferred anonymity. For that reason, nation-states supplying weapons to the Middle East preferred to collaborate with him.

Omar fully understood the impact of his actions. He slept well at night.

✌

July 2018
Abu Dhabi, United Arab Emirates

Omar was now forty-nine years old. He had remained single and obsessively focused on his work as an established supplier of both black-market arms in the Middle East, and Middle Eastern antiquities to the world. He led a comfortable, albeit solitary, life in Abu Dhabi.

Last week, however, he received a disturbing phone call from an associate at the United Arab Emirates embassy in Washington, D.C., who told him the American government was aware of his involvement in the Hobby Lobby scandal, and they had uncovered other "information of interest," a euphemism for his arms trading.

Most of his acquaintances knew he was a collector of Middle Eastern antiquities. Many realized he also traded antiquities on the world market. Only a few knew he financed looting the ancient sites. None of them were aware of his arms dealings.

Omar operated on anonymity. He could not have anyone prying into his other dealings. He knew he needed to leave the Middle East.

ॐॐ

September 2018
Abu Dhabi, United Arab Emirates

Two months later, as he sealed a packing container, he reflected upon his move to Colombia. The Hobby Lobby scandal started about eight years earlier when U.S. Customs seized cartons of artifacts from the Middle East bought by Steve Green, the CEO of Hobby Lobby, destined for his Museum of the Bible.

Omar's problems began in 2017 when the Justice Department filed a formal indictment involving Hobby Lobby for smuggling illegal artifacts into the United States.

The indictment named four dealers, three in Israel and one in the United Arab Emirates. Although he was not the actual "UAE Dealer" listed, Omar had likely supplied some of the stolen antiquities to that UAE Dealer. It was only a matter of time before Homeland Security would uncover his involvement.

The story for Omar, however, went back even further to the March 2003 invasion of Iraq by the Coalition forces led by the U.S. looking for weapons of mass destruction. During the ensuing chaos, Omar had looted the Iraq Museum and then warehoused many of the antiquities. Some of these artifacts were likely included in the sale to Hobby Lobby.

Ultimately, the Green family would work out a deal where the company returned $1,600,000 worth of artifacts to Iraq and agreed to a fine of another $3,000,000.

As he oversaw the packing of the last boxes of his abrupt move to Colombia, he made sure each item had a proper provenance and proof of ownership, even if they were fraudulent. Although he was bypassing the United States, he did not want any troubles entering Colombia.

His empty home was now cavernous. He would miss Abu Dhabi, but he was always a loner and ready for a change.

After looking at several countries, Colombia emerged as his best option, as it already had strained relations with the United States, and offered enough stability for him to live comfortably. He wanted a country where he could enjoy his wealth, but still be at arms-length from the United States. He also needed a warm climate—and a new adventure.

The Bear's Den

Thursday, October 18, 2018
Computer Lab
The University of Maine
Orono, Maine

Tom had been waiting all week for tonight. He was more presentable with a light blue short-sleeved shirt, and he had combed his hair, which was getting long, but nothing to be done about it now. Although the session wasn't until seven o'clock, Tom left the Pizza Palace early to grab a quick bite at the Bear's Den and then hang out at the Computer Lab. He wanted to finish *Valverde's Gold.*

Jenny arrived a few minutes early. As they settled in front of the monitor, Tom noticed the fresh smell again as he nudged closer to her.

She was a quick learner, easily grasping the material, and the hour sailed by.

As he hoisted his backpack, he cleared his throat and asked again, "I know you have a quiz tomorrow, but do you want to grab a bite at the Bear's Den?"

"Sure. I do have a big day tomorrow, so I can only stay for a bit."

His plan to meet an hour earlier had worked. It was a quick walk up the stairs to the Bear's Den. He fought the urge to take two steps at a time.

The Bear's Den was a popular meeting place, especially in the evening. Most of the Memorial Union had been renovated at one point or another, but the Bear's Den kept a 1950s vibe, with chrome Formica tables and red aluminum chairs. It had the same linoleum as the computer lab, which made the room even louder when filled with students. It was a wide, open area with dozens of large circular tables and smaller square tables lining the walls. Tom preferred the square tables, and he had one favorite on the back wall.

He grabbed a small coffee and Jenny a Diet Coke. They split a bear claw, which was usually a little chewy this time of day, but still good.

Tom pointed to his table near the back. Jenny said hi to a group of girls on the way to the table.

As they sat down, he used the line he'd been practicing for days. "Dr. Wade mentioned you were in the Honors College?"

"Yep. I haven't declared a major yet, but I'm leaning toward English."

"Really. I assumed you were a computer science major. Nobody else usually takes this course."

"Yeah, I figured that out too late to drop it. Thanks again for saving me."

She didn't have a Maine accent.

"Where are you from?" he asked.

"Amherst, a small town in the middle of Vermont, but I've lived all over the world growing up. My dad was a physician in the Foreign Service, so we moved every three to five years, like in the military. Before Vermont, we lived in Washington, D.C., and before that in Colombia. I was actually born in Hong Kong."

She continued, "My mom is a nurse. My parents met in New Hampshire at Dartmouth where my dad was an intern, and she was in nursing school. My mom is from Vermont, close to where we live now. Her Vermont roots are partly why we moved back to Amherst when my dad retired about six years ago."

"I've never been to Vermont. Why did you pick the University of Maine?"

"I want to marry a lobsterman."

"Well, I grew up in Limerock, the lobster capital of the world—I'm not sure that's a good ide..."

Tom stopped as Jenny smiled. He cleared his throat. "Orono is about two hours from the closest lobsterman."

"Yeah, well, I didn't have a map in front of me when I applied." He noticed her left eye twinkled when she smiled. "But I love the outdoors and Maine has lots of it. Maine was a perfect fit, but my parents were a little surprised. My dad always wanted me to go to Yale, his alma mater, and my mom suggested either Dartmouth or Middlebury to be closer to home. It took a while to convince them, but when they learned more about the Honors College, they were on board."

Tom suspected Jenny was well-to-do. Most out-of-state kids were.

After a chewy bite of bear claw, Jenny said, "Dr. Wade mentioned you were also in the Honors College. How do you like it?"

"It's been great. A good advisor is the key. Dr. Wade is mine."

"Yeah, he seems like a good professor. Do you tutor a lot?" she asked.

"As much as I can. I need the money. I'm dual majoring in anthropology and computer science, and I tutor in both. Anthropology is easier."

"No argument here. Why computer science and anthropology? It seems like an odd combination."

"Yeah, I hear that a lot. I'm interested in combining artificial intelligence and archaeology. I'm not sure it will work, but I want to do something innovative. Have you ever heard of Dr. Sarah Parcak and space archaeology?"

"Yeah. I signed up for her GlobalXplorer project, but I haven't done much with it yet."

"I want to do something like that. She generates hundreds of thousands of satellite images of Peru, and I hope to use artificial intelligence to find the good stuff."

Tom continued, "Ideally, a satellite could scan a region of interest and then hand off the images to a neural network.

But the challenge is that every site is unique. The learning for one doesn't necessarily help with another."

He was trying not to sound like a nerd.

"What do you like about computers?" asked Jenny.

She sure asks a lot of questions. Is she really interested?

Someone dropped a book nearby. They both jumped.

"I enjoy programming, getting a computer to follow my commands to do something new or interesting."

"Sounds like you may have control issues," she said. He noticed the twinkle in her left eye again when she smiled.

Tom enjoyed her smile, and she was right, on a certain level.

It was getting late. As they finished their drinks and the bear claw, Tom offered to escort Jenny back to her dorm.

"No thanks. I know the way." As she got up, she simply repeated, "Same time next week?"

"Sounds great. Good luck tomorrow on your quiz."

After Jenny left, Tom spent a moment collecting his thoughts.

"What just happened?" he asked himself, apparently out loud, as a couple of nearby heads turned.

❧

Tuesday, October 23, 2018
The University of Maine
Orono, Maine

The next Tuesday, Jenny texted Tom.

< Sorry Tom. Need to cancel this week. Big
project due Friday and group meets
Thursday night. >

< Do you want to meet tonight or
tomorrow? >

< Sorry I can't 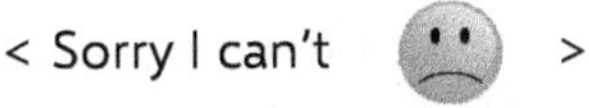 >

Tom rubbed his unintentional stubble. The sad emoji cheered him up a little.

❧

Thursday, November 1, 2018
Computer Lab
The University of Maine
Orono, Maine

For the next week, he checked his phone with trepidation every time he received a text, worried he'd get another message from Jenny canceling another session. On Tuesday, he changed her text tone to the refrain from Don Campbell's "You and Me."

> *Lots of love birds just like us and they're all*
> *around as far as I can see...*

Now, at least, he would know if the text was from her.
The text never came.
When Jenny finally arrived at the Computer Lab, Tom dove right in. They had a couple of weeks to review and Jenny had a mid-term next week, and he hoped they'd still have time for the Bear's Den.
Jenny came prepared, and they were up to date within the hour.
She agreed again to the Bear's Den, this time with no time constraints.
Tom had learned a lot about Jenny from the last session. Tonight, she started the questions. After they settled into their back table, she asked, "Why did you pick Maine?"
"I always planned to attend college, which was my parent's plan as far back as I can remember. I was never sure why they were so insistent. Neither of them attended college.

"My teachers in high school wanted me to look around, but I only applied to Maine. Most of them thought it was a lazy choice, but the University has a great computer science program, anthropology department, and the Honors College. It's also affordable with my tutoring. And a few of my friends from high school were coming here too."

"You said you grew up in Limerock. Where's that?" she asked.

"There's an old expression—Camden by the sea, Limerock by the smell. It's on the coast by Camden."

Jenny smiled. "Is that Maine humor?"

"Yeah, Maine humor."

"Tell me more about Limerock by the smell."

"Well, Limerock doesn't smell anymore. Commercial fishing is pretty much gone. I wasn't kidding when I said it used to be the lobster capital of the world."

He thought Jenny's eyes widened.

"My mom and dad are Maine natives. When I was growing up, my dad did various jobs, but now he sells and installs carpets. He has an office and showroom at the end of the house." Talking was like moving. It relaxed him. "My mom also has a small upholstery business at home."

"Do you have any brothers or sisters?" she asked.

"Nope, only me."

"Me neither—only child."

Tom was taking his time with his coffee, but Jenny had finished her bear claw.

"Do you have a quiz tomorrow in English?" he asked.

"Nope, we have a break this week after the project last Friday, but I should get along. I've a test in another class tomorrow."

After she left, Tom wondered if these meetings were still only tutoring, or possibly something more. They planned to meet again next Thursday. He'd offered to see her in between if she ever needed extra help, but he didn't really expect her to call.

He hoped she wouldn't learn too much too quickly and end the tutoring.

Inca Gold

November 2018
Cartagena, Colombia

Before Omar left Abu Dhabi, he wound down his antiquities business, which required too much time and oversight. Looting, on the other hand, was much more lucrative and less hands on, so he would continue to search for hidden treasures and fabricating provenances.

The Hobby Lobby scandal shook his world, and opened a window into his other businesses, a window he needed closed. Homeland Security traced some of the Hobby Lobby documents and fraudulent provenances back to him. All his endeavors over the years were at risk, which led to his relatively abrupt move to Cartagena, a city of about a million people on the northern coast of Colombia. He found a compound on the water, on the outskirts of the city, that provided him with the security he needed and was large enough to accommodate his staff. Although the compound was not for sale, Omar had convinced the owner to sell. The property was on a peninsula, so he would only have to secure one side.

The main house was a little smaller than his home in Abu Dhabi, but the surrounding grounds were expansive. He looked forward each afternoon to the sea breeze that helped with the oppressive humidity.

Initially, he spent most of his time organizing his personal collection in a room he called the museum. But it would take more than a collection of Middle Eastern artifacts for him to feel truly at home. He buried himself in his work, rarely leaving the compound.

He always thought it ironic that Hobby Lobby had landed him in trouble and not his arms dealing.

He would continue his arms dealing in the Middle East, but he was looking for a change here as well. His whole life had been in the Middle East, with its inherent turmoil. Now that he had accumulated sufficient wealth, he looked forward to pursuing other interests.

One reason he chose South America was the legend of the lost Inca gold that he had studied years ago at Birzeit. The legend had always intrigued him. He was a voracious reader and almost everything he read about the Incas typically included some reference to the lost gold. The notion of gold just waiting for him to discover was compelling.

It was a fascinating story, but there was not just one story. He understood a tale with this many narratives is often a myth, but he was still captivated. It rekindled the spark he had felt as a young man when he had first entered the antiquities market to search for treasures.

After finally settling into his new home, Omar pulled out the notes he had accumulated over the last few years on the Inca treasure.

- *The Spanish Conquistador, Francisco Pizarro, captured the Inca king Atahualpa in Cajamarca, Peru in November 1532.*
- *Atahualpa offered a ransom of a room full of gold and two smaller rooms of silver.*
- *Pizarro agreed - gold and silver trickled into Cajamarca.*
- *Pizarro became impatient. Worried Atahualpa was planning an attack, with only a portion of the gold delivered, Pizarro executed Atahualpa in July 1533.*

- *The legend holds that the Inca General Rumiñahui was on his way to Cajamarca with the rest of the ransom.*
- *When General Rumiñahui learned of the execution of Atahualpa, he turned his army back into the Llanganatis, a remote mountain chain in Ecuador where he hid the rest of the ransom gold.*
- *Along with gold grains and nuggets, General Rumiñahui transported the gold as plates, tiles, jars, cups, figurines, and other trinkets.*
- *Silver was the same along with silver ingots.*

To fill the ransom room in Cajamarca, the value of the gold today could easily exceed a billion dollars. He was not interested in silver. His singular focus was on the gold.

Omar then pulled out Valverde's Derrotero, directions to the hidden gold dictated by Valverde, a common Spanish soldier. This is the document used by almost all explorers in the last one hundred and fifty years.

The legend says Valverde married an Inca princess and her father, who had helped hide the gold, showed him the location of the treasure. Valverde became wealthy.

Later in life, Valverde returned to Spain. On his deathbed, he dictated the Derrotero for the King of Spain. Omar used the translation found in a book by Richard Spruce, a botanist, who explored the Amazon and Llanganatis around 1860. Spruce uncovered the Derrotero in Banos, a small town in the eastern Andes.

Omar had read the Derrotero many times over the years, but he always focused on the first sentence.

Placed in the town of Pillaro, ask for the farm of Moya, and sleep (the first night) a good distance above it; and ask there for the mountain of Guapa, from whose top, if the day be fine, look to the east, so that thy back be towards the town

> *of Ambato, and from thence thou shalt perceive the three Cerros Llanganati, in the form of a triangle, on whose declivity there is a lake, made by hand, into which the ancients threw the gold they had prepared for the ransom of the Inca when they heard of his death.*

Although the Derrotero continued for two pages, his index finger traced the end of the first sentence—*there is a lake, made by hand....*

He did not necessarily believe in the literal translation of the Derrotero. Too many had carefully followed the guide, only to return empty-handed, or not at all.

Instead, he fixated on the reference of a man-made lake. Virtually all accounts of expeditions following the Derrotero looked for the gold in a cave or mine. No one had seriously searched for an artificial lake or gold underwater because no one could see underwater—until Depth Cam.

Omar first saw Depth Cam a couple of years ago.

Ren Zheng was the CEO of Zheng Enterprises, a technology company headquartered in Hangzhou, China. Zheng was one of Omar's closest business associates and they often shared information with each other that might be mutually beneficial. Zheng was intrigued by a camera developed by a graduate student at Stanford around 2015. The camera, mounted on a plane or drone, could see about ten meters under water by eliminating the surface distortion of the waves. It was called FluidCam and the technology Fluid Lensing. The clarity of the images was remarkable, but the technology was limited to drones or airplanes.

Zheng thought it might have a military application, especially if mounted on a satellite, so he stole the design specifications and the software. Stanford never discovered the theft. Zheng Enterprises re-built the FluidCam in about six months, with enhanced optics, and called it Depth Cam. Shortly thereafter, Depth Cam was on a satellite in low Earth orbit. The images from space were equally remarkable, but still limited to a depth of ten meters under water.

Its military applications were not apparent, so Zheng put the project aside.

Omar agreed that the military applications were limited, but he had always wondered if the camera system might help him find the Inca gold.

Omar then pulled out a dissertation he had come across over ten years ago from a Yale doctoral graduate student. The thesis, postulating where satellites might lead the field of archaeology, had planted the idea that this technology might help Omar find the lost Inca gold. The dissertation also touched upon the use of artificial intelligence to interpret the imagery from satellites.

Jerome Westhoven, the graduate student, successfully defended his thesis and was now a tenured professor in archaeology at Yale.

On and off over the years, Omar had reviewed the biography of Dr. Westhoven on the Yale website. It had changed little. Dr. Westhoven still listed his interests as pre-Colombian civilizations and technology in archaeology. Under hobbies, he listed expeditions, mentioning one to the Llanganatis.

Dr. Westhoven had become the editor of *Modern Archaeology* about four years ago, a reputable journal. Omar had found an editorial by Dr. Westhoven from a couple of years ago about the potential use of artificial intelligence and deep learning. His editorial focused on the inadequate training data sets, which hampered machine learning, and some potential solutions. He referenced the satellite work by Dr. Sarah Parcak.

Omar was already intimately familiar with the work by Dr. Parcak. She had found evidence of looting, which she called "waffles" in some Iraqi sites. He was impressed she had detected his handiwork from space.

He had read her textbook, *Satellite Remote Sensing for Archaeology*, published in 2009. It was technical, but he understood what she could do with satellite imagery. Omar imagined the potential of combining artificial intelligence with satellite imagery.

He had also studied artificial intelligence and deep learning. Much of what he read was heavily ladened with jargon, but he understood the principles. You train a neural network with a data set. Once it has learned, it could then find similar images or objects, sometimes with better accuracy than a human, and a lot faster.

All the pieces circulated in his head.

Omar had established a routine of walking around his estate after lunch, when the sea breeze was just starting, and the oppressive humidity was yet to come. This is when he would let his mind wander.

It was on one of these walks that he decided he would fund a "virtual" expedition in the Llanganatis, using Depth Cam and artificial intelligence to identify *a lake, made by hand, into which the ancients threw the gold.*

If the virtual expedition found a lake or lakes with possible treasure, the second phase of his plan would be an actual expedition to the Llanganatis, but not the traditional, on-the-ground expedition. He would use a helicopter.

After years of contemplating the Inca gold, the time had come to move forward.

He needed someone like Dr. Westhoven to pull this together. With his reputation in the world of antiquities, however, Omar could not approach him directly. Once again, he needed an intermediary, preferably one already with a connection to Dr. Westhoven. With a little research, he found an antiquities dealer in Bogotá often mentioned in connection with artifacts authenticated by Dr. Westhoven.

The pieces were falling into place.

Capstone

Thursday, November 15, 2018
The University of Maine
Orono, Maine

Now, in his senior year, Tom's capstone or honors thesis was due the next semester. He met monthly with his advisor, Dr. Gordon Wade, about the capstone, as well as tutoring. Today, they will review the final draft of his capstone project. Tom was always early. Dr. Wade was always late. He was a popular professor and faculty advisor for several graduate students and was pulled in many directions. But no matter, once they got down to business, Tom had his full attention.

He fidgeted in the armless chair outside Dr. Wade's office, pretending to do important work on his iPhone. While waiting, he reflected back to his freshman year on how he had chosen Dr. Wade to be his advisor. With his dual major, he had a choice of an advisor in either computer science or anthropology. Because Tom had envisioned his capstone project overlapping both disciplines, he wanted someone comfortable in both fields.

Tom remembered his interview as a freshman with Dr. Wade for a work-study job. Tom's parents couldn't help a lot financially, and he needed the cash. Back then, he checked the online job board daily. He wanted something in computer science, if possible. In mid-October, when a tutoring job in computer science was posted, his online application resulted in an interview with Dr. Wade.

During the interview, Tom mentioned he was interested in deep learning. He still remembers Dr. Wade chuckling when he told the professor about the neural network he had programmed in high school to recognize the image of a lobster.

When Dr. Wade realized Tom was a first-year student, however, he explained that tutoring is usually reserved for upper-class students and apologized for not making that clear on the job board.

At the end of the interview, Dr. Wade told Tom he was teaching an upper-level class the next semester on artificial intelligence, and invited Tom to enroll if he was interested. He said this might set him up for tutoring the next year as a sophomore. Dr. Wade also mentioned he needed some help on a machine learning project. It was only a few hours a week for a few weeks, but Tom readily accepted.

Although the project did not last too long, Tom realized Dr. Wade understood how artificial intelligence could cross over to other disciplines. After that, it was a simple choice to ask Dr. Wade to be his advisor, which he did just before the Christmas break. They met again after the break when the professor finally agreed. As unpretentiously as possible, Tom suggested Dr. Sarah Parcak's textbook, *Satellite Remote Sensing for Archaeology*, as a great resource.

Tom continued to fiddle with his iPhone, as Dr. Wade was a bit later today than usual.

His vision of intersecting deep learning and archaeology had begun in a sand trap.

Tom worked at the Limerock Golf Course the summer after high school. He loved the precision of the hole cutter—a perfect circle—4.25 inches.

But raking the sand traps is where he would often daydream. He remembered the day and the trap. It was early morning, the day after the solstice, and the sand was still damp from the morning dew in the kidney-shaped trap on the seventeenth green, when he wondered if he could use artificial intelligence to identify sand traps on a golf course. This was the first time he thought of using satellite images.

A little over a year ago, in January 2017, Dr. Parcak launched GlobalXplorer, a virtual expedition to scan satellite images of Peru. About this time last year, Tom proposed using a neural network to study these images for his capstone.

Dr. Wade, however, had other ideas. Tom recalled the uneasy discussion. He remembered wondering if he had made a mistake asking Dr. Wade to be his advisor.

"This is too much like the neural network you trained in high school to identify a lobster. It's not a stretch goal. Don't limit yourself to satellite images in one location. Also, there are other imaging modalities, like drones, airplanes, sonar, LIDAR, boats, or underwater vehicles, which might also benefit from deep learning.

"Present the notion that deep learning is a powerful tool that has many potential applications in archaeology. Discuss the challenges with image acquisition, the training data set, the variety of archaeology sites, and offer potential solutions. Think bigger.

"Tom, I don't want to discourage you from actual programming. But, for your capstone, I want you to think more broadly. Remember why you picked your two majors? This project has a lot of potential."

At the time, Tom remembered how frustrated he was, even a little angry. If what Dr. Wade suggested made any sense, someone would have already done it. Tom felt overwhelmed. Other student's capstones were glorified book reports, nothing like this.

But last summer, Tom poured over Dr. Parcak's textbook again and again, taking notes on three-by-five-inch index cards. He was still old school in a lot of ways. Her textbook detailed how to get the most out of satellites and the images by identifying important domains like landscape types, site types, satellite bands, and pre-processing of the images.

Tom had always struggled with starting new projects, but an idea had begun to percolate. He envisioned a unique neural network for each of the various combinations. A desert-urban locale, for instance, would have a different network than a mountainous-rural site, but he could re-use the basic neural network.

A separate software application sitting on top of all the neural networks would manage the entire process and choose the appropriate neural network.

It might work....

Tom had procrastinated throughout the summer before he finally put his ideas to paper. Programming the neural network would be the easy part, but nothing about this project was easy. This was all new. There was no model to guide him. Creating the training data set for the different locations and site features around the globe to teach the neural network would be the challenge. Fortunately, Dr. Wade had told him he did not need to actually train a neural network, but he did need to show how it could be done.

He would use the neural network he developed in high school to recognize the image of a lobster, which was a convolutional neural network, or CNN, called VGG-16 that was developed by the Visual Geometry Group at the University of Oxford. It revolutionized image recognition, but it required significant hardware, including graphics processing units or GPUs to process the thousands, if not millions, of images. Fortunately, the University of Maine had the necessary hardware, which allowed Tom to test his ideas.

He had submitted a final draft of his capstone to Dr. Wade a couple of weeks ago, although he hesitated to call anything final. Today, he would hear his advisor's feedback.

When Dr. Wade finally arrived, harried as usual, Tom smelled a whiff of pipe tobacco as the professor ushered him into the office. The room had changed little over the last three years. It always seemed too small, or he had too many books lining his walls. Through the large window overlooking the mall, the slanting November sun highlighted his oversize oak desk that added to the muddle. He could see the tops of the maple trees that lined the mall with a few stubborn, brown leaves still holding on.

Dr. Wade leaned back in his cracked leather chair that squeaked when he leaned way back, which he often did when he was thinking. Tom had heard that squeak a lot over the years.

In his early forties, with some slight graying of his short sideburns and hair but a youthful vibrance to his eyes, his advisor was a few inches shorter than Tom, and rounder, but Tom had noticed most professors softened after forty.

"Good morning, Tom. Sorry I'm late."

"Good morning. By the way, thanks for connecting Jenny with me."

"Jenny who?"

"She's the student having trouble in your COS 140. You set her up with me for tutoring."

"Oh, yes, I remember now." Dr. Wade had connected Tom with dozens of students over the last few years. This was the first time Tom thanked him for a particular student.

Dr. Wade continued. "I finished reading your draft last week."

Tom took the creeping grin as a good sign.

"Impressive, Tom, very impressive. You've incorporated all we've talked about, and this is an excellent piece of writing.

"You start by presenting the notion that machine learning, specifically deep learning, can use images from any source and learn to detect items of interest. Then you segue into the heart of your paper saying that each archaeology site is unique. You acknowledge the biggest challenge is defining all the key elements like site and landscape types, which vary from one location to another, and then you suggest that a unique neural network can be trained for each combination with an adequate training data set.

"To tie it all together, your software Manager is a brilliant idea to organize all the important domains and then choose the appropriate convolutional neural network. Your example of Stonehenge is perfect.

"Although the last section diving into VGG-16 is technical, it's an excellent summary of how all this would work. Great job, Tom."

Dr. Wade leaned back. Tom heard the familiar squeak. "I hope you don't mind, but I shared this with a colleague. His name is Dr. Westhoven, and he's a professor of archaeology at Yale. We were undergraduates together. He's authored a few articles about technology in archaeology, and I thought he'd find this interesting."

"But it's not finished yet," said Tom.

Dr. Wade leaned forward onto his elbows. The chair only squeaked when he leaned back, never forward. Dr. Wade had the same look from three years ago when he told Tom to think more broadly about his capstone. Tersely, he said, "It's finished enough, and you knew I'd always need someone in archaeology to read the paper to be sure it makes sense to them."

After a brief pause, he continued, "Also, with some editing for length, you might be able to publish your capstone. Dr. Westhoven is the editor of *Modern Archaeology*. Here Tom, look at this."

He handed Tom an editorial Dr. Westhoven had written a couple of years ago. Tom skimmed it. The gist was how technology opened new doors in archaeology. The last paragraph caught Tom's attention.

> The new technology threatens many archaeologists, but every new potential site discovered is an opportunity to get our hands dirty, which is why most of us are archaeologists.

"I sent your capstone to Dr. Westhoven last week, and we talked on Monday. He was intrigued. He asked if he could talk to you. I can set up an email introduction if that's okay?"

Tom sat upright. "Sure," he said, a little louder than he intended. Tom had always planned to pursue a graduate degree in archaeology. Connecting with Dr. Westhoven would be great.

Dr. Wade's smile returned. It had been a while since they had discussed Tom's capstone in this much detail. Usually, their monthly meetings revolved around tutoring or Tom's plans for graduate school. Tom thought he was on the right track with his capstone, but he wasn't expecting this much approbation.

Dr. Wade tapped a few keys on the keyboard. He must have already drafted the email to his friend. Things were moving quickly. Tom was usually more deliberate.

"I know you haven't settled on graduate school yet, but you've got to decide in the next couple of months. Yale has an outstanding anthropology department, and archaeology is a major division. Dr. Parcak was an undergraduate there. Meeting with Dr. Westhoven will be helpful if you want to pursue archaeology."

Tom cleared his throat. He'd been giving this some thought, even before he met Jenny. "Actually, Dr. Wade, I think I might stay at Orono to complete a two-year master's in computer science, if you'll have me, and then look at a doctoral program in archaeology."

Tom knew that staying at Maine probably seemed like a copout to Dr. Wade, something safe, but he really did like programming.

"We'd be delighted to have you, Tom, but why don't you meet with Dr. Westhoven before you make that decision?"

As the meeting ended, Dr. Wade squeaked his chair again. "Tell me about Jenny. Is she doing okay in the class?"

"Yeah. She's in the Honors College and majoring in English. She didn't realize COS 140 was for computer science majors."

"Yes, I remember. She came in just after add/drop and was stuck with the class. She looked like a fish out of water. Good job, Tom."

"It's kind of fun."

"Kind of fun?"

"Yeah. Thanks again Dr. Wade. See you next month."

He would look for the email from Dr. Westhoven, but he was now more focused on seeing Jenny tonight.

The email from Dr. Westhoven hadn't arrived by the time he left the Pizza Palace to meet with Jenny. Tonight would be the fifth session.

He'd had dates on and off over the years, more so in high school, but he still was not comfortable around girls. He'd never had a steady girlfriend. He rationalized relationships involved too many variables and unknowns, which he didn't handle well. He was, in fact, a nerd with a dash of insecurity, which he managed with a touch of OCD. Structure was his comfort zone. He enjoyed a beginning and a clean end, like a computer program. Relationships were too inexact.

But Jenny stirred up new feelings that he was still trying to understand. He wasn't sure why, which also bothered him. He was careful about what he said around her and how he said it. Before, he'd never cared too much about his appearance. Now, he actually timed the clothes dryer to take out his T-shirts before they wrinkled. Their fledgling relationship had some complexity, which he embraced like a convolutional neural network, or so he thought.

She also seemed more engaged. Possibly she'd been a little nervous, too, when they first met. She smiled more now. She even called him a nerd once, which he took as a term of endearment. After each tutoring session, she stayed longer and longer at the Bear's Den.

But Tom was a pragmatist, which many saw as a glass-half-empty kind of guy. One of his high school friends once told him, "You could play rock-paper-scissors with yourself and always lose." The thought of a bad outcome would often cripple him. He considered asking Jenny on an actual date, but what if she said no? He understood she was there because she needed help. He was her tutor.

The Bear's Den was enough for now, but next Thursday was Thanksgiving. Including tonight, Tom counted four more sessions out on his fingers until finals, and then tutoring would be over.

After another productive session, they headed back to their table in the Bear's Den. Tom noticed Doug, a friend from Limerock, sitting by himself with a book. Doug motioned them over to sit with him, but Tom waved him off. Tom would see Doug, along with Mike, another friend from Limerock, next week when he gave them a ride home. He did not want to share Jenny.

As they settled into their regular table, Jenny asked, "What do you do for fun, besides tutor me?"

Tom smiled. "I enjoy running and the outdoors. I like reading, mainly nonfiction. But most of all, I enjoy programming."

"I guess I was hoping for something more interesting so I could convince my roommate you're not a nerd."

Tom laughed. "I was wondering how long it would take you to figure that out."

"I had an inkling after the first session."

He noticed the reassuring twinkle in her left eye with her smile.

Tom also learned she enjoyed creative writing, but that was not a specific major at Maine, so she had chosen English.

"I'm also interested in climate change. That's another reason I'm at Maine, other than to find a lobsterman," she said with a grin. "Maine has a great Quaternary Center, which studies climate events like the last glacier about 10,000 years ago."

Good thing she explained the Quaternary Age. Creative writing and quaternary science seemed like an odd combination, but he was one to talk.

Jenny took her time finishing her bear claw and hot chocolate. And she finally accepted Tom's offer to walk her back to her dorm. They bundled up against the wind and took their time, which stretched the usual five-minute walk into ten minutes. Even though nothing remarkable happened, like a goodnight kiss, Tom still felt like he'd moved up another rung, on what seemed like a very long ladder.

Back at the Pizza Palace, Tom read the email he finally received from Dr. Westhoven.

To: Tom Kirkpatrick
Date: Thursday, November 15, 2018
From: Jerome Westhoven, PhD

Subject: Capstone

Dear Tom,

My good friend, Dr. Wade, sent me the draft of your capstone. It is an excellent review of technology in archaeology and a look at where technology could take us.

This might make a good commentary piece for Modern Archaeology.

If you are interested, we could Zoom, or meet here in New Haven at your convenience. I'd love to show you the campus, but I know this is a busy time of year.

I am around the Sunday of Thanksgiving weekend, or we could set something up in December.

Sincerely,

Jerome Westhoven, PhD
Council on Archaeological Studies
Yale University

Tom replied he would be delighted to Zoom call the Sunday after Thanksgiving. He had already promised Mike and Doug a ride back to Orono that Sunday.

As Tom was brushing his teeth before bed, he reflected on his day. He hadn't expected Dr. Wade to be so enthusiastic about his capstone. His session with Jenny this evening was the most engaging so far, including the walk back to her dorm. And he was meeting with a professor from Yale.

With Thanksgiving coming up, he wouldn't see Jenny again for a couple weeks, but he was content for now with the Jenny situation. As he finished brushing his teeth, he told his reflection that he'd get a haircut over Thanksgiving before the next tutoring session.

⚜

Thanksgiving
Thursday, November 22, 2018
Limerock, Maine

Tom's mom, who was half Finnish, always prepared a traditional Thanksgiving dinner with a Finnish twist of Kaalikääryleet, or cabbage rolls. The sweet smell filled the house. He wondered what Thanksgiving was like for Jenny.

He spent a lot of the holiday morning debating if he should send her a quick text. Finally, he realized, once again, that he was over thinking it and just did it.

< Happy Thanksgiving! >

He wondered about adding a turkey emoji, but he decided to keep it simple. Now he had to wait for a reply, or even if she would reply at all.

After fifteen minutes with nothing, he wandered into the kitchen to help his mother with the vegetables. Just as he finished chopping up a turnip, he heard Don Campbell, her text tone he'd set in October.

< You too. See you next week. >

That was all he needed.

Sunday, November 25, 2018
Zoom Call
Limerock, Maine - New Haven, Connecticut

Dr. Westhoven started the Zoom call a minute after ten o'clock. He was behind a large oak desk, much like Dr. Wade's. Tom could see bookshelves distorted by the webcam on each side, teeming with books in disarray. A large window behind him streamed in sunlight between the lowered wooden slats, darkening his image slightly. It looked like he was calling from his office at school.

"Good morning, Tom. Thank you for taking some time to talk this morning. I know you're busy at this point in the semester."

Tom was at his dad's much more modest desk in the showroom office, the walls behind him lined with a rainbow of carpet samples.

"Good morning, Dr. Westhoven. My dad sells carpets. I'm in his office."

"Wow, that's quite a selection," said Dr. Westhoven, putting Tom at ease. "I love the sun, but this time of year, it streams into the office. Can you see me okay? I can try a virtual background."

The sunlight created a halo effect, but Tom said, "It looks fine."

Dr. Westhoven was clean shaven with sandy-brown hair down to his shoulders, much longer than Tom's even before his haircut yesterday. He also wore wire-rimmed glasses and had an infectious smile. Although he and Dr. Wade had been undergraduates together, he looked younger than Dr. Wade, probably because of the long hair.

Tom had found some background on Dr. Westhoven online. He did his undergraduate and graduate work at Yale and became a tenured professor there about six years ago. His biography on the Yale website revealed his interest in pre-Colombian cultures in South America and that he had authored a book, *Metallurgy of the Incas.*

Dr. Westhoven had a copy of Tom's capstone in front of him. "I think Dr. Wade already mentioned to you that your capstone might be an appropriate commentary piece for *Modern Archaeology*. I think we could get this into the spring issue if you're interested."

"Sure, absolutely." replied Tom, clearing his throat.

"Great, Tom. I've highlighted what I think our readers would want. I'll send this along in an email. Review my suggestions and let's try to wrap this up by early January. I need to get this to the publisher by late January for the spring issue."

Dr. Westhoven continued, "There's another reason I wanted to talk to you. I host an annual conference in Boston every February, sponsored by *Modern Archaeology*. Would you like to present your ideas at the conference? The content would overlap the article. What do you think?"

This took Tom by surprise. He looked down to fiddle with the volume with his right hand while running his left hand through his hair. It felt different, so short.

He looked up and cleared his throat again. "I'm not much of a public speaker." He grabbed the mouse and moved his self-image across the screen to the right. "I guess I'm also not sure my capstone is finished. I'm not ready to present."

"I disagree. Even the grammar is near perfect."

Tom knew this was an incredible opportunity, but public speaking about his capstone, finished or not, was too much.

After an awkward pause, Dr. Westhoven said, "Look, I finalize the speakers by the end of next month. If you change your mind, let me know. I think this would be a wonderful experience for you."

"Thanks, Dr. Westhoven. I'll give it some thought."

"I also know from Dr. Wade that you're thinking of pursuing a graduate degree in archaeology. From what he tells me, I think you'd be a good fit at Yale. I'd love to show you around the campus."

Tom didn't know what to say. He was running out of things to tinker with. He caught himself before he cleared his throat again.

"Dr. Wade and I've talked a few times about graduate school. I'm not sure what direction I'm headed, but I'm leaning toward a master's in computer science at the University of Maine. It's a strong program. After that, probably a doctoral program in archaeology. But thank you for the kind words."

"Okay Tom. When the time is right, please let me know.

The call lasted about fifteen minutes. Tom thanked him again, and they arranged another Zoom call during the Christmas break to give Tom a few weeks to review his suggestions for the article.

"How did the call go?" his mother asked, while Tom finished packing to head back to campus.

"The professor at Yale offered to publish a condensed version of my capstone."

"That sounds wonderful. Congratulations."

He didn't mention the invitation to speak at the conference. He did not want to get into it with his mother. He knew what she'd say.

And Dr. Westhoven was right. Tom would tweak the capstone for months, but he was essentially done. He'd always struggled to complete a project. To this day, he still considered his lobster convolutional neural network a work in progress. The combination of his need for perfection and his fear of failure was sometimes paralyzing, always causing him to agonize over the details.

Antigüedades Sur

Friday, November 16, 2018
Antigüedades Sur
Bogotá, Colombia

Miguel Titere was admiring the morning skyline out of his office window in downtown Bogotá. The sun streamed in through the large window behind his desk, striking the bookcase to his right, highlighting his collection of gold Inca figurines and his treasured brass sculpture by Oswaldo Guayasamín. From the bookcase, he picked out a golden llama dwarfed by the brass sculpture. It was warm from the sun. He carefully wrapped it in his monogrammed handkerchief and placed it in his inside suit pocket.

He was a broker specializing in pre-Colombian artifacts, in particular the Inca empire. Antigüedades Sur was his company. His limited, high-end clientele worked through similar high-end dealers around the world in New York, London, and Hong Kong. He did not deal with a lot of South American buyers and none from the Middle East, which is why Omar Al Tajir surprised him when he asked to meet through a mutual acquaintance.

The office for Antigüedades Sur was fairly small, but most of his work was on the phone. His office was a hodgepodge of books, antiquities, and photographs of the rich and famous, including one from a dig at Ollantaytambo in the Cusco region, the only time he was on an actual site at a dig. His large desk was an extension of the disorganization.

He had one secretary who had been with him from the beginning. Her reception area was as large as his office, but much more neatly appointed. Unless he was with a client, the wooden door to the reception area was usually open. But even the casual observer would notice the thickness of the door to his office, and a more careful observer might notice the security cameras perched high on the walls.

Miguel's business dealings were always legitimate. He only handled antiquities with proper provenance and documentation. Antigüedades Sur had been in business now for over twenty years and provided Miguel and his family a comfortable life.

He looked forward to meeting the Arab this afternoon. Apparently, he had just moved to South America and hoped for some advice. What advice he sought, Miguel was unsure of.

Miguel searched online, but could not find much about him. Like Miguel, he kept a low profile. Miguel did learn he was an antiquities dealer from Abu Dhabi, but he had no website or social media presence. He wondered what prompted his move to Cartagena.

Señor Omar Al Tajir was still learning Spanish, so when they talked on the phone last week, they spoke in English, which Al Tajir spoke fluently with a British accent. He told Miguel he was going to be in Bogotá today and asked if they could meet. Miguel suggested a late lunch.

They agreed to meet at the Restaurante Julio in the early afternoon to avoid the crowd. It was a short walk from his office, and Miguel often used the restaurant for meetings. His secretary reserved his usual table by the window.

Even though it was comfortable today, he wiped a little sweat off his brow with the back of his hand as he entered the air-conditioned restaurant, remembering he had used his handkerchief to wrap the golden llama.

Miguel was early and took his seat by the window. Restaurante Julio was small but not intimate. It was quiet this time of day. His window table allowed for a conversation that was comfortably private. He also preferred the window seat overlooking the street, as the restaurant otherwise seemed too dark due to the wood paneling. Only a couple at the bar and a half-dozen other patrons at various tables in the shadows remained. His stomach growled from the lingering smells of the lunch hour.

The server brought his coffee. As he took his first sip, a dark Mercedes limousine quietly pulled up in front of the restaurant. From the backseat a large, at least by Colombian standards, well-dressed man stepped out. His closely cropped black hair and dark complexion highlighted a well-fitted, probably Armani, light blue suit, with an equally well-coiffed beard. His most striking feature, however, was his sullen eyes.

Miguel was slightly rotund. He loosened another button on his suit. Standing by the Mercedes, Al Tajir looked like he would tower over him by a good ten centimeters. Miguel shifted in his seat.

As he entered the restaurant, Al Tajir did not wait for the maître d' to seat him. When he met Miguel's eyes, he made his way to the table by the window. He must know what I look like, thought Miguel, although the restaurant was almost empty by then. He had a firm handshake, which also surprised Miguel. Perhaps this is the custom in the Middle East.

Al Tajir was about Miguel's age, perhaps slightly older. He genuinely seemed delighted to meet Miguel and thanked him again for taking the time.

"My pleasure, Señor Al Tajir. I'm happy to assist you to settle into Colombia."

"Please, call me Omar. May I call you Miguel or do you prefer Señor Titere?"

"Miguel is perfect. Please, Omar, sit down."

Although they had spoken English on the phone last week, as a courtesy, Miguel asked him again, "Do you prefer Spanish or English?"

"English, if you please. I'm still learning your wonderful language."

As he sat down, Omar asked for his advice for a good cup of Colombian coffee and what he would recommend for lunch. Miguel noticed the trace scent of cigar.

They spent most of the lunch talking about Miguel's family and upbringing.

"I have lived in Colombia my whole life, growing up on my family's coffee farm. After college, I employed with a Colombian antiquities dealer and learned the business quickly. My father desired me to take over the coffee farm, but eventually he supported my new company of Antigüedades Sur. Shortly after, I married and now have two wonderful children. That was about twenty years ago."

Miguel thought it odd that Omar shared nothing about his family. After a sip of coffee, Miguel continued, "I learned early that connections to the high-end dealers in New York, London, and occasionally Hong Kong were important. The dealers did the selling. I simply supplied the artifacts.

"I also realized the importance of provenance and I have a few experts in pre-Colombian art and artifacts around the world on retainer."

He retrieved the handkerchief from his suit pocket and gently unwrapped the golden llama. "Here señor—this is an example of an artifact I deliver."

He handed Omar the unwrapped llama. It glowed in the bright midday sun. It easily fit in the palm of Omar's hand, who examined it from all angles, turning it over and over. Miguel could tell he was being careful to avoid undue attention.

"This must be worth about $20,000, if this is twenty-two karats," Omar murmured, which impressed Miguel. Omar knew his gold.

"Even more as an artifact," replied Miguel. "The Incas did not know about—what is the word—alloys like steel, but they did know how to work with gold and silver. The Spanish stole and melted down all the Inca gold and silver they found, which is why this llama, with proper provenance, is even more valuable."

Miguel explained the Inca fascination with gold. "The ancients worshipped the sun. They believed gold was the sweat of the sun. To them, gold had no intrinsic monetary value, but by fashioning the gold into artifacts like this llama, they worshipped their god."

Omar asked, "How much gold did the Incas possess?"

"No one knows for sure, señor. The Incas did not have a written language. They recorded information on quipus or colored knotted strings, which no one has been able to decipher. We know the Spanish invaders stole more than hundreds of millions of dollars of gold, but legend says the Incas hid even more gold in the mountains of the Llanganatis in Ecuador."

After the server cleared their plates, Omar shared some of his past that Miguel already knew from his internet search. The sun emphasized his sunken eyes.

"But my business has become too competitive," said Omar. "After Hobby Lobby, it was not the same." He did not elaborate.

Then Omar started sharing his plans for his future in South America. "Moving my business in Middle Eastern antiquities to South America makes little sense to me. So, I am looking for something new, a new venture. But I do not want to start or run a new business. I would prefer to be a partner, a silent partner, in an established business."

Miguel stiffened.

Omar turned his gaze to the street, which was darkened by a passing cloud. Miguel's gaze followed. The Mercedes was waiting. He could not see the driver through the tinted windows. Instead, he focused on an old man with a cane across the street, following an equally small, frail dog.

Omar continued, "Preferably one dealing in antiquities like yours. I know of your reputation, and honestly, I was hoping you might be interested in a partner, a silent partner."

Now it was Miguel's turn to be coy. He carefully wrapped the llama in his handkerchief and returned it to his inside suit pocket. "I'm flattered, señor, you would consider me for such an opportunity. May I ask how much of an investment you are considering?"

Omar returned his gaze from the street to face Miguel. "These are important questions, Miguel. I'm looking to invest up to forty-nine percent of the equity into Antigüedades Sur, up to five million dollars."

The sun burst through, highlighting the street. Miguel squinted and returned to his coffee. He tried to stay collected while gently rocking almost imperceptibly. Omar must have also done some research. This was more than he could refuse.

Miguel sipped his coffee, now too cool to enjoy. They were the only ones left in the restaurant. He rubbed his hands together under the table. This was almost too good to be true. He had wanted to expand his business for some time, but access to capital had limited him.

Did Al Tajir seek him out, knowing he would be amenable to a partnership? Most of his competition was larger, acquiring smaller businesses like his. But Miguel was never interested in selling. He had a niche market. He had considered expanding, bringing on a younger partner, but this opportunity seemed perfect, if Al Tajir was truly silent.

Miguel also understood it would be better to partner with Al Tajir than compete. With his apparent wealth, he would be a formidable competitor.

"May I have a few days to consider your kind offer, señor?"

"Yes, of course, and thank you, Miguel, for your consideration. I'll be in Colombia another few weeks before I fly back to Abu Dhabi over your holidays to finish up some business. Perhaps we can connect before I leave?"

"How about we talk next Friday? I'll be in my office. I think you have the number." But Miguel handed him his business card anyway.

Miguel offered to help with travel arrangements, but Omar deferred.

"Thank you, Miguel, but I brought my jet from Abu Dhabi."

Omar insisted on paying for lunch. He was again effusive in his thanks and looked forward to talking in a week. He offered Miguel a ride back to his office, but Miguel wanted to walk the short distance.

Back at his desk, Miguel replaced the llama in the bookcase and carefully folded his handkerchief. He knew little more about the Arab than he had before the lunch, except that he knew his gold and he was wealthy.

Al Tajir had mentioned Hobby Lobby, which Miguel thought was curious. Everyone in the antiquities trade knew about the Hobby Lobby scandal. Miguel knew the UAE dealer named in the indictment was not Al Tajir.

How did the Hobby Lobby affair affect his business so dramatically that he moved to South America? Miguel found a press release from May. It looked like the last chapter in the scandal. So why did Al Tajir move five months later?

Miguel had a lot to consider. He needed to be sure Al Tajir would truly be a silent partner. What did Al Tajir expect to get out of this relationship? He had the means to start his own business. Why did he seek me out as a partner?

Antigüedades Sur was successful and self-sustaining, but stagnant. His business would need to grow to support a new partner, silent or otherwise. Al Tajir's connections might open new markets around the world.

Miguel asked his secretary to schedule a meeting with his lawyer.

⌘

Friday, November 23, 2018
Bogotá, Colombia

This afternoon, he would talk with Al Tajir. His lawyer had drafted an agreement that offered him protections, including the option to buy out the Arab. Yesterday, preparing for today's phone call,

Miguel had sent the draft for Al Tajir to review, assuming this would be a negotiation.

To his surprise, Al Tajir returned the agreement, signed this morning.

The afternoon phone call was perfunctory. Al Tajir suggested they celebrate the new partnership after the holidays, when he returned from Abu Dhabi.

This was happening so fast, but the contract gave Miguel all the options. He continued to search online about Al Tajir, but nothing new turned up. There was no obvious connection to the Hobby Lobby imbroglio. Al Tajir's online presence was reputable, but Miguel still harbored a nagging feeling everything was falling into place too easily. There was just not a lot he knew about Omar Al Tajir. He was clearly wealthy. Were antiquities just a hobby for him?

In the back of his mind, though, Miguel thought perhaps he was finally getting what he deserved after twenty years in the business.

Monday, November 26, 2018
Bogotá, Colombia

It took Miguel the weekend and a few more phone calls to his lawyer before he signed the agreement. Antigüedades Sur was now a partnership with $2,500,000 in the bank. He decided to keep the money in deposit until he was comfortable with his new silent partner.

He understood Al Tajir was affluent and continued to wonder about the source of his wealth. You do not make this kind of money selling trinkets from the desert. Miguel assumed he was born into money, likely oil money.

Monday, November 26, 2018
Cartagena, Colombia

Omar was pleased Miguel had signed the partnership today, and he wired the money to Miguel's bank. The ease with which he recruited Miguel reminded him of how easily Ayyash had recruited him, as a young man, to support Hamas.

With this important step out of the way, he could now focus on the Inca gold. Finding over a billion dollars of lost Inca gold was a long shot, but finding even a fraction would still be worthwhile, if it truly existed.

The legend stated that General Rumiñahui hid the gold in the Llanganatis in Ecuador, which was now a national park. Although the entire park was open to the public, the government rarely granted permission for expeditions. They always failed, sometimes with fatalities, which was bad for tourism. Omar learned, however, with proper bribes to the proper people, he might receive permission for an expedition, but Ecuador kept half of any gold recovered. He decided to move forward without permission, not sharing any of the gold with the government. He was comfortable working clandestinely.

But Miguel would balk at anything illegal. Forging documents was Omar's specialty, and the fraudulent permissions would easily pass as legitimate if Miguel did not examine them too closely.

Evenrood's

Thursday, December 13, 2018
The University of Maine
Orono, Maine

Tonight was the last tutoring session. This could be the last time Tom would see Jenny. That reality was in the back of his mind throughout the session, which seemed to pass even more quickly than usual.

As the session ended, she said, "Thank you again, Tom. I'm so much more comfortable with the material. I'm not struggling like I was when we first met."

He had noticed it, too. She now seemed confident and inquisitive, with a good grasp of the material. He did not want this to end.

The Bear's Den had become part of their routine. They had their favorite table at the back. As they settled into their seats, Jenny pulled out a small bottle of Vermont maple syrup for Tom as a thank you.

"Is this as good as Maine maple syrup?"

"It should be," she said earnestly, but his grin revealed he was teasing.

The maple syrup gave him hope. He had never received a gift from a student before.

Jenny didn't appear to have a boyfriend at Maine or back home in Vermont. He still wondered if this time together was just tutoring or something more. He would find out shortly, one way or the other.

They talked about their Christmas vacation plans while he was waiting for the right moment. Although he was more comfortable around her after two months of tutoring, he understood that their only interactions so far had been across a computer screen or a Diet Coke.

It was getting late. Time was running out. He flushed a little. He waited for Jenny to take a sip of her soda, then cleared his throat, and asked as calmly as possible, "I know you're busy with finals next week, but how about taking a study break on Saturday night, or, if you're too busy now, maybe we could get together after the Christmas break, maybe here at the Bear's Den or downtown at Pat's?"

"What did you have in mind?"

Tom thought he saw the twinkle in her left eye and the beginning of a smile. "There's a nice restaurant, Evenrood's, in Bangor."

"Sounds great. Is this a date?"

"Yeah, I guess so. Is that okay?"

Jenny just smiled. "How about six o'clock?"

"Great. I'll pick you up at Somerset."

That wasn't so hard—but it was—for Tom. He dealt with his insecurity by not taking risks. He made himself available for any last-minute questions. But he knew she wouldn't call. She was prepared. No matter, he was now focused on Saturday night.

She stood up and thanked him again for his help and turned to leave, flipping her hair just like she had done the night they met two months ago. She seemed lighter than usual as she left. He certainly was.

Maybe Dave was right—maybe she was a gestalt. He really needed to look that up.

Saturday, December 15, 2018
Somerset Hall
The University of Maine
Orono, Maine

Jenny was finishing her eyeliner in a small mirror, propped up on some books on her desk in her dorm room. She could see her roommate smiling in the reflection behind her.

"He must be some nerd," said Robin with a chuckle.

"Yeah, he's a nerd, for sure." Jenny turned quickly. "How do I look? It's been a while since I put on make-up."

"Fabulous. Just be careful you don't scare him away. He may not be able to handle all that beauty. When is he picking you up? You can tell a lot by the car he drives."

Jenny checked her wristwatch. "Now! Wish me luck. See you later," said Jenny as she rushed out the door, stuffing an arm into her jacket.

Tom was pacing outside the entrance to Somerset. The cold kept him alert, even though he could have easily followed someone in and waited in the lobby.

Just as he looked up one more time to the elevator in the lobby, Jenny burst through the security door with her signature smile. He was speechless, again, just like the first time they met.

Jenny finally broke the silence. "Ready?"

"Oh, yeah, sorry. You look great. This way."

Tom headed to the F-150, a hand-me-down truck from his dad, and opened the door for Jenny. He noticed a little rust starting by the floorboard.

"Nice truck. I like the bench seat. Brrrr. It's a little colder tonight than I expected."

Tom was also chilled from waiting outside. "Yeah. It will warm up quickly," he said as he started the truck and turned the heater up.

Rubbing her mittens together, Jenny said, "It's a beautiful night. The stars are so bright. And look, the moon is peeking out from behind that cloud." As they drove by the Versant Astronomy Center, she asked, "Have you ever been in there?"

"Not yet. Dave, my roommate, said it was worth the trip."

"Maybe we can check it out together sometime."

"Yeah." This date was off to a good start.

The Penobscot Country Club was on the way and hosting a holiday event. The moon gently illuminated the rolling golf course.

"Do you play golf?" asked Jenny.

"I played a lot when I was a kid. The Limerock Country Club was my summer job in high school, but I haven't played much since then. Joe, a friend from high school, and I'll play once or twice a summer until we run out of golf balls."

"What do you mean?"

"Most end up in the woods and quarries."

"Quarries?"

"Yeah, remember I mentioned the vein of limestone that runs behind Limerock. It also runs by the golf course. You actually hit over a small quarry on the eighteenth hole."

"My dad plays, but I only went along for the ride on the golf cart. Do you tutor in golf, too?"

Tom smiled. This was going way better than he expected.

Soon they were headed down State Street hill into the heart of downtown Bangor, a maze of one-way streets, but Tom knew his way, weaving back and forth through the lanes.

Everything was festive and a large holiday tree lit up West Market Square as they rounded Central Street.

"Evenrood's is there on the corner." Tom pointed to a rounded building just past the square to the right.

As they passed 11 Central Downtown Eatery, Jenny remarked, "I didn't know there were so many restaurants huddled together here."

Tom found a parking spot along the Kenduskeag Stream, which ran through downtown. As they walked to the nearby restaurant, the wind hit them head on. He felt the urge to hold her hand through his gloves and her mittens. Too soon, maybe later, he thought.

The glow from the restaurant's circular picture windows greeted them as they crossed the street. They instantly warmed up as they entered the lobby.

An elderly woman with a kind smile looked up. "Good evening, Tom. We've been expecting you." She grabbed two menus and motioned them to follow her.

He had reserved a special table between two large pillars, which provided them with a little privacy. Jenny looked out over West Market Square. He was content to look at her.

Once they settled into their seats, Jenny asked, "Is this where you bring all your dates?"

Tom was trying to impress her, but not in that way. "No, not at all. You're the first date I've brought here."

"Well then, where do you usually bring them?"

Tom was a little flustered. "I don't date a lot, especially the students I tutor. I'm pretty busy."

"Well, I guess I should be flattered. So why me? And how do they know you so well here?"

Tom ignored the first question and answered the second. "I've dined here a few times with the owner's son. I tutored him a couple of years ago and we stay in touch."

Just then, the server arrived from behind Jenny and turned to her. "Good evening. I'm Joshua, and I will take care of you this evening."

A not-so-subtle grin crept across Tom's face. "Hey Josh. This is Jenny. Jenny, this is Josh, the owner's son."

"Nice to meet you, Jenny. May I offer you two a drink besides water?"

"I suggest the chardonnay," said Tom.

"Thanks, but I'll have some sparkling water. I may crack a book later."

"Very good," said Josh as he turned and left with a quick wink directed at Tom.

Jenny watched as Joshua headed to another table. "What's the wink about?" she asked. "And I'm underage, so no alcohol for me."

Back on the defensive, Tom replied, "I may have mentioned to him I was bringing a date here this evening. He graduated last year and now has a day job managing a startup fiber optic company, but he still helps on weekends.

"And the woman who greeted us is his grandmother. His mom owns the restaurant."

"So, you don't bring a lot of dates here?"

"Nope, you're the first actual date—at Evenrood's." Tom was now enjoying this again.

"Alright, I'll drop it." Jenny looked around the restaurant. All the tables were occupied, and a festive atmosphere filled the restaurant. "Is Evenrood their last name?"

As "Carol of the Bells" started in the background, Jenny continued, "I love this song."

"Me too. No. His grandmother told me the story. Josh loved the dragonfly called Evinrude in the Disney film, *The Rescuers*, but he always misspelled it as Evenrood. Pretty unique name for a restaurant."

Josh came back with their drinks, and Jenny ordered the fish tacos and Tom, the grilled scallops.

"By the way, how many finals do you have?" asked Tom.

"One on Monday, two on Wednesday, and COS 140 on Friday morning, and then home to Amherst. How about you?"

"One on Wednesday."

"Only one. What's the deal?"

"Well, the capstone project doesn't have a final and two professors in two courses told me not to bother with the final, so that leaves only one. How are you getting back to Vermont?"

"Nice segue, nerd. I ride with a guy from Rutland."

"You mean like a boyfriend?"

Jenny grinned while cocking her head, which immediately made Tom uncomfortable for asking. "No, just a ride-share, but he is cute. My old boyfriend goes to UVM."

Tom took a long sip of chardonnay. He hung onto the "old" part. "How long does it take you to get home?"

"About five hours. It's a long ride, especially back and forth over Thanksgiving. But Christmas is a nice break. I'm looking forward to seeing some friends, skiing, and reading. I may even work a little at the Tyson Store."

"Is that a gift shop?"

"More like a mom-and-pop convenience store in between Okemo and Killington. It gets busy during ski season. I've worked there the last couple of summers. Jeff and Tina, the owners, helped us settle in when we first moved to Amherst. How about you?"

"Same. I usually help my dad a little, but mostly I reconnect with friends and do a little skiing. There's a ski area in Camden, and I meet up with my roommate at Sugarloaf for a few days after New Year's. It's a nice mental break."

Josh delivered their meals with a little extra flourish, for Jenny's benefit.

They talked about their friends they hoped to see over the holiday. Jenny was particularly close to Jackie, her best friend from high school, and Tom talked a lot about Joe.

"Oh, I almost forgot. Dr. Wade sent my capstone to a colleague at Yale, who's the editor of *Modern Archaeology*. He asked me to write a commentary piece about my capstone. That will also keep me busy over the break."

"Wow. That sounds like a big deal." Jenny took a bite of her fish taco.

Tom was finishing his scallops. "I guess. But I did pass on his offer to speak at a conference in Boston."

"Why?"

"I don't know. I'm not much for public speaking and I'm not sure my capstone is ready."

"It seems odd he'd have asked you to write an article and speak at a conference if he didn't think you were ready and had something worthwhile to say."

Tom changed the subject. "His name is Dr. Westhoven. I looked him up online. His research interest is pre-Colombian cultures, particularly the Incas. He authored a book titled *Metallurgy of the Incas.* It has a lot of reviews on Amazon, so it must be a textbook."

"Neat. I've been fascinated with the Incas since we lived in Colombia. My dad has quite a collection of books at home."

Josh reappeared, and they passed on dessert. Jenny offered to split the tab, but Tom insisted. "I've got to find some way to spend all my tutoring money."

The evening air was crisp, and the night was young. Tom suggested a stroll around downtown, all decked out for Christmas. It was hard to see any stars with the streetlights overhead, and the moon was hiding behind the clouds. As they turned left onto Main Street, they saw Rebecca's Gift Shop across the street, brightly lit for holiday shoppers. Patrons filled Nocturnem Draft Haus with the large picture window dripping with condensation on the inside.

As they wandered back to the truck, he deftly held her hand, albeit through his gloves and her mittens. The best part, however, was when Jenny hopped in the cab and slid over the bench seat to sit next to Tom on the ride back to Orono.

As they passed the old state hospital on their left and the abandoned water works on their right, Jenny broke the silence. "What are your plans for next year? Are you still thinking about a graduate program in archaeology?"

"Eventually, but I've been talking with Dr. Wade about a master's in computer science at Maine first."

"That's a two-year program, right?"

"Yeah."

Jenny gently leaned into Tom. "It's good to know you'll be around if I need any more tutoring."

He'd been wondering if staying at Maine was the right decision. This helped.

Tom had carefully planned out the evening, including Josh as their server, but he wasn't sure how to end it. "Any chance you'd want to get together after Christmas break, maybe at the Bear's Den or downtown at Pat's?"

"Yeah, but I don't have a car, so how about the Bear's Den? We can figure out a time once we get our class schedules."

Tom forgot about the car.

"Neat."

He purposely parked the F-150 in the back lot to walk with Jenny a little more, again glove in mitten. He was headed around the building to the main entrance when she pulled him suddenly toward the back entrance.

As they approached the security door, she led him into a hidden alcove. She reached up to kiss him gently on the lips, wrapping her mittens around his neck to pull him closer.

"That should last until the Bear's Den," she said, as she quickly turned and disappeared through the security door and up the stairs.

Christmas Break

Friday, December 21, 2018
Limerock, Maine

Tom usually gave Mike and Doug, two good friends from high school, a ride home on school breaks. The F-150 was showing its age, but had plenty of miles left on it, or so Tom hoped. They'd made the two-hour trip together many times over the years, with Doug always riding shotgun and Mike spread out on the backseat.

As an entering freshman, Tom had planned to room with Doug in Gannett Hall, but they ended up doubled up in a single room. The week before classes began, however, a double room opened up and Tom moved in with Dave, and Doug got the single.

Tom and Doug played football and baseball in high school. Tom was glad he'd attended a small school. Anything much bigger and he probably would not have made the sports teams. Doug played fullback. He was short and stocky, which led to his nickname, "Cannonball." Tom always admired his tenacity.

Mike was more of a nerd, like Tom. Although Tom spent a lot of time with Doug during football and baseball season, he hung out with Mike during the long winters.

Tom was preoccupied on the ride home, thinking about Jenny. Other than a quick thank you text from almost a week ago last Sunday, he hadn't heard from her since their date. She was probably focused on her finals. They never really texted a lot, anyway, he told himself.

He had planned to send her a text over the break, but he wasn't sure when, or what to say other than the obvious Merry Christmas, or maybe to check on her grade in COS 140. He wasn't sure of the proper protocol.

Doug broke the silence. "Are you ever going to get the cruise control fixed?" Part of the ritual of the drive home was Doug complaining about Tom's slow driving. "Then maybe you could approach the speed limit."

The F-150 had served Tom well over the years, but there were a few mechanical issues, like the broken cruise control, but nothing significant, especially when you don't have the cash to fix them.

Tom was quieter than usual, but Doug knew how to fix that. Around Northport, he asked, "Hey, tell me again who thought up the 'hubcap caper?' I can't remember."

Besides his tenacity, Tom also envied Doug's memory. He could remember the scores of games and plays from years ago. Both Tom and Mike knew what he was doing. He remembered the hubcap caper better than they did.

Tom looked back at Mike in the rearview mirror, who just rolled his eyes. The hubcap caper was something Mike would rather forget, and Doug knew it.

Mike wasn't going for the bait, so Tom started. "I think it was Hans' idea, but we all jumped onboard." Hans was the foreign exchange student from Sweden during their senior year.

Tom continued, "The idea was to 'kidnap' the teachers' hubcaps and then hold them for ransom for better grades. We hit Gartley, Morrill, and Foote. And Mike wanted to include the principal."

Tom had always thought including the principal was a brilliant idea. He never would have suspected Mike was in on this. The principal was Mike's father.

He also liked having Hans involved. Other than getting someone pregnant or getting pregnant, a foreign exchange student couldn't get into too much trouble. What could go wrong?

Mike then filled in the details, yet again. "On that late December afternoon, under the cover of darkness, we easily pulled all the hubcaps. Gartley, however, was already missing his right rear."

Tom picked up the story. "The caper didn't last long. Although we always intended to return the hubcaps, we never intended to confess. The ransom was just a joke." He looked at Mike in the rearview mirror. "Somehow, they figured out who did it."

"It was your lousy ransom note," said Mike.

"Whatever," said Tom. "Anyway, the next day all our hubcaps were missing, and only ours. Somehow, they knew it was Hans, Mike, and me. Each of us found a note in our locker arranging a hubcap swap in Gartley's room the next day after school."

"Then Tom's OCD kicked in. He just had to replace Gartley's missing hubcap, one he probably didn't even know was missing. And the new one was shiny. It didn't match the others, and Tom was out $80."

"It was very shiny," said Tom, nodding his head.

"The best part of the story is Tom actually tried scuffing it up, so it matched the other three, but it was still obvious," Mike said. "Everyone got their hubcaps back, plus one. Christmas break started the next day, so the whole affair was forgotten by the time we returned in January."

"And your dad handled it well, too," said Tom, smiling at Mike in the rearview mirror.

Doug turned around to face Mike. "That was probably the only time you ever did anything remotely nefarious, or at least the only time you got caught," chuckled Doug.

Mike and Doug then talked about their classes for next semester, their last semester at Maine, bragging about who had the easier course load. They had learned not to ask Tom. Neither of them understood what he was doing, and he took his studies way too seriously.

But Doug finally asked, "Are you still doing two majors? I don't know why. If I had my choice, I wouldn't major in anything."

Tom just nodded, hoping to end the conversation.

"What are you ever going to do with anthropology? You know, you'll eventually have to get a job."

"I'm interested in archaeology, and do you want me to start on convolutional neural networks?"

Both Mike and Doug shook their heads no.

"All right—knock it off."

The rest of the ride went quickly, as it did when they reminisced. Tom didn't mention Jenny, though she was on his mind. Even driving through Camden, with crosswalks littering Main Street, wasn't as annoying as usual.

They made plans to connect at The Garage tomorrow night. Tom would text Joe, his best friend from high school. Doug and Mike would let the rest of the crew know. Tom dropped them off at their houses and headed home.

On his way, he reflected on what Mike said about his possible OCD. As a kid, his mom often called him a perfectionist. Perhaps this was a euphemism for OCD.

He did have trouble finishing projects. He was more comfortable saying, "I'm working on it," rather than presenting a finished product and then being judged on something that might not be perfect. Good was not good enough for Tom. Besides, everyone has trouble finishing stuff occasionally.

And the new hubcap was very shiny.

320 Park Street
Limerock, Maine

His mom met him at the door with a big hug. "Dad's still at work, but he'll be home in an hour or so. He's finishing a job in Thomaston."

"Great. What's for supper?"

"Your favorite."

Tom had only four days to embrace the Christmas spirit, but his mom made it easy. She decorated the house, inside and out. He had a half-dozen Christmas movies to watch, culminating with *A Christmas Carol* on Christmas Eve, dozens of gingerbread cookies to eat, and Christmas shopping tomorrow.

Tom loved the four-week Christmas break. Although he liked to keep busy, it was still a mental break. No tutoring, studying, exams, or finals.

Christmas break was also a time to reconnect with high school friends, although the crew had dwindled after four years. He was especially looking forward to seeing Joe, who usually had an interesting girlfriend he rotated out about every three months.

Limerock's population hovered around 9,000. Growing up, it was a working harbor. It really was "Camden by the sea, Limerock by the smell." Tom remembered that no matter which way the wind blew, there was a distinctive smell. The burning dump from the north, commercial fishing from the east, a processing plant for fish guts from the south, and the cement plant in Thomaston from the west. But all of that had been cleaned up years ago.

The name Limerock came from the limestone quarries, mined in the mid to late 1800s. Jenny would be interested in the geology. The quarries, which ran from Thomaston to Rockport, were striking from satellite views on Google Earth.

But the limestone industry played itself out in the early 1900s. And, more recently, when fishing collapsed, the current arts and tourist scene followed. Now the harbor was full of sailing boats and yachts.

His dad sold and installed carpets, which afforded him a reasonably stable income.

Tom was proud of his heritage. Both parents' ancestors had been in Maine long enough for Tom to be a Maine "native." His mom's family immigrated from Finland in the late 1800s to work the granite quarries on the islands off the coast. His dad's family came from southern Scotland about the same time to work in the limestone quarries. They were high school sweethearts.

Tom was up in his room putting away his stuff when his phone started playing "Radioactive" by Imagine Dragons. It was Joe's text tone.

< Call me when you can - nothing urgent. >

Tom wanted to swing by the high school to catch Mr. Gartley, and it was getting late, so he would call Joe on the way.

Joe was a bright kid, but struggled with discipline. Tom was the opposite. He wondered if possibly that was why they got along so well. Joe was also a gifted athlete, but he only played baseball in high school. He struggled with the commitment required by the other sports, but baseball was more pastoral, he said.

After graduation from high school, he started at the University of Southern Maine but left after a semester. He had plenty of work and opportunities at home and always seemed to have three or four jobs. His latest was digging graves.

Joe answered quickly when Tom called. "Hey Joe. What's up? I'm going to see you tomorrow at The Garage, right?"

"Yeah. Just wanted to give you a heads up. I have a new girlfriend. I like her a lot, and I just want you to be nice."

Tom chuckled. "I'm always nice. Are you getting weird on me? It's not my fault you change girlfriends every season. Let me check. Ayuh, winter starts today."

But now Tom understood how it felt to be with a girl you really liked. You want everything to be right. He'd known Joe for years, and they had never had a conversation like this. She must be special.

"Okay, okay. See you tomorrow, geek," said Joe.

"I prefer nerd."

Limerock District High School
Limerock, Maine

Tom stopped in to see Mr. Gartley whenever he could. Although today was Friday, Tom was home early enough to catch him at the high school. Mr. Gartley had been his math teacher, the one with the shiny right rear hubcap. He was Tom's first true mentor.

In the summer before Tom's senior year, the school received a gift of a small IBM zEnterprise computer from Tom Watson, Jr., the former CEO of IBM who summered on North Haven, off the coast of Limerock. He had donated to many causes in the mid-coast area and the computer was yet another example of his generosity.

The principal placed Mr. Gartley in charge of the new computer, which he affectionately named the "Beast."

Even before the Beast, Mr. Gartley knew Tom was interested in programming. He had seen a video game Tom had designed for his friends. The Beast was already set up for machine learning, so Mr. Gartley encouraged Tom to try deep learning, a subset of machine learning.

Tom had been familiar with Python, the language of choice for machine learning from programming his video game. He also knew some of the early work in machine learning was to recognize the image of a cat. To learn more about deep learning, he programmed the open-source VGG-16 convolutional neural network to recognize the image of a lobster.

After weeks of programming, training, and tweaking the hyperparameters or variables, it worked. His neural network could accurately recognize a lobster. It was not perfect, which always nagged at him, but this foundation would serve him well.

Mr. Gartley's door was open, and Tom poked his head in. He was erasing the whiteboard.

"Hey..."

Mr. Gartley turned around with a smile. "Hey yourself, Tom. Come on in. You can help me clean these whiteboards."

Tom extended his hand to shake, and Mr. Gartley handed him an eraser. "I was hoping you'd swing by. These whiteboards are filthy. No one cleans them as well as you. How are you doing?"

"Great. I met a girl." Tom couldn't believe his ears, but he had to tell someone.

"Well, that's great, Tom, but I meant academically. Anyone I know?"

"Nope. She's from Vermont. I met her tutoring."

"Tutoring. Hopefully, you smartened her up. Are you going to see her over the break?"

"No, but we have a date when we get back."

"So, how are you doing with your studies? Everything on track? Any new majors? Any interesting projects?"

"Yep. Everything's on track. I'm doing well with grades and stuff but..."

"But what?"

Tom started cleaning the whiteboard. He always started at the lower left. "To be honest, I feel like I'm spinning my wheels a little. I'm learning a lot. I'm enjoying my studies. I'm having fun and all. But meeting Jenny started me thinking about my goals, my future.

"I'm also wrapping up my capstone, but I'm having trouble finishing."

Mr. Gartley smiled. "You've heard the expression the last ten percent of a project is ninety percent of the work. For you, the last one percent always seemed like ninety-nine percent of the work. I'd be happy to look at it if that would help."

Tom's need for perfection, along with his insecurity, was a tough combination. Mr. Gartley took the eraser back from him and motioned him to take a seat in his old desk near the front row. Then Mr. Gartley took his seat behind his desk, adjusting his Yoda paperweight with the inscription—**Do or do not. There is no try**. Tom knew a teaching moment was coming.

After settling into his old desk that seemed to shrink a little every year since graduation, Tom replied, "Yeah, my advisor says something similar, without the percentages."

Mr. Gartley smiled again, knowingly.

"He sent a draft of my capstone to a colleague of his at Yale, who wants me to write a condensed version for *Modern Archaeology*. He also asked me to speak at a conference in Boston."

"That's wonderful, Tom. When is the conference?"

"In February—I declined."

"What! Why?"

"I don't like public speaking."

"Tom, you're a bright kid, or I wouldn't trust you to clean my whiteboard, but you're always playing it too safe. You don't challenge yourself. You could have gone to an Ivy League school, but you didn't even try. It sounds like you're doing well at Maine, which is great, but think bigger. You underestimate yourself."

Tom was weary of hearing about his potential.

"Let me offer you two pieces of advice." Mr. Gartley was one of the few people whose advice he'd listen to, but it still made him uncomfortable.

"First, be open to opportunities. Put yourself in situations where those opportunities exist. Don't always take the path of least resistance.

"And second, don't get in the way of your future."

Tom looked puzzled. "What do you mean, don't get in the way?"

"Your future will happen. You don't have to plan everything out. Don't be too prescriptive. You're a bright, inquisitive kid. Put yourself out there. Let things happen—unfold. These two pieces of advice go together. Take some risks and see where it takes you."

Sometimes Mr. Gartley sounded like Obi-Wan or Yoda, probably on purpose. He was always weaving *Star Wars* into his classes.

"That's enough of that. Any plans over the break?" asked Mr. Gartley as he stood up and handed the eraser back to Tom.

"The Garage tomorrow night with the Hubcap Caper gang, a little skiing, you know, the usual."

While finishing the whiteboard, Tom filled him in on his classes for the next semester. They talked a bit about graduate school. After talking with Mr. Gartley, he realized he was perhaps planning too far ahead with Jenny. They'd only had one date. But he needed to decide in the next month or two about the next couple of years.

Almost like he could read Tom's mind, Mr. Gartley said, "Remember, Tom, don't get in the way of your future. Let it happen."

The whiteboard sparkled, and Tom had kept Mr. Gartley long enough. It was Friday, and the sun had set.

"Thanks, Mr. Gartley. Have a great Christmas break. And thanks for the advice. I'll try to figure out what you meant." Tom smiled and turned to go.

"Enjoy your break, Tom. And I hope things work out with Jenny. She sounds nice."

Since when are girls nice? "Yeah, she's nice."

"And tell everyone tomorrow I said hi. And give that Boston opportunity some more consideration.

"Oh, by the way, I lost my hubcap again off the right rear wheel. You know, the shiny one. It's okay. Now I have three hubcaps that match."

On the way home, Tom heard Don Campbell. It was a text from Jenny.

< Almost home. Glad finals are over.
I think I did okay in COS 140. >

< Great. I knew you would.
Have fun skiing. >

She broke the ice. Now, instead of fussing about if he should text, he could focus on what to text. He was glad he had asked her to Evenrood's before the break.

ॐ

320 Park Street
Limerock, Maine

Tom was looking forward to lasagna, his favorite. His dad came home a little early. Dinner was about the only time they could all get together.

320 Park Street was a modest, blue, two-story colonial clapboard house on the edge of town. It sat on about six acres, mostly field with woods in the distance, which Tom explored as a kid searching for hidden treasures.

As they sat down to dinner, his dad was favoring his left knee.

Tom dug into the lasagna. "How's work going?" he asked his dad.

"Pretty good, you know, up and down. It'll pick up after the holidays."

"I'm caught up at school. I'll help while I'm home."

"Yeah. That would be great. I could use the help, and the company."

After a bite, Tom continued, "You know that professor I talked to after Thanksgiving? He asked me to present at a conference in Boston in February. I declined, but it was nice he offered."

"Why did you decline?" asked his mom.

"I don't think I'm ready to present my capstone."

She continued, "Tom, I've been hearing you're not ready since you were a little fella. I doubt the professor would have asked you to speak if he didn't think you were ready. I don't know how college works, but I can't imagine an opportunity like this comes along too often."

"That sounds a lot more interesting than laying carpet," said his dad.

Tom cleared his throat and shifted in his chair. His dad changed the subject. "How are your finances?"

"Okay. Tutoring helps, but I'll need another loan for next semester. I have an appointment at Merrill Trust next week. It shouldn't be a problem."

"I wish we could help more, Tom, but things are so tight. How about if I pay you for helping me after the holidays?"

Tom laughed. "That would be a first. No, I'm okay."

His dad smiled. It would be a first.

Tom said nothing about Jenny or that he had a follow-up Zoom call with Dr. Westhoven the next week. His mother was right. Speaking at a national conference was a big deal. Maybe he was getting in the way of his future.

The Garage

Saturday, December 22, 2018
The Garage
Limerock, Maine

Although he was more of an introvert, Tom always enjoyed meeting up with his friends. In the old days, when none of them were legal, they gathered at someone's home, usually Doug's. Now, everyone was over twenty-one, and they typically met at The Garage, a downtown bar in the basement underneath one of Main Street's art galleries.

A large, commercial garage door, suitably distressed, faced the harbor, with the actual entrance cut into the larger door. This time of year, the dark tones of the bar were even darker, although the mirror that lined the back wall was decorated with Christmas lights, which brightened the place.

Marcia was thinking of college out west somewhere. Ann was applying to medical school. Mike and Doug were still considering their options after graduation. Ferolyn, Doug's girlfriend since high school, was finishing her teaching degree at the University of Southern Maine, hoping to land a job in Limerock. She already had a student teaching assignment in Limerock lined up for next semester. Hans was back home in Sweden.

Joe showed up about eight o'clock with a girl that Tom did not recognize. Joe wasn't trying to be fashionably late. He just went to his own time, his own flow.

Her name was Lynda. She was also a schoolteacher in South Thomaston where Joe grew up, and she and Ferolyn hit it off. Tom noticed Joe seemed subdued, in a good way.

Tom wasn't sure why Joe's girlfriends had never lasted more than a few months. He was an acquired taste for sure, but a good guy at heart. He also understood Tom better than the rest. He was the one who said Tom could play rock-paper-scissors with himself and always lose.

The bar was filling up and a few others joined the table. Everyone was having side conversations, and Tom heard snippets here and there.

"Have you heard from Hans?" Ann asked Mike. "He's gone dark on Facebook."

"When does your student teaching start?" Doug asked Ferolyn, who was already in a conversation with Lynda about what teaching grade school was really like.

Joe still worked with his father, but he'd started a side job this fall as a sexton. He started telling Doug and Tom a story about digging a grave last week in Waldoboro when Tom's watch vibrated.

His spine stiffened. He barely heard Don Campbell above the din. He cleared his throat. It was a text from Jenny. He glanced at his watch. The text was brief....

< Good to be home.

Thanks again for your help. >

Two texts in two days. He had decided to send her a "Merry Christmas" text in a day or two, hoping to stay in touch over the break, but this was way better, and unexpected. While Joe was animating his story about digging into the frozen ground, Tom tapped on his watch...

He needed something more than an emoji. He ordered another IPA and pulled out his iPhone, but before he could think of a reply, Jenny replied.

< And Merry Christmas. >

< And a Happy New Year. >

"Who are you texting?" the ever-observant Doug asked Tom.

"It's just someone I tutored last semester."

Doug asked, "Does this have anything to do with the babe at the Bear's Den?" Then Tom remembered he had seen Doug at the Bear's Den after a tutoring session with Jenny just before Thanksgiving.

Ferolyn gave him a kick, which jiggled the table. Doug must wear shin pads. He didn't flinch.

"I'm not sure," replied Tom.

"How many babes were you with at the Bear's Den? She was incredible. I figured she was a tutoring session."

Apparently giving up, Ferolyn just rolled her eyes.

Mike then asked if anyone was interested in a trip to Sugarloaf. Thankfully, that changed the subject quickly.

While the rest of them were busy with travel plans, Tom spent the rest of the night talking mainly with Lynda, being "nice," but he was a little distracted.

"How did you guys meet?" asked Tom.

"At Mr. Kites."

Meeting in a bar is never a good start, thought Tom as Lynda continued. "I was with a bunch of friends celebrating one of their birthdays last September, just after school started. And Joe was there, too, looking lonely and lost, so I asked him to dance."

That was summer, and yesterday was the first day of winter. Three seasons with the same girl set a new record for Joe.

She must be special.

⤜∗⤛

Friday, December 28, 2018
Zoom Call
Limerock, Maine - New Haven, Connecticut

Christmas was an enjoyable day with his family. Mom always gave him an L.L. Bean Oxford shirt and chino pants. His dad scheduled an appointment at Fuller Ford to replace the cruise control. Doug, who was always complaining about his slow driving, must have gotten to his dad.

This morning was the follow-up call with Dr. Westhoven. Tom had thought about Mr. Gartley's advice. He'd also refined his capstone, which he'd submitted to Dr. Westhoven a couple of days ago.

Tom settled at his dad's desk in the showroom, surrounded by new 2019 carpet samples hung neatly on the walls. Dr. Westhoven called at ten as scheduled. "Good morning, Tom. How was your Christmas?"

Tom thought Dr. Westhoven had had a haircut since Thanksgiving, but it was still long as he anchored it behind his ears.

"Great. It's always a good break."

"Good. Thanks for sending along your latest draft. Tom, I can't speak for Dr. Wade, but it looks like you're done. It's time to start working on the article for *Modern Archaeology*. By the way, have you given any more consideration to the conference? It's not too late."

"I've given it a lot of thought." Tom cleared his throat. "If the offer is still open, I'd like to present."

"Wonderful, Tom. I hoped you'd change your mind. Your presentation will complement your article. I'll send along some presentations from past conferences to guide you. Focus on the talk for now, which will then help you write the piece for *Modern Archaeology.*

"Let's connect next Friday, after New Year's. How does that sound?" said Dr. Westhoven.

"Great. And thanks again, Dr. Westhoven, for the opportunities."

Tom knew the presentation was the right thing to do, but now he had to prepare a talk and a paper, neither of which he'd ever done before. So much for the senior slide.

He stared out the window at the vacant sandlot across the street where he had played pickup baseball as a kid. Scrub brush had grown up all over the diamond, covered yesterday by a couple of inches of snow that sparkled with the low winter sun, transforming the sandlot into a Hallmark card.

Tom's head swirled with emotions. He would take Dr. Westhoven's advice and call his capstone done. After almost a year, it was time to wrap it up. But he wasn't relieved or pleased. He still struggled with completing a project, and the more complex the project, the more he struggled. And, remembering back to how long it took him to actually start writing his capstone last summer, he knew beginnings were also a challenge for him as he thought about how to begin the article and now the conference.

These feelings were genuine for Tom. He wished he understood them. He wanted to enjoy the moment, but the conference was eight weeks away, which seemed so close, but the start of the new semester and Jenny were only three weeks away, and seemed so far.

∼∽∽

January 2019
Limerock, Maine

Doug had his traditional New Year's Eve party. Someone brought some André Cold Duck for midnight, which had an interesting taste. Joe and Lynda were there. Everyone was a couple except Tom.

He sent Jenny a Happy New Year text message, and she responded promptly that she was looking forward to seeing him in a couple of weeks. The best start ever to a new year, he thought.

To take his mind off Jenny, he kept busy. He spent some time learning about Google CoLab, a free, online hosting solution for Python, ideally suited for machine learning. He would no longer be tied to the University mainframe.

Dr. Westhoven sent along some presentations from past conferences. Tom had a few questions, which the professor had answered on the Zoom call last Friday. Tom had already started outlining his talk.

He also helped his dad finish the job in Thomaston, skied a few days at the Snow Bowl with Mike and Ann, saw *The Last Jedi* at the Strand with Joe and Lynda, and met up with Dave and his girlfriend, Amanda, at Sugarloaf for a couple of days. Without his usual distractions, he missed Jenny the most at Sugarloaf.

They had texted every couple of days about the snow conditions and weather, but nothing again about how she was looking forward to seeing him. Back home, while packing for Orono, he sent her a text, the one he had been wanting to send since the new year. Classes started on Tuesday, so she would have to be back on campus by then.

< Do you want to hook-up Tuesday at the
Bear's Den to compare schedules? >

< What time? >

< How about 3? >

< See you then. >

This was much better than texting about ski conditions. Still, he wondered what it would be like to be with Jenny at the Bear's Den and not as her tutor.

The Offer

Monday, January 7, 2019
Bogotá, Colombia

It was a quick commute for Omar from Cartagena to Bogotá in his Gulfstream. Miguel did not think today's meeting would be anything but lunch with his new partner to review the December financials. They met again just after the lunch hour at the Restaurante Julio at their usual table by the window.

After going over the books, Omar fell silent, turning his gaze to the street, darkened by the afternoon clouds. Miguel took a sip of his coffee, signaling for a refill from the server. In their brief time together, he had already learned to wait and let Omar break the silence. And when he did speak, he was usually to the point.

Omar finally turned to him and said, "Miguel, I'm going to look for the lost Inca gold in the Llanganatis, and I hope you will join me."

Miguel put down his coffee. "Many have tried, señor, but none have succeeded in five hundred years. Some doubt it even exists, or if it did, that it has already been found."

He thought Omar was annoyed with him. His new partner was hard to read.

Miguel continued. "And don't forget the curse. Everyone who has ever come close to the gold has died an untimely death."

With a gradual smile, Omar replied, "I know, my friend, but I have a different approach in mind. Let me fill you in and then you can decide if you're interested. I know it is understood, but please use our usual discretion and do not share what I tell you with anyone."

The secrecy heightened Miguel's interest. He sat forward in his chair.

Omar pulled out a folded document and laid the two pages in front of Miguel, who recognized it was a copy of Valverde's Derrotero. Omar leaned in and whispered the first sentence. Miguel listened carefully....

Placed in the town of Pillaro, ask for the farm of

Moya, and sleep (the first night) a good distance

above it; and ask there for the mountain of

Guapa, from whose top, if the day be fine, look

to the east, so that thy back be towards the

town of Ambato, and from thence thou shalt

perceive the three Cerros Llanganati, in the form

of a triangle, on whose declivity there is a lake,

made by hand, into which the ancients threw

the gold they had prepared for the ransom of

the Inca when they heard of his death.

Omar emphasized, "there is a lake, made by hand, into which the ancients threw the gold," pointing to the words with his manicured index finger as he read them. Miguel had read the Derrotero dozens of times over the years, but he had never paid attention to the reference to the lake.

Omar continued, "Most expeditions have looked for the gold in a cave or mine that is described in the next two pages of the Derrotero. I'm going to focus on these lakes made by hand.

"I will use satellites to find lakes possibly made by man, and then use artificial intelligence to determine which of those lakes might harbor the Inca gold hidden in their depths. The actual expedition will be by helicopter. There will be no trekking through the Llanganatis. The team will be small, well trained and equipped."

"Interesting, señor." It was Miguel's turn to look reflective. "It sounds like this will cost a small fortune."

Again, he thought Omar seemed annoyed with him.

"You are correct, my friend, but I will finance the entire operation."

"What would be my role?"

"I need someone with your abilities to oversee the operation," explained Omar.

Miguel wondered what his abilities were.

"I have already taken care of the necessary permissions from the Ecuadorian government, but there's still a lot of work to do, and I wish to remain in the background."

"My business has become busy, thanks to you, señor. It would be difficult to step back," said Miguel, who actually had the time but not the inclination to commit, knowing the history of prior expeditions into the Llanganatis.

"I understand," said Omar, again turning his gaze to the street, which Miguel followed. The sun peeked out from a cloud, causing Miguel to squint, but not Omar. "Ecuador will take half of any gold we find. Besides a monthly retainer for you, I will share ten percent of any gold we find with you after expenses."

Miguel knew the lost Inca gold could be worth over a billion dollars, if it existed.

Things move fast with the Arab, thought Miguel. Why must he always be in the background? If he is hiding something, he is hiding it well.

Since they had first met, Miguel had continued to plumb for information, but so far, he had found nothing new. He still wondered about the earlier reference to the Hobby Lobby scandal.

"Please tell me, señor, in more detail, what you need for me to do if I accept this generous offer?"

Omar looked back at him. "I have identified an archaeologist to lead the project. I think he is our best chance to find the lakes made by man. His name is Jerome Westhoven. He is a professor at Yale. Your first job is to engage with him. Have you ever heard of him?"

Miguel smiled. "Yes, señor, I have. I have worked with Dr. Westhoven on several occasions. He is an expert in pre-Colombian artifacts. Buyers and museums often use him to authenticate pieces I offer for sale. Why him?"

"Wonderful," replied Omar. This was about as ebullient as Miguel had seen him.

Omar continued. "He is the editor of *Modern Archaeology*. Either he would possess or know someone who does possess the skills to look for the gold.

"Miguel, please give my offer some consideration. Remember, your discretion is important. Let's reconnect in a week or two. I hope I have interested you in this adventure. If we can engage Dr. Westhoven, I'm prepared to offer him a stipend to cover all his costs and five percent of the gold, after expenses."

Miguel rocked ever so slightly. It was a habit, his tell. Yes, he was interested, extremely interested. He had only known Omar for a short period of time. Even though the man appeared to make quick decisions, Miguel understood he was methodical. He had likely already put a lot of thought into this. If anyone could find the Inca treasure, it would be Omar Al Tajir.

Miguel was not a deep thinker. That Omar may have sought him out as a silent partner of Antigüedades Sur because of his connection with Dr. Westhoven never occurred to him.

But Miguel was good at math, and ten percent of a fortune was still a fortune.

Tuesday, January 8, 2019
Bogotá, Colombia

Miguel did some research after the meeting. His share could be millions, or nothing, which he thought was more likely. But he did not need to wait a week or two to decide. He reached out to the Arab to let him know he was interested, but needed to learn more about the proposal.

Omar suggested they meet face-to-face again, this time at his home. Omar would fly him to Cartagena and have him back to Bogotá by late afternoon.

Unbeknownst to Miguel, Omar had already set up a holding company with four subsidiaries in Nevis, an offshore tax haven. Miguel would be the titular head of three, but Omar would control the financials. The other subsidiary listed Tarek Sharif as its head. This would be the company that would manage logistics and materials.

&

Wednesday, January 23, 2019
La Casa Occidental
Cartagena, Colombia

Two weeks later, Miguel was boarding a private jet to Cartagena. Omar was wealthy. Miguel understood that, but he had never flown in a private jet. The only markings on the sleek white Gulfstream were G280 over *A6-V5W* on the tail. The pilot and flight attendant welcomed him on board at the bottom of the airstairs. It would be a quick flight.

The top of the airstairs opened into an impressive galley with a bar with a subtle whiff of leather. The interior of the cabin was creamy white with wood paneling. Natural light streamed in through over a dozen windows running down the fuselage. The cabin was divided into two sections, with the forward cabin set up for meetings with four leather seats, two on each side of the aisle facing each other, around two polished tables. The aft cabin was longer, with two large, reclining seats facing each other on the left and a matching leather sofa against the right cabin wall. Miguel settled into a reclining chair in the aft cabin.

On the flight, Miguel skimmed through a couple of books he had brought along about the lost Inca treasure. By the time he arrived in Cajamarca, he was fairly certain he would join his new partner in his quest to find the lost Inca gold. And he was anxious to learn more about his role in the adventure.

With his customers, Miguel dealt with extraordinary wealth. These were the only ones who could afford the artifacts he brokered. He expected an impressive home, but when the limousine passed through the gates, the opulence still took him aback. The compound was on a peninsula. It looked about ten hectares, although he could not see the entire property because of the lush trees.

A well-manicured lawn with a central fountain surrounded by a colorful flower bed led to the main entrance of the large, white, two-story house, likely constructed during the colonial-era, situated toward the back of the compound by the ocean. Several smaller, matching white bungalows partially hidden in the trees surrounded the main house.

As he walked to the entrance, beads of sweat formed on his forehead and upper lip. It was warmer here than Bogotá, even with the gentle sea breeze. He was not used to the oppressive humidity.

A stocky, middle-aged man casually dressed in a white suit met him at the door. "Welcome Señor Titere to La Casa Occidental. I'm Tarek. Please follow me if you will."

His English was crisp, with a Middle Eastern accent. Omar probably brought him from Abu Dhabi, although Cartagena was becoming a popular destination for immigrants from the Middle East.

The beige grand entrance was as large as his office of Antigüedades Sur, and twice as high, with an ornate crystal chandelier. A grand staircase graced the back of the entrance. Tarek brought Miguel to a long rectangular room off to the right, filled with antiquities from the Middle East. A large oak table centered the room. A marble fireplace at the far end looked like it had not been used in a while. There were no pre-Colombian artifacts. A slight echo from his Oxford shoes on the tile followed him and Tarek to the back of the museum room.

Motioning to a large leather chair next to the empty fireplace, Tarek asked, "May I offer you a coffee or tea, or a cold beverage?"

Miguel could feel the air conditioning as he sat down. He noticed the hint of cigar in the cool air. "No, thank you." Miguel dabbed his forehead with his handkerchief. He was still adjusting to the humidity. Tarek bowed and left. He wondered how the man looked and stayed so cool.

Alone, Miguel rose from his seat and circled the room, admiring the artifacts. Omar startled him a few minutes later when he entered from a small office off the back of the museum.

Omar gave him a brief tour of the room, skipping the three dated photographs on the fireplace mantle. One showed Omar towering over a distinguished-looking individual in the desert. No family photographs anywhere. They circled back to Omar's office, which was smaller and darker than Miguel expected. More items from the Middle East decorated his office, but still no family photographs.

Miguel settled into a comfortable leather chair, with Omar behind his large desk, covered with papers in disarray. Miguel noticed dozens of books about the Incas in a bookcase behind Omar, all within arm's reach. There was one small window up high over the bookcase, which supplemented the dim lights over the desk. Tarek appeared again to offer some coffee, which Miguel accepted now that he had cooled off.

He had come to Cartagena to accept the offer, but he wanted to hear the details again. Miguel needed to convince himself that he was doing due diligence. He asked several questions. Many were redundant. Omar patiently answered all of them.

After a dozen questions, and a brief pause, Omar mentioned again he hoped the expedition leader would be Dr. Westhoven.

"If Dr. Westhoven identifies some lakes, we will also want him on the ground in the Llanganatis. He has the experience we need."

Miguel noticed the use of "we" instead of "I." Omar must know he was here to accept the offer.

"I agree, señor." Miguel was gently rocking, almost imperceptibly. It was time to end the charade. "I'm honored you have considered me for this opportunity. Please include me in this adventure."

A rare smile by Omar. "This is certainly good news, my friend. Now, let me fill you in on more of the details.

"I have a few considerations to follow, but we will otherwise leave the satellite search and virtual expedition to Dr. Westhoven."

"The most important consideration is the underwater search needs to be limited to a depth of about ten meters. I have a satellite that can only see to that depth," he explained.

"Also, we will limit the first expedition to five lakes, which I hope we can survey in one week given the weather in the Llanganatis. Dr. Westhoven needs to find the five most promising lakes that might harbor the hidden Inca gold.

"I already have a helicopter, an MD600N, which I have retrofitted with pontoons for water landings. I removed the back seats so there is plenty of room for equipment. A Zodiac watercraft fits between the pontoons.

"The actual expedition will be from a base camp in the Llanganatis to minimize flight time. Again, there will be no trekking through the Llanganatis."

Miguel caught himself rocking again. He clasped his hands in his lap and straightened his spine. He wished he could take notes.

"We will place a six-man team in the Llanganatis that includes the pilot, a diver, the base camp manager, Dr. Westhoven, his assistant, and you. Tarek, the gentleman who greeted you this morning, will be our base camp manager."

Miguel continued to be impressed with Omar's methodical planning. "When do you hope to enter the Llanganatis, if all goes well?" he asked.

"Next March, a year from now. That is the best combination of weather, including temperature, rain, and most important, the wind."

Omar then returned to Dr. Westhoven. "I have a draft email to Dr. Westhoven under your signature. Please edit my attempt to make it personal, more like a typical email you would send to him."

Miguel made a few minor changes and logged into his Gmail account to send the email to Dr. Westhoven.

To: Dr. Jerome Westhoven
Date: Wednesday, January 23, 2019
From: Miguel Titere

Subject: Llanganatis

Dear Dr. Westhoven,

I hope you're doing well. It's been a while since we have worked together, but I have always appreciated your expertise and help in the past.

I have a proposal I hope will interest you.

With the backing of the Ecuadorian government, I'm mounting an expedition into the Llanganatis.

If this is of interest, I would love to talk with you in more detail.

Sincerely yours,

Miguel Titere
Antigüedades Sur

Miguel understood that Dr. Westhoven was important to the operation. He was one of only a handful in the world with the required skill set. Replacing him would probably significantly delay the operation, and Miguel suspected Omar did not handle delays well.

Omar then presented Miguel with a nondisclosure agreement. He described it as a formality. Miguel's profession dictated discretion, but he had never signed a nondisclosure agreement. It was simple, less than one page. Omar, so far, had been a good partner, so Miguel signed the agreement after a cursory review.

They took a break for lunch. Miguel followed Omar back through the museum into the grand entrance, into a smaller room off the back left of the entrance, behind the kitchen. The informality, along with the clatter in the kitchen, helped relax Miguel. He was still not comfortable with how quickly things were unfolding.

During lunch, Omar asked about some of his old clients from the Middle East. Over the last month, many had approached Antigüedades Sur directly. They did not go through dealers, which further helped Miguel's margin. And, they did not have the same standards for provenance and documentation as Miguel's usual clients. Their new business would easily cover Omar's investment.

"It has made a difference, señor. You will see for yourself when we review the financials next month."

After lunch, they returned to the office, where Omar laid out the corporate structure of the operation. Without getting into the details of the holding company in Nevis, Omar explained to Miguel he was the head of three new companies. One would provide grant money to fund Dr. Westhoven. Another would own the helicopter. And a third company would hire the people and pay for other incidentals during the operation. Omar would fund all the corporations. He did not mention the fourth company headed by Tarek.

"My friend, in addition to ten percent of the gold, I will also compensate you for your time and effort. I will match your median monthly income until we complete the operation. Does that sound fair?"

"Yes, señor, very fair. It looks like we are prospecting, if that is the word, for gold," said Miguel.

The final document Omar presented to Miguel was a simple agreement. Without specifically mentioning gold or silver, Miguel would share in any profit, after expenses, at ten percent. The document was on the letterhead of the third company.

It did dawn on him that Omar had already laid a lot of groundwork even before Miguel committed. Evidently, Omar was moving forward, with or without him. Miguel was glad he committed. He had nothing to lose. And how fortuitous that he already had a working relationship with Dr. Westhoven.

❧

While Miguel was on his way back to Bogotá. Omar leaned back in his office chair and watched the ceiling fan dissipate the smoke from his cigar.

"He took the bait, Tarek."

Tarek looked much more relaxed not playing a domestic. "It appears so." Tarek took a sip of arak.

Omar met Tarek during his third year at Birzeit. Tarek Sharif was ex-military, and now a trusted associate. He was the intermediary for illegal arms trading and supervised the looting of antiquity sites that Dr. Parcak identified as "waffles" on her satellites.

Omar had never notified the Ecuadorian government or sought their permission for the expedition. He was not concerned about the percentages he had promised, as he had other plans for sharing the gold.

"You look troubled, my friend. What is it?" asked Omar.

"He almost seems too gullible. I worry we can trust his discretion."

"Yes, but we only tell him what we need him to know. He does not seem bright enough to figure it out."

Another silence while Omar enjoyed his cigar and Tarek his drink.

Omar had another reason for bringing Tarek back to La Casa Occidental. "Tell me about the rumors."

"I hear stories of another expedition next summer. The guy working on our helicopter likes to talk. He has also retrofitted another."

"Do you know who is financing the other expedition?"

"No, but the lettering on some of the equipment in the hangar is Japanese. Also, Luis Alvarez, an old partner of the famous Llanganatis explorer Andrés Fernández, has been spotted in Quito. He may be connected to the expedition, but I'm not sure yet."

"Interesting. Fernández died in 2017. He was supposed to have an extensive collection of maps and documents. I wonder if someone found something of interest after his death."

Omar carefully placed his cigar down into an intricate ashtray. "If someone else can lead us to the gold, I want to know about it. This will not directly affect our plan, but if they find gold before us, I want it."

⁂

Wednesday, January 23, 2019
Antigüedades Sur
Bogotá, Colombia

The flight from Cartagena lasted less than ninety minutes. On the flight, Miguel tracked down the ownership of the Gulfstream. The jet was owned by an offshore company in Nevis but registered in the United Arab Emirates under the name of Tarek Sharif. Was this the Tarek he met at Cartagena? He did not remember Tarek's last name.

Miguel was back in his office by late afternoon. He knew from experience it would often be a few days before Dr. Westhoven would reply to an email, so he was surprised when there was one already waiting for him.

To: Miguel Titere
Date: Wednesday, January 23, 2019
From: Jerome Westhoven, PhD

Subject: Re: Llanganatis

Dear Miguel,

It's good to hear from you.

You have piqued my interest. When may we connect?

Sincerely,

Jerome Westhoven, PhD
Council on Archaeological Studies
Yale University

Miguel looked up "piqued" in his English translation. He forwarded the email to Omar, who suggested Miguel meet with Dr. Westhoven face-to-face in New Haven. Miguel would fly on the Gulfstream, which had a range well within a flight from Bogotá to New Haven.

Dr. Westhoven and Miguel settled on a date the following Friday. Miguel asked Dr. Westhoven if he would mind meeting on the jet. It would give them more time to talk.

How would he present this to Dr. Westhoven? Their interactions in the past were always professional, focused on an artifact they both understood well. Miguel was good at brokering artifacts. They sold themselves to willing buyers. Selling a virtual expedition was unfamiliar territory.

The Pizza Palace

Tuesday, January 22, 2019
Bear's Den
The University of Maine
Orono, Maine

Today was the first day of classes. Tom arrived early to the Bear's Den, grabbed a coffee, and made his way back to their table. As he hung his winter coat on the back of the chair, he pulled out his class schedule and flattened it on the table, almost knocking over his coffee.

He only had four classes this semester and one was finishing the capstone, which was now, after his Zoom call with Dr. Westhoven, essentially done. He had also decided over the Christmas break to enroll in the master's degree program for computer science and signed up for a graduate level course to get a head start on his degree.

Jenny arrived on time. After she pulled off her mittens and a quick wave, she picked up her Diet Coke and made her way back to Tom. Tom noticed how well her green jacket fit.

He stood up to give her a quick hug and almost spilled his coffee again. The hug felt a little perfunctory, but he wasn't sure what to expect.

"Hey, is that a new coat?" he asked.

"Yeah, a Christmas present."

"Looks nice." Tom had worn his new Oxford shirt. "What do you think of my new shirt?"

"Very nice, too, but probably not as warm as my jacket," she said with her smile that Tom had missed for the last four weeks.

As she settled into her chair, she pulled out her schedule. Hers was a lot busier than Tom's, but he noticed she was always done by three o'clock.

He only had three actual classes, plus his capstone, which didn't show up on the schedule.

"What's the deal?" she asked. "Are you part time now?"

"The schedule doesn't show the capstone and I'm pretty well caught up on credit hours. You know, the senior slide."

"One of those looks like a graduate course in computer science. Does this mean you decided to stay for a master's?"

"Yeah. I have to formally apply, but Dr. Wade said he would be delighted to have me another couple years."

"Me too. We should celebrate."

Tom didn't know how to respond, so he smiled and took a long sip of his coffee. This was as good a time as any to ask. "How about the Woodman's on Thursday?"

"Yeah, that's a great idea. I have an early class on Friday, so could we go out early?"

"Sure. I'll pick you up around five o'clock?"

"Perfect."

As they chatted about their Christmas vacations, Tom remembered his Zoom calls with Dr. Westhoven. "By the way, remember that conference in Boston I mentioned last semester?"

"The one you declined?"

"I decided to do it."

"Really. When is it again?"

"President's Day Weekend."

"Darn. I already told Robin I would spend the weekend with her. She lives in Bethel, near Sunday River. I'm sorry."

Tom didn't expect she would have any interest in coming with him. "It will probably be pretty dull. You'll have a lot more fun skiing at Sunday River."

Tom had been fussing about reuniting with Jenny for a month. It surprised him how comfortable he felt around her.

As they were walking out of the Bear's Den, Tom mentioned that he usually grabs a cup of coffee around three o'clock every afternoon for a mental break, if she wanted to swing by. Tom had noticed she had a two o'clock class the next day in Stevens Hall, which was next door to the Bear's Den.

"Yeah, I should be able to make it, but if I don't, I'll see you at five o'clock on Thursday."

❧❦

Thursday, January 24, 2019
Woodman's Grill
Orono, Maine

They met yesterday and today at the Bear's Den. After a coffee and Diet Coke, they took off for the Woodman's Grill. Tutoring hadn't started yet, so Tom had to be careful with his expenses. Hopefully, Jenny would order a hamburger and not a steak.

"The hamburgers are great at the Woodman's," said Tom, hoping to steer her in the right direction.

"I was thinking of the fish tacos."

That was affordable. "Yeah, they're good too."

Jenny had an early class tomorrow, so after dinner, they headed back to campus. Tom remembered Fridays from last semester were also busy for Jenny, which sometimes limited their Bear's Den time together after tutoring. The Pizza Palace was just across the street, but showing her the Palace would have to wait.

As they bundled into the truck, Tom asked, "Do you want to get together Saturday for a Pat's pizza? We could maybe stream a movie?"

"Sounds great. I've never had a Pat's pizza."

Tom found this hard to believe, but then, she didn't have a car.

"Well, you're in luck. The Pizza Palace is also above Pat's."

"What's the Pizza Palace?"

"That's what we named our apartment. I'll swing by at five."

$$\approx\!\infty$$

Saturday, January 26, 2019

Pizza Palace

Orono, Maine

Jenny was already waiting by the curb when he arrived at Somerset. He panicked he was late but saw he was actually five minutes early, which he took as a good sign that she was looking forward to tonight.

When they arrived at Pat's, Dave was in the back making and baking pizzas when Tom caught his attention and sent him a quick text.

< 1 p & m >

< She's a nice gestalt. >

He still hadn't looked up gestalt.

Fifteen minutes later, Tom and Jenny were heading upstairs to the Pizza Palace with a pepperoni and mushroom pizza.

The stairs to the apartment opened into a small kitchen, too small to do any serious cooking, but why cook when you live above a restaurant? Pizza smells from Pat's below permeated the apartment. A tattered sofa and coffee table separated the kitchen from the living room. Two bedrooms in the back, with a large bathroom between, completed the apartment. Remarkably, everything was clean, but then no one had been here for over a month. It had a retro vibe with the kitschy Formica kitchen table with aluminum edging.

They settled on the sofa to eat the pizza.

"Now I understand why everyone raves about Pat's Pizza. This is great, even better than the pizzas I made at the Tyson Store."

After another bite, and a look around the Palace, Jenny asked, "Which bedroom is yours?"

"The one with the broken ski tip on the door. You want a tour?" This was out of character for Tom, and he immediately flushed.

Jenny just chuckled. Tom wasn't sure what that meant.

After they finished the pizza, Jenny settled back on the sofa and rested her head on his shoulder.

Tom pulled Jenny closer. "That was the bestest pizza ever."

Jenny reached up with her free hand and pulled him down for a long kiss while caressing his neck. When she finally released her lips, she whispered, "Bestest isn't a word." Tom noticed she was gently biting her lower lip. "And maybe this would be a good time for a tour of your bedroom."

The movie would have to wait....

Afterwards, Tom made a note to fix the squeak in the bedsprings.

The next day, after lunch, they drove back to Somerset. Tom walked with her up to her room. He had never been in Somerset. Robin, her roommate, sat up on her bed when they entered.

"So, you're the computer geek?" she said with a wide grin. "I've heard a lot about you."

"I prefer nerd, but I'll answer to either."

Jenny blushed. Tom noticed a few novels scattered amongst her textbooks, including a Stephen King book, *The Outsider.*

"Nice to meet you, Robin."

Jenny ushered Tom into the hall.

"Sorry about that," she said.

"What? And miss seeing you blush?"

"I wasn't blu...."
Before she could finish, Tom gave her a proper kiss.
"See you tomorrow," he said as he turned to the stairs.
"Ayuh," replied Jenny, a little breathless.

Dr. Westhoven

Friday, February 1, 2019
Bogotá, Colombia to New Haven, Connecticut

Today was Miguel's flight to New Haven. Once again, the same pilot and flight attendant greeted him. Customs was perfunctory. For this trip, he chose a seat in the forward cabin with a table so he could do some work. They were in the air within thirty minutes, headed to Tweed-New Haven Airport. The four-hour flight was uneventful, and gave Miguel time to read about artificial intelligence.

Omar had told Miguel to offer Dr. Westhoven five percent of the gold and a grant to fund his work, but only after he expressed a serious interest. Dr. Westhoven could then split his five percent as he chose with his team.

The Gulfstream touched down about one o'clock locally to clear skies. Even though it was the middle of winter here, Miguel did not notice any snow. The pilot positioned the plane facing the sun, which softly illuminated the cabin.

Dr. Westhoven was already waiting on the tarmac, bundled up against the cold, when Miguel walked down the airstairs to greet him.

"Dr. Westhoven, it's so good to see you again," said Miguel with a hearty handshake he had learned from Omar. Miguel still thought it odd a professor with his reputation had hair to his shoulders.

"Likewise, Miguel. My goodness, business must be good," said Dr. Westhoven, admiring the plane.

"It has its ups and downs, as you know, but it has been a good year. I wish I could say I own this plane, but I lease it when I must travel. It's more convenient and set up for meetings such as ours."

Miguel shivered and motioned Dr. Westhoven to follow him up the airstairs. "Come aboard and let me show you around." Miguel could tell he was impressed.

Dr. Westhoven accepted an offer of coffee from the flight attendant.

They settled in the forward cabin with a table between them. A two-page paper-clipped document lay face down on the polished surface.

Once the cabin was secure, and they had warmed up, Miguel started. "Dr. Westhoven, I will get directly to the point. I'm looking for the lost Inca gold in the Llanganatis. You and I both know the history of these expeditions, but please listen to my proposal."

He expected some reaction from Dr. Westhoven but so far, only a quick nod of his head, and hair.

Miguel flipped over the two-page document and pushed it toward Dr. Westhoven.

"Here is a translation of the Derrotero. Please read the first sentence and pay particular attention to the end of the sentence."

Dr. Westhoven traced the words with his index finger. When he reached the end of the first sentence, he looked up.

Miguel said, "I'm intrigued by 'there is a lake, made by hand, into which the ancients threw the gold they had prepared for the ransom of the Inca.'"

Using some jargon he learned on the flight, he continued, "What I'm proposing is a virtual expedition of the Llanganatis using satellites to find lakes made by the hand of man, and then using artificial intelligence to look into those lakes to find the gold."

As Dr. Westhoven scanned the rest of the Derrotero, Miguel caught himself rocking in the leather seat.

"Hopefully, with artificial intelligence, we can narrow the search down to about five lakes and conduct an actual expedition to the Llanganatis, but without trekking. We will use a helicopter I have specially outfitted to survey each lake. The team on the ground in the Llanganatis would be small, only six, including yourself and your assistant."

Miguel waited. He could tell the professor was listening intently, but still had no reaction. Dr. Westhoven finally looked up from the Derrotero.

"Any questions?" asked Miguel.

"Not yet. Intrigued is the right word, Miguel. Please continue."

"I selected you, Dr. Westhoven, because I need someone familiar with the Incas, someone comfortable with technology such as artificial intelligence and satellite imagery, and someone who has been on the ground in the Llanganatis."

He paused. He was uncomfortable going further without some affirmation from Dr. Westhoven, who had turned his gaze out the cabin window to the tarmac, rubbing his pursed lips slowly with his right hand. The sun entering the cabin highlighted his stubble.

"Miguel, there are hundreds of lakes in the Llanganatis. How do we find the lakes made by hand referenced in the Derrotero?"

Good—a question, thought Miguel. He is interested. "That is an important consideration. I will leave the details to your expertise, but I will provide high-resolution images from the Llanganatis. Perhaps you could focus on lakes with a river or stream but with no clear outflow. This might suggest a lake made by the hand of man. The Derrotero also references a declivity. Possibly looking for lakes on a slope would also help narrow the search."

Dr. Westhoven looked like he was now thinking, not listening, so Miguel waited.

"I like the concept, Miguel, but the challenge is the training data set for the deep learning neural network. There is none. This has never been done. We will need to make assumptions, which may or may not be true. We don't know what the Inca gold would look like underwater."

Dr. Westhoven took a long reflective sip from his coffee.

Miguel did not reply, but he was rocking again, ever so slightly. He was not sure what Dr. Westhoven meant by the training data set.

The professor continued, "Success will depend entirely upon the training. We will need to model Inca gold and silver underwater to train the neural network." Another sip of coffee. "Assuming we can overcome that hurdle, how do we see underwater?"

Miguel did not understand the importance of training, but he could tell Dr. Westhoven was concerned. Omar wanted Dr. Westhoven. He needed to hook him.

"You are—how do you say—astute, my friend. I have already engaged a special camera mounted on a satellite to see underwater up to ten meters. The camera reduces the impact of the surface waves, but the water still needs to be reasonably clear."

He skipped over the issue of the training data set. "Are you at least interested, my friend?"

"Tell me, Miguel, how is the Ecuadorian government handling your request?"

"We expect formal permission in the next couple of weeks. They will, of course, want half of any gold we find."

They both took another long sip of coffee.

"Yes, Miguel, I'm interested," said Dr. Westhoven. "Fill me in on your timeline and funding."

"Wonderful. The project will have two distinct parts. The first phase, under your direction, will identify up to five lakes that might hide the gold. I hope you can complete this by the fall of this year. The second part is an actual expedition into the Llanganatis by helicopter, specially outfitted for the expedition.

"As you know, the weather in the Llanganatis can be unforgiving. We have a narrow window of opportunity, and my goal is to be in the Llanganatis about a year from now in March 2020.

"I will fund the entire project. You will receive a grant to support your work, and if we find any gold, I will share five percent, after expenses, with you. You can split this with your team in any way you desire. You and I both know this could be worth millions."

Dr. Westhoven leaned back. "This might be a good time for a scotch," he said. Miguel buzzed the flight attendant.

He understood Dr. Westhoven needed a moment. "I know this is a lot to process, my friend. I don't expect a firm commitment this afternoon, but you are my first choice for this project. If we do head into the Llanganatis, I also hope you will lead the actual expedition next March. Please take some time to consider my proposal. Give it some thought. We can reconnect when you've made a decision."

They had been meeting for an hour. Dr. Westhoven sipped his scotch deliberately. Miguel could tell he was interested. Omar would be pleased.

"This is indeed intriguing, Miguel, but there are a lot of loose ends. Let me give this some thought. I think I can put together a team, but the training data set will be the key. How about I commit to an answer in a couple of weeks? Is that acceptable?"

"Perfectly. I know you will give this the consideration it deserves. Frankly Dr. Westhoven, if this does not interest you, I will question the merit of this project."

Miguel was in the air by three o'clock. He had dinner on the plane and was back home by evening. He thought Dr. Westhoven would ultimately join, and he updated Omar during the flight back.

Omar did seem pleased, but it was not always apparent to Miguel.

⊱⊰

The Yale campus was quiet on Friday afternoon by the time Dr. Westhoven returned to his office. Miguel had always seemed like a measured man. This all seemed so fanciful. But no one had ever presented him with a fully funded project without a lot of strings attached. Even at Yale, he had to scrape for funding, especially in archaeology.

He wasn't sure why Miguel had reached out to him. Dr. Westhoven did not have the expertise to program and train a convolutional neural network—but Tom Kirkpatrick did. He had said nothing to Miguel about Tom, but he'd need someone like him.

He also knew enough about machine learning to understand the importance of the training. There was no existing training data set to find underwater gold or silver. He would have to develop a model, but no one had ever seen Inca gold or silver underwater.

He pulled up a copy of the Derrotero online and read it carefully. The first sentence was at odds with the rest of the document. It plainly says the Incas threw the gold into a man-made lake.

So why did everyone look for the gold in caves or mines? Perhaps it was easier than looking underwater.

Miguel was right. Satellite imaging could narrow the search by selecting lakes in the Llanganatis, with features suggesting the Incas had created a lake "by hand." Dr. Parcak had already laid the groundwork for imaging dried-up riverbeds.

Tom will be at the conference in two weeks to present his paper. Dr. Westhoven decided to connect with him then, face-to-face. If Tom wasn't willing or able to join him, Dr. Westhoven didn't have anyone else in mind. And he already knew Tom had difficulty committing. It would be a long two weeks, but he also needed the time to process the offer by Miguel.

Friday, February 8, 2019
La Casa Occidental
Bogotá, Colombia

Tarek had been in Quito for the last couple of weeks, laying the preliminary groundwork for the expedition, still over a year away. Tarek had also learned more about the other expedition, which Omar expected him to share this afternoon on their regularly scheduled phone call.

Omar had reached out to his contact at the Ecuadorian embassy in the United Arab Emirates, who confirmed an expedition headed by Luis Alvarez, with funding from a Japanese conglomerate or *keiretsu*, was heading into the Llanganatis next summer. A small team was planning to helicopter into the mountains, but he did not know when or where. He needed Tarek to confirm what he already had learned.

Omar did not panic easily, but he also understood the importance of planning and expecting loose ends. As he mulled over his options about the competing expedition, his phone rang.

"Hello—Tarek, it is good to hear your voice. What did you find out?"

"An expedition has requested permission to conduct a survey of a lake in the eastern park this summer, probably in August. They will use Quito as their base, flying by helicopter back and forth each day to the lake. The application indicates they are looking for a lost Inca settlement. There is no mention of gold."

"Do you know who is leading the expedition?"

"Luis Alvarez, the former partner of Andrés Fernández. The money backing the expedition is Japanese. If Alvarez is involved with Japanese backing, this expedition is not looking for Inca settlements."

"Agreed. Good work Tarek."

Omar had already been formulating a plan. The helicopter would only make it easier to execute.

"What about the conference next weekend? Is everything in place? Based upon the timetable Dr. Westhoven gave to Miguel, I believe he plans to connect with someone at the conference before he makes his final decision. I will be interested in your opinion of Dr. Westhoven. Also, there is a young man speaking about artificial intelligence. Check him out, too."

"I have already registered for his talk," said Tarek. "He is an undergraduate at the University of Maine."

"Interesting," replied Omar.

The Conference

Friday, February 8, 2019
Orono, Maine

Dave and Amanda typically were at Sugarloaf on the weekends, and Jenny had fallen into the weekend routine of staying overnight at the Palace. Occasionally, when they were all at the Palace, weekend mornings were chaotic, but in a fun way.

Both Tom and Jenny were busy, she with her classes, and Tom preparing his talk, which was only a week away. This afternoon, however, they were packing for a weekend at Sugarloaf with Dave and Amanda at his family's A-frame in Spring Farm, a small community off the mountain in Carrabassett Valley. Tom had been there a dozen times over the years, but this was Jenny's first visit.

Dr. Westhoven had emailed Tom last weekend that he wanted to meet at the conference about an opportunity, which usually meant more work for Tom, and not the paying kind. They arranged to meet on Sunday afternoon after the conference ended. Even though he had a light class load, he was already stretched with tutoring, and he hadn't even started the article he owed Dr. Westhoven for *Modern Archaeology*. He just wanted to get this presentation over with.

Although not a fan of buses, Tom was planning to take the Concord bus to Boston until a plane ticket arrived from Dr. Westhoven. He really didn't want to fly, but he would not share this with Jenny. He reluctantly returned the bus tickets.

Tom had been working on his presentation since Christmas break and had condensed his forty-page capstone into a forty-minute talk titled "Expanding Archaeology with Artificial Intelligence." He was finally comfortable with the content. Now he needed to get comfortable with public speaking.

On the way to Sugarloaf, he mentioned to Jenny, "Dr. Westhoven wants to meet with me next weekend in Boston."

"Why?"

"It's probably about starting the article for *Modern Archaeology*. Or maybe about Yale again. I'm not ready for that conversation." Tom had formally applied and had been accepted into the master's program in computer science.

Dave and Amanda were already there when they arrived. Tom enjoyed spending time at the A-frame. It was built back in the 1950s when the Valley was the center of activity at Sugarloaf. Dave's family bought it in the late 1970s. Plenty of windows supplied natural light. The inside was pine board. The camp also seemed larger than it was, with an open ceiling, except for a small, second-story loft bedroom at one end over a couple of other bedrooms on the first floor, separated by a small bathroom. A wood stove provided ambiance.

They left for dinner early enough to get a booth at Tufulio's, Tom's favorite restaurant in Carrabassett Valley, just minutes from the A-frame. Vintage posters of Sugarloaf from the 1960s and '70s decorated the place, with framed stained glass separating the booths. The background music was from the same era as the posters. The wait staff was always welcoming, and the food was great.

The restaurant filled up quickly as happy hour ended. The server commiserated with them about the rain tomorrow afternoon, but mentioned a nor'easter was brewing next week, just in time for February vacation. This only reminded Tom about the conference next weekend.

The next morning, they hit the mountain early, knowing afternoon rain would shorten their ski day. In the afternoon, the weather was too foul to do anything outdoors, so they all huddled around the wood stove and read with their warm drink of choice.

While Tom and Jenny were preparing spaghetti for supper, she asked, "How's your talk coming? When are you going to present it to me?"

"How about tomorrow on the way back to Orono?"

"Great. I'm sorry I won't be there, but I promised Robin months ago."

"That's ok. You'd just make me more nervous than I already am."

Thankfully, she didn't ask about the article. Tom did not want to talk about it, but he also didn't want it to be another in a long line of projects he would almost finish. Not because they were hard. He just did not want to be judged. Having a work that was in progress was easier, safer.

Tom had never presented at a national conference, or any conference, for that matter. Even though he had a decent presentation, he was still uncomfortable with public speaking. He dealt with it like he usually did, by over preparing. Anything worth doing is worth doing to excess. But he needed to practice presenting to someone.

The next day, Jenny drove home so Tom could give his talk. He got through the presentation three times, making changes each time. Jenny seemed to lose interest the third time through, but the repetition helped.

As she turned off the Kelley Road exit near Orono, she said, "Tom, I can give this talk I've heard it so many times. You've got this. It's time to stop fussing and enjoy the experience."

"You mean like smell the roses?"

"Yeah."

"It's winter—there are no roses."

"There are on Valentine's Day."

Tom got the hint. Their first Valentine's Day together was Thursday.

Now, where to buy roses....

❧☙

Friday, February 15, 2019
Hotel Commonwealth
Boston, Massachusetts

Dr. Westhoven had asked Tom to touch base when he arrived at the Hotel Commonwealth. After checking in, Tom walked up the stairs to the conference level on the second floor to register. The number of name tags splayed out over three large tables surprised him. The young woman at the registration table mentioned this was the largest conference ever, and she was looking forward to his talk.

Tom recognized Dr. Westhoven talking to an older gentleman near the elevator. He waved to Tom. He was a little taller than Tom expected, but still not as tall as Tom.

"Nice to meet you in person, Tom. I just wanted to double check everything is all set for you for tomorrow."

Tom was the opening talk of the conference at eight o'clock, which was fine by him. Once he finished his presentation, he could then relax and enjoy the rest of the conference.

"I think so. The audiovisual folks asked me to show up a half-hour early for sound check, and then off I go."

"Great. Get a good night's sleep and I'll see you in the morning."

All checked-in and registered, Tom took the elevator to his room, which was larger than he expected, with a large desk in a small alcove with a built-in settee by the window. He had a partial view of Fenway and the Green Monster. When he bounced on the king-size bed, he wished Jenny had been able to come along. He practiced his talk one more time and then texted Jenny goodnight with a picture of the bed.

< Wish you were here. >

< Me too. >

After a restless night and a quick cup of coffee, Tom headed to the small conference room for sound check. He was taken aback by how many people were milling around so early. By the time Dr. Westhoven introduced him, the crowd was standing-room-only.

From reading the program, Tom knew his talk was unique at the conference, more theoretical as opposed to actual artifacts or digs, but he did not expect to attract this much attention.

Although he had practiced dozens of times, this was his first time giving the presentation before an audience other than Jenny. He was not sure his talk would resonate with the attendees.

After clearing his throat and taking a deep breath, he started with an overview of artificial intelligence, and then introduced the notion of using deep learning to help review the reams of images often produced by satellites, drones, sonar, or any device looking for potential archaeological sites.

The next forty minutes flew by. He had to slow down to coincide with his PowerPoint. He used his nervousness to his advantage. He was in the flow.

After clearing his throat a couple more times, he highlighted the challenges of deep learning. "Many archaeological sites do not have a defined training data set, which can be the limiting step. We are just learning what ancient sites look like on satellite. Combining more images with ground-truthing to verify the findings will facilitate training, at least for these specific sites. The work by Dr. Parcak categorizing landscape and site types establishes a firm foundation."

He also referenced GlobalXplorer. "This crowdsourcing initiative has already generated millions of images in Peru of heavily forested mountains that are being validated. Ultimately, this could be a training data set for other similar landscape types."

Although Tom left time for questions, there were not a lot. He hoped that was not from a lack of interest. Dr. Westhoven had to leave to prepare for the next talk, but before he left, he gave Tom a thumbs up.

Afterward, when everyone was waiting for the next speaker, a Middle Eastern gentleman came up to Tom and asked a question, one that Tom had been pondering but did not specifically address in his presentation. Tom glanced at his name tag.

Dr. Tarek Sharif
Ministry of Antiquities

"Wonderful talk, Mr. Kirkpatrick. I understand the challenges of defining a training data set, but are there ways to simulate or model a data set for training?" he asked.

Tom cleared his throat and nodded. "That's the crux of the issue and why deep learning has not developed as quickly in archaeology as it has in other fields. Frankly, we don't always know what an ancient site will look like from space, and until we have a clearer understanding, it's difficult to develop a training data set to simulate accurately a find in the real world.

"Eventually, the work being done by Dr. Parcak and her team with GlobalXplorer, coupled with ground-truthing, may provide an adequate training data set, although probably only for the mountains in Peru, but it's a start."

"Thank you, Mr. Kirkpatrick. Exciting work." Dr. Sharif bowed and left.

After all the angst, it was over. Now he could relax and enjoy the rest of the conference. Tom wondered if things would have turned out okay without all the fussing, or if fussing was a necessary ingredient. He started to text Jenny, but remembered she'd already be on the hill with Robin.

His presentation had more of an impact than he realized. Over the next few weeks, he would receive several emails with congratulations and questions. He saved the questions to help him frame his article for *Modern Archaeology.*

Also, Tom did not yet realize the impact his talk had upon Dr. Westhoven—and Tarek Sharif.

∽∾

Tom enjoyed the first day of the conference, but he felt a little like an imposter. After the last lecture, he texted Jenny. This was her first-time skiing Sunday River. She was enjoying the mountain, even though it was busier than Sugarloaf. Tonight was dinner at the Bethel Inn with Robin and her family. Tom let her know his talk went well, and he missed her. After an "I told you so," she sent a kiss emoji.

He filled up on hors d'oeuvres at the afternoon reception and then headed back to his hotel room for an early night.

As he lay in bed, staring at the ceiling, wondering why hotel rooms never had an overhead light, he felt a peculiar combination of loneliness and fulfillment. He rarely had time to reflect. It was too early to text or call Jenny, but he was not ready for bed. He spent a few minutes looking out over the Fens to quiet his mind.

∽∾

Sunday, February 17, 2019
Hotel Commonwealth
Boston, Massachusetts

The conference ended, and by all accounts, it was a success. After packing, and before heading to Logan, Tom took the elevator to the fifth floor to meet with Dr. Westhoven. He hoped it was not another push to attend Yale. He didn't want to disappoint the professor. And he needed to unwind before he started on the article for *Modern Archaeology.*

As he exited the elevator and turned the corner, the low afternoon sun streamed through the window at the far end of the hall. Sunshine in the winter always lifted his spirits, but he felt a little claustrophobic as he walked down the long hallway to Dr. Westhoven's room at the end of the hall.

Dr. Westhoven welcomed him into his corner suite, which had a separate room with a couple of chairs arranged around a small circular table next to a window. Otherwise, it had the same cream-colored hotel furniture as his room. As Tom pulled a chair up to the table, he could see Fenway Park.

"Thanks again, Dr. Westhoven, for this opportunity. The feedback's been great. There was one gentleman, I think he was from Egypt, who asked a great question about modeling training data sets. He seemed to understand the challenges."

Dr. Westhoven grabbed a document from the bed. "Interesting. Tom, your presentation was great. You started a lot of old school folks thinking in new ways, including me."

He followed Tom's gaze to the Green Monster. "Do you ever get down to see the Red Sox?"

Tom turned to look at the document that Dr. Westhoven had placed on the table. "Not in years, but I follow them. The pitchers and catchers report tomorrow." Tom was not one for small talk, but he enjoyed the Red Sox.

"Look, Tom, there's no subtle way to introduce this. I've been asked to lead a virtual expedition to find the lost Inca gold underwater in the lakes of the Llanganatis of Ecuador. The virtual aspect is we will look with satellite imagery and use deep learning to refine the search. I want you to join me."

Dr. Westhoven laid it all out for Tom—gold, Llanganatis, lakes, satellites, and artificial intelligence. He waited for Tom to absorb all this.

Tom pursed his lips as his gaze wandered back to the shadow of a cloud moving across the Green Monster.

"Tom, this is the next step of what you've proposed for deep learning. This is an opportunity to make it happen."

He brought his gaze back to Dr. Westhoven and leaned in slightly, eyebrows raised. Did Dr. Westhoven listen to his talk? There's no training data set for gold on the bottom of a lake. Without a training data set, a virtual expedition is destined to fail.

As if on cue, Dr. Westhoven said, "The challenge will be the training data set. There is none. We'll need to model what a pile of Inca gold and silver looks like underwater, and then image it from space, much like Dr. Parcak has done in Egypt and Peru."

Tom had been quiet. He needed to say something. After clearing his throat, he asked, "Why underwater?"

"Are you familiar with Valverde's Derrotero?"

Tom nodded yes, and Dr. Westhoven pushed the document on the table toward him.

"In the very first, albeit long sentence, it references 'a lake, made by hand.' I highlighted it here." He pointed to the passage. "There may be other gold in the Llanganatis, but the focus of this virtual expedition is the man-made lake 'into which the ancients threw the gold.'"

Tom carefully read the first sentence. He took a deep breath, leaned back in his chair, and ran both hands through his hair, clasping them together behind his head. He had never trained a neural network without a well-defined data set.

Dr. Westhoven waited a moment to let Tom ponder and then brought him back.

"If we have a reasonable level of confidence we found something, the second phase would be an actual expedition in the Llanganatis. But there would be no trekking. We would travel by helicopter."

Helicopter. Tom laid his hands on the table. Friday was his first time on a plane. Now a helicopter?

"Who is sponsoring the expedition?"

"A gentleman in South America. His name is Miguel Titere. He's a broker of pre-Colombian antiquities. I've collaborated with him on and off over the years.

"I know this is a lot to process, Tom. Do you have any other questions?"

Tom was already thinking about the training data set. Dr. Westhoven was right. That's the core of deep learning, and typically a training data set already exists.

"Yes, this is a lot to process," said Tom. He leaned back in his chair. "The neural network will depend on how closely we can model a pile of Inca gold and silver. Do we even know what a pile of gold and silver looks like underwater? And even with a great model, how can we see underwater?"

"You've identified the issues. A lot of moving parts for sure, and I need someone like you, someone who understands all the moving parts."

Dr. Westhoven continued. "We'll have access to a unique camera called Depth Cam mounted on a satellite that can see underwater to about thirty feet, if the water is reasonably clear and there's no cloud cover. From the ransom the Incas had already brought to Cajamarca, I also have a sense of what they might have dumped into the lake."

Silence again. Tom leaned forward and rested his chin on his left hand, staring at the document. He cleared his throat again. "What's the timeline?"

"The goal is to be on the ground in the Llanganatis in March 2020. That means we must complete the virtual expedition by fall. If we do go into the Llanganatis, Miguel asked me to lead the actual expedition and I hope you'll join me.

"Finally, Miguel has offered me five percent of whatever gold we find. How about two percent for you out of that five? I'll let you review the legend yourself, but you'll find this could be millions." Dr. Westhoven's eyebrows tented on his forehead.

After a moment, he continued, "This will require a significant time commitment from you over the next year. I'll pay you a stipend of $1,000 a week during the semester and $2,000 during the summer. You'll also have an expense account for travel and incidentals.

"Honestly, Tom, we both know the likelihood of success is quite low. Dozens if not hundreds of explorers have ventured into the Llanganatis and no one, at least no one we know of, has ever found any gold in caves, mines, lost cities, or certainly underwater. But I'm excited to try. Even if we fail, we'll have advanced the field of archaeology."

"Will we be able to publish our findings?"

"No, we can't publish, but we can still write about the framework, the overall approach, like your capstone."

Tom's mind raced, which was not necessarily unpleasant if there was an actual answer or discrete solution. This, however, all seemed so obscure.

He finally muttered. "I need some time to think this through." He had gotten treasure hunting out of his system as a kid.

"Understood. Let's connect next Saturday morning. How about a Zoom call?"

"Sounds good, Dr. Westhoven. Thanks again for the opportunity to speak at the conference. I've learned a lot."

"Your welcome, Tom." Dr. Westhoven handed him the copy of the Derrotero. Tom sat there for a moment before he realized the meeting was over.

Last night, back in his hotel room, Tom felt like a weight had been lifted. Finally, he could focus on Jenny and enjoy the last semester of his senior year. Now, as he slunk down the hallway, following his long shadow to the elevator, his mind was a swirl. He did not like that disorganized feeling.

Waiting at the elevator, he could not get past the idea that this was an enormous distraction, with no chance of success. It was a waste of time, and he wasn't one to waste time. Everything he did had a purpose. This was a "needle in a haystack" without a haystack.

And yet, what Dr. Westhoven had said sparked a subtle interest in the project, along with the stipend.

The elevator arrived. Back to reality, time to check out, Uber to Logan, and back to the Pizza Palace, and Jenny. He was suddenly tired. Possibly a quick nap on the plane. He would be back in Orono in a couple of hours.

On the plane, he reread Valverde's Derrotero. There it was, in the first sentence.

> *... on whose declivity there is a lake,*
>
> *made by hand, into which the ancients*
>
> *threw the gold...*

He closed his eyes....

He awoke when the jet rumbled into its descent. Jenny would pick him up in the F-150. He wanted to hear about her weekend, but she'd also want to know why Dr. Westhoven had wanted to meet.

❧❦

Knowing Tom struggled with decisions, Dr. Westhoven had intentionally scheduled the Zoom call in only one week, hoping to push Tom along. After the meeting, Dr. Westhoven emailed Miguel from the hotel. He painted perhaps an overly optimistic picture.

To: Miguel Titere
Date: Sunday, February 17, 2019
From: Jerome Westhoven, PhD

Subject: Llanganatis

Dear Miguel,

I met with a potential member of my team, and he is interested. I have a follow-up meeting next Saturday morning.

Perhaps we should plan to talk next weekend?

Sincerely yours,

Jerome Westhoven, PhD
Council on Archaeological Studies
Yale University

Miguel replied to Dr. Westhoven's email with an invitation for a phone call the next Saturday afternoon. He also attached some images from Depth Cam, the underwater camera.

That evening, once Dr. Westhoven was back home in New Haven, he poked around on the internet. He had read about a camera a couple of years ago that could "see below the waves."

He found an article from 2016 about a research scientist, Dr. Ved Chirayath, who had developed a camera and software platform to reduce the distortion of waves. Dr. Chirayath called it FluidCam, which he mounted on a plane or drone. Depth Cam was on a satellite. FluidCam must be something different.

The Decision

Sunday, February 17, 2019
Orono, Maine

Jenny tossed Tom the keys when she picked him up at the airport. Tom was hoping to hear about her weekend with Robin, but after a quick hug and kiss, and before he could say anything, she asked, "Why did Dr. Westhoven want to meet?"

It felt good to be back on the ground in the F-150. He would have preferred to talk about the conference, and then ease into the afternoon discussion with Dr. Westhoven, but he said, "He wants me to join him in a virtual expedition using satellites and artificial intelligence to look for the lost Inca gold underwater in the lakes of the mountains of Ecuador."

There—it's out. What a nice synopsis, he thought. He left out the helicopter for now.

"You mean the Llanganatis? Finally! It's about time someone found the gold."

He expected Jenny to be interested, but she took it a step further. He forgot about her interest in the Incas.

"Can I help?" she asked.

"I don't know, Jenny. This seems like a waste of time. I'm not even sure the lost Inca gold exists. And there is no training data set. Satellites can't see underwater. There are too many variables, too many unknowns. And we'll fly around in a helicopter."

"I get your concerns about the data set and the satellite, but what does the helicopter have to do with it?"

"Nothing. It just seems dangerous to fly around in a helicopter in the mountains."

"Are you scared of flying? You didn't seem yourself when I dropped you off Friday at the airport."

Tom wouldn't admit that to her. "No. It's just a hassle to fly with TSA, the lines, the boarding process, and crowded seating. Concord has an excellent bus service to Boston, at a fraction of the cost."

Tom knew Jenny was aware of his control issues. He didn't want to accentuate his shortcomings. It was a long, twenty-minute ride to the Pizza Palace with only light, safe conversation.

As Tom backed into a parking spot behind Pat's, Jenny finally returned to the Inca gold. "Don't focus on whether you'll find the gold. You probably won't. Think about the process, the adventure, the journey. What did Mr. Gartley tell you? Be open to opportunities and don't get in the way of your future, or something like that. You're not doing either. And why would Dr. Westhoven get involved if he didn't think it was worthwhile?"

"He has tenure. He already has a job. He has funding. This will be a lot of work, and I don't want to derail my academic career on a fool's errand."

"Well, you got the 'fool' part right. And we can work on your fear of flying."

"I'm not afraid of flying." Tom felt his "beet head" coming on. As a kid, whenever he had a tantrum, he would first hold his breath and then his face would turn beet red, which his mother called his beet head. It happened infrequently now, but when it did, he didn't have to start the sequence by holding his breath. He could just beet head. Jenny had never seen a full-blown beet head. Sometimes slowing down his breathing helped.

As they climbed the stairs to the Palace, Jenny asked, "Don't you need to train the computer? How would you model the underwater gold?"

"I don't know. What I do know is it's a considerable time commitment. It's going to take time away from everything else, including you."

"I want to help. Remember, I pulled an A- in COS 140, and I know more about the Incas than you do. This will be fun. It's an adventure, a virtual adventure. I can't believe you're not excited. This is the stuff of legends. This is your capstone."

Tom opened the fridge. "You want anything to drink?" as he grabbed a Hipster Apocalypse.

"I'm good." Jenny settled on the sofa and put her feet up on the coffee table. He knew this would not be a quick conversation. He joined her on the sofa.

"This is a big leap from my capstone. I've always assumed I'd have a starting point, something to use as a training data set. Here there is nothing."

"If you build it, they will come." She used this line now and then, and it drove Tom nuts. She never used this quote correctly.

"It's 'If you build it, *he* will come,' not *they* will come."

With the distraction, his beet head was dissipating. Maybe Jenny hadn't noticed.

"Whatever. For once, Tom, go with your gut."

"If you go with your gut, it comes out crap."

"Arrrgh. I'll loan you my copy of Malcolm Gladwell's *Blink*. It's a quick read about how we make decisions."

"And let's watch *Field of Dreams*, so you get the quote right."

She had a week to convince him, and she was off to a slow start.

Tuesday, February 19, 2019
The University of Maine
Orono, Maine

Dr. Wade was in his office waiting for Tom. They had a scheduled meeting next week, but Tom had asked to meet early. He had never asked for a meeting off schedule, and Dr. Wade was concerned. He heard footsteps and a knock on his office door. Tom poked his head in.

"Hey Tom, come on in. What's up?"

Tom cleared his throat. "Thanks for seeing me. I want to run something by you." He sat down. Dr. Wade noticed him squirming a little in the seat, trying to get comfortable.

"I have an opportunity to work on an archaeology project with Dr. Westhoven over the next year. It will be time-consuming and, if I accept, I'll need to back off on tutoring, and it might delay my master's degree. I told him I would decide by this weekend, and I would appreciate your advice."

"This must be quite an opportunity. I'd hate to lose you as a tutor, and I thought you needed the money?"

"I do, but the project has a stipend. I'm more worried about my master's program. This project might delay my graduation."

Dr. Wade pulled out his pipe from an inner jacket pocket. He knew smoking was not allowed on campus, but fiddling with the bowl relaxed him.

"A lot of students delay their programs. The important thing is you complete your degree. Tell me more about the project."

"It's a virtual expedition using artificial intelligence to review satellite data. I've serious doubts it will succeed. I'm not sure I want to delay my master's on something so pointless."

Dr. Wade really wanted to light his pipe.

Tom continued, "I'm just having a tough time committing to something I know will fail."

Dr. Wade stared at his pipe as he leaned back. The squeak from his chair seemed louder.

"A couple of thoughts. I doubt Dr. Westhoven would engage you with something entirely pointless. You may not succeed, but it's still often a worthwhile experience. What you describe sounds a lot like your capstone. This seems like a natural progression.

"And you know I'm not a philosophical guy, but when I do reflect upon my life, some of the best things were happenstance. I happened to be in the right place at the right time.

"Think about your own life. You didn't plan to meet Jenny, but you put yourself in the right place at the right time. You're young, Tom. Experience as many opportunities as you can. There's plenty of time later to fiddle with this," said Dr. Wade, holding up his pipe.

"I guess what I'm trying to say is to be open to opportunities. Let them happen and see where they take you."

This reminded Tom of Mr. Gartley's advice. Is the universe really this random?

Dr. Wade continued, "As a side note, I guess I always hoped you would change your mind and stay with computer science. You have a knack for deep learning that goes beyond archaeology. I understand why Dr. Westhoven sought you out. This may give you a chance to reflect upon your own future."

This was not exactly what he wanted to hear from Dr. Wade.

∽⍟

Saturday, February 23, 2019
Pizza Palace
Orono, Maine

This morning was the Zoom call with Dr. Westhoven. Dave and Amanda were at Sugarloaf, so they had the Palace to themselves. Jenny usually slept in on Saturday mornings, but this morning she was up early, preparing bacon and eggs, while Tom dragged himself out of bed. Saturday had arrived quicker than he wanted. Over the last week, he had thought a lot about the project and the multiple logistical issues. It still seemed like a fool's errand, but Jenny remained supportive, almost too supportive, and Dr. Wade did not dissuade him, as he had hoped.

On Wednesday, Dr. Westhoven emailed him about the Depth Cam, the software and camera combination that could visualize underwater up to ten meters. Tom had to admit the demonstration images were impressive.

On Thursday, he received an Indiana Jones hat with a note from Dr. Westhoven. "You'll need this for the Llanganatis."

He reread parts of *Valverde's Gold* by Mark Honigsbaum. This was the "fun" book he was reading when he first met Jenny. Now, it was not as fun to read.

He found the passage he was looking for. Andrés Fernández-Salvador probably had taken more trips into the Llanganatis than anyone else. One of those trips was by helicopter, which crashed on an island in a river near Cerro Hermosa. It took over a month to rescue him and his team.

Perhaps the gold exists, wondered Tom, but the lack of any written history by the Incas was frustrating. Everything was secondhand through the Spanish. Searching for the gold hidden five hundred years ago following the Derrotero was challenging enough. Trying to find it underwater seemed impossible.

Jenny wanted to be part of this. He also heard the "build it and they will come" line a few more times. They would watch *Field of Dreams* tonight. Then maybe Jenny would at least get the quote right.

If he agreed to the project, he could not talk with Dr. Wade about the expedition, which also bothered him. He would be on his own.

He had a few questions left to ask Dr. Westhoven this morning, but unless the answers differed from what he expected, he had decided.

Yale University
New Haven, Connecticut

Dr. Westhoven was in his office, finishing a cup of coffee. His Zoom call with Tom was in an hour. A week had gone by since the conference, and he was worried that pushing Tom to decide by today might backfire. He did not have a backup plan. He hoped Tom would commit on this morning's call.

Dr. Westhoven had a superficial understanding of artificial intelligence, but Tom's knowledge of convolutional neural networks was much deeper than his. He remembered when Dr. Wade told him about Tom's VGG-16 lobster neural network from high school.

He had also looked at the satellite images of the Llanganatis provided by Miguel. The details were amazing. The resolution was less than a meter. This would be crucial in the search for the gold.

He also reviewed the underwater demonstration images Miguel had provided from Depth Cam. They were equally impressive. But the real-life images from the Llanganatis would need to live up to the resolution of these examples.

Dr. Westhoven put the final touches on a couple of PowerPoint slides he hoped to present to Tom this morning, if he were on board.

The PowerPoint

Saturday, February 23, 2019
Zoom Call
New Haven, Connecticut - Orono, Maine

Tom propped his pillow on the headboard, trying to get comfortable with his laptop while waiting for Dr. Westhoven's call. Jenny was reading at the kitchen table.

Dr. Westhoven called at eleven.

"Good morning, Tom. Tell me some good news," he said with a smile.

Tom turned the volume down a little. "I've thought a lot about your proposal, but I still have a few questions."

"Shoot."

"First, do you really think there's gold to find?"

"I think so. We don't have any written records, but what we do have from the Spanish suggests the ransom room in Cajamarca was not filled when Pizarro executed Atahualpa. And a large amount of gold and silver was on the way to Cajamarca.

"So, I do think the Incas hid some gold and silver. I'm not sure how much, and I'm not sure where, but that's what I aim to find out, with your help."

Dr. Westhoven continued, "Also, I'm not sure what the lost Inca gold and silver looks like underwater, but we can guess based upon what the Incas had already brought to Cajamarca. The gold and silver in the ransom room was a combination of cups, jars, plates, medallions, wall tiles, and figurines of people and camelids.

"There are also references to carrying the silver as ingots and the gold in bags as grains and nuggets. The silver ingots may be at the resolution of Depth Cam, but the grains of gold in bags, which will have disintegrated after five hundred years, will be too small for the satellite. We'll need to focus on the trinkets and the shape and edge of the pile."

"Makes sense. A deep learner is typically based upon edge and shape recognition," said Tom.

Clearing his throat, he waited a moment before asking his next question. "Realistically, Dr. Westhoven, how much time do you think this will take?"

"This will need to be a priority. For now, it's mostly planning, but I suspect the project will consume most of your summer.

"Also, you may need to lighten your class load for next year, and if this goes forward, we will be in the Llanganatis in March 2020. You might need to finish your degree the following summer, but that's your call."

Tom was glad he was taking a graduate course this semester. This might help keep him on track academically.

Tom also wondered if Dr. Westhoven really understood the importance of the training data set.

"Another thing that bothers me is this Depth Cam. I can't find anything about it online. Do you think it works? If we can't see underwater, we're dead in the water, so to speak." Tom wasn't trying to be funny.

Dr. Westhoven relaxed his gaze a little. "That was one of my biggest concerns, too, so I took some Depth Cam images of Maltby Lake, a nearby pond. I'll send along the images. It does work, but it needs to be a sunny day and the water reasonably clear. I can see a fish in the pond."

"Thanks, and if you could also send along any specifications." Tom looked at his notes beside him on the bed. "Will you also tell me more about the sponsor of the expedition?"

"Sure. His name is Miguel Titere, and his company is Antiquities South. We've worked together on several occasions. He's reputable," said Dr. Westhoven. "The virtual expedition was his idea. He reached out to me to oversee the technology and, if we go, the ground expedition."

"Okay, just a couple more questions. This one is important to me." Tom lowered his voice, suspecting Jenny was listening. "I'll need another set of hands. I have a friend, Jenny, who's willing to help."

"Understood, Tom. I assumed you'd need some help, particularly next summer. What's her background?"

"She's an English major, but she also has an extensive knowledge of the Incas. Her family lived in Colombia when she was growing up. I don't need her so much for the AI stuff, but next summer sounds like a two-person job."

Dr. Westhoven took a slow sip of coffee. Until now, he'd been accommodating. Tom started to realize this was not just an academic exercise for Dr. Westhoven. He really wanted to find the gold.

"Jenny's knowledge of the Incas may also help as we model the gold." He realized how this sounded as soon as it came out. Dr. Westhoven was the expert. Tom needed another reason for Jenny to be a part of this.

"How much help do you think you'll need next summer? I could arrange for an internship with one of my graduate students. I have one in mind, and she's knowledgeable about satellite imagery."

Tom had to think fast. "Thanks, Dr. Westhoven, but all I really need is just another set of hands."

Another sip of coffee and then Dr. Westhoven stared at the screen. "Pardon me for asking Tom, but I get the sense that Jenny is more than a friend willing to help. What happens if you two drift apart over the next few months?"

"I don't think that will happen, but I have someone else who can also help me on the water next summer, if necessary." Tom hadn't considered that and pulled Dave out of thin air.

Another sip of coffee by Dr. Westhoven. It must be getting cooler by now.

"Jenny sounds okay, but she needs to understand the importance of discretion with this project. I'll send along a couple of NDAs, one for you and one for her."

"NDAs?"

"Non-disclosure agreements, standard for a project like this. Also, you'll need to pay her out of the $1,000 stipend. Is that okay?"

Tom nodded.

"Okay, you had one more question?"

Tom gazed down for a moment and stared at his clasped hands. "Well, I know this whole thing is a long shot, but how safe is an actual expedition to the Llanganatis? Hundreds have ventured into those mountains. Some did not return."

"That was another of my concerns. I was in the Llanganatis about ten years ago and its reputation is well deserved. Although the Llanganatis is a national park, the tourism is in the western part of the park. The interior and eastern part are still mostly uncharted. Even satellite images on Google Maps are sketchy, but we'll have our own set of images.

"Miguel plans to join us in the Llanganatis, and he isn't the outdoors type, so I think we'll be safe. His life depends upon it, too, but obviously I can't make any guarantees. The helicopter is the key."

"Would Jenny join us in the Llanganatis?" asked Tom.

"No, the team will be small. The helicopter only accommodates six, so it would be you and me with the rest of the team."

After a few moments of silence, Dr. Westhoven finally asked, "What do you think Tom, are you in?"

Tom's chin was numb from his rubbing. It also bothered him that Dr. Westhoven pushed back on Jenny, but he understood. After a deep breath and subtle sigh, "Yeah, I just don't want you to have unrealistic expectations. Success without an actual training data set is unlikely, but I'll give it a shot."

"That's all I can ask, Tom. Is Jenny there?"

Tom nodded.

"Why don't you have her join the call?"

"Okay—hang on."

Even before he got off the bed, Jenny bounced in and grabbed her pillow to prop herself against the headboard next to Tom. As he suspected, she'd been listening. Hopefully, she hadn't heard his description of her as "just another set of hands." He turned his laptop slightly to bring her into view. She rubbed her foot against his shin, which jiggled the laptop and self-image.

"Hi Jenny. Nice to meet you. Welcome aboard."

Then they got to work.

Dr. Westhoven presented his screen. "I'm hoping this will organize our work."

Tom chuckled when a PowerPoint appeared on his screen. "Are we going to be graded on this?"

"Sorry, Tom, habit. I always reduce everything to a PowerPoint."

Dr. Westhoven continued. "So, although our interest is the gold, the underwater pile or piles are a combination of gold and silver. We'll need to model both and see what they look like on Depth Cam. This will be the training data set. Simple—right?"

Tom's eyes widened.

"Yeah, I know. We have some work to do. How about we assign some tasks this morning?"

Dr. Westhoven updated the slide as they reviewed each task. After about fifteen minutes, all the tasks were assigned, along with a timeline for completion.

Expedition to Llanganatis

- Assumptions (Today)—DR W
- Model for Gold and Silver (March)—DR W & TOM
- Size of Training Data Set (March)—TOM
- Depth Cam Satellite (April)—DR W
- Lakes for Training (June)—TOM
- Training the Neural Network (September)—TOM
- Choose Llanganatis Lakes to Scan (September)—DR W
- Scan the Llanganatis Lakes (October)—DR W & TOM

"Okay, let's start with the assumptions I've made. Let me know if you think any of them are off. Here's what I'm thinking. Again, pardon the PowerPoint."

Assumptions

- Silver Ingots - Gold Bags
- 100 to 150 pieces per Inca boat
- Multiple boat loads per pile
- Tiles - Plates - Medallions - Jars - Cups - Figurines
- Depth Cam - 10 meters or 30 feet
- Pile of gold visible by Depth Cam
- Man-made lake
- Thermal quality of gold and silver
- Multiple sites

Dr. Westhoven continued, "The legend says the gold on the way to Cajamarca would fill the other half of the ransom room, which was seventeen feet by twenty-two feet by nine feet high.

"Also, we don't know for sure how many pieces are in a pile. Depth Cam will probably not see anything less than eight to twelve inches anyway, but based upon the weight of gold and silver, one loaded Inca boat would likely carry only about one hundred to one hundred-fifty pieces.

"It also makes sense that the Incas probably dumped several boat loads into one pile. This would make subsequent recovery easier."

Tom realized the number of items in a pile was a scaling issue. He could increase or decrease the size of the pile by manipulating the images of the training data.

"Our focus is on the gold, but we must also account for silver in the pile in the model," said Dr. Westhoven. "Fortunately, on satellite, gold and silver look the same. The biggest decision we need to make is how to model the pieces of Inca gold and silver. We will not be perfect, but this is where good enough will have to be good enough."

Tom squirmed. Instead of the usual elbow to his ribs, Jenny kicked him in the shin, which jiggled their computer self-image again. Good enough was not typically good enough for Tom.

Dr. Westhoven continued, "Trinkets like wall tiles, plates, medallions, jars, and cups would be in the six-to-fifteen-inch range. I'll send you more precise measurements, but the wall tiles were about twelve inches and wider, and plates and medallions about twelve to fifteen inches. Jars varied, but most were about six inches in diameter and twelve to fifteen inches high. Cups, figurines of camelids and people were smaller, although occasionally the figurines were quite large. The straight edges of the wall tiles will likely emulate any silver ingots in the pile.

"Also, ten meters underwater is the limit of Depth Cam, so we'll confine our search to thirty feet. I doubt the Incas would have dumped the gold much deeper. Recovering the gold and silver would have been too difficult."

Dr. Westhoven took another sip of coffee.

"Another key assumption is Depth Cam will actually see the gold and silver underwater. This has never been done before."

The assumptions were adding up. With each one, Tom realized the likelihood of success dropped. In the small, self-image window, he noticed Jenny had a subtle smile.

Dr. Westhoven was still displaying his screen. "The Derrotero is also quite specific. The ancients threw the gold and silver into a lake made by the hand of man. Identifying features of a man-made lake will narrow the search. I have some ideas to help here.

"Ultimately, I also wonder if we can use the thermal qualities of gold and silver. In direct sunlight, the metals will heat quicker than the surrounding water. Infrared may help us here.

"Finally, the Derrotero suggests the ancients threw everything into one lake, but there may be more than one pile in one lake or possibly multiple lakes.

"I don't think we should take the directions in the Derrotero too literally. Many have followed these directions, and no one has yet found the gold. Fortunately, the satellite casts a wide net."

Dr. Westhoven took a deep breath. "I think that's enough. We've covered the major challenges. Are you guys available in a couple of weeks to pick up where we left off?"

Tom nodded his head. "Sounds good, Dr. Westhoven. This is a lot to digest. We'll start thinking about a model for a pile of gold."

"Thanks, Tom. I'll send along the NDAs. I'm glad you guys are on board. I'm looking forward to collaborating with you both. Honestly, I'm not sure we'll find any gold. But I love the idea of breaking new ground, and, if we follow our instincts, who knows...."

An email arrived just after the call ended. Dr. Westhoven wrote he would send precise measurements of the Inca artifacts later this weekend and he attached the two PowerPoint slides along with two nondisclosure agreements. As Tom read the

NDA, he noticed a paragraph that he could not reference the project in any scientific work or writings. Tom shook his head as he finished reading the NDA.

"What's the matter?" asked Jenny.

He pointed to the paragraph. "I'm going to spend the next year working on this and I can't publish or reference any of the work."

"The experience will be great, even if you can't publish, even if we don't find any gold. This is the chance of a lifetime, a chance to do something never done before. I thought that was your dream?"

"This isn't a dream, it's a nightmare. My dream is to do something worthwhile."

Jenny pivoted and asked Tom the same question she had asked when she picked him up at the airport. "What do you think the Inca gold will look like underwater?"

"I've no idea, but we need to have something by the next call." Clenching his teeth for a moment, he then said, "Jenny, what have I gotten myself into? Did you see all the work on the PowerPoint?"

"Since when are you afraid of work? You do this stuff for fun. You're just struggling with the uncertainty, the unknown. Let it go—go with the flow.

"And it's what have 'we' gotten ourselves into. I'm part of this, too, remember? And it's almost spring. You're basically done. You're on the senior slide. For $1,000 a week, this looks like a pretty good gig to me."

"I almost forgot. I'm supposed to pay you out of the $1,000."

"No worries. I'm in this for the fringe benefits," she said, patting the bed, making it squeak.

Tom smiled. They both knew she didn't need the money. "I'll try to make it worth your while," he said as he leaned in for a kiss. "In the meantime, I need to clear my head. Do you want to go for a run with me?"

"No. Unlike you, I still have work to do, and my head is clear."

2 Feet Brewing

Saturday, February 23, 2019
Pizza Palace
Orono, Maine

The Zoom call left Tom in a muddle. He enjoyed running when he'd something to ponder, something to think about, like a problem to solve, like how to find a pile of gold thirty feet underwater. Today should be a good run.

It was a clear but blustery day, hovering around ten degrees. As he headed down Main Street toward the Stillwater River, the wind was at his back. He thought about the PowerPoint. He needed to model a pile of Inca gold and silver on a lake bottom, realistic enough to train a convolutional neural network. If he could come up with a training data set, he would use the same VGG-16 he had used in high school.

But he had no training data set—none. He would have to build one—from scratch.

He crossed the bridge over the Stillwater and turned left toward the University on College Avenue. The river was clear of ice except for an occasional chunk floating by.

How could he model a pile of ingots, plates, tiles, jars, cups, medallions, and figurines? He chuckled and shook his head. A bit of frozen sweat on his hair hit his forehead. "This isn't computer science," he mumbled to himself.

He understood the satellite sees shapes, sizes, edges, and contrast. It can't see mass, so he could create a model out of anything—like plastic. The model also had to be light enough to transport onto a lake—like plastic. But how would he retrieve the plastic? He couldn't leave it on the bottom. Maybe he could use biodegradable plastic.

He turned onto campus at the Alfond Arena. He'd worked up a sweat. The buildings on campus broke the wind as he passed the athletic fields and headed for Somerset Hall, Jenny's dorm, at the far end of campus. He remembered their first kiss as he passed her dorm and turned right onto Rangeley Road.

He assumed he should use an actual lake to model the gold, but maybe he should just use a pool, or just photoshop a pile of gold. He knew, however, the better he could emulate the actual gold underwater, the better the training data set.

As he left campus and turned right into the gusting wind onto Route 2 and back toward downtown, tiny icicles formed on his eyelids from his breath. Even on a clear day in February, you can always count on the wind.

By the time he jogged up the steps to the Pizza Palace, he had the start of a plan, a shaky one, but a plan. Jenny was finishing up the dishes. After a quick pat on her butt, he jumped in the shower.

Tom spent the rest of the afternoon at his desk with his Pilot Precise V7 fine point rolling ball pen and a wide-lined white notepad, his preferred pondering combination. He had tried other pens and papers over the years, but nothing matched the flow of the V7, and the texture of sugarcane-based paper. He recognized this was a minor obsession, but he was sure it helped him think better.

When faced with a complex problem like this, he typically "chunked" it, broke it down into smaller problems, just like modular programming. The V7 flowed onto the sugarcane with ideas.

After a few minutes, he looked over at Jenny, studying at the kitchen table. "Hey, now that I'm getting a stupend, are you up for 2 Feet tonight?" Tom's favorite microbrewery in Bangor.

"Sure, but what's a stupend?"

"A stupid stipend."

All Jenny could do was sigh.

Back to chunking. According to Dr. Westhoven, the satellite could make out an object about a foot in length, so he decided to start with one-by-one meter images, which was a little over three-by-three feet or about eleven square feet. This should have enough detail.

He also needed to know how the actual gold and silver dispersed onto the bottom of a lake in the Llanganatis when dumped five hundred years ago by the Incas. And then how would he model this dispersion with plastic? This would determine how many one-meter satellite images he could get from each pile.

Fabricating the plastic was another issue. Dave could 3D-print some prototypes, but 3D printing thousands of plastic items was beyond his capacity.

Finally, how would he actually dump hundreds of pieces of plastic into an actual lake?

Normally, chunking a problem was a satisfying experience, one step closer to a solution. This afternoon, however, left him with more questions than when he started. He wasn't even sure plastic was the best choice to model gold and silver.

By four o'clock, Jenny needed a break from studying, and it was time to head to 2 Feet Brewing. She wandered over to Tom's desk and rubbed his shoulders as she peered over his right shoulder. She knew the spot to rub.

"What are you up to?"

Tom capped his Pilot. "I'm trying to break this down into manageable pieces or chunks. The only one I get so far is the number of images I'll need to train the neural network—at least 75,000—and that's a guess until I figure out the rest. Otherwise, it's a mess."

Jenny looked at his list.

1. *75,000 minimum images to train the VGG-16*
2. *Model gold and silver with biodegradable plastic*
3. *Fabricate the plastic gold*
4. *Guess what a pile of actual gold looks like underwater*
5. *Guess how plastic gold disperses in water*
6. *Guess the number of items per pile*
7. *Calculate how many Maine lakes to dump the plastic gold*
8. *Select the Maine lakes to dump the plastic gold*
9. *Dump the plastic gold*
10. *Image the plastic gold with Depth Cam*
11. *Program the VGG-16*
12. *Train the VGG-16*
13. *Select the "man-made" lakes in Llanganatis*
14. *Image the "man-made" lakes with Depth Cam*
15. *Find the gold and silver*

"Impressive." She grabbed his pen, uncapped it, and wrote...

16. *And have fun*

"Nice pen," she said as she tossed the uncapped V7 onto the kitchen table. "Done. Let's go."

Tom resisted the urge to re-cap the pen.

The sun was low as they headed down the interstate to 2 Feet Brewing in Bangor.

"What do you think about Vermont for spring break?"

Tom had been wondering about spring break. "Is this some elaborate scheme to get a free ride to Vermont?"

Jenny just smiled.

They were early enough to get the wrap-around window seat in the front. It wasn't much of a view, a parking lot and Baptist church across the street, but it was intimate and comfy, surrounded by cushions. The bar occupied the left wall, and the beer choices were on an ever-changing chalkboard behind it. They could smell the appetizers. The bartender pointed to a new IPA for Tom. They ordered enchiladas, lobster bisque, and with his new stipend, lobster pot pie, for dinner along with the new IPA for Tom and a cider for Jenny, who was still underage until October.

As Tom was taking a pull from his IPA, Jenny placed a printout of Dr. Westhoven's PowerPoint slides in front of him. He used it as a coaster.

"I thought I was the nerd?" said Tom, hoping to drink in peace.

"It must be catching," she said with the twinkle in her left eye, moving his beer to better see the *Expedition to Llanganatis* PowerPoint.

The sun was setting through the trees behind the parking lot across the street. Tom took the bait. "Okay, on my run today, I thought we could use plastic to model the gold and silver. We're only interested in shapes and edges, not the mass."

"I noticed the plastic on your chunking list. Doesn't plastic float?"

"I found a biodegradable plastic with a density of 1.3 grams per milliliter."

Jenny chuckled. "What does that mean?"

"It sinks." Tom wasn't always this parsimonious.

"If we use plastic," Jenny said, "I know a company in Vermont near Ludlow called Mack Molding that fabricates plastic stuff like this. We can connect with them on spring break in Vermont next month."

"Neat." The enchiladas arrived. "I bet Dave can 3D-print some models to bring to Vermont. All he would need are the measurements from Dr. Westhoven. And if we use biodegradable plastic, we could take additional images after the pile dissolves as control images."

Tom took a bite of his enchiladas. He didn't know how much the plastic would cost, but he didn't really care.

As he finished his IPA, he said, "You know, if this works, we're going to have a busy summer, dumping plastic gold in lakes all over Maine. And the more piles and images to train the VGG-16, the better. We'll have a lot of work in the next month or two, but next summer might be fun."

"Absolutely. That's the spirit."

They devoured the rest of the enchiladas.

"By the way, what are our plans for the summer?" she asked, in between bites.

"I guess I was hoping you'd stay at the Pizza Palace."

The bartender brought two lobster pot pies and Tom another beer. He took a long swig.

Jenny cocked her head and took a spoonful of pot pie. "This is good." Taking her time, she finally continued. "I don't know. Would I have my own bedroom, a bathroom, a parking spot? What's the rent?"

Tom smiled. "You don't own a car, so you don't need a parking spot. There's one bathroom and I can learn to keep the toilet seat down. The bedroom has a full-size bed, and I fixed the squeak. You'd also have at least two drawers of your own and part of a closet. And I can take the rent out of your stupend." Tom was hoping for a smile. Sometimes she was hard to read.

Jenny took another spoonful. "Is Dave okay with this?"

"He should be. He and Amanda will be in Bath for the summer. Dave has an internship at BIW."

"What about a job? Jeff and Tina were planning on me at the Tyson Store next summer. What's your assumption here?"

"I'm making enough with the stipend to cover both of us. We could split it."

"I want my own job, and I want to be more than just another set of hands," she said, waving her palms in Tom's face.

As he suspected, she had overheard his conversation with Dr. Westhoven, and his comment about just needing another set of hands.

Tom saw the beginning of a smile. The bartender brought over the last appetizer of lobster bisque. He tried a different tack.

"You know, I can arrange a showing of the Pizza Palace tonight, even a sleep over, if you're interested." Jenny had already spent every weekend at the Pizza Palace since the start of the semester.

Jenny chuckled. "Let me think about it."

After finishing her second cider, she changed the subject. "Will you explain a VG 16?"

"VGG-16. It's a convolutional neural network, or deep learning program, developed in 2014. It was a fundamental change in image recognition. And it's open-source or free."

2 Feet started to fill up. He could tell by the crooked look on her face that he needed to flesh out his explanation. After a sip of lobster bisque, followed by another swig of IPA, he drew out a diagram on the napkin he was now using as a coaster. He started with the outer beer ring from his mug and drew smaller and smaller circles inside one another down to VGG-16 in the middle. The mug was broad, so he could fit in all the circles. He pointed to the DL ring.

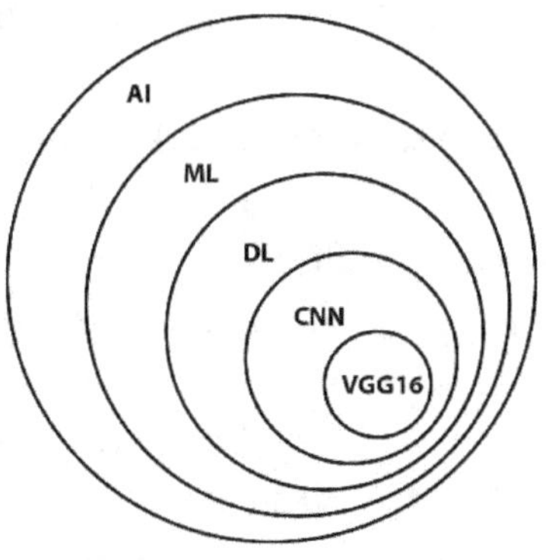

"Deep learning is a type of machine learning based upon layers or neural networks, trying to replicate how the brain processes information. CNN, or a convolutional neural network, is a type of deep learning with three or more network layers. VGG-16 is a type of convolutional neural network with sixteen layers. The last two or three layers of the VGG-16 are the ones you change. This is what I used in high school. Still, there are no shortcuts. You must teach the VGG-16 with training data, and the better the training data, the better and quicker it learns. VGG-16 is really good at image recognition, which is why we'll use it to look for the gold."

She still looked puzzled. "Well, what's AI and machine learning and deep learning? Are they all the same thing?"

"The popular press uses them interchangeably, but they're different. AI is an all-encompassing term for any program that makes decisions. Machine learning is a type of AI that makes decisions based upon some type of training or learning."

Jenny folded the napkin with the diagram and put it in her fanny pack. Using her smile to her advantage, she said, "You really are a good tutor."

Tom smiled back, but as he finished his second IPA, he remembered he'd never trained a convolutional neural network without a well-defined training set, and he was using biodegradable plastic for gold and silver. He took on a more somber mood.

"No one really knows what a pile of gold and silver looks like underwater. Modeling the Inca gold and silver will be the key. We'll need thousands of plastic pieces and dozens of underwater piles to image by satellite. And a satellite that can see underwater. And a neural network that works."

As he stared into the empty glass, he said, "This is overwhelming."

"Have another beer," suggested Jenny. "I'll drive back."

A third IPA did not help.

Tom finished his IPA, and they headed back to Orono. She tried to cheer him up on the way, but it wasn't always easy shaking him out of his doldrums.

She tried anyway. "Are you doing okay?"

"Yeah, this is just a lot to process."

"Well, I guess I better hang out at the Palace until you sober up." Tom noticed she gently bit her lower lip.

"I only had three beers." It took him a moment to catch on. "But yeah, that's a good idea. Maybe we could watch a movie or something." After another pause, "I could also give you a proper tour of the apartment."

"I'd like that."

Phone Call
New Haven, Connecticut - Bogotá, Colombia

Shortly after the Zoom call, Dr. Westhoven called Miguel. He still had concerns about Tom's girlfriend, but he did not share these with Miguel.

"It's good news, Miguel. Everyone is on board. The team has already started."

"Wonderful. I knew you were the right person. I will set up the funding mechanism. By the way, I would prefer this not go through the regular channels with your University for obvious reasons. Will that be a problem?"

"I'll work it through on my end. We have protocols for sensitive projects, like defense contracts."

"Good, good. Now, tell me more about your team."

"I have kept the team small. I have a programmer who will develop the neural network, and his assistant."

"Wonderful. Please keep me posted. I'll send you an email with the grant and funding information. Good work, Dr. Westhoven."

"Oh Miguel, will you send me more information on Depth Cam? It's so important to see underwater. I need to fully understand how it works."

"Certainly, my friend."

Early Afternoon
Bogotá, Colombia

As soon as Miguel completed the call with Dr. Westhoven, he emailed the good news to Omar.

> *To: Omar Al Tajir*
> *Date: Saturday, February 23, 2019*
> *From: Miguel Titere*
>
> *Subject: Expedition*
>
> *Dear Omar,*
>
> *We have Dr. Westhoven on board. Please release the funding.*
>
> *Also, he is looking for more background information on the Depth Cam.*
>
> *Sincerely,*
>
> *Miguel*
> *Antigüedades Sur*

Keiretsu

Saturday, February 23, 2019
La Casa Occidental
Cartagena, Colombia

Omar read Miguel's email in his office. The beginnings of his plan were falling nicely into place. He was pleased how easily Miguel had recruited Dr. Westhoven. But he was not so naïve to expect everything would continue so smoothly.

Tarek would arrive later this afternoon from Quito. Omar had a few things to review with him. Omar had learned the competing expedition would explore the eastern Llanganatis. He had studied satellite images, and so far, he had not detected any unusual activity. He did note the terrain in this region was undulating, which fit nicely into his plan.

When Tarek arrived, Omar had a rare smile when he greeted him. "It is good to see you, my friend. Did you learn anything at the conference?"

They settled into Omar's office off the museum. Omar already had a glass of arak poured for Tarek.

"Yes. Dr. Westhoven seems reliable, certainly more than Titere, but I was intrigued by the talk of the undergraduate. He laid the foundation for what you are trying to accomplish with artificial intelligence.

"I watched him throughout the weekend. Although he was unaccompanied at the conference, he met with Westhoven on Sunday after the conference for about an hour. Afterwards, when he checked out, he seemed preoccupied. I wonder if Westhoven had tried to recruit him then."

"Interesting. I always assumed Dr. Westhoven would need a programmer, but I did not expect an undergraduate. Perhaps someone low-profile, assuming he can get the job done, would be best. Find out as much as you can about him. He may come in handy if Dr. Westhoven ever bows out."

Omar turned around to switch on the ceiling fan and then lit a cigar.

After another sip of arak, Tarek continued. "I've also learned more about the other expedition."

"Good, Tarek. Tell me what you know."

"This expedition does have something to do with Andrés Fernández. He died a couple years ago, but apparently a former partner, Luis Alvarez, acquired some of his old documents, maybe related to the Barth Blake expedition of the late 1880s, that located the gold in a cave by a lake. I do not know the exact lake. The expedition is scheduled for August."

The smoke disappeared from the tip of his cigar as Omar took a long drag. "Our focus will remain on our project, but we'll need to monitor this other expedition as well."

After another drag on his cigar, Omar continued. "Antigüedades Sur will never replace the revenue stream I left in Abu Dhabi. Unfortunately, the political unrest here does not match the Middle East, but discontent has been rising in the region, particularly in Mexico, where the drug lords have the resources to buy our matériel.

"I have gathered some items in Abu Dhabi that I think will interest them. I need you to return to Abu Dhabi and bring back a sampling of what we have to offer.

"Once everything is in place, my plan is to work with the existing supply chains and avoid an internecine war. Where this leads remains to be seen."

Another drag on his cigar.

"Finally, on your way back, I have also arranged for you to meet a helicopter pilot in Portugal. He is from New Zealand but works out of Lisbon. He comes highly recommended."

Tarek would spend another few days at La Casa Occidental before flying back to Abu Dhabi. Omar knew Tarek needed the break. One way or the other, Tarek would have a busy summer.

⇛⇝

While Tarek was in Abu Dhabi, Omar learned even more about the competing expedition from his contact in Ecuador. Nihon Aeronautics was the keiretsu, or Japanese conglomerate, backing the expedition. As Tarek had learned, the leader was Luis Alvarez, who seemed focused on a cave identified by Barth Blake from the late 1880s. The expedition was scheduled for early August, with at least six planned trips by helicopter and perhaps more, depending upon what they found.

Omar still did not have the location of the cave in the eastern Llanganatis, but he would use Zheng satellites to pinpoint the lake once the actual expedition started.

He doubted the keiretsu was using artificial intelligence if the expedition was focused on a single location, but he could not afford to have unwanted attention drawn to the Llanganatis.

He already had a plan for dealing with the competing expedition. The terrain in the eastern park made access difficult, which explained the helicopter, and the mountains fit nicely into his scheme. Now, he simply needed to wait for the right time.

⇛⇝

Friday, March 8, 2019
La Casa Occidental
Cartagena, Colombia

Two weeks later, Tarek was back. He had safely warehoused the matériel in Bogotá. Tarek and Omar were reviewing the inventory in Omar's office. Once Omar was assured everything was accounted for, he looked up through his veil of cigar smoke and poured Tarek another tumbler of arak. He then flipped on the ceiling fan, which emitted a soothing hum.

"What did you think of the pilot?" asked Omar.

"He will be adequate."

Tarek never enthusiastically endorsed anyone. Probably a wise approach with the clientele they dealt with.

"Good work, Tarek. Now, I have another job for you. You have a meeting with Sebastián Escobar, the son of the Colombian drug lord, in Medellín in two weeks. Use the Gulfstream and bring a sampling of the matériel, except the Stinger missiles and launchers. I have other plans for them."

Omar carefully placed his cigar in the ashtray. He unlocked the middle drawer on his desk. He pulled out a stack of photographs and handed them to Tarek. "Here, look these over."

While Tarek thumbed through the photographs of Inca treasures with detailed measurements handwritten by Dr. Westhoven on each item, Omar continued, "You were correct, Tarek. The undergraduate from the University of Maine is working with Dr. Westhoven."

The smoke from his cigar dispersed quickly with the overhead fan. "I need to verify his program works. I want you to create some fake gold based on these photographs. As I understand, these programs focus on shapes and sizes. I think we can replicate the Inca gold with bricks, plates, jugs, cups, and small statues.

"Once Dr. Westhoven has selected the twenty or so lakes made by man in the Llanganatis, we will dump the fake gold in one of these lakes."

"I'll pull this together quickly," said Tarek.

"No rush. I want to coordinate this trip into the Llanganatis with the other keiretsu expedition this August. We will just need those twenty lakes from Dr. Westhoven by then."

Catch a Wave

Sunday, March 3, 2019
Pizza Palace
Orono, Maine

For the third time this week, Jenny asked, "Have you decided on how to model the gold and silver?" She stood over Tom, who was at the kitchen table reading a journal, her arms akimbo.

And for the third time this week, Tom replied, perhaps a bit too loudly, "I don't know." But when he looked up at her expression, he knew this would not be a casual conversation and quickly added, "But I have some ideas. Do you have a minute?"

Jenny pulled up a chair.

He opened his laptop. "I started with two of the assumptions we discussed last weekend with Dr. Westhoven. First, based upon what the Incas already brought to the ransom room in Cajamarca, the underwater pile of gold and silver is probably a combination of silver ingots, wall tiles, plates, medallions of the sun and moon, jars, cups, and figurines. So, we'll need a combination of these items to model all the shapes and edges. And for Depth Cam to see the items underwater, they need to be at least eight to twelve inches, like the fish in Maltby Pond that Dr. Westhoven saw.

"Second, each pile would probably be several boat loads with one hundred to one hundred-fifty pieces per load, the limit of what an Inca raft or boat could transport onto the water."

Tom tapped a few keys. "Here, I put together a quick spreadsheet."

He turned his laptop to show Jenny. "As Dr. Westhoven suggested, I ignored the bags of gold."

Item	w (inches)	l (inches)	h (inches)	Volume cubic feet per item	Number in Pile	Volume cubic feet per pile
Ingot Silver	4	7.75	1.75	0.031	18	0.6
Tile Wall Small	12	12	0.125	0.010	8	0.1
Tile Wall Large	15	15	0.125	0.016	8	0.1
Plate	12	12	0.125	0.010	8	0.1
Medallion Sun	15	15	0.125	0.016	8	0.1
Jar Large	6	6	12	0.196	9	1.8
Jar Small	4	4	8	0.058	16	0.9
Cup Large	6	6	12	0.196	18	3.5
Cup Small	4.5	4.5	8	0.074	18	1.3
Figurines	2	6	12	0.083	12	1.0
					123	9.5

"Wow, my little nerd's been busy."

He ignored her. "The measurements are from Dr. Westhoven. I guessed at the number of each item per boat load, but the total of 123 items is within the parameters he set last weekend.

"I already sent this along to Dr. Westhoven, but you get the idea. I can easily adjust the numbers. Also, Dave said he can 3D print a sample of the items. He should have them ready by next week. Once I get the samples, we can then experiment to see how they disperse in water."

Jenny looked puzzled. "What do you mean, experiment?"

"First, we need to see how the Inca gold and silver would actually disperse in water, and then try to emulate that with plastic. This will define the number of one-meter squares or images in a pile for Depth Cam. This is important. It's a Goldilocks."

"Goldilocks?"

"It must be precise. If we image too big an area, we include empty bottom in the satellite grid. Too small and we miss important edges for the VGG-16.

"I think the ingots and figurines will simply drop, so I won't bother to model their dispersion, but the tiles, plates, medallions, cups, and jars will scatter on their way down because of their shapes.

"To model the actual gold and silver, I thought we could use pewter plates for the plates and medallions, and pottery for jars and cups. They should have all this stuff at the Antique Marketplace in Bangor. We may have to look around for ceiling tile made of tin to model the Inca wall tiles, but it should work."

Jenny's eyes brightened. "They also have a ton of books in the basement."

Tom continued, "We can then compare the dispersion of the pewter and pottery with the plastic gold. We just need a pool to dump all this stuff."

"Hey, what about the Wave Tank?" she asked. "I did a paper on it last year. It's plenty big enough and about fifteen feet at the deep end."

"I forgot about the Wave Tank. With his engineering major, Dave probably has access. I'll text him to see if we can get into the tank after hours."

"See, I knew you'd come up with something."

"This is the easy part, but I still don't think a pile of plastic at the bottom of a lake will actually train a convolutional neural network to find gold. I know it's about the journey, but I'd rather be on the yellow brick road to somewhere else."

"Stop whining."

"I'm not whining." But Tom knew he was whining, a little. As he closed his laptop, signaling he was done, he received a text from Dave.

< Surfs up next Saturday at 7. 11 Central. >

"Looks like this is going to cost Dr. Westhoven a dinner at 11 Central," he said.

Tom was busy the following week. First, he purchased a bodyboard to float the fake gold and 3-D printed plastic onto the Wave Tank. Then, he found a small wooden frame for raised bed gardening at the farmer's market to hold the fake gold and plastic on the bodyboard. He would simply pull the frame off the board with a rope to get a consistent dump, and the frame would float out of the way.

The big purchase was a Chasing M2 underwater drone to photograph the dispersion on the bottom of the tank. After skimming the instructions, he handed the drone to Jenny. "Here, you're officially in charge of underwater photography." He didn't have the patience to work through an instruction manual. Jenny, on the other hand, enjoyed reading them, editing for grammar, and overall clarity.

He also needed to recover the items from the bottom of the Wave Tank after each dump. He decided to use a blue tarp that would cover the bottom of the tank. To easily measure the dispersion, he outlined a one-meter grid on the tarp using duct tape.

He charged all of this with the credit card provided by Dr. Westhoven.

Saturday, March 9, 2019, 7 p.m.
Wave Tank
The University of Maine
Orono, Maine

Dr. Westhoven had rescheduled this morning's Zoom call for next weekend, which was fine with Tom. He still had a lot of work to do before the call. Tonight, they were at the Wave Tank. He planned five dumps of the fake gold and silver from the Antique Marketplace, and another five of the 3-D printed plastic.

He had also planned to give Dave the bodyboard when they finished. "Careful, don't scratch my new board," said Dave, every time Tom pulled the wooden frame to dump the gold.

It took a couple of dumps to get the hang of it, but it worked. And Jenny was adept at maneuvering the M2 drone to get quality pictures of the dispersion piles.

As Tom was loading the bodyboard for the last dump of plastic, Dave wasn't helping. Tom turned around and saw he had changed into a swimsuit.

"Hurry up. I'm freezing," Dave said.

"What are you doing?"

"I want to try out my new bodyboard."

"There are security cameras all over the place?"

"You think I'm the first guy to surf in the Wave Tank? Let's move it. My goosebumps are getting goosebumps."

After they picked up the last dump, Dave turned on the waves. He was quickly body surfing a two-foot wave in the middle of the Wave Tank, and freezing, just like in the ocean off the coast of Maine.

"If you drown, you're on your own," yelled Tom.

Fortunately, Dave didn't last long.

On the way back to the Pizza Palace, Jenny smiled.

"What's the grin about?" asked Tom.

"I was just thinking. I can't remember a more interesting Saturday night."

"Ayuh."

❦❧

Sunday, March 10, 2019
Pizza Palace
Orono, Maine

Tom looked at all the photographs the next morning. The resolution of the M2 drone was amazing. The dispersion patterns were very consistent, with the plastic only slightly wider, but still very close to the dispersion of the fake gold and silver from the Antique Marketplace. He had asked Dave to 3-D print the cups and jars without bottoms so they would not float too far before sinking, just like actual gold and silver, and it worked.

Tom then scaled the dispersion pattern to a depth of thirty feet, and an eleven-by-eleven-meter grid captured all the edges at a depth of ten meters, the maximum depth of Depth Cam, with about seventy percent of the items within a five-by-five-meter circle in the center.

It looked so precise, but Tom understood his handsome grid pattern was based upon a lot of assumptions that were probably at least partially wrong. Short of using actual gold, this was as good as he could get. But he was still not comfortable with the uncertainty.

One lingering question was the actual size of each image to train the neural network.

0	0.1	0.15	0.2	0.25	0.25	0.25	0.2	0.15	0.1	0
0.1	0.2	0.25	0.3	0.5	0.5	0.5	0.3	0.25	0.2	0.1
0.15	0.25	0.5	0.6	0.8	1	0.8	0.6	0.5	0.25	0.15
0.2	0.3	0.6	1.5	2	3	2	1.5	0.6	0.3	0.2
0.25	0.5	0.8	2	4	6	4	2	0.8	0.5	0.25
0.25	0.5	1	3	6	10	6	3	1	0.5	0.25
0.25	0.5	0.8	2	4	6	4	2	0.8	0.5	0.25
0.2	0.3	0.6	1.5	2	3	2	1.5	0.6	0.3	0.2
0.15	0.25	0.5	0.6	0.8	1	0.8	0.6	0.5	0.25	0.15
0.1	0.2	0.25	0.3	0.5	0.5	0.5	0.3	0.25	0.2	0.1
0	0.1	0.15	0.2	0.25	0.25	0.25	0.2	0.15	0.1	0

One meter, the distance he had outlined on the blue tarp seemed like an obvious choice. Most of the Inca gold objects were less than one meter. Also, an eleven-by-eleven-meter satellite image would have 121 one-meter images, a manageable number for training. He would email his recommendation to Dr. Westhoven, and they could decide on the next Zoom call.

As he was admiring his spreadsheet, he wondered if he could just use the images from the Wave Tank to train the neural network. It would certainly be easier, but there were already too many loose ends or variables. He needed to get as close as he could to what a pile of Inca gold would look like underwater in the Llanganatis. And Dr. Westhoven would probably not approve.

"Whatever," he said aloud to himself.

Jenny looked up from her book. "What?"

"Nothing. I was just admiring my spreadsheet."

"Oh." She returned to her book.

Two thoughts floated through his mind. First, he was a nerd, and second, Jenny knew he was a nerd and didn't bat an eyelash when he acted like one.

༄

Wednesday, March 13, 2019
Fogler Library
The University of Maine
Orono, Maine

Tom was in the library waiting for Jenny to finish her last class. He wasn't looking forward to the rescheduled Zoom call on Saturday with Dr. Westhoven. Tom was still struggling with all the ambiguity built into the assumptions.

His last assignment was to estimate the size of the training data set, which typically includes tens of thousands of images, sometimes more.

Training the neural network in high school to recognize a lobster took about 35,000 images of lobsters to get an accuracy of eighty percent. He could have added more images to improve the accuracy, but there came a point of diminishing returns. Now, Tom needed to guess that number for the gold, the "elbow" in the curve of diminishing returns.

There were also so many variables affecting the calculations, like the lake depth, turbidity, and the size and shape of the pile of gold. He had that sinking feeling again that this was all hopeless.

A lot was riding on his guesses.

When it was time to meet Jenny at the Bear's Den, he gathered his papers and stuffed them into his backpack.

She was waiting at their table in the back. "Why the sourpuss?"

"I'm trying to estimate, really guess, the size of the training data set. It's overwhelming."

He changed the subject. "What time do we meet Amanda and Dave?"

This was the payback dinner at 11 Central for Dave and Amanda's help at the Wave Tank, courtesy of Dr. Westhoven.

"Seven. By the way, how did you explain the Wave Tank to Dave?" asked Jenny.

"He didn't ask. I told him this was an archaeology project. He was more concerned I didn't scratch his bodyboard."

The next morning while making coffee, Jenny casually mentioned, "The squeak is back."

"You noticed."

"I certainly did," she said as she poured the coffee.

"I'll oil it again, but I never had this much trouble before."

Jenny smiled. "Are you ready for the Zoom call this weekend?"

"Almost. I'm guessing we'll need a minimum of about 75,000 one-meter satellite images. More would be better, but that's the minimum."

Even though he had double- and triple-checked his calculations, this estimate was still a guess, and if he guessed wrong, his calculations would affect everything that followed.

"That seems like a lot," said Jenny.

"It is, but remember, each pile will generate thousands of images depending upon scaling, and I'll use multiple bands and manipulate the images."

"You can explain that tonight. Let's get going. I have a nine o'clock class."

That evening, back at the Palace over a pepperoni and mushroom pizza, they returned to the conversation about how many unique images Tom could generate from each pile of plastic.

"Okay, what were you talking about this morning with bands and manipulating the images?" asked Jenny.

In between bites, Tom explained, "A satellite has various lenses or bands. Some, like infrared, are invisible to our eyes, but they may highlight key features. I'm not sure how well infrared works underwater, but it does on land. I'll use the usual visible red, green, and blue or RGB bands, and infrared or IR-RG bands.

"I can also process or manipulate each image with software. I'll augment each image with edge and contrast enhancement, and rotate them by 30 degrees, 45 degrees, and 90 degrees, and repeat everything after enlarging each image to 150 percent and shrinking to 75 percent.

"Slow down, nerd. What do you mean, rotate and enlarge each image?"

Tom took his napkin. "Here, ignore the dab of pizza sauce. Pretend the napkin is one image. Because everything is digital, I can rotate the image like this." Tom then rotated the napkin 30 degrees, 45 degrees, and 90 degrees.

"Also, I can make it smaller," as he folded it a couple times, hiding the pizza sauce, "or larger," as he unfolded the napkin entirely.

"So, I can manipulate each image by three sizes and four rotations for twelve unique images. And for each image, I can enhance the edges and contrast."

"Wow, you can do all that?"

"Manipulating the image is easy. Getting the images will be the tough part. You want a beer?" asked Tom on his way to the refrigerator.

"Sure. Have you thought about how much gold and silver the Inca dumped in a pile?"

"Dr. Westhoven estimated a single Inca boat could only handle the weight of one hundred to one hundred-fifty pieces of gold and silver. It seems unlikely the Incas would dump loads all over the place. I bet they dumped several boat loads in one place to make recovery easier.

"So, I'm thinking we should dump four loads for a total of about five hundred items in each pile. From the dispersion data from the Wave Pool, the pile at ten meters depth will look like a fried egg about eleven meters in diameter with a big yellow gold yolk in the middle. With all the imaging processing, this will generate about 5,600 images and another set of control images after the biodegradable plastic dissolves.

"In shallower depth, the dispersion pattern is tighter. At seven meters, the dispersion pattern will be about eight meters in diameter and generate about 3,000 images. A depth of five meters is about 1,500 images.

"I'd like to try for twenty piles. The deeper the water, the more images, but the less clarity of the Depth Cam images. Too deep and we may not get enough quality images to train."

As Tom took a swig of his Hipster Apocalypse, Jenny asked, "So, how do you put this all together?"

He swallowed. "Let's take an average of 3,500 images per pile and multiply by twenty piles. What do you get?"

She reflexively pulled out her iPhone and then realized she could do this in her head. "70,000."

"By adding the infrared band, we can double that to 140,000. That's well over my estimate of 75,000 test images, but I'm concerned the infrared band won't see deep enough to add any additional information. So, this may cut the number of images in half back to about 70,000."

"This all makes sense, I think," she said.

"I'm glad this makes sense to you, because I'm not so sure."

Jenny passed over his comment and moved on. "So, where are we actually going to dump the plastic?"

"I want to use as many lakes as possible to mitigate the variables like depth, water temperature, turbidity, and water flow. I'm thinking ten to twelve lakes with one or two dumps per lake."

He added after a moment of reflection. "It seems doable."

At least it did on this day in March.

Friday, March 15, 2019
Bear's Den
Orono, Maine

The Bear's Den was quiet on the Friday before spring break. After the Zoom call with Dr. Westhoven tomorrow morning, they were off to Amherst. Although he had been preoccupied with preparing for the Zoom call, he wondered about Jenny's plans for the summer. "How is the job hunting going for summer?"

"Not great. There's a ton of waitressing jobs, but I was hoping to do something a little more interesting. I'm still looking."

After Jenny took a long sip of her Diet Coke, she changed the subject. "Have you thought about erratics?"

"You mean like your behavior?"

She just rolled her eyes. She had decided to minor in Earth Sciences, one of the reasons she had chosen Maine. "When the last glacier receded about 10,000 years ago, the rocks trapped in the glacier from Canada dropped all over New England when the ice melted. They're called erratics. You see them everywhere if you look. Lake bottoms are often littered with them. This may confuse your program. We probably need to be sure the lake bottom is clear before we dump the plastic."

Tom thought for a moment. "We could use the underwater drone, but that's time consuming. I wonder if a fish finder would work. It outlines the bottom and can record the depth, too. I'll check the Old Town Trading Post."

"I'm in charge of underwater imaging, remember? Let me handle this," she said.

"Great. Will you check out GPS units, too?" Tom took a long sip of coffee. "I think we're ready for Dr. Westhoven tomorrow."

"And I'm ready for spring break," she added.

Road Trip

Saturday, March 16, 2019
Zoom Call
New Haven, Connecticut - Orono, Maine

Jenny had spent last night at the Pizza Palace, and she was quieter than usual this morning. Tom wondered if she had lost some of her enthusiasm for the project, as she understood more about the challenges. Or maybe she was just thinking about the road trip to Vermont. Or maybe it was the uncomfortable conversation they had last evening about him sleeping in the separate guest room in Vermont. Jenny had not yet told her parents about staying with him for the summer.

Tom did not like early morning Zoom calls if it was sunny in New Haven. Even with the shades drawn, the backlighting from the early morning sun made it difficult to see Dr. Westhoven's facial expressions.

Prompt as always, Dr. Westhoven's video feed came up. "Good morning, guys. Thanks again, Tom, for sending along the dispersion data. It all makes sense."

It must be cloudy there. Tom could easily see the professor.

Dr. Westhoven continued, "Before your update, I want to talk a bit about the lake 'made by hand' and get your thoughts on how to narrow the search. Sorry, another PowerPoint."

Artificial Lake

- River inflow
- No outflow
- Mound on shore
- Ancient riverbed
- Rivers
- Declivity
- Number of lakes to scan

"The Derrotero states the lakes were 'made by hand' so I'm going to focus on lakes with a river or stream flowing in with no obvious outflow. This would suggest the Incas made a dam or other obstruction to create the artificial lake.

"In addition, if I can find a lake with a mound or heap on the shore, especially next to a dried-up riverbed, that would also suggest a dam or man-made element. That lake would deserve a closer look. We can use satellite infrared images to detect any evidence of an old riverbed connected to a lake," Dr. Westhoven explained.

"It's possible that a dam created by the Incas failed in the last 500 years and reverted to a river or stream, but we'll focus on lakes. There are too many rivers to include in the analysis.

"I'm not sure if looking for lakes on a declivity will be helpful since everything seems to be on a slope in the Llanganatis, but I added it anyway.

"By the way, thanks for emailing me with your thoughts on the size of each image. One meter makes sense. If we go with one meter, I was wondering how many lakes we can scan with your neural network. A large lake that's one-mile-by-one-mile is about 2,500,000 images. Even a small lake is over 700,000 one-meter images."

Tom had already thought this through. Assuming his neural network could process about one image per second, with ten GPUs, 25,000,000 images would take about a month.

Tom took a deep breath. "With the time frame you have laid out, 25,000,000 images is the limit. If we assume an average lake is about one million images, that's about twenty-five lakes."

"That helps. Thanks Tom."

Tom added, "I also like your idea of looking for evidence of an old riverbed or mound on the shore. There should be some Landsat images with IR-RG bands, which will help. Hopefully, it will significantly narrow the search."

"Agreed." The professor leaned back. Even though his backlighting was dim, his image briefly washed out as the camera readjusted. "I reviewed your spreadsheets on the contents of a pile. It all fits within our assumptions.

"I've also learned more about Depth Cam. It has seven bands like Landsat with a resolution to thirty centimeters or about a foot, like the fish I spotted in Maltby Lake, but it depends upon the turbidity. We will only use the RGB and possibly IR-RG, but it also includes Thermal IR.

"One other thing, Tom. Remember that Depth Cam images are rectangular? This means all the lakes I image will include some land surrounding the lake. Is that going to be an issue?"

"No, not at all. Land is easy to distinguish from water. I'll be able to remove it from the data."

Dr. Westhoven took a sip of coffee.

"So, tell me, what have you guys been up to?" Dr. Westhoven sat back in his chair and folded his arms across his chest.

The subtle shadows highlighted his features. He looked tired, thought Tom, but it probably was just the lighting.

He updated Dr. Westhoven on their progress. "I estimate the minimum training data set is about 75,000 images and each pile will generate between 3,000 and 11,000 one-meter square images, depending upon the depth.

"We'll want to use as many different lakes as possible to mitigate differences in turbidity, water temperature, flow, bottom debris, and the like. I think, realistically, we can visit ten to twelve lakes this summer, doing one to two lakes per weekend. This would generate over 100,000 training images."

"Where are you setting all this up?"

"Google CoLab. Is there anything at Yale?"

"No, that's why I asked," Dr. Westhoven said. "This will take a while, even with a mainframe. Are you going to be able to run all this data through by October?"

"I think so, but if I can't get the hyperparameters right, it might take longer."

Tom tried to hide his discomfort with all the guesswork going into this project.

"Once the ice is out at Pushaw, a lake outside of Bangor, we plan to dump some plastic and iron out the bugs."

Dr. Westhoven chuckled. "You still have ice on the lakes? Tulips are coming up down here."

He continued, "I'm impressed with what you've accomplished. Let's connect in another couple of weeks. If anything comes up in the meantime, we can schedule a Zoom call. Keep up the great work."

After the call, Tom did a check-in with Jenny. "You know, this is all guesswork, right? I've spent hours this week doing calculations, all based upon pretend numbers with pretend plastic gold. About the only thing I know for sure is the training data set will be small, and I'm not sure it will be enough."

"I get all that, Tom, but you're so energized talking with Dr. Westhoven. You're not going to flunk a course if this doesn't succeed. You're getting paid. Aren't you enjoying any of this?"

He was quiet for a few moments. Clearly, Jenny had not lost her enthusiasm.

"I guess a little. At least this summer will be fun."

"Good. And I mean this in the kindest way. Please stop whining. I can't be your cheerleader for the next year. You need to find some joy in this on your own."

"I'm not whining."

"You're whining now, my little nerd. Now let's hit the road."

⊷⊶

Saturday, March 16, 2019
Orono, Maine to Amherst, Vermont

Tom was understandably anxious about his first trip to Vermont and meeting her parents. So much had happened since their first date at Evenrood's only three months ago. They left after the Zoom call under overcast skies, hoping to get to Amherst by sunset. It had snowed a little during the night, but the roads were clear on the interstate. The F-150 was showing its age but was mechanically sound. Whether the truck would make it to Vermont was the last thing on Tom's mind.

His mom was right. Meeting Jenny's parents was a big deal. He'd gotten a haircut last week. As he eased onto I-95, he tried to loosen his grip on the steering wheel. Only five hours to go.

Jenny filled him in, again, about her parents. They moved to Vermont about six years ago when her dad retired as a physician from the Foreign Service. Her mom was a nurse, still doing some per diem work at a local hospital. She grew up in Proctor not too far from Amherst, where her family settled after immigrating from Finland to work in the marble quarry.

Jenny attended nearby Woodstock Union High School, which was about the same size as Tom's.

The clouds cleared when they crossed the Connecticut River. With cruise control, they would arrive a little early, around five o'clock, just in time for a New England winter sunset.

Last week, Tom had done some reading about color transmission through water and bored Jenny with his concerns through New Hampshire.

"Do you remember Roy G Biv?" asked Tom.

"Who?"

"Roy G Biv, the acronym for visible light—red, orange, yellow, green..."

"Yeah, I think so. Why?"

"It turns out different wavelengths transmit differently through water. Yellow is still visible at ten meters, but red washes out at three to five, and infrared even quicker."

"Is this really a concern or just something else for you to fuss about?"

They both got a little cranky after three hours in the truck.

"We should be okay with the yellow plastic, but we may not be able to use the infrared bands like I hoped. That would reduce the number of usable training images. So yeah, this is really a concern."

With a little less sarcasm, Jenny asked, "What are you going to do?"

"I'll know more after we start getting Depth Cam images. Even poor-quality infrared images might help, but to be on the safe side, let's add a few more dumps."

"Sounds good. Remember, you're on vacation, too. Maybe you should read something fun to take your mind off Roy."

Jenny's phone chimed. It was a text message from her mom.

< We're on our way to Rutland to get some
scallops. None in Ludlow. Back by 5:30. Love
Mom. >

"Looks like we're having scallops tonight. I'd told my mom you liked them," said Jenny.

With Jenny's directions, he easily found the camp road and the house. He expected something more rustic, but in the plowed driveway, he surveyed a modern, white, two-story home with gables and a large wrap-around deck, nestled next to Lake Amherst, which peeked through the pines. A foot of fresh snow blanketed the yard. The frozen lake in the distance had snowmobile tracks down the middle.

Tom sat for a moment in the F-150, squeezing and releasing his grip on the steering wheel. Feeling a little flushed, like the first time they met, he grabbed their gear from the back seat and followed Jenny up the neatly shoveled walkway to the front door. He was careful not to squish the whoopie pies he had brought along. At the door, he took a deep breath and cleared his throat.

Before opening the door, Jenny turned around and wrapped her free arm around his neck, and pulled him down for a kiss.

"We made it. Welcome to Vermont. Let me show you around before they get back. Let's stow the skis first."

Tom followed her downstairs. This clearly was a skiing family with a collection of all kinds of equipment. It made sense with Okemo and Killington at your front door. His skis were beat up compared to the others, all neatly lined up against the wall in the basement.

"Do you want to try another pair of skis?" asked Jenny. "Maybe you could fit into my dad's bindings."

"No way. These are handmade, and I ski on the bottoms, not the tops."

After Tom hung his skis, Jenny gently turned him around and buried her head in his jacket with a hug. "I'm so glad you came home with me to Vermont."

"Me, too." Tom was glad her parents weren't there yet.

Jenny grabbed his hand and led him back upstairs, where she gave him a quick tour. The first floor was an open design with the entry opening into the kitchen and dining area, and a large living room behind some stairs with a cathedral ceiling overlooking the deck and lake, both covered with snow.

Tom wondered if she was as nervous as he was. If she was, she hid it well.

As they entered the living room, the setting sun over the lake was spectacular, reflecting off the snow of the frozen lake.

Tom noticed some embers in the fireplace to his left. Tom loved the smell of a wood fire.

Books were tucked in everywhere. A lot were fiction, like a collection of Stephen King novels by the fireplace. Some were medical. Many were history.

"Let me show you your room," said Jenny, as she headed for the stairs separating the dining room from the living room. Tom grabbed his duffle bag and followed her up the stairs, enjoying the view with every step she took.

"The weather is supposed to be great for the next few days. I thought we could ski Okemo tomorrow. It that okay?" she asked.

"Great. I'll ski anywhere with you." That sounded corny. "I mean anywhere you want." Not much better, he thought.

Upstairs was three bedrooms and a small office for her dad. Her parent's bedroom was in the middle, at the top of the stairs. The guest room with two twin beds overlooked the driveway, and Jenny's bedroom, on the opposite end, faced the lake with a view of the waning sunset.

"Here you go. I'll let you unpack and meet you downstairs. Let me know if you need anything." After one more quick kiss, she flipped around and down the stairs.

Alone, a smile slowly emerged. Here he was, actually in Vermont. He'd been fussing about this for a month. After a few deep breaths, he finished unpacking and wandered downstairs as Jenny's parents drove in the driveway.

Skiing in Vermont

Saturday, March 16, 2019
Orono, Maine to Amherst, Vermont

Her dad looked younger than Tom expected. He had a closely cropped haircut, almost a crewcut. Tom was glad he'd gotten a haircut. He was about his height, which was good. His mom always said he stooped around shorter people.

Jenny resembled her mother with her blue eyes and blond hair.

Her dad extended his hand. "Hey, Tom. I'm John. Nice to meet you. Sorry we're late. We wanted Maine scallops for dinner, but evidently scallops aren't a popular seafood in Ludlow, so we had to go to Rutland."

Her mom gave him a hug. "Hi Tom. Welcome. I'm Ingrid." She eyed the whoopie pies Tom had brought. "The official Maine dessert. They look decadent."

"Ayuh, and they are," said Tom in his best Downeast accent he could muster.

The scallops were delicious, and the chardonnay helped him relax. Jenny also had some wine with dinner. Being underage evidently didn't matter at home.

During dinner, her dad asked, "Any chance you're a lobsterman in your spare time?" while smiling at Jenny, obviously aware of her plans to marry a lobsterman.

"No, but my best friend in Limerock has a recreational license. Does that count?" Joe always had a few traps out in the summer.

Jenny scowled at her dad.

After dinner, they sat in the living room overlooking Lake Amherst and enjoyed the whoopie pies. The fire gave off a warm orange glow. Tom and Jenny sat next to each other on the couch. Across the lake, he could see the headlights of an occasional car driving by on Route 100, too far away to be heard. The Sonos played some background classical music, which he recognized but couldn't name.

Her parents were great. Maybe it was the chardonnay, but for the first time in a while, Tom felt oddly at ease, enjoying the moment.

Then the questions started. Jenny must have talked him up a bit. Her parents knew about his capstone project.

"Jenny tells us you're a computer whiz, that you're working on something interesting, combining artificial intelligence and archaeology," said her dad.

"Usually, she calls me a nerd. Whiz sounds better," replied Tom.

Jenny blushed and tried a gentle elbow to his ribs, but they were too close.

"I learned machine learning in high school. The potential applications are enormous, but my real passion is archaeology. I am hoping to combine deep learning with archaeology."

Tom rarely talked about his capstone with anyone except Dr. Wade.

"What sparked your interest in archaeology?" asked her mom.

"Well, probably the Incas," he said with a chuckle.

He took another sip of wine. He needed a break from talking about himself.

"I also became fascinated by the Incas. We all did when we lived in Colombia, especially Jenny. The Incas were her go-to subject for book reports in high school." Her dad pointed to a collection of books about the Incas in the living room next to the fireplace. "I think she's read every book."

Tom quickly scanned the titles. He didn't see the textbook by Dr. Westhoven on metallurgy by the Incas.

Her dad continued. "In about one hundred years, the Incas expanded from their capital in Cusco to over three thousand miles in the western Andes with ten million subjects, the largest pre-Colombian culture, and then lost it all to the Spanish in a couple of years. It's an incredible story."

While adding a log to the fire, Jenny picked up the story. "The Incas accumulated gold to worship the sun, and silver to worship the moon. Although the gold and silver had no monetary value to the Incas, they amassed vast treasures. Gold and silver were everywhere."

Tom was impressed. Jenny really did know a lot about the Incas.

Her mom added, "I was always amazed at what the Incas did not have. Their empire formed about the same time as the Italian Renaissance halfway around the world, but they had no written language. Everything we know about them is secondhand from the Spanish invaders. The Incas did not use the wheel. They had no working knowledge of alloys like bronze or steel. They seemed so primitive compared to Europe but still created beautiful architecture and a system of government."

"Remember our trip to Machu Picchu?" asked Jenny. "I was ten or eleven years old. The tiered gardens running down the mountain were amazing. I can't remember the details, but I thought there was gold hidden somewhere in the mountains."

Jenny's dad took a more philosophical turn. "Scholars still debate how the Spanish could conquer the Incas so easily, with only a handful of soldiers. Some suggest the subjects of the Inca empire may have viewed the Spanish, at least initially, as liberators from the Inca rule."

After a moment of thought, Tom replied. "I never considered that, but the Incas did force the vanquished tribes to follow their rule, often against their will."

It was getting late, and the fire was dying out. Her mom and dad finished their wine and said their goodnights. Day one with her parents went well, thought Tom.

As her parents climbed the stairs, Jenny put another log on the fire, signaling she had no intention of bedtime yet. She poured Tom some more chardonnay and cuddled a little closer on the sofa. He wondered if Jenny felt as relaxed as he did.

She leaned over and gave him a kiss on the cheek, followed by a soft, "Thank you for being my nerd," and then another kiss, this time on his lips. After some gentle exploring with their tongues, Jenny finally broke off the kiss and buried her head on his shoulder.

He placed his arm around her. The new log crackled, and the flickering yellow light highlighted her blonde hair. Tom closed his eyes. He remembered the freshness of her hair the first time they had met.

"This was the first time I heard about your capstone in that much detail. It sounds impressive. I can see why Dr. Westhoven wanted you to speak in Boston."

"And I didn't realize you were such an Inca fan. Your family has quite a collection of books." He pointed to the collection by the fireplace.

They sat quietly for a few minutes, watching the crackling fire consume Jenny's log. Tom hoped it was oak, so it would burn longer.

He wondered how she had become such a good kisser. He also wondered when she would tell her parents about her summer plans.

The fire gradually turned to embers. It was time for bed. They headed for the stairs and after one more kiss at the top of the stairs, and a gentle unintentional brush across her breast, Tom said, "Enjoy your room with a view."

As they each opened the door to their bedroom, they both looked back one more time down the long hallway. Even in the dim light of the hallway, Tom thought he saw the twinkle in her left eye. He really wanted a room with a view.

❧

Monday, March 18, 2019
Okemo Mountain
Ludlow, Vermont

Skiers pack the slopes on weekends, especially during spring break, so Tom and Jenny didn't bother to ski yesterday. Today was a bluebird day, and there was still plenty of good snow left from the last snowstorm.

On the way up the Quantum Four lift, Jenny looked down at Tom's skis. "What's the metal plate under your boot?"

"It's a homemade ski by John Howe. He was a retired engineer at the Head Ski company who had this idea for an innovative dampening system. He made these skis in his barn in western Maine and called them The Claw."

"The Claw?"

Tom held up his glove like a claw. "They grip the ice like a claw. I met John at Sugarloaf a couple of years ago, and I've skied on them ever since. This is my only pair now since I delaminated a tip last spring in the bumps at Sugarloaf. That's the ski on my bedroom door. Unfortunately, John passed away last summer."

"Sorry to hear that. By the way, if you want to ski bumps, you're on your own."

Although Jenny considered herself a beginner, Tom thought she was much better. They skied from one side of Okemo to the other. Tom was comfortable anywhere on the mountain, so he let her pick the trails and lead. He enjoyed watching her, as much as the skiing.

He knew Jenny had a boyfriend in high school. On the next lift ride up, as they approached the bull wheel, he asked, "Have you ever had a serious boyfriend?"

"Serious? Not yet," she said with a laugh as she pushed off the lift and headed to Sunset Strip toward the middle of the mountain.

They grabbed an early lunch at the Summit Lodge and sat on the deck, basking in the noonday sun overlooking the valley. He felt a calmness as he leaned back and closed his eyes against the warmth of the sun. His mind was freed of convolutional neural networks.

That evening, after dinner, they settled in again in the living room with another roaring fire. Her dad headed to the Sonos. But before he could press the play button, Jenny interrupted. "How about if we listen to someone who's still breathing?"

Her dad had a pleasant laugh, like Jenny's. She loaded her playlist on Sonos. Tom recognized *Night Sail* by Devonsquare, his favorite Maine pop group from the 1970s. Maybe he'd mentioned it to her at the Bear's Den.

Her dad circled back to the Incas. "What do you think about the legend of the lost Inca gold?" he asked Tom.

"I'm not sure. I read a book called *Valverde's Gold* last semester. It was about the author's journey in Ecuador to find the lost gold in the Llanganatis. He reviewed all the history. It was fascinating." He had noticed the same book by the fireplace with a well-worn book jacket.

Jenny's dad continued, "I've always been intrigued by the capture of the Inca king and the gold ransom he offered to the Spanish. The ransom room still exists in Cajamarca. I visited it once on a diplomatic trip to Ecuador."

Tom knew the story well. Atahualpa, the Inca king, was in Cajamarca when the Spanish quickly overwhelmed the Inca soldiers. They were no match for the small contingent of well-armed Spanish.

"The Valverde story is interesting in its own right," said her dad. "A few years after the death of Atahualpa, Valverde, who was a poor Spanish soldier, married an Inca and became wealthy overnight. According to legend, his bride was an Inca princess and her father an Inca chieftain who had taken part in hiding the ransom gold. Valverde, on his deathbed, dictated the

Derrotero as a guide for the Spanish king to find the hidden gold."

Tom didn't realize the father was an Inca Chieftain.

Her dad continued, "Many have followed the Derrotero, some have lost their lives, but no one we know of has found the lost Inca treasure, if it exists at all. The Llanganatis are now a National Park in Ecuador. It's still some of the most remote terrain in the world."

Jenny tried to hide a yawn. Tom hoped this was just a subtle sign for her parents to go to bed, and not that she was really tired. He had been looking forward to some couch time with her.

It worked. Her parents said goodnight and after another chardonnay and log on the fire, they picked up where they left off last night.

Tuesday, March 19, 2019
Amherst, Vermont

This morning, Tom had an appointment at Mack Molding. The meeting went well. Tom confirmed the plastic would sink and dissolve in about a month, with no harmful or residual effects. The entire order would be about 10,000 pieces.

By the time Tom returned, it was too late to go skiing, so they snowshoed at the Coolidge State Park with some rentals from the Tyson Store. They had the park to themselves except for another couple cross-country skiing.

Wednesday, March 20, 2019
Okemo Ski Resort
Ludlow, Vermont

Wednesday was another beautiful day as Okemo transitioned into spring. By afternoon, they had shed their outer layers.

On the Sunrise Quad, Jenny mentioned, "I did some checking. I found a job online at the Hudson Museum as a docent."

"What do you know about being a docent?"

"The description said no experience was necessary. They will train me. It really sounds interesting."

She applied online for the job later that afternoon. The director of the museum replied by email that evening, and she had a telephone interview the following afternoon.

That evening, Jenny showed Tom the email. "Look at this. It's nine-to-five Monday through Thursday. It's perfect. We can get an early start on Fridays. Will that work?"

"I guess so." He had hoped they would have even more time off together, but a three-day weekend would work.

He changed the subject. "When do you think your parents will let us sleep together? Your room has a much better view."

"You can see the lake from the living room."

"That's not why I want a room with a view."

Jenny chuckled. "Just give it a little more time."

෨෴ඐ

Thursday, March 21, 2019
Amherst, Vermont

The next day, they cut their ski day short so Jenny could prepare for her interview in the afternoon. Her parents were out running a few errands, so she set up for her video call in the living room. Tom drifted upstairs to the guest room to check his email.

About thirty minutes later, he heard footsteps running up the stairs. Jenny burst in and tackled him on his bed. "I got the job, pending reference checks!"

After Jenny rolled off him, and he caught his breath, he said, "It's official—we're living together this summer. Now you can tell your parents."

"Easy. One step at a time."

After a few minutes on the bed, Jenny broke the silence. "Do you think it's true that opposites attract?"

"I certainly hope so," said Tom. "What was it like moving around so much when you were younger?"

"I didn't mind it too much until I was about twelve. I had some good friends in Colombia, and I didn't want to move to Washington. I still stay in touch with some of them on Facebook. And then, when the time came to move to Vermont, I didn't want to leave my friends in D.C."

Tom had lived in the same town, the same house, with the same friends his entire life. He wondered how moving every three to five years affected Jenny. She only talked about Vermont and a bit about Washington. He hadn't heard much about Colombia until this week.

ॐ

Friday, March 22, 2019
Amherst, Vermont

Today was raining, and after four days of skiing, they needed a break anyway. They planned to see a movie in Ludlow this afternoon. This morning, Jenny went grocery shopping with her mom. Meanwhile, Tom pulled a book from the living room library about the Inca treasure, the *Sweat of the Sun, Tears of the Moon* by Peter Lourie. Jenny's dad had piqued his interest again. He settled onto the couch overlooking the lake.

At the Tyson Store, Jenny's mom casually said, "Tom seems nice."

"Yeah."

"Why did you invite him over?"

"He likes to ski."

A wobbly wheel on the cart annoyed Jenny.

"So do I, but why did you invite <u>him</u> over?"

"I like him. I wanted to see if he would come over with me, and I wanted you to meet him."

"What if he just wanted to ski Killington?"

"Killington's not that gre...." Then she saw the grin on her mother's face.

"One last question and then I'll leave you alone. What do you like about him? He doesn't seem the lobsterman type."

"I'm not sure. He's focused, centered, thoughtful—all the things I'm not."

"You're thoughtful," said her mom.

"Not 'nice' thoughtful but deliberate thoughtful, although he's nice thoughtful, too."

"Well, your dad likes him. And so do I. What about you, now?"

"Yeah, I do, but I don't have a lot of experience being a girlfriend since high school. This is different. I don't want to screw it up."

Jenny was becoming increasingly annoyed by the errant wheel.

"By the way, I have a job at the University's Hudson Museum, and I'm staying with Tom at his apartment for the summer."

Her mom just smiled again and took over steering the wobbly cart. "We figured."

Later, after the movie in Ludlow, Jenny suggested to Tom that he move his gear to her room—for a better view.

Llanganatis in Maine

Sunday, March 24, 2019
Amherst, Vermont to Orono, Maine

The week went by too fast, but Tom had been able to push the expedition out of his mind, for the most part. Today, they were heading back to Orono.

Jenny was in her center seat next to Tom. It was a little over five hours to Orono. As they headed back to Route 100, Tom asked, "Do you know a shortcut? I was going down to Portsmouth and then up I-95."

"Not in the winter. Sometimes in the summer it's fun to go over the White Mountains, but this time of year, it can be nasty. Let's head south."

The conversation was light. They talked about their individual goals. Jenny wanted to do something with writing. "My Aunt Lisa in Burlington is a freelance travel writer, and she loves it. I hope I can do something similar with geology or climate change."

She also shared some of her frustrations as a kid, moving every few years. "I experienced some incredible stuff growing up all over the world, but I never felt settled until Amherst. Vermont is my home."

Tom had already done a lot of talking with her parents during the visit. He was content to listen. Letting her talk was safe, and she was sharing things that made him feel closer to her.

As they turned north on I-95 at Portsmouth, Tom suggested lunch at Bob's Clam Hut in Kittery. "It's a tourist trap, but it's open year-round. In the winter, it's quiet and although the indoor seating is a little dark and cool, the clams still taste great."

"I love clams. How did you find this place?"

"They used to have a small takeout place at Sugarloaf."

While waiting for their order, they rubbed shoulders on the heated patio to stay warm.

"Thanks for telling your mom and dad about our summer plans. The view in your room really was awesome." Tom hesitated. "The view of the lake was nice, too."

Jenny smiled. "It was nice to share a bed without a squeak."

They arrived in Orono in the late afternoon with the usual caravan after a school break heading north on I-95 to Orono. Although they were both still stuffed from Bob's, Tom suggested splitting a Pat's pizza.

A few minutes later, they were on the sofa with a pizza. After a bite, Tom went to the fridge and came back with a bottle of André Cold Duck with two plastic champagne glasses.

"What's this?" asked Jenny as Tom poured.

"I'm not sure, but I had some on New Year's Eve. It was good, so I bought a couple of bottles at the IGA. It fits into my budget."

"Nice bubbles," she said as she raised her glass to Tom for a plastic clink.

"Do you want to catch-up on the depth finders while we eat?" asked Tom.

"Sure. I'm leaning toward the Raymarine. It pairs with an iPad for a bigger display, and we can also take screen shots. They have one at the Old Town Trading Post."

"Neat," he said. "Let's pick it up this week, so it's ready to go by ice-out at Pushaw. What about a GPS unit?"

"I'm not so sure about that. I didn't see any online with the resolution we need."

"Okay. By the way, if we ever make it to the Llanganatis, Dr. Westhoven wants some type of sonar device to scan the bottom of the entire lake. I didn't even know something like that existed, but he gave me the name of a company to check out. Here it is—Aeolus." Tom handed her a sticky note from his wallet. "It sounds like an underwater Roomba."

Jenny pulled out her iPhone and googled Aeolus.

"Did you know Aeolus was the Greek god of wind? There are dozens of hits."

Tom shook his head no.

After a few minutes of scrolling, she finally found the company. "Here it is. It's called the Triton. It's 1.75 meters long and weighs seventeen kilograms. The Triton is programmable and can scan for twenty-four hours on a single charge in water as cold as four degrees Celsius. To avoid the impact of waves, it operates about one meter below the surface. Obstacle avoidance is also embedded. It comes with a remote satellite uplink to make it truly independent and uploads images in real time to anywhere in the world."

"How much?" asked Tom.

"It doesn't say. There's a contact number. I'll call tomorrow to find out more. This may work."

"Okay. Let's look at some lakes to dump the plastic gold," said Tom as he placed a battered *Maine Gazetteer* on the coffee table. After he poured some more Cold Duck, Jenny flipped through the pages of the oversized book of maps. "So this is the famous *Gazetteer.*" She tried but couldn't find Limerock. "How do you find anything?"

Tom flipped it over to the back cover, where a map of the state of Maine was carved up into seventy rectangular quadrants. This was the index to the maps.

Pointing to the map on the back cover, he said, "Here's Bangor." He then traced a large circle around it with his index finger. "Let's pick some lakes within the circle to visit this summer."

Jenny found Penobscot Bay on the large map and then Limerock.

He reviewed the criteria for lakes again with Jenny.

A little exasperated by his attention to detail, she finally said, "Tom, I get it. We're looking for remote lakes that aren't too deep and not too far from Bangor, right? Oh, and fun to explore."

Ignoring her attitude, "Right. Let's start with Pushaw."

He pulled up the online depth chart of Pushaw on his laptop.

While he was studying Pushaw, Jenny was thumbing through the *Gazetteer*. "Where's Nahmakanta?" She had heard a lot about this remote lake from Tom.

He found it quickly. It crossed two pages.

"Where's the road?"

"It's the tiny dotted line there."

She squinted.

"Next to Nahmakanta are the Debsconeag Lakes. They'll be fun to paddle, too," he said.

While Jenny googled Nahmakanta, Tom studied the map on the back and circled ten lakes around Bangor and added them to a PowerPoint slide with a background of Nahmakanta for next weekend's Zoom call.

Llanganatis in Maine

- Pushaw - Orono
- Fields Pond - Orland
- Alligator Lake - T34MD and T28MD
- Little Pond - Smithfield
- Pleasant River Lake - Beddington Twp
- Hopkins Pond - Mariaville Township
- Duck Lake - T4 ND
- Sebec Lake - Bowerbank
- Flagstaff - Bigelow Township
- Nahmakanta - T1 R11 and T2 R11

"Do you think Dr. Westhoven will be impressed with my PowerPoint?"

"I don't know, but I certainly am," said Jenny, pouring the last of the Cold Duck. "Will this be enough to get 75,000 images?"

"I think so."

As Jenny handed him his drink, he asked, "I know it's Sunday night, but do you want to pretend we're camping at Nahmakanta?"

"Okay, but no campfire. And we must break camp early. I have a nine o'clock class."

੭৽৶

Monday, March 25, 2019
Orono, Maine

Jenny found time at lunch to connect with Aeolus about the Triton. Its maximum speed was six knots per hour, so a large lake one-mile by one-mile would scan in about eighteen hours.

Fortunately, most of the lakes of interest in the Llanganatis were smaller.

Later, at the Bear's Den, Tom asked, "How much?"

"Depends."

"On what?"

"Each one with the satellite uplink package is $55,000. If you order five or more, the price drops to $50,000 apiece. A large lake could still be scanning into the next day, so even if you go back and recover the Triton, you'll still need at least three, which includes one backup."

Tom agreed. "We'll need more than one for sure, maybe four, depending upon how many lakes we can visit in one day. This is Dr. Westhoven's call. I'll send him the specs. Thanks for tracking this down."

∾∞

Saturday, March 30, 2019
Zoom Call
New Haven, Connecticut - Orono, Maine

Once Dr. Westhoven's image stabilized, he started, "One year from now, hopefully we'll be in the Llanganatis. How's it going, guys?"

"Hey, Dr. Westhoven. Great. We had a good break in Vermont, and we hope to be on Pushaw in the next few weeks," said Tom.

After a sip of coffee, Tom continued. "By the way, how do I trigger the Depth Cam satellite?"

"You email Zheng Enterprises. I'll forward the format. Here, can you see my screen?"

"Yep."

"The subject line is the GPS coordinates in decimal degrees format, followed by the size of the image in meters, east-west first, then north-south. The body contains the date and the Greenwich Mean Time to start the scan. Zheng Enterprises has a dozen satellites in orbit with Depth Cam and will select the closest satellite. Imaging will start within 90 to 120 minutes of the time you specify.

"In this example, Depth Cam will photograph a grid of four meters on the latitude by five meters on the longitude. The actual GPS coordinates are the center of the grid.

"Once you get the image from Zheng, you'll need to partition it into one-meter grids. Does that make sense?"

Tom checked his email. "Yeah. I'll try it now. Here are the coordinates for home plate on the Mahaney Diamond, the baseball field at the University. It's a sunny day here and home plate is clear of snow." Tom replaced the coordinates and time in the email from Dr. Westhoven and sent it off to Zheng Enterprises.

To: Zheng Enterprises
Date: Saturday, March 30, 2019
From: Thomas Kirkpatrick

Subject: 44.904715,-68.669383,4,5

2019-03-30T17:00:00

Dr. Westhoven replied, "Let me know how it goes. The key, of course, is timing the satellite for a clear day."

"Do you have any idea how much this costs?" asked Tom.

"No. Zheng must be billing Miguel. It doesn't matter. We need to understand how Depth Cam works. Take as many images as you need."

"How do I actually get the image?" asked Tom.

"Once Zheng acquires the image, you'll receive an email with a hyperlink. You'll need plenty of bandwidth to download the image."

"The University belongs to Gig.U Network. Bandwidth shouldn't be an issue."

Dr. Westhoven then said he was about halfway through the lakes in the Llanganatis. "My goal is to have them all reviewed by summer and narrowed down to about twenty-five high-value targets by September."

Tom filled him in on his meeting with Mack Molding.

"We also picked ten lakes for this summer. We're shooting for about twenty piles, or two piles in each lake, with about five hundred pieces all jumbled together in each pile, hopefully imitating a pile of Inca gold. I hope it's enough." Tom shared his screen with the PowerPoint of the lakes.

"Jenny also connected with Aeolus. It sounds like the Triton will do the job. It can transmit real-time data to a satellite uplink, but it will take twelve to eighteen hours to scan a large lake. Although most of the lakes in the Llanganatis are smaller, we'll probably need more than one Triton."

"Understood. Thanks for sending the information along. I expected this to be expensive. This will be Miguel's call. Otherwise, everything seems on track. How about we connect in four weeks?" asked Dr. Westhoven. "And let me know how Pushaw goes."

"Sounds good, Dr. Westhoven."

"Great. Well, keep up the good work, guys." He signed off with a wave.

Both Dr. Westhoven and Jenny were glass-half-full people. Tom was not necessarily a glass-half-empty type, but he still didn't think they would find any gold.

At a high level, he told himself, all this nonsense would eventually be over, probably sooner rather than later. The VGG-16 would not find any gold, and Mr. Titere, with his carefully chosen team, would not go to the Llanganatis. Tom was just biding his time.

In the meantime, his stipend would soon increase to $2,000 a week, which was way more money than any tutoring or summer job, and he was looking forward to the summer with Jenny.

Tiltin' Hilton

Friday, April 12, 2019
320 Park Street
Limerock, Maine

This was the first free weekend since Vermont, and Jenny had said she wanted to meet Tom's parents before graduation, which was only five weeks away. She also wanted to meet Joe and Lynda. Tom had something planned with them for tonight, but wouldn't tell her what.

They hit the road just after lunch. Although Jenny thought she already knew the answer, she asked anyway, "Have you ever brought a girl home to meet your parents?"

"Only one."

She'd expected a simple no.

"When was that?"

"I was a freshman at Maine. Her name was Chrissy. She was a bitch."

"What?"

"Joe asked me if my parents could watch her for the weekend."

"Watch her? What does Joe have to do with this?"

"Joe and I were heading to Nahmakanta. Chrissy was his dog, and my parents were delighted to watch her for the weekend. Other than Chrissy, nope."

"Let me guess, Maine humor."

"Ayuh."

"Well, I'm a little nervous, to be honest, whether or not I'm the first."

"You should be. I'm their pride and joy."

She turned to face him as a grin spread across his face. "You're not helping, Tom."

"Jenny, my parents already know all about you, and they're probably more nervous than you are. Just be yourself. They know how much you mean to me."

After a few moments, Jenny broke the silence. "I bet your mom has some good stories."

"Now you're making me nervous."

"What was it like visiting me the first time in Vermont?"

"I was anxious, but that was a little different. I wasn't official."

"Official?"

"Official boyfriend and besides, I was just there for the skiing." Tom dropped his right arm, but not in time to block a direct hit to his ribs.

As they entered Limerock, Tom veered off Route 1. "I'm going to take a quick detour before we head to the house." A few moments later, they pulled up to the high school. "I want you to meet Mr. Gartley."

The high school was quiet, but he hoped Mr. Gartley might still be there. When Tom poked his head into the classroom, he was at his desk grading papers. Tom reached for Jenny's hand and walked in.

"Hey, Mr. Gartley."

"Hey yourself, Tom. You timed that perfectly. I just finished cleaning my whiteboard. Who's this?"

Tom was a little flustered, so Jenny introduced herself. "Hi, Mr. Gartley. I'm Jenny."

"Nice to meet you, Jenny." He turned to Tom. "Is this the same Jenny you told me about at Christmas?"

"I better be," she answered with a smile. She noticed Tom's hand was getting sweaty, so she let go. "We're down for the weekend so I can meet Tom's parents."

The three of them talked a bit. Tom updated Mr. Gartley on his master's program for the next year. He did not mention the Llanganatis.

"It sounds like you two are all set for the next couple years."

"I think so. I also took your advice and presented at the conference in Boston. It went okay. I'm trying to stay out of my future, whatever it is."

Tom smiled and Mr. Gartley chuckled and held up his Yoda paperweight.

It was getting late, and they said their goodbyes.

On the way out, Tom poked his head into the principal's office, but Mike's dad was on the phone. Tom waved.

On the last leg to Tom's house, Jenny said, "I've never been back to Woodstock High. It's nice you have someone like Mr. Gartley. I wish I had a guiding star like him."

"Yeah. He's a lot more than a math teacher to me."

Tom honked as he drove in the driveway, shouldered between two tall oak trees that shaded a rusted basketball hoop at the end of the driveway. His mom came out, waved at Tom, and went directly to Jenny for a big hug.

"It's so nice to finally meet you, Jenny. Here, let me help you with your stuff. Tom's dad will be home any time now. I should have checked, but I hope you like lasagna. It's Tom's favorite."

Jenny was the center of attention, and Tom was loving it. The peeling blue paint on the side of the modest, colonial, two-story clapboard house caught his eye. He wondered how long it had been peeling.

There were two doors on the front. The one closest to the driveway led into an enclosed porch and the other, on the far end, had a sign over the door, Knox Floor Covering, which opened into his dad's business.

The house was on a six-acre lot on the outskirts of town, mostly fields with woods in the distance. "Those woods have treasures," said Tom, pointing. "They looked farther away when I was a kid."

Entering the porch, Jenny remarked, "That's a lot of tools," motioning to a wall of hammers, pliers, and other tools, all neatly hung and organized.

"Those are my dad's tools."

While his mom put the finishing touches on the lasagna, Tom gave Jenny a tour of his home.

The porch opened into a large kitchen with a dining room table. To the left, through an archway, was an equally large living room with a worn couch and two comfy chairs around a mid-sized TV.

Beyond the living room, his dad's showroom was just as Tom had described. A rainbow of perfectly arranged carpet samples lined the walls. This was the most private room in the house and where they'd sleep.

"It doesn't have the same view as your bedroom in Amherst, but the carpet will soften our sleeping bags," commented Tom.

They dumped their gear in the showroom and headed up the back stairs.

Upstairs, over the showroom, was his parents' bedroom. Tom's room, with no door and no privacy, was at the other end of the house, over the kitchen. In between the two bedrooms was the music-library-study room with a worn table and chair. A taupe carpet with a tight pile lined the walls, with bookshelves everywhere.

"I've never seen carpet on walls before."

"It was cheaper and easier than wallpaper for my dad to install. And it muffled the sound when I played my music too loud."

Jenny looked at the books. Most of them were nonfiction, but he also had a collection of Michael Crichton and John le Carre.

"Where are your Stephen King books?" she asked.

"I don't have any. I guess I'm more partial to nonfiction." From the well-worn encyclopedia for kids, he pulled out the

Helminth - Infrared volume. "This is where I first read about the Incas." He found the Inca entry quickly from the worn edges.

There was a chess set on a small table in the corner. "I didn't know you played chess."

"I was the seventh grade chess champion," he said, pointing to a small trophy on the top shelf.

She looked out back over the field and the woods in the distance. She turned around and gave Tom a hug. "Is this where you evolved into a nerd?"

He chuckled. "It does look like a nerd kingdom. I did spend a lot of time in this room. It brings back good memories."

Dinner conversation focused on Jenny and her family. Tom's parents had never met anyone who'd lived in so many places all over the world. His parents were what she expected and, so far, no surprises about Tom from his mom, other than some stories about his beet head. Jenny had seen hints of it now and then, and it was nice to have a name for it. She appreciated how Tom must have felt, being the center of attention, when he visited Vermont for the first time.

࿇

Tiltin' Hilton
Owls Head, Maine

After dinner, Tom and Jenny headed to Owls Head to meet Joe and Lynda. Tom had been evasive about where. A light rain started. He hoped fog, which always seemed worse in Owls Head, would not follow it.

"So, where are we going?"

"The Tiltin' Hilton."

"The tilting what?"

"You'll see."

Jenny would not turn twenty-one until October, so Tom needed to find a bar with a "liberal" carding policy. It had been four years since Tom lived in Limerock, so he hoped Joe could help.

It turned out his sister worked at the Crescent Beach Inn, or CBI, known locally as the "Tiltin' Hilton." She would make sure Jenny got in. The CBI wasn't what Tom had in mind for a night out with Jenny, but the more he thought about it....

"What are you grinning about?" asked Jenny.

"It's on the water. You'll love it. There might even be a lobsterman kicking around," he said.

The CBI had seen better days. The entire building resembled an army barracks about twenty feet wide by sixty feet long, complete with a rusted, gable metal roof. White peeling paint over gray primer greeted them at the entrance. There was no kitchen or entertainment, at least in the traditional sense. The constant drizzle added to the ambiance.

The most enchanting feature of the CBI, however, was that the entire building tilted about fifteen degrees toward the water. The building was a huge parallelogram with thick guy wires attached to the roof rafters of the landward side every ten feet that were anchored to the ground to keep the building from toppling into the sea. Rain dripping off the rusted roof seemed to defy gravity.

Tom recognized Joe's Subaru in the parking lot. Somehow Lynda had convinced him to trade his Mustang for a Subaru, a sensible choice for Maine winters, but Joe wasn't typically sensible, at least when it came to cars.

Tom and Jenny took off their raincoats in the alcove. Once inside, the bar was in the front to the right so you could pick up your drink on your way by. Joe and Lynda were chatting with Marcia, his sister, by the door when Tom and Jenny stepped inside.

Lynda gave Jenny a hug. "It's so nice to meet you, Jenny. Joe has told me so much about you."

From the bar to his right, Joe's sister asked Tom, "Nice to see you again, Tom. What can I get you guys?"

Jenny ordered a lager and Tom his usual IPA. They were in.

The inside was as lovely as the outside. At least there was no peeling paint on the bare pine board. Water stains here and there from leaks decorated the walls. Grimy lights in the rafters cast angular shadows on the pine tables that lined the walls. A wide center aisle led to the bathrooms in the back, with posts every ten feet, which had been installed too late to stop the Hilton from tilting. Small windows, just above eye level, dotted the walls with a half-dozen replaced by warped plywood. The rain pattering on the thin metal roof added to the allure. The floor had a pleasing bounce as they found a table halfway down on the landward side.

Tom and Joe knew the landward side would be important later on. Although there was no formal entertainment at the CBI, watching patrons—after a few beers—navigate around the center posts to the bathroom in the back was entertaining enough. If they happened to bring along their beer to the bathroom, you wanted to be uphill.

Joe had his usual collection of jobs, but grave digging had taken off since spring. He was digging all over the Midcoast area and was busy.

Although this was Jenny's first time in a bar, she easily negotiated the "perp walk" to the bathroom.

When she returned to the table, Tom turned to Joe and Lynda. "Bob Marley has a couple of shows at the Strand in June. Are you guys interested?"

Joe started, "She's shade in the summer and warmth in the winter."

"That's Tim Sample," said Tom. "Marley's the guy whose mother eats clams and gets the runs."

Joe and Lynda had already planned that weekend to visit Lynda's parents in Otis, so they had to pass.

Jenny had heard about Bob Marley, Bert and I, and Tim Sample, but she still wasn't sure what they all meant by Maine humor. "Tell me again what's so special about Maine humor."

Joe explained in his best Downeast accent, trying to copy a bit from Tim Sample. "Maine humor is different. It's not like the humor you see on the TV. A lot of Maine humor will go right over your head. It doesn't mean it's not funny. You just don't get it. But be careful driving home. That's when it's apt to hit you—and take you right off the road."

Although Joe did his best, Jenny still didn't get it.

"I guess you'll have to wait for the ride home," said Joe with a smile.

The CBI always tilted more as the evening wore on, so when the rain finally stopped, and before it started again, they called it a night with promises to connect again after Tom's graduation.

Limerock grounded Tom. He was glad they finally caught up with Joe and Lynda. On the way home, he asked Jenny, "What did you think of Lynda?"

"She's great—and so is Joe."

Jenny was otherwise uncharacteristically quiet on the way home from the CBI. As they pulled into the driveway, she finally said, "It's nice you have such good friends and a history with Joe. I have friends all over the world, but none with the stories you guys tell. It's special. I hope you appreciate it."

"I've never thought of it like that." Tom realized, once again, that Jenny noticed things he did not.

戉执

On Sunday morning, on the way back to Orono, while waiting for crosswalk traffic in Camden, Jenny asked, "Could you do an independent study project this summer that might take some of the pressure off next year?"

She continued, "I bet Dr. Wade would sponsor something for three or four credit hours. You can't work on the algorithm all the time."

Tom reflected as the road cleared of pedestrians. "I've always wanted to do something with the Popham Colony. The part on private land has never been excavated. It's about two hours from Orono."

"You certainly were a quirky kid growing up. What's the Popham Colony." Jenny quickly pulled out her iPhone to google Popham Colony.

Tom started to flush. "I don't have that many quirks."

"Not according to your mother."

Before he could respond, she paraphrased the Wikipedia entry. "Popham Colony was one of the earliest European settlements in North America. Although most of the site on public land has been explored, a part on private land has never been excavated."

"You know, there would be satellite images before and after the excavations, with ground-truthing on the site. I could use these images as the training data set and the VGG-16 neural network to look for good stuff on the private property by satellite. This might work. I could also use this as a case study in my article for *Modern Archaeology*."

Pushaw

Wednesday, April 17, 2019
Orono, Maine

The plastic had arrived on Monday at MaineSpace, a climate-controlled storage unit on Stillwater Avenue in Bangor. Today was the first chance Tom and Jenny had to check out the delivery. The entire load wasn't that heavy, but it filled most of the ten-by-ten-foot storage unit.

Staring at the yellow plastic almost touching the ceiling, Tom asked, "How are we going to get all this plastic gold onto the lakes?" He needed to figure this out quickly, as they planned a shakedown trip to Pushaw the first weekend that the weather cooperated.

"What about an inflatable raft?" asked Jenny. "There's no way we can fit this into the canoe with all our other gear."

"Yeah. I was considering a second canoe, but that would be a pain to transport. Let's swing by Walmart on the way home and see what they have."

They found an inflatable raft that could hold all the plastic for two piles. Deflated, it would be easy to transport.

Jenny had already picked up a Raymarine Dragonfly Pro Chirp Fish Finder from the Old Town Trading Post and paired it with her iPad. "It's not much to see out of water, but everything's ready to go."

Upon reviewing the specifications of the off-the-shelf GPS units, Tom found they were only accurate to within three to five meters on land, and only slightly better on the water without obstructions. To get a tight image pattern from Depth Cam, he needed accuracy to a meter or better.

He knew the military had much better precision, so he emailed Dr. Westhoven. Perhaps Zheng Enterprises had a recommendation. Being able to pinpoint each pile for the satellite was essential.

⮞⮜

Saturday, April 20, 2019
Zoom Call
New Haven, Connecticut - Orono, Maine

This was the first Zoom call in almost a month, and Dr. Westhoven started the call promptly, as usual. Tom and Jenny were still on the bed in his bedroom.

"Good morning, guys. Congratulations Tom on Phi Beta Kappa."

Jenny gave Tom a gentle nudge, which jiggled the laptop.

"Thanks Dr. Westhoven. We've been so busy it hasn't sunk in. Graduation is only three weeks away."

Tom continued, "I think we're all set here except for the GPS unit."

Dr. Westhoven's eyes brightened. "I have some good news. I checked with Zheng Enterprises. With Miguel's intervention, I purchased a military grade GPS unit from Zheng that combines GPS with GLONASS, the Russian system. It also corrects for atmospheric influences in real time. The accuracy is down to one meter and even better on the water."

"Wow, when do you think it will arrive? We need it before we head out onto Pushaw."

"Zheng Enterprises is shipping directly to you. It should be there early next week. I'll send you the tracking number."

"Neat. By the way, the ice is out. We hope to be on the water in the next week or two. We have all the equipment ready to go except the GPS."

"Wonderful. Are you all set with targeting Depth Cam?"

"Yeah. It was spot on home plate at Mahaney Diamond," said Tom, swinging an imaginary baseball bat.

Tom continued, "One last thing. If someone confronts us on a lake asking what we're doing, we need a cover story. I'm going to say we're modeling fish habitat with the plastic, and I'll give you as a reference. Does that make sense?"

"You know Tom, that does makes sense. Let me know how Pushaw goes. Let's reconnect after graduation. Congratulations again on Phi Beta Kappa, and good luck to both of you with your finals."

❧◦❧

Thursday, April 25, 2019
The University of Maine
Orono, Maine

Tom met with Dr. Wade last week, who enthusiastically endorsed the Popham Colony project. Tom also found Landsat images both before and after an excavation by Jeffrey Brain that he had started in 1994 and continued on and off for about twenty years.

He hoped his VGG-16 for the Llanganatis would come together as easily.

❧◦❧

Saturday, May 4, 2019
Pushaw Lake
Orono, Maine

Today was a beautiful spring day in the mid-fifties, which felt even warmer after the long winter. Finals were next week. Tom only had one, and Jenny, who was well prepared, wanted a break. So, they headed out to Pushaw. Tom planned to dump two piles in about fourteen feet of water near Dollar Island.

He checked Windy.com. There was only a gentle breeze coming off the water. He figured it would take a couple of hours once they were on Pushaw.

Last week, he organized the plastic at the storage unit. It was claustrophobic, surrounded by yellow plastic gold almost to the ceiling. He decided each pile would be four dumps of plastic, two off the starboard and two off the port side of the canoe. After dumping the four loads, each pile would have about five hundred pieces all jumbled together.

Jenny would then photograph everything with the M2 underwater drone.

Transporting the plastic on the lake was another challenge. To reduce the volume of all the plastic, Tom stuffed ingots inside the smaller cups, and then the smaller cups inside the larger cups. He hoped it would be easy to separate and then mix everything up when they were on the lake.

By mid-morning, they had loaded the truck with enough plastic for two piles, the deflated raft, and topped it all off with the canoe. They headed out Essex Street to Gould's Landing on the southern tip of Pushaw.

A busy lake in the summer, Pushaw was quiet in early May. It's also shallow, which Tom wanted until he was comfortable with the images from Depth Cam. Dollar Island was about a mile paddle.

Although Jenny had canoed on Lake Amherst, this was the first time they had paddled together. It took fifteen minutes and a bit of effort with a hand pump to inflate the raft. He made a mental note to get a battery-operated pump. They packed the raft with the eight loads, in the order they would dump them, and covered everything with an elastic mesh. Together, they hauled the loaded raft, which was surprisingly light, and then the canoe to the shore.

The breeze wafted in from the north, back toward Gould's Landing, just as predicted by Windy.com, but not enough to slow them down. Tom, aware of the dangers of hypothermia this time of year, ensured Jenny's floatation device fit properly in case they capsized.

Tom was now familiar with the GPS/GLONASS unit. After about twenty minutes of paddling, they were over the spot Tom had picked from the depth charts. It must have been quite a sight to see two kids paddling a canoe and towing an inflatable raft piled high with yellow plastic, intently studying a fish finder. Fortunately, very few year-round residents were around to view the spectacle.

They paddled around off Dollar Island until Jenny confirmed the bottom was clear with the fish finder. Tom paddled about twenty more feet north, into the wind, and Jenny dropped the grapnel anchor. She let out about thirty feet of rode, and the canoe gently drifted back to the clear spot on the bottom.

Jenny recorded the depth and then launched the M2 drone to visualize and photograph the bottom. If the drone verified the bottom was clear, they would rely upon the fish finder for the rest of the lakes and save some time on the water.

"This looks good," she said. She took a screenshot of the depth finder with the iPad and then handed the iPad to him. "See, everything is clear."

Tom dropped the Seechi disk to record turbidity and locked in the GPS/GLONASS coordinates.

He then pulled the inflatable around on the starboard side of the canoe, away from shore, to minimize undue attention. They needed to separate the cups and ingots, which took them about twenty minutes, longer than he had expected.

Tom started dumping the first load on the port side, the side opposite the raft. Jenny repeated the process from the bow seat. Then he pulled the raft around to the port side to dump the other two loads on the starboard side. When they were done, they could see yellow on the bottom but no discernible shapes because of the waves.

Jenny adroitly maneuvered the M2 drone to video the pile from all angles. These images would hopefully validate his estimates of the dispersion pile from the Wave Tank, but it took extra time to get these images.

She showed Tom the screen. "It looks like a giant yellow egg, over easy."

He looked at his watch. He was surprised to see it was after one o'clock. This was taking longer than he had expected, and the wind was picking up as it usually did in the afternoon.

"We need to hustle," he said.

"All done. It looks like most of the plastic fell within a few feet of the center, but the plates and tiles did scatter. I'll bring up the drone."

"Let's leave the drone in the water and drift downwind another hundred feet to dump the last pile," he said. "With the drone in the water, you can get some video of how the plastic disperses in real time."

"Sounds good."

Tom pulled the anchor and let the canoe drift downwind. He didn't bother to cover the remaining plastic in the raft with the elastic mesh. After Jenny confirmed the bottom was clear, they repeated the process for the second dump, this time with Jenny getting some video of the plastic sinking.

By the time they finished, it was about three p.m. Tom's estimate of a couple of hours turned into about four. Even though it was still sunny, the temperature with windchill dropped to about 40 degrees. They were ready to come in.

They followed the inflatable raft downwind to Gould's Landing. He realized paddling upwind with the raft with the afternoon wind would have been a challenge. The wind and weather would be more of a factor than he had realized.

The raft beached first, followed by the canoe. Together, they loaded the canoe on the F-150. While Tom secured it, Jenny collapsed the raft. This entire process took another thirty minutes.

It was after four o'clock by the time they were back at the Pizza Palace. No 2 Feet Brewing tonight. Jenny had finals, and Tom had video and photographs to review. If his dispersion model was off, he would have to re-configure the Depth Cam image grid.

They'd had a pizza last night, so Tom made some tacos, Jenny's favorite, so she could study for her finals.

Wednesday, May 8, 2019
Finals Week
Orono, Maine

Tom was up early to study for his one final this morning. More important, today was a clear day on Pushaw, so he could trigger Depth Cam to take the grid pictures of the two dumps from last weekend. On the M2 drone photographs by Jenny, it looked like the dispersion piles were about fourteen feet or five meters in diameter, with most of the pile—or the yolk—within five or six feet of the center. The dispersion would enlarge at deeper depths, but he suspected the yolk would stay small. At least that is what he predicted based upon the dispersion in the Wave Tank.

He set up a ten-by-ten meter grid for Depth Cam, realizing this was way beyond the edge of the actual pile, but he would use these images to validate the satellite's capabilities.

To determine the best time of day for imaging, he scheduled a set of images just after dawn, another complete set at noontime, and then again, a couple of hours before dusk. The noontime photos were the clearest. He was glad the plastic was yellow.

After he carved up the Depth Cam image into one-meter grids, he was a little surprised. He was expecting a fractal pattern where one grid would scale up or down and look similar to each other, but that wasn't the case. Each one-meter grid looked unique. He wondered how this might affect training.

After Jenny's last final this afternoon, they spent the rest of the day packing and moving her stuff to the Pizza Palace.

That evening, after Jenny had settled in, she popped a bottle of Cold Duck and said, "We're done. The summer has officially started."

Saturday, May 11, 2019
Graduation
Orono, Maine

Tom graduated with highest honors. His parents attended his graduation. This was the first time they'd been on campus since Parent's Weekend his freshman year. This was a milestone for Tom, and he was happy to share it with his parents and Jenny. They celebrated at Evenrood's in Bangor.

On Monday, they were heading over to Vermont for a few days before a busy summer.

Friday, May 17, 2019
Amherst, Vermont

The week in Vermont went quickly. They paddled a little and hiked a lot. Jenny showed Tom her favorite run around Lake Amherst. Jackie, Jenny's best friend from high school, arrived home mid-week for the summer from Occidental College, and they grabbed a pizza at Goodman's American Pie.

Tom was also becoming more comfortable around Jenny's parents. By the end of the week, he was able to clear his mind a little.

They were heading back to Orono later this morning for a Zoom call with Dr. Westhoven tomorrow morning.

Saturday, May 18, 2019
Zoom Call
New Haven, Connecticut - Bangor, Maine

Dave and Amanda were in Bath, so they had the Pizza Palace to themselves for the summer. Last night, the squeak returned.

As usual, Dr. Westhoven started the call promptly. "Good morning, guys. Are you ready for summer? It sounds like Pushaw was a success."

"It went well. We learned a lot. The GPS worked. The satellite was spot on, and Jenny verified the accuracy of the dispersion model with her drone.

"By the way, the best images were at noontime with a polarizing lens. I'm glad we picked yellow for the plastic gold. Also, there might be fewer fish swimming around at noontime to disrupt the image."

"That all makes sense. I'll use noontime when it comes time to image the lakes in the Llanganatis."

Tom continued, "The images from Depth Cam are interesting. You can't always see detail, particularly on the periphery, but you can see what looks like a pile in shallow water. I also noticed each grid is unique. I guess I was expecting a fractal pattern. We're generating thousands of expensive images. I hope this all works."

"Understood. Not knowing is the tough part, but we should have some answers by fall, don't you think?" asked Dr. Westhoven.

"I think so. We have a tentative schedule to visit nine more lakes. We should be able to visit them all by the end of summer."

Dr. Westhoven asked, "Have you thought about just banging away at all the lakes at once, instead of a weekend at a time?"

"I did, but it will take a few months for you to narrow down the lakes in the Llanganatis, anyway. Even if I had all the images at once, it still takes time to pre-process and process each lake. Then we have to wait at least a month for the plastic to dissolve. Even with Jenny's help, it still would take a week or two to dump twenty loads of plastic. I'm eager to see if this neural network learns, but there are no shortcuts."

"Understood. I'm glad Jenny's on board. How about if we connect in four to six weeks? Let me know if you're running into any problems in the meantime."

"Sounds good, Dr. Westhoven. How about if we Zoom on a weekday? We'll probably be on the water most weekends," suggested Tom.

"Great. I'm still working my way through the Llanganatis. So far, I've ten lakes. I hope to have this done by late summer. Hopefully, everything will fall into place by August."

"Neat. By the way," Tom said with a smile, "I'm glad Jenny's on board, too."

"Me too," said Jenny, who rarely spoke during the Zoom calls.

Dr. Westhoven returned the smiles and signed off. It still amazed Tom how short these calls lasted. They condensed four weeks of work into a fifteen-minute Zoom call.

The Summer Palace

Saturday, May 25, 2019
Orono, Maine

Everything went smoothly at Fields Pond this morning. They finished by early afternoon and the weather was favorable for tomorrow to dump another two piles, this time in thirty feet of water. By the end of the weekend, they would have six piles in two lakes, with the entire summer ahead.

Tom had watched Jenny make macaroni and cheese for dinner. She was a striking figure from behind as she stirred the elbow macaroni. After watching for a few minutes, he snuck up on her and gently kissed her on the neck.

"I didn't realize you were such a fan of elbow macaroni," she said with a twinkle in her left eye.

After dinner, they walked to Marsh Island Brewing and stretched out on the deck to watch the sunset.

"Red sky at night, sailors' delight," Tom uttered as they gazed out over the Stillwater.

"What?"

"Red sky at dawn, sailors be warned. A lobsterman's wife would know that." He had heard this saying dozens of times growing up.

"As best as you can predict Maine weather, a beautiful sunset usually means a nice day tomorrow, but color in the morning is trouble."

As the waning rays of the sun slipped below the horizon, Jenny mentioned, "I finished *Lust for Inca Gold* by Steven Charbonneau this afternoon. It was a good read. It seems like the gold might really exist. I don't understand why you're so convinced it doesn't."

"Why would anyone write a book that the gold doesn't exist?" asked Tom. "Those books are just modern-day *Hardy Boys* mysteries."

Jenny huffed, "Well, I thought it was well written and researched."

After a sip of her root beer, she mentioned, "Saturday night in downtown Orono. It's quieter than I thought."

"Aren't you glad you decided to stay at the Pizza Palace?"

Jenny chuckled. "What do you think if we changed the name to the Summer Palace, you know, just for the summer?"

"Fine by me, but don't let Dave know. He was the one who named it the Pizza Palace."

After another sip, Jenny asked, "How's the Popham Colony coming along?" Tom had made a trip down on Thursday to check out the site.

"So far, so good. No one has threatened to shoot me yet. I met a couple of landowners and explained the project. I asked to get some GPS readings from their property, but they weren't interested. They said they did not want a bunch of scruffy looking college kids digging up their backyard. That's why no one has excavated this piece of the Colony."

"You could use a haircut."

Running his left hand through his hair, Tom replied, "It's okay. There are a ton of Landsat satellite images going back years. This is a textbook example of how to use satellite imaging. It's nice to have at least one project this summer that might find something worthwhile."

"Stop whining...."

Sunday, June 23, 2019
Summer Palace
Orono, Maine

A month later, the summer was going fast, and the weather had not been cooperating. They only had four lakes done—Pushaw, Fields Pond, Alligator Lake, and Little Pond in Smithfield, which was out of the way, but Jenny wanted to see a hermit's hidden encampment in the nearby woods.

Jenny loved her job at the Hudson Museum. The director had her writing copy for the exhibitions and promotional material. This was her first paying gig for writing.

This evening after dinner, Jenny asked, "How's the training going? Do you have the images from Little Pond?"

Tom had not talked too much lately about the Inca gold, focusing instead on his Popham Colony project. She wasn't sure if that was a good sign or not.

"Yeah, I loaded them on Thursday, but there's still not enough data to see any learning. I'm used to feeding tens of thousands of images all at once. These dribs and drabs are driving me nuts. The pre-processing of the images is also taking more time than I expected. But there's plenty of summer left. I just hope I've something to show for it by Labor Day, besides a sunburn."

Not as much whining as she expected, which she took as a good sign.

✷

Thursday, July 4, 2019
Summer Palace
Orono, Maine

Last weekend had been another washout. Jenny knew Tom was getting frustrated. Patience wasn't one of his virtues. He had done his beet head thing last week when he had to redo the images from Little Pond. No wonder he was an only child.

They were coming up on seven weeks. The weather over the weekend looked like it would cooperate for Pleasant River Lake tomorrow, and Hopkins Pond on Saturday. Both were off Route 9 or the Airline, and both lakes were deep. Tom wanted a couple of dumps in about thirty feet of water, the limit of Depth Cam.

As he shuffled through the mail, Jenny went at it head-on. "You don't seem yourself Tom. Not a fan of fireworks?"

"What, no, I mean yeah. I'm just starting to worry this has been a huge, although profitable, waste of time."

"Starting to worry. You've been fussing since graduation. It's only the 4th of July."

Tom ignored her. "We've only done four lakes, but the neural network isn't learning. I probably don't have enough images yet, but still, it's frustrating. I can't believe I thought yellow plastic would work."

"What about the follow-up or control images after the plastic biodegrades? Aren't they just as important?" she asked. "We'll add Pleasant River Lake and Hopkins Pond this weekend. That'll be fourteen piles. We'll be more than halfway there."

"Yeah, I know, and I'm not fussing. I'm just a pragmatist."

Jenny rolled her eyes. "Whatever. Let's just enjoy the fireworks tonight."

⤳⤲

Friday, July 26, 2019
Zoom Call
Cape Cod, Massachusetts - Orono, Maine

The three weeks after the Fourth of July were busy. They added Pleasant River Lake, Hopkins Pond, and Duck Lake. They now had seven lakes with sixteen dumps. After the Zoom call this morning, they were heading to Fire Road 9 on the Bowerbank side of Sebec Lake to visit Mike and dump one load of plastic.

Mike's dad, who was the principal at the high school and part of the Hubcap Caper, had summers off, and ever since they were kids, Mike's family had summered at Sebec.

Tom worried a little that Mike might ask some questions about the plastic, which is why he was only bringing one load, thinking one load would be less suspicious. So far, no one had asked questions, but Mike was more inquisitive. Sebec was also a busy lake in summer, so Tom planned to dump the plastic up around the Narrows in the big lake, where it was quieter.

Dr. Westhoven started the Zoom call at nine. "Good morning, Tom, Jenny. Both of you have nice tans."

"Yeah, we've been on the water a lot this summer."

Tom noticed Dr. Westhoven's background was different. He was expecting the streaming summer sun behind him in his office on the early morning call. Instead, soft lighting highlighted his features. But he still looked pasty.

"Your background is different. Are you home?" asked Tom.

Behind Dr. Westhoven, a couple of kids in swimsuits ran out a screen door that whapped when it closed and startled him.

"No, I'm on vacation on the Cape. My family owns a cottage in Chatham. I have a few minutes before I'm expected on the beach. I'm working on my tan, too."

"It looks like they're having fun," said Jenny.

"Yeah, it's something we all look forward to every year."

"Neat. It's another good weekend here, and Jenny and I plan to visit a lake in central Maine. That'll get us up to eight. How are you doing with the lakes in the Llanganatis?"

"I'm done. I've narrowed it down to twenty-four lakes that the 'hand of man' could have made. Most of the lakes have infrared evidence of a dried-up riverbed. The work by Dr. Parcak on infrared imaging was helpful. I just followed her textbook.

"I had hoped we'd find the lakes in the same general region of the Llanganatis, but that's not the case. They're scattered all over. It shouldn't be much of a factor, though, with the helicopter. The entire park is only about 850 square miles.

"Zheng Enterprises will start deep scanning the lakes with Depth Cam in the next week or two, but the weather is the determining factor. As you suggested, I'll scan about noontime with the polarizing filter. Hopefully, we'll have all the images from the twenty-four lakes quickly, and then you can do your magic with the neural network."

An attractive woman in a one-piece bathing suit with shorter hair than his walked up behind him and whispered something, and he nodded. She then turned to leave. The screen door startled him again.

He ran his fingers through his hair and tucked it behind his ears. "When do you think your neural network will be ready?" he asked Tom.

"I've been uploading the satellite images from the plastic as soon as we get them. To be honest, I was discouraged earlier this month, but with the last couple of lakes and with the follow-up images after the plastic dissolves, I'm finally seeing some learning. It's not as accurate as it needs to be, but tweaking the hyperparameters this week made a difference. It will be another four to six weeks before I'll know for sure.

"Jenny and I plan to finish dropping all the plastic in a couple of weeks, but it might go into November to run all your lakes through the neural network. Does that still fit into the timeframe for March 2020?"

"I'm not sure, Tom. It'll be tight. I'll check with Miguel. Anything I can do to help speed up the process?"

"No, not really. This is a massive amount of data, and it just takes time, if it works at all."

"All right. I'll send you the coordinates for the twenty-four lakes. Most are less than a square mile. I'll update Miguel and let you know if the timeline is an issue. Let's connect after Labor Day. Have a great rest of the summer."

"You too, Dr. Westhoven, and try to get a little sun."

This was a milestone that made everything more real. Tom's neural network, based on piles of yellow plastic in Maine lakes, needed to identify the top five lakes in the Llanganatis out of the twenty-four selected by Dr. Westhoven that might harbor the lost Inca gold.

While reviewing the map of the Llanganatis, Tom wondered why the Derrotero was so confusing. Maybe General Rumiñahui hid the ransom gold in multiple locations across the Llanganatis, in caves and mines, as well as lakes "made by the hand of man." Perhaps he buried some. Perhaps they'll find gold in more than one lake, but more likely, Tom thought, there's no gold to find.

Fool's Gold

Friday, July 12, 2019
Syria

The Iran-backed Lebanese Shia movement of Hezbollah announced today it was reducing its presence in Syria. The Syrian Army under President al-Assad had regained control of most of the country. This news disappointed Omar. He was a supplier to Hezbollah. This would affect his bottom line. The opportunities in South and Central America took on added importance.

Sunday, August 4, 2019
Quito, Ecuador

Omar finally received the list of twenty-four lakes in the Llanganatis from Miguel last weekend and acted quickly. The timing was perfect. He had always wanted to coordinate the dumping of his fool's gold with a visit to the lake being explored by the keiretsu. The keiretsu had already made three trips into the Llanganatis, but the weather had grounded them for the last three days, and tomorrow's weather was still uncertain.

He still did not know what was directing their search, but it did not matter. With Zheng satellites, he followed the expedition helicopter to a remote lake in the eastern park. The activity on the lake focused on the southeast shore, but cloud cover made any detailed observations difficult. Fortunately, the lake was not one of the twenty-four selected by Dr. Westhoven.

Omar had carefully studied the Derrotero, looking for any clues that might have led Luis Alvarez, the head of the expedition, to this lake, but he found none other than an oblique reference to "the entrance of the *socabón* (tunnel), which is in the form of a church-porch." Alvarez must have another document or map.

Earlier in the week, upon instructions from Omar, Tarek brought the FIM-92 MANPADS Stinger launcher with three warheads from the secure warehouse in Bogotá to Quito.

Omar arrived in Quito this afternoon on the Gulfstream. After an hour's ride through the old and new Quito, he arrived at the Hotel Grande, where he met Tarek in the lobby.

"It is good to see you, my friend," said Omar. "We have a busy few days ahead. I'll fill you in on the details at dinner. Let me settle in and let's meet in the restaurant in about an hour."

Omar had already shared the outline of the plan with Tarek, who would construct the base camp in the Llanganatis and be on site as the base camp manager. Although the actual decision to go forward with the expedition was still months away, the timetable would be tight. That was why Tarek was already in Quito, busy with preparations.

An hour later, at a discrete table off to the side in the hotel restaurant, Omar explained why he took the risk of bringing the Stinger missiles to Quito. This was yet another reason he needed Tarek. For his plan to succeed, he needed Tarek's unique skill set, someone who would do whatever needed to be done.

After ordering, Omar began. "Are we ready to fly tomorrow?"

"I have already loaded the fool's gold and missiles onto the helicopter. We will be ready as soon as the weather breaks."

"Good. Now let's review the twenty-four lakes selected by Dr. Westhoven."

Omar laid out a map of the twenty-four lakes. They were all over the Llanganatis. He had circled one lake just north of the park in red. He pointed it out to Tarek.

"This is 'Ground Zero' where we will dump the fool's gold," said Omar.

Although Dr. Westhoven would actually trigger the Zheng satellite based upon the weather in the Llanganatis, Zheng Enterprises would not start deep scanning the twenty-four lakes until Omar gave the okay after he and Tarek had dumped the fool's gold.

Ultimately, the program by the undergraduate needed to detect the fool's gold in Ground Zero or Omar would not commit the resources to the ground expedition.

Tarek looked up. "How long for Zheng to scan the Llanganatis lakes?"

"A lot depends upon the weather, but likely four to six weeks. I'm not sure how long it will take the undergraduate to process the images, but Miguel told Dr. Westhoven we need the top five lakes by late October. Assuming his program finds the fool's gold, we can then choose the site of the base camp from the location of the five lakes. There will be no flying in and out of Quito everyday like the keiretsu. Too conspicuous and too dependent upon the weather."

After a few minutes of enjoying their meal, Omar continued. "The weather does not look good for tomorrow, but we need to be ready the next time the keiretsu flies."

❧❦

Tuesday, August 6, 2019
Ground Zero
Llanganatis, Ecuador

After a couple of days in Quito, today was the first day to fly safely to Ground Zero to dump the fool's gold, and the keiretsu was also in the air to the Llanganatis. With Tarek at the stick of the MD600N helicopter, they took off for the sixty-minute flight to Ground Zero. Omar had on coveralls that looked custom fitted. The helicopter had been equipped with pontoons, with a Zodiac attached between the pontoons, and an auxiliary gas tank.

The fool's gold occupied the back of the cabin where the last row of seats had been removed. Tarek had also carefully packed the Stinger launcher, along with three missiles, on the floor behind them.

Tarek easily located Ground Zero just outside the northern boundary of the National Park and gently brought the helicopter down. Bobbing on pontoons on the lake, they might be the first to visit this lake since the Incas. Omar was glad he had chosen a helicopter without a tail rotor, as the tail moved up and down like a vertical pendulum.

With a weighted rope to sound the bottom, they dumped the fool's gold in about five meters of water. They did not scan the bottom for rocks or other debris, nor did they record the turbidity. But they did record the GPS coordinates. It was now almost two o'clock.

Before they took off, Omar moved to the second-row seats. He methodically unpacked the launcher and loaded a Stinger warhead, which protruded from the cockpit on the starboard side. He then directed Tarek to a new GPS location south-east of their current location. The weather continued to hold.

Over the last week, Omar had been carefully tracking the keiretsu expedition with Zheng satellites. Like Omar and Tarek, the weather had also grounded the conglomerate, but today they were back at the same small lake in the eastern part of the Llanganatis.

Following Omar's directions, Tarek landed in a pond about five kilometers west of the keiretsu team. A steep ridge on the east separated them from the expedition. An even steeper peak loomed above them on the western side. Omar had chosen this spot as the expedition helicopter would pass overhead on its return to Quito.

Omar had never actually spelled out his plan, but he knew Tarek had figured it out when Omar instructed him to bring back the Stinger missiles from Abu Dhabi.

They both were quiet while Tarek surveyed the horizon with binoculars, and Omar focused intently on the live satellite feed on his monitor.

Around three o'clock, the satellite showed the expedition preparing to leave. Omar knew from watching the expedition that it took about thirty to forty minutes for them to secure everything before they returned to Quito.

Thirty-five minutes later, they both heard the distant thumping of a helicopter approaching from the east.

From the second-row seat, Omar said calmly, "I need you facing east."

Still on the pond, Tarek swung the MD600N into position. As the thumping intensified, Omar flipped the switch to activate the Stinger missile. The expedition helicopter broke the ridge to the east and passed overhead at high speed, just to their north. Omar had about eight seconds to sight the helicopter before it would pass out of view. He had tone. He waited until it started to climb the steep ridge to the west and then launched the missile. The propellent dropped onto the floor and rolled into the water with a splash.

A fireball followed. The MD600N shuddered from the explosion. The flaming expedition helicopter rotated slowly down onto the eastern side of the steep ridge bordering the pond, crashing onto the mountainside with another fireball and explosion.

Omar had intentionally dropped the expedition helicopter onto the mountainside. Even though the keiretsu in Quito would know the expedition did not return this afternoon, it would still take some time to piece together what happened, and even longer to recover the wreckage from the mountainside.

Omar carefully replaced the Stinger launcher into its case and returned to the port side seat in front, next to Tarek.

"Now, let's see what is so interesting at this lake they have been visiting."

Tarek ascended and turned the MD600N east, following the contours of the land. They arrived at the lake in about five minutes. From the satellite images, Omar had watched the expedition working on the southeastern shore close to what seemed like a sheer cliff, yet he could not make out the details.

The lake was oval, about one kilometer north to south, and nestled in between two ridge lines. At this altitude, the shoreline, other than the cliff, was scrub brush. The lake was in shadows this time of day, except for the top of the cliff, which reflected the harsh yellow light from the sun onto the rippling water below.

As they approached the cliff, they both saw it. A rough opening in the light gray, fine grained rock, about five meters off the water. Tarek landed the helicopter about one hundred meters from the cliff and approached slowly, gently bobbing on the water. As they got closer, they could see the shiny rungs of a crude ladder driven into the cliff starting about one meter off the water leading to the opening. The opening was about three meters in diameter. A make-shift hoist protruded from the top of the opening.

"This must be the place. The rungs look new," said Omar.

Tarek dropped the anchor, and they slid into the Zodiac underneath. Tarek piloted the Zodiac to the base of the cliff below the socabón.

A couple minutes later, Omar, followed by Tarek, was climbing the ladder. At the opening, they stood up and looked into the dark tunnel. The floor was about a meter and a half wide at the opening, with enough room for two men, but not much more.

Tarek flipped on the flashlights and gave one to Omar. The tunnel was only about five meters deep and ended abruptly with a wall of crushed rock. Various equipment like a generator, jack hammer and pickaxes littered the floor on each side. As they approached the wall of stones, they could see where the jack hammer had tried to clear some rocks near the top of the tunnel.

"This looks like a collapsed cave," said Tarek.

"It does not look like the expedition has made much progress. They seemed to have underestimated the project," replied Omar as he looked around at the rudimentary equipment. "It will take more than these toys to clear this rock."

As they turned to leave, they could see the billowing smoke from the crash over the ridge to the west.

"It should be easy to locate the crash, but not so easy to reach the wreckage in this part of the Llanganatis," said Tarek.

Satisfied that the expedition had not found gold, they returned to the helicopter and headed back to Quito. On the trip back, Omar contemplated his next move. Once the dust settled, perhaps he would approach the keiretsu for a joint project, but his focus for now needed to be on the lakes in the Llanganatis.

Expedition Missing Deep in Llanganatis

El Comercio - Wednesday, August 7th, 2019

A helicopter ferrying an expedition deep into the Llanganatis, led by Luis Alvarez, former partner of famed explorer Andrés Fernández-Salvador, failed to return Tuesday evening. Unsubstantiated reports suggest a crash site in the eastern National Park. The authorities are not providing further information pending a flyover of the area when the weather improves, hopefully later this week.

Friday, August 9, 2019
Cartagena, Colombia

The weather turned the day after the crash, which hampered any investigation. Perhaps today the authorities could at least fly over to locate the wreckage, but it would still be weeks before anyone could reach the actual crash site. The climb up the ridge to the wreckage would be demanding.

The newspapers correctly identified Luis Alvarez as leader, but did not mention Nihon Aeronautics, the keiretsu financing the expedition. After a few more days, with no new information, the story would fade away, as they typically do.

Back in Cartagena, Omar reviewed how his plan was progressing. Dr. Westhoven had selected the twenty-four lakes in the Llanganatis for deep scanning with Depth Cam. He and Tarek had planted the fool's gold. Omar had cleared Depth Cam to start scanning the twenty-four lakes. Now he was waiting for the undergraduate to finish the program, which, according to Miguel, would be another six weeks. It would then be yet another six weeks after that to select the five lakes. By early November at the latest, Omar would know if the program had found Ground Zero. This was bumping up against the timetable for a March expedition.

Once he had the five lakes, he and Tarek would then select a location for the base camp. Tarek could actually build it in a few weeks, but he would spread out the construction over three months to avoid drawing any attention. Omar had also hired the helicopter pilot, who would help Tarek.

In the meantime, Omar would focus on developing relationships with the militants and drug lords of Central and South America. He needed the revenue. Antigüedades Sur was not enough.

He had also tentatively reached out to Nihon Aeronautics through a trusted intermediary in Abu Dhabi, being careful not to draw too much attention to himself. The keiretsu would eventually determine the expedition helicopter was brought down, and not by a malfunction.

The program needed to find the fake gold at Ground Zero or it was back to arms dealing—or working with the keiretsu.

Flagstaff

Friday, August 9, 2019
Carrabassett Valley, Maine

Even though the weather was uncertain, Tom needed Flagstaff Lake this weekend to stay on schedule. After loading up the F-150 with two loads of plastic in Bangor, they set out for Sugarloaf. Flagstaff was nearby, only six miles from Spring Farm on the Carriage Road, and Dave offered to let them stay at the A-frame.

So far, they'd dumped plastic in eight lakes, with Flagstaff and Nahmakanta left. Tom had Depth Cam images on seven of the lakes, but only four after the plastic dissolved.

The weather had not cooperated in June, but since then, they had gotten back on track. Acquiring the actual Depth Cam images, however, was another challenge. It was tough coordinating the satellite with decent weather.

But his biggest concern wasn't the weather.

"Why so grumpy?" asked Jenny as they turned left on Route 16 at North Anson.

"Oh, the usual. I thought the neural network would need five or six lakes, but it's still not learning a lot after Duck Lake, the seventh lake. I wonder if the hyperparameters are right. I'm also worried about underfitting or overfitting the data."

"I'm not sure what under or overfitting means, but you'll figure it out."

Tom wasn't as confident as Jenny. He was also concerned about how long it was taking Google CoLab to process the images. He needed to look at other options for computing power, or he might not meet the deadlines.

Something else to figure out while he was running out of time and patience.

∾∾

Saturday, August 10, 2019
Flagstaff Lake, Maine

They woke up to an overcast day. The treetops around the camp swayed slowly in the wind. In winter, this often meant wind hold on some of the upper lifts at Sugarloaf. Tom wasn't sure what this meant in summer and, more importantly, on Flagstaff. Windy.com predicted winds starting from the northwest, and then shifting and intensifying from the north throughout the day. If they didn't get to Flagstaff this weekend, they could not try again until September, which would further delay training the neural network.

Tom had been careful to avoid foul weather. Jenny had not paddled on a nasty day. It was about eight in the morning when Tom, trying to hide his concern, said, "Hey Jenny, let's get an early start. If we finish by late morning, we can go for a hike later."

The carriage road was in decent shape, so they made good time. When they arrived at the private gate at the end of the dirt road, the wind was not too bad. They could not see it, but Tom knew Hurricane Island was behind the peninsula of land blocked by the gate.

They were on the water and over the first site just after nine. Tom looked up at West Peak on Bigelow and wondered how the mountain affected the wind.

He hoped to have both sites done by late morning, but he hadn't counted on the debris all over the bottom. Flagstaff had also been "made by hand" back in the 1950s when the power company dammed the Dead River, which flooded the town of Flagstaff and its surroundings. This created the fourth largest lake in Maine. Remnants of the town and farms littered the bottom everywhere.

"I didn't realize how much debris would be on the bottom. That looked like an old foundation back there," said Tom, pointing to the last spot they checked.

"At least there are no erratics," replied Jenny. "Farmers collected them to build stone walls. They picked this area clean."

She finally found a clear area in about twenty feet of water. They dumped the first load of plastic, and she finished the drone photographs around eleven when Tom noticed whitecaps out on the main lake to the east. He saw Hurricane Island in the distance.

They were heading southeast toward Ferry Farm and were only halfway there when the wind started shifting and intensifying from the north. Tom yelled over the waves, "Jenny, the wind's coming up quicker than predicted. Let's head back."

"Can we dump some plastic on the way?" she asked.

"I don't think so. We need to get off the lake."

Tom needed to turn and paddle directly into the wind or slightly off. Sideways to the wind is when you get into trouble.

The wind had blown the bobbing raft along the port side of the canoe. Although Jenny had become a strong paddler, she hadn't experienced rough water like this before.

Jenny brought up the drone and secured it in the canoe. Tom pushed as much gear as possible to the bow where she was paddling. Heading into the wind, he wanted the bow as low as possible.

He had to pivot the canoe quickly once he started. He tried to sound calm, but it was difficult as he had to yell over the wind and waves. "I'm going to paddle us clockwise, away from the raft. Okay?"

"Okay. Let me know when to paddle."

Tom sensed anxiety in her voice, but it was hard to hear above the sound of the wind and waves.

"Okay—now!"

Tom pushed the raft out of the way with his paddle and started paddling furiously. It was working. His paddle churned the water. The canoe was turning easier than he expected.

Just as they passed through the most vulnerable position, the line from the raft tangled his paddle. He lost steering only for a moment, but that's all it took. Without the raft as a buffer, a wave came up and flipped the canoe.

Tom never went under, but he couldn't see or hear Jenny. The waves were crashing over his head. He quickly took a deep breath to go under.

Then he thought he heard laughing.

He looked again and saw Jenny on the other side of the upside-down raft, bobbing up and down with the waves with a huge grin. He let out his deep breath slowly.

The wind was blowing them to shore toward Ferry Farm. Tom worked his way back to the raft and gave Jenny a wet hug. The water was warm, so he let the wind blow them back to shore. There was no point in trying anything else at this point.

The rest of the plastic had tumbled out of the raft when it flipped.

Jenny always carried the GPS in her pocket. "I took a GPS reading when we flipped. This is the quickest we ever dumped a load of plastic. Maybe we should capsize more often."

If Tom had been by himself, or with Dave, he probably would have done his beet head, but he couldn't help laughing along with her. Fortunately, there was no risk of hypothermia, and they were close to shore.

Once they were safely on shore, they didn't have any towels, but they'd dry off quickly enough in the wind. While Jenny deflated the raft and organized all the equipment, Tom jogged back to the gate to Hurricane Island to get the F-150, his wet sneakers squeaking all the way. By the time he returned, they both were mostly dry, but a little chilly with the overcast sky and wind.

The A-frame had a small shower, and Tom and Jenny squeezed in together. It was dinnertime by the time they warmed up and changed into dry clothes.

One of the other reasons Tom wanted to visit Flagstaff was Tufulio's, one of his favorite restaurants. They headed over early to get a booth by the window.

After they settled in, Tom raised his IPA to Jenny and said, "Half a lake is better than none."

"Since when did my nerd become a lake half-full kind of guy?" Jenny smiled and raised her Diet Coke to toast him. She was looking forward to October when she'd be twenty-one.

Tom reluctantly joined in the revised toast.

After dinner, they rode up to the mountain. Clouds still hung over the valley, but the wind had died down. As they turned onto Oh My Gosh corner on Route 27, the setting sun peaked in between the clouds and the distant Western Mountains, highlighting their first view of Sugarloaf in the summer. It was as spectacular as in the winter.

Flagstaff was by far the most challenging lake this summer. Although they were both tuckered out by bedtime, they took full advantage of the queen-size bed, without a squeak.

ବେଷ

Sunday, August 11, 2019
Carrabassett Valley, Maine

They slept in this morning. Flagstaff had taken more out of them than they realized. Before leaving, Tom suggested a morning hike on the Narrow Gauge Trail. The trail was an old narrow-gauge railroad bed that went about nine miles from Carrabassett Valley to the Access Road by the mountain. They wouldn't walk the whole trail today. Just enough for Tom to muster up some courage, maybe at the fork in the road by the bridge to the airport, to ask her a question that had been on his mind for a few weeks.

As they passed the bridge, Tom abruptly stopped, which startled Jenny, and asked, "What do you think about getting an apartment together?"

She gave him a gentle nudge, much gentler than her usual, which he took as a good sign. "I was wondering if you were ever going to ask. Were you thinking about the Pizza Palace or something else?"

That was easy, thought Tom. He let out a deep breath. "Something else, like in Bangor."

"I like Bangor. It has a vibe."

They were back at the A-frame by noon. As Tom fumbled with the key, Jenny said, "I read somewhere Bangor has more microbreweries per capita than anywhere else, just in time for my birthday."

"Yeah. Dr. Wade lives in Bangor. I'm meeting with him on Tuesday about the Popham project. I'll ask him if he has any suggestions. If we can't find an apartment by September, you can always stay at the Pizza Palace until we find a place."

As Tom finally opened the door, he asked, "Are you sure you want to give up Somerset?"

"Well, I will miss Robin—and the guys checking out my ass in the cafeteria, but yeah, I think I can give it up."

Tom was a little surprised, which was probably her intent. But it was true. He had noticed the boys checking her out, and more than just her ass.

"Then I'll try to pay more attention to your as..." Tom never got it out as Jenny gently pulled him down to her for a very sensual kiss.

Tuesday, August 13, 2019
Summer Palace
Orono, Maine

When Tom arrived early for his meeting with Dr. Wade, he was in his office, looking relaxed in short pants.

Tom was already getting some results of the Landsat images of the Popham Colony. A real training data set made all the difference.

"You know Tom, you may have another paper to publish here. This is remarkable work and easily worth four credits. I wish I could award you more." Four credit hours was the maximum for independent study.

They talked about Tom's classes for the fall semester. He was enrolling in only four classes.

"Is everything else on track with your project with Dr. Westhoven?" Dr. Wade asked. "Is dropping one class enough? I guess there's no chance you could tutor or teach a section?"

"I don't think so, Dr. Wade. I'm still not sure dropping one class will be enough."

After the Popham update, Tom casually mentioned he and Jenny were looking for an apartment in Bangor. "Do you have any suggestions?"

Tom thought Dr. Wade looked a little surprised.

"I didn't realize things were that serious between you two, but I should have guessed. I know Jenny is why I got you another couple of years.

"You know, Tom, I have a mother-in-law apartment already set up in the back of my house. It's furnished. My mother-in-law planned to move to Bangor about a year ago from Florida. Unfortunately, before she moved, she fell and broke her hip and never bounced back. She's in Bangor now but in assisted living."

Dr. Wade lived on French Street. Tom had been there a few times for dinner, but he had never seen the interior other than the entryway and dining room. French Street ran parallel to

Broadway, one of the historic districts in Bangor, and was near St. Joseph Hospital, where Dr. Wade's wife worked as a nurse.

"I know it's a big house, but I didn't realize there was an apartment," said Tom.

"My wife has held onto the apartment until she was sure there was no hope her mother could navigate the stairs to the apartment. Her mother is doing okay, but she'll never be able to climb those stairs.

"If you're interested, I'll talk with my wife to see if she's ready to rent the apartment. If she's okay, we can show it this weekend."

"That would be great, Dr. Wade. Thanks."

Back at the Summer Palace, Tom texted Dave.

< Jenny and I are looking for an apartment in
Bangor. I know this is sudden and I can help
with the rent until you find a roommate. >

< That's great. I was going to ask you if
Amanda could stay at the Pizza Palace. This
is perfect. >

Tom suspected that might be Dave's reaction, but he was still relieved.

Then Tom started fussing. What if Jenny was uncomfortable renting from Dr. Wade? What if the rent was beyond their means? What if it was a crappy apartment, although that seemed unlikely if this was for his mother-in-law? What if they didn't like the furniture? What if his wife did not like Jenny, or Jenny didn't like her?

He was overthinking again. One step at a time. Deep breath. Ultimately, he wanted this to be Jenny's decision.

But he was tired of the smell of pepperoni.

Later, when Tom told Jenny about the apartment, she was excited, which relieved a lot of the pressure. Dr. Wade emailed Tom the next day that he could show them the apartment this weekend.

❧

Saturday, August 17, 2019
Bangor, Maine

Jenny's job at the Hudson Museum ended yesterday. Today, they were heading to Bangor to look at the apartment, and then onto Limerock. On the drive to Bangor, she reflected on her perfect summer.

"I had a great summer, and it's not over yet."

"We'll remember this summer when we're old and gray," said Tom.

Interesting, thought Jenny. Tom rarely commented on their future. She thought it made him uncomfortable, so she avoided these discussions.

"I just wish the neural network was done," he added.

Me too, she thought.

He continued, "Too bad about the red fish. If it weren't for the smell, you might have found a lobsterman."

Joe had taken them out lobstering this summer, and Jenny baited the traps. She did not like the smell of red fish, the preferred bait for lobstering.

Jenny crinkled her nose, but then said, "I did find my lobsterman. And he doesn't stink."

Tom had placed the apartment decision in her hands, and she wanted to make a good impression.

"The weather sure is a lot different from last weekend," she said as they drove into Dr. Wade's driveway. She had mentioned Flagstaff a few times this week. Tom always over planned everything, and she enjoyed needling him about the capsizing on Flagstaff.

This was the first time Tom had seen the Wades' house during the day. It was a traditional two-story white clapboard with a wraparound veranda on the left and a small front yard that looked out onto the Broadway Park. Small junipers lined the brick walkway.

"I didn't realize the park with so big," said Jenny, looking across French Street.

Broadway split the park down the middle into two large sections. There was a playground across the street, but it was mostly open space. On this side of Broadway, one group of boys played touch football while another played soccer.

Dr. Wade came out with his wife and met them in the driveway. Jenny suddenly felt unsettled.

"Nice to see you again, Jenny. This is my wife, Vicki," he said. "I remember you were an English major. An A- in COS 140 is impressive." By now, Dr. Wade had a big grin. "Either you're really smart or Tom is a great tutor."

That broke the ice. "Well, we both know Tom is a great tutor." And when she said her mom was also a nurse, his wife took an immediate liking to Jenny.

They talked about parking. Tom reassured them they only had the F-150 and had no plans or money for another vehicle.

Dr. Wade then led them around the veranda to the apartment in back. There were seventeen steep steps up to the apartment. That explained the lofty ceilings in the dining room and why the mother-in-law would need to be in decent shape.

The stairs opened into a warm, off-white kitchen. Jenny's eyes widened. It was a new apartment with all new appliances. Sunlight filled the apartment. A gentle breeze flowed through the open windows. Everything smelled so fresh.

A dining room table nestled against a wall in the kitchen would be a perfect place to study. Through the kitchen was the living room.

"This is lovely," said Jenny, as they entered the living room with a maple floor, which further lightened the room. A small couch and a recliner surrounded a flatscreen television.

And there was no clutter.

"The furniture is beautiful," said Jenny. Everything was a shade of blue. "It matches perfectly."

Off to the right was the bedroom. Jenny squeezed Tom's hand. She wanted him to know she liked what she saw.

In the spacious bathroom was a stacked washer and dryer.

Dr. Wade asked if they thought $900 a month was fair.

Another squeeze by Jenny.

"That sounds great, Dr. Wade," she said. "This is a really cute apartment. I'm sorry your mother never had a chance to enjoy it," she said, turning to his wife.

His wife's voice choked a little. "I know, but it's nice she's in Bangor. When do you think you might move in?"

"How about Labor Day weekend?" asked Jenny. "Classes start the following Tuesday."

"That sounds perfect," his wife said.

Dr. Wade would forward the lease to Tom by email. They said their goodbyes.

In the driveway, Tom said, "That was easy. I don't think we're too far from downtown. It'll be fun to explore the neighborhood once we settle in."

Jenny held his arm as they walked to the truck. "Hey Roomy, when should we tell Dave?"

"I texted him on Tuesday after I met with Dr. Wade. He was relieved. Amanda was already planning to move into the Pizza Palace.

"By the way, what's a Roomy?" he asked.

"You, you're a Roomy, R-O-O-M-Y, my roommate."

"It sounds like something you'd cough up. Any chance I can just be your nerd?"

"Nope. You're now my Roomy."

"Okay, then you'll be <u>my</u> Roomie, R-O-O-M-I-E. Let's hit the road, Roomie. We can celebrate tonight, Roomie."

Jenny chuckled. "You know, maybe you're right. Maybe Roomy-Nerd does sound better. I'll have to think about it. Yeah, I like it—Roomy-Nerd."

Tom rarely came out on top of these exchanges.

Nahmakanta

Wednesday, August 21, 2019
Nahmakanta Lake, Maine

Last weekend, they celebrated their new apartment with Joe and Lynda at Waterman's Beach. Joe's recreational lobster license was getting a lot of use this summer.

To prove she'd found her lobsterman, Jenny bought Tom a yellow lobsterman's Sou'Wester hat at the Keag Store. It fit perfectly.

Tom had left the last two weeks of summer flexible to catch up, but everything, remarkably, was on track. Nahmakanta was the last dump, followed by a week at Amherst, and then moving day. Although they had been on a lot of lakes this summer, Nahmakanta was the first lake where they would camp overnight. He wanted it to be special.

Tom and Joe discovered Nahmakanta when they were in high school. It's a Maine Public Reserve Land in the Maine woods between Moosehead Lake and Millinocket. Tom had been back every summer since, with either Joe or Dave.

Today, they were on their way to Nahmakanta. Originally, they had planned to go tomorrow, but the weather was uncertain later in the week, so they moved everything up a day. Tom had only packed one load of plastic, so they would have enough room for their camping gear. He had also saved Nahmakanta for the end of summer, with warm days, cool nights, and fewer bugs.

Nahmakanta would be the tenth and final lake. It was the most remote lake they would visit this summer, which added to the excitement for Jenny. There were many places in Maine without cell coverage, but this was truly off the grid. A sporting camp on the north shore and the nearby Appalachian Trail were the only signs of civilization. The camp sites were only accessible by canoe. Once they finished dumping the plastic, they also planned to canoe the nearby Fourth Debsconeag.

It was about a three-hour drive. As they exited the interstate going north at Lagrange and headed to Milo, Tom said, "It's hard to believe summer's almost over. I've dragged you all over Maine."

"It couldn't have been any better. Even capsizing on Flagstaff was fun. By the way, you can take off your hat now. It looks hot." Tom was wearing his Sou'Wester.

Jenny had spotted her first moose a couple weeks ago, so now she was rubbernecking every clearing they passed.

After another pothole and confirming he still had the yellow gold, he noticed Jenny biting her lower lip. "Tom, do you think we have any chance of finding gold?"

"I doubt it. Now that we're wrapping up, it still feels like the neural network needs more data. The infrared images haven't added a lot. The timeline is too tight. It would be better to have two to three times the training data and a few more months, but we don't. I feel like I'm just going through the motions."

He continued, "I'm not sure I even believe the legend. It just doesn't seem possible that the Incas hid that much gold and silver in the Llanganatis."

"Well, I've also done a lot of reading this summer, and I think the lost gold does exist—somewhere," she said.

Tom turned left onto a dirt road north of Brownville Junction towards Jo-Mary Campground and used Dr. Westhoven's credit card to pay the tithe at the checkpoint, the last semblance of civilization, for a couple of days.

Logging roads in the Maine woods were like driving through a canyon of pine trees, and Tom loved the smell.

Occasionally you would see a logging truck, but otherwise, you would have the canyon to yourself.

After a particularly deep pothole, he turned to Jenny and asked, "Have you thought about what we'd do with the money, you know, just dreaming?"

"Not really. I don't think a pile of gold would make me any happier. But it would be fun to find out, wouldn't it?"

"Yeah, it'd be fun to find out."

After a few minutes and another jaw rattling pothole, Jenny pulled out the *Gazetteer*. "Are you sure you know where you're going? We've been on this dirt road for almost an hour. In Vermont, dirt roads usually end."

Tom just smiled. He knew the road went on and on, and he knew the way. And he enjoyed seeing Jenny wound up a little, once in a while.

After a few more turns, they arrived at a parking lot with a bright blue porta-potty with a bunch of posted signs on what to do and what not to do.

"Where's the lake? I was expecting a view, not a porta-potty."

"It's a short portage down to the lake and then about a forty-five minute paddle to the site," said Tom. He was enjoying this.

"Okay, I was worried this was it."

"Nah, our site doesn't have the luxury of a porta-potty."

Tom led her down the path. As they broke the tree line by the shore, Jenny let out a gentle gasp. "It's beautiful, and so quiet and so green." Her eyes followed the shoreline to the hills in the distance. "It looks like the glacier created Nahmakanta. Look at the hill over there," she said, pointing to Nesuntabunt Mountain on the western shore.

A gentle breeze came in off the lake. The wind typically kicked up in the afternoon, so Tom wanted to get on the water.

Both pine and hardwood trees enveloped Nahmakanta except for a small beach in the distance on the eastern shore.

"That's where we're headed," he said as he pointed to a beach on the right, about a mile down the lake.

The sun was behind them. It was an easy paddle into the gentle breeze. There would be no re-enactment of Flagstaff today. Tom initially headed to the left toward the western shore. After a few minutes of paddling, he said, "Here you can see the entire lake. It's quite a view from back here."

Jenny lifted some water with her paddle into Tom's lap.

"Good shot."

"Pay attention to paddling and not me."

Perhaps Jenny was more unnerved by capsizing in Flagstaff than she'd let on.

There were a couple of sites on the eastern shore. Tom had his eyes on the farther one by the narrows. The sites are first come, first serve, but usually during the week, you would have your choice.

He pointed to a sandy beach. "There it is, about two o'clock. You can see the picnic table by the trees and the fire ring."

She turned back a little toward Tom. "Have you ever been skinny-dipping?" she asked in between strokes.

"Nope."

"Me neither. This place is so remote...."

Although Nahmakanta was remote, the Appalachian Trail followed a ridge along the western shore, and a sporting camp was on the north end. Occasionally, someone from the sporting camp would troll down the center of the lake. Skinny dipping was probably not going to happen, but it occupied Tom's thoughts for a few strokes.

When they beached the canoe and raft, warm sand greeted their feet. Driftwood was scattered about on the beach, and Tom knew there was also plenty of down wood behind the site. A wobbly but sturdy picnic table was at the back, just under the trees. The fire ring by the shore showed some wear but was plenty big for a warming fire. Scrub brush grew here and there on the sandy beach. Across the lake, pine trees ascended the gentle hill from the western shore. The Appalachian Trail was hidden in the trees. As they unpacked the canoe and pitched the tent, Tom noticed Jenny had a bounce, the same bounce she had on his first visit to Vermont.

As expected, there was no cell coverage. Tom had printed out the forecast from Wunderground.com and Windy.com for the next couple of days, but the weather could change quickly in Maine. Good practice for the weather in the Llanganatis, he thought.

Both weather apps predicted tomorrow morning into the afternoon would be clear with little wind, which would give them plenty of opportunity to dump one load on Nahmakanta and then drive to Fourth Debsconeag to explore. The next day on Friday, however, Wunderground predicted rain later in the day.

Today, they would relax and enjoy the site.

Tom had slipped a bottle of Cold Duck into the bottom of his stuff sack. One of the first things he did while Jenny pitched the tent was tie a rope around the neck of the bottle and hide it in the lake. It would be cool by dinner. They had learned Cold Duck pairs well with everything.

Once they had the site set up, they stretched out on their camp chairs on the beach to read. Tom wanted to read Dr. Parcak's new book, *Archaeology from Space: How the Future Shapes Our Past*, but Jenny had another idea.

Stephen King was her favorite author, even before she attended the University of Maine, where he had also been an English major. She loved his "rags to riches" story.

Jenny wanted Tom to read at least one Stephen King book, but Tom didn't like scary books or movies. *Star Wars* was his limit. Years ago, he saw *Pet Sematary* with friends, but only because it was set in Maine. After some persistence by Jenny, however, Tom agreed to read *Pet Sematary*.

"I thought I was supposed to be the whiny one," Tom had said.

"I learned from the best."

He had assumed if he knew the ending, it might not be so scary.

He was wrong. The book was still scary—from the beginning.

Jenny had brought along Dr. Parcak's new book to read. Tom wondered if this was payback for capsizing at Flagstaff.

"How's Dr. Parcak's book?" he asked.

"I'll let you know Roomy, you just read yours."

He planned rib eye steaks for tonight, along with fried potatoes and onions, and surprised Jenny with the chilled Cold Duck, which he poured with a flourish.

By late August, the sun starts to set around 7:30. The temperature also drops in the evening, but tonight was still comfortable. A light breeze kept the black flies away.

After dinner, Tom spread out the permethrin-impregnated picnic blanket. The sand gently warmed the blanket, which was pleasantly squishy on the sand. It was getting dark, so he put his book down.

He opened the blue cheese and crackers and brought over the rest of the Cold Duck. The sand and fire kept them warm.

"I remember meeting you for the first time in the computer lab. I was tongue-tied. I couldn't even remember your name. When I got back to the Pizza Palace, I couldn't describe you to Dave. I couldn't find the words. He said you were a gestalt. I'm still not sure what it means."

"The whole is greater than the sum of the parts," replied Jenny. She had an amazing vocabulary. She put her head on his shoulder. "You were not what I expected for a tutor, either. I told Robin she needed to sign up for a computer class and screw it up so she could get her own tutor."

Jenny continued, "It's hard for me to find the words, too, but it feels like what we have is special. I guess every couple probably feels this way. It doesn't matter. That's how I feel."

She leaned over and softly kissed him. He loved to read, but this was way more fun.

"You know, I was nervous too. I never needed tutoring before. I wasn't sure what you thought of me. You were a senior, and I was only a sophomore. I didn't think you would have the time or interest for me. I thought the Bear's Den was part of the tutoring. It took me a few weeks to realize you were interested in me, too."

He just grinned. "If you want to go skinny-dipping, now is the best time. There's still a bit of last light."

Jenny poured the rest of the Cold Duck. Last light was waning fast. She finished her drink with one swig and threw her fancy paper cup into the fire. The sizzling cup gave her blonde hair a sparkling orange glow.

She stood up and then helped him up. Her back was to the lake. Tom expected a kiss, but Jenny went for his belt buckle. She started undressing him, motioning with her eyes for him to undress her, too. She took her time. Tom did not.

Jenny neatly folded his clothes on the blanket, topped by his socks and boxers. Her clothes were in a pile on the sand.

She then led him by the hand to the water in the last of the last light. No one would see them. The sand slid between their toes. Tom stole a glance at her by the last of twilight. Although the lake was chilly, it was a refreshing walk out to waist deep.

Jenny dove in headfirst, followed by Tom.

This is the stuff of dreams, or at least my dreams, he thought. He couldn't believe this was happening.

The swim didn't last as long as he had hoped, but he was chilly too. He worried the invigorating water might have sobered Jenny up.

Apparently not.

As they dried off, she took more time than perhaps necessary, even with the tiny camp towel. It was at times like this that he wondered what a girl like Jenny was doing with a nerd like him.

As he reached for his neatly folded clothes, she gently pulled him down onto the blanket. They embraced and shared each other's body heat. Then she kissed him. They had kissed before, but this was different. It was coming from a deeper place. Maybe it was the Cold Duck, being naked on the beach at Nahmakanta. He wasn't sure. He was trying not to be so analytical about things like this.

He felt goosebumps on her arms, and maybe her nipples on his chest.

He could also feel his bulge near her inguen.

When they made love, Tom typically took the lead, and he always wondered about boundaries.

Tonight was different. Tonight, she took the lead.

She slowly reached down. Although Tom wasn't her first, she was inexperienced, as was he. They were both learning to know each other together.

She broke off her kiss and gradually moved down. They touched each other in ways they had not done so before. Something was happening that Tom had only imagined.

Afterwards, collapsing into each other's arms, they wrapped the blanket around themselves, and tracked shooting stars until the chill took over.

As the fire flickered its last light, they raced to the tent and jumped in their pajamas to warm up, and then returned to the campfire to watch the dying embers.

With Tom in her arms, she whispered, "I'm so happy I found my lobsterman."

Tomorrow was for exploring the surrounding lakes. Tonight was for exploring each other.

❧❦

Thursday, August 22, 2019
Nahmakanta Lake, Maine

When Tom woke, he was still glowing. But he needed to focus on the day ahead. With no cell signal, there were no updates on the weather. Things could change quickly, but so far, Wunderground was spot on, with a few cumulus clouds and a light breeze from the southwest, just as predicted.

As he tossed the DEET to Jenny, he said, "It's going to be warmer today with no wind. The black flies will be out."

On the water, Tom wore his Sou'Wester hat. Jenny took a picture, but she couldn't post it without a cell signal.

They finished Nahmakanta by late morning. After ten lakes and twenty piles, they were done with the yellow plastic gold. Jenny gingerly stood up and did a little victory dance in the bow. Tom noticed her trail pants fit particularly well.

Jenny had packed a lunch, so they paddled directly back to the parking lot for the twenty-minute ride to Fourth Debsconeag. After a picnic, they were on the water by early afternoon. The canoe launch was near Chewonki's Wilderness Camps. On the northern shore, Jenny spotted a moose with a calf.

They were back at the campsite by dinner time for their last night on Nahmakanta. Tom wished he'd brought another bottle of Cold Duck to celebrate. With no Cold Duck, he also wondered how this evening would go.

After dinner, they once again stretched out on their blanket. The fire was still lively. Tom reminded Jenny that they needed to wash off the DEET at some point with a dip in the lake. "We also need to do a tick check, which is more thorough when you do it together." He thought he saw the twinkle in her left eye.

As the sun started its slow descent behind Nesuntabunt Mountain, Jenny became reflective. She nestled closer to him. "How do you see your future, our future? And not the school stuff. I already know you're a nerd, but what about you and me?"

Tom had been looking forward to doing a tick check on Jenny. This was an unnecessary distraction.

"I'd like to have a dog at some point," he replied. "Ouch!" as he rubbed where her elbow hit his ribs. Quickly regrouping, "Jenny, I can't imagine a future without you. I just hope we can find a way to stay in Maine, but the more degrees we get, the fewer options we may have. For me, being with you is what's important."

Jenny rubbed his ribs where she had poked him. "I know talking about this makes you uncomfortable, but I've always envisioned a family. I like cats, but I could live with a dog."

Feeling a little emboldened, Tom continued, "Now, when you say a family?"

"You know, kids, a family. Is that a problem?" she answered with a scowl.

"A dog wouldn't do it for you?" Tom pulled Jenny closer, which mitigated the impact of her elbow. He was getting better at predicting them, but she varied the spot.

After a moment, she asked, "How many degrees do you plan on getting?"

"I'll probably apply to a doctoral program in archaeology. Where depends upon you. What about you? Are you looking past an undergraduate degree?"

"I'm thinking of an MFA in creative writing. I always envisioned myself as a freelance writer like my Aunt Lisa, writing about geology or the climate, and raising a family."

He turned to kiss her on her cheek and closed his eyes. This weekend was the first time they had talked so much about their relationship and their future. Everything weaved together, except for the cat—and kids—but the cat was the bigger issue.

The sun was setting with another beautiful sunset.

"Red sky at night, Tom and Jenny's delight," she said, as she got up to add some driftwood to the fire.

As the last light waned, he gently wrapped his arms around her and whispered, "It's time to wash off the DEET."

He found out Cold Duck was not necessary to enjoy the water at Nahmakanta.

Later, after they warmed up in the tent, they did a tick check. It was very thorough.

As Tom drifted off to sleep, he tried to imagine a future where they found the gold. It didn't work. He could not get past the fact that the VGG-16 was stalled. It was not learning.

He remembered the old computer adage, garbage in-garbage out.

Friday, August 23, 2019
Nahmakanta Lake, Maine

They were up early. Tom started the camp stove and readied the French press while Jenny started breaking camp. He wanted to get on the water before the afternoon breeze. At least it would be behind them on the way back to the parking lot. There was also some weather predicted to come in later today.

Nahmakanta had always been a special place for Tom. Now, it was a special place for Jenny, too.

They headed back to the Summer Palace for a Zoom call with Dr. Westhoven in the morning, and then they would then head to Amherst for a week.

Jenny surprised Tom on the way back to Orono when she said, "Let me decide when to tell my parents about living together, okay?"

"Why? I assumed you'd already told them."

"I don't want any drama. I don't expect any, but my dad still thinks of me as his little girl." Jenny's gaze drifted away, pretending she was looking for a moose.

"Okay, it's your call, Jenny." Tom tried not to sound annoyed, but he was.

The Lost Inca Gold

Moving Day

Friday, August 23, 2019
Summer Palace
Orono, Maine

They were back in Orono by mid-afternoon. Nahmakanta had been a much-needed mental break for Tom. Otherwise, he was constantly fiddling with hyperparameters with each new batch of data. Although he still had Flagstaff and Nahmakanta left to image, which was almost twenty percent of the training data set, the VGG-16 was still sluggish to learn. It improved only marginally with data from each new lake.

By now, Tom had expected to see the learning level off, but there was nothing yet to level off. Usually the solution was more data, but he was running out of lakes—and time. And waiting another month for the plastic to dissolve was also frustrating, although with the warmer water, the plastic was now dissolving in about two to three weeks.

Tom reviewed the actual Depth Cam images many times. Occasionally, he could make out something at five meters deep, but only shadows any deeper. He knew, however, the neural network saw the images differently. It focused on edges, shapes, and contrast.

Also, Tom realized that even if his neural network learned how to recognize a pile of gold underwater, the Inca gold still needed to be in one of the twenty-four lakes selected by Dr. Westhoven. And the Incas would have needed to drop the gold in less than thirty feet of water to be seen by Depth Cam. Tom did not handle uncertainty well, even in the best of circumstances. All of this was almost incomprehensible.

Also, Google CoLab was slowing down as he added more lakes, so he had to add more GPUs.

He had some ideas to run by Dr. Westhoven on their Zoom call tomorrow. Tom had little good news to report. As usual, he wasn't looking forward to the call.

After the call, they would head over to Amherst. Jenny was looking forward to seeing Jackie, who would be home a few more days before leaving for Occidental.

❧❦

Saturday, August 24, 2019
Zoom Call
New Haven, Connecticut - Orono, Maine

Tom didn't want to worry Dr. Westhoven, but the neural network was not learning. He was still waiting for more data, but he'd been telling himself that all summer.

Dr. Westhoven started the call from his office. It was a sunny day in New Haven, and even with the shades down, the highlighted background darkened his face along with his tan from the Cape.

"Hey Tom, Jenny. Any improvement in learning?" asked Dr. Westhoven. No small talk today. Tom was glad Jenny was at his side.

"Not yet, but if the weather holds tomorrow, we'll get Depth Cam images on Flagstaff and Nahmakanta. Then, another few weeks before all the plastic dissolves but, honestly," Tom took a breath and cleared his throat, "I expected to see some learning by now. I'm worrying about the loss function or optimizer or both. I think the representational space is okay, but we're not looking at cats or dogs or lobsters. Even with intensive image pre-processing, we're still peering at a pile of yellow plastic up to thirty feet underwater."

"Understood, Tom. What's your next move?"

Tom noticed the change from "our" to "your" next move.

"Weather permitting, I'll hopefully have all the Depth Cam images in the neural network by early September, and then another week or two to fine-tune it. I may not meet the end-of-October deadline."

Dr. Westhoven pursed his lips and blinked a few times. It was hard to tell with the backlighting, but Tom thought he saw a new expression on Dr. Westhoven. Was it concern, disappointment? Usually, he was always positive, upbeat, no matter what Tom threw at him. Maybe the timeline was more important than Tom realized.

With his gaze still fixed on his desk, Dr. Westhoven adjusted his glasses. Sliding his hair behind his left ear, he looked up and asked, "Realistically, when will your algorithm finish scanning the lakes in the Llanganatis?"

"Probably early November, assuming I can get the VGG-16 to learn."

Tom knew this was over the deadline, but before Dr. Westhoven could respond, he continued. "I do have some good news. When I looked at the Depth Cam images from the eight lakes in the Llanganatis you've surveyed so far, some are deeper than thirty feet in the middle, beyond the range of Depth Cam. There's no value in running them through the neural network, so I'm working on some code to remove these deeper images from the data set, which is about fifteen percent of the images. This will speed things up."

Then, in a more somber tone, he added, "I just hope the ancients didn't drop the gold in anything deeper than thirty feet. If they did, we'll never find the gold."

Tom wondered if Dr. Westhoven's screen had frozen. His expression did not change.

Then Dr. Westhoven looked down again at his desk. His long hair fell forward. "Anything to speed up the processing is great. I've always assumed the Incas didn't dump the gold and silver too deep if they ever planned to recover it. Hopefully, I'm right.

"Miguel needed the five lakes by October. I'll update him this weekend that it might not be until November. I'm hoping he built in some elbow room if we want to get to the Llanganatis in March."

Dr. Westhoven took a deep breath. "I'm struggling to get Depth Cam images, too. There are still sixteen lakes to image. The weather has been so lousy, but I hope to have all the lakes imaged in the next couple weeks. The Llanganatis looks like a miserable place, at least on satellite. I hope March has better weather. But without a functioning neural network, it doesn't matter."

Nothing like stating the obvious, thought Tom. An uneasy quiet followed.

Finally, Dr. Westhoven broke the silence. "I know this is taking even more time than you planned. Don't get over extended once the semester starts."

"I think I'm okay. I did an independent study project this summer with Popham Colony for four credits, so I can reduce my classes by one this semester. And no tutoring for now. Dr. Wade understands this project is time intensive."

"Good. So, tell me about your Popham Colony project."

"I found some neat stuff using old Landsat images and VGG-16 on the private land that had never been excavated. I used some of the image processing I developed for the Llanganatis project."

"That sounds interesting. Will you send along what you found? Possibly it's something you can publish. By the way, where are you with the original article you owe me?"

Tom thought he could see Dr. Westhoven smiling, but he wasn't sure with the bright backlighting. The article for *Modern Archaeology* was the last thing on Tom's agenda.

Dr. Westhoven chuckled. "I know, Tom. We'll get to it. There'll be some downtime this winter." After a brief pause, "Okay, let's connect in a few weeks."

The call ended, and they hit the road. The sun was on its way to a beautiful day, and Jenny suggested a new route over the White Mountains on the Kancamagus Highway.

"That was a tough call," said Jenny. "Did you see the look on his face when you said it might not be ready until November?"

"Yeah. It's nice to see someone else fussing for once."

After a moment, Tom continued, "By the way, did you decide when to tell your parents we're shacking up?"

"Not yet. It'll work out. And sharing an apartment sounds better than shacking up."

They didn't talk much about the gold on the way over. Instead, Jenny skirted around their future, stuff like graduate programs, kids, cats, and dogs. Sirius XM labored in the mountains, but Tom appreciated the timing of *Wouldn't It Be Nice* when Jenny mentioned marriage. He had learned his lesson earlier. He nodded and let her do most of the talking.

Tom liked the alternate route over the White Mountains. The F-150 was quieter at fifty miles per hour, driving through small towns instead of seventy miles per hour on the turnpike.

As they passed Loon Mountain, Tom asked, "What was the best part of this summer?"

"That's easy—being with you. We were together 'All Summer Long'," singing like the Beach Boys.

"Nice voice. Any other talents I don't know about?"

"A few. I'll sprinkle them in, here and there."

There was still a lot to learn about Jenny.

They arrived at Amherst later in the afternoon. It was still a five-hour drive, but more relaxing than the interstate. Tom also appreciated looking in the rearview mirror and not seeing a pile of yellow plastic gold.

Maine weather was often fickle. It never seemed to be the same for more than two or three days. But in Vermont, Wunderground predicted a perfect week, warm days and cool nights. A much-needed break after a damp summer.

Jenny's parents met them in the yard. "Wow, look at your tans," exclaimed her mom.

"Don't worry Mom. We used sunscreen all summer." Her mom had always been concerned about sun exposure since Jenny was a kid in Bogotá.

After hugs, Jenny nonchalantly mentioned, "If it's okay with you guys, Tom and I hope to sleep on the deck, if that's okay. The other good news is we have an apartment together in Bangor. We're renting from Tom's advisor. I'll get you the address. Do you know where the bug nets are?"

She had not mentioned to Tom about sleeping on the deck. There was no drama. As they unpacked their bags upstairs in her bedroom, he gently pulled her onto him on her bed.

"Smooth," he said. "I love the deck idea."

"And I have my lobsterman." Jenny smiled, followed by a kiss. Tom could tell she was relieved the apartment discussion was done.

Jenny's friend Jackie joined them for dinner. Tom took over the kitchen. They'd stopped at McLaughlin's in Bangor for lobsters, steamers, butter, Humpty Dumpty BBQ potato chips, and whoopie pies.

They ate on the deck where Tom showed everyone how to eat a lobster, the Maine way. Even Jenny helped with the intricacies. The Cold Duck was also a hit.

The sunset matched the lobsters. "Red sky at night, Tom and Jenny's delight," she said, explaining to everyone what it meant. She was becoming a real Mainer, thought Tom.

They camped the entire week on the deck. Most nights were clear, and Tom pointed out some constellations. The moon was waning crescent throughout the week with a new moon on Friday. It was comfortable on the deck, even though it wasn't carpeted like the showroom in Limerock. For the first time in months, they were not dumping plastic. This was an actual vacation.

On the back road to Woodstock, they stopped at the Vermont Farmstead Cheese factory and picked up some curds for her dad. Tom enjoyed driving the back roads through the mountains, following a meandering river or stream, but sometimes he felt claustrophobic in the deep valleys.

They played tourist in Woodstock and occasionally would run into one of Jenny's old high school classmates. Tom wasn't sure, but he wondered if the guy who gave her a long hug was her old boyfriend.

"He was just a good friend," was all Jenny would say.

By the end of the week, they were both rested, ready for the new semester, and their new apartment. The only blip was a text from his mother yesterday that his dad's knee had finally given out. Tom was not too worried. His dad's knee had bothered him on and off for years, but he always bounced back. He texted he would connect with them on Monday when they were back in Maine.

⁎

Sunday, September 1, 2019
Bangor, Maine

The move to their new apartment went smoothly. It only took one trip with the F-150 and Dave's car. Dave had been a good roommate and friend. Tom would miss his wit, but he was no match for Jenny.

The new apartment was furnished, but the walls were bare.

"We need some posters," said Jenny. "Making this homier will be fun."

They also needed another bookshelf, and Tom needed a desk, as Jenny had claimed dibs on the kitchen table to study. Other than that, they were set.

They reconnected with Dave and Amanda that evening at Evenrood's to thank them for their help with the move. Tom and Jenny reminisced about their first date here last December. The boys toasted to their new roommates. After dessert at Happy Endings on Main Street, they said goodnight to Dave and Amanda and walked back to their new apartment.

The night was still young, so they stopped at Bangor Wine and Cheese on their walk home. Jenny suggested some inexpensive champagne and blue cheese to celebrate.

They snuggled on their new couch and listened to the oldies on Sirius XM. This was the first time Tom had tried champagne. He liked it almost as much as Cold Duck.

It was a warm night, and Tom had intentionally left the mini split off. By bedtime, they were more comfortable without pajamas as they slipped into their new bed.

❧❦

Labor Day
Monday, September 2, 2019
Bangor, Maine

"He's scheduled in two weeks."

Tom could hear the weariness in his mother's voice. A pang of guilt swept over him for not calling sooner.

"Is this a serious operation?" he asked.

"I don't think so. He should be home the next day, but he can't use his new knee for a few months."

Although his dad sold and installed carpets, Tom knew he made his money from the installation.

"Are you going to be okay, you know, financially? Does dad have disability?"

"No. We have some value in the house if we need. We'll get by."

"Let me know if I can help. I've saved some from my tutoring."

"Thanks Tom, but we'll get by."

Although Tom did not know the details of his parents' financials, except that they could not help with his tuition, he knew six to eight weeks out of work would be tough. His dad worked all the time, taking no vacations, just to make ends meet.

"Okay. I'll come down when he is discharged to help get him settled."

Wednesday, September 4, 2019
Bangor, Maine

Tom had no classes today. He had not told Jenny about his dad's surgery. He was still processing the news himself. Maybe this weekend.

This was the first day since Vermont that he could fully devote himself to the VGG-16. He now had Depth Cam images on all the Maine lakes and eight with follow-up images after the plastic dissolved.

As he looked at the training data output, however, he slowly panicked. The accuracy was still only sixty percent. The extra GPUs only underscored more quickly that the neural network was not learning. As he sat at the kitchen table, his panic mixed with bitterness. What a waste of time.

He continued to fiddle, looking closer at the representational space. He highlighted the edges and contrast even more. But every change took time to assess, and he could only make one or two changes at a time. It was slow work and Tom's already limited patience was wearing thin.

He was running out of time.

Friday, September 6, 2019
Antigüedades Sur
Bogotá, Colombia

Omar was calling Miguel this afternoon. Omar had not made the trip to Bogotá in a couple of months, but they stayed in touch by phone every two weeks. A typical phone call would start with some perfunctory discussion of Antigüedades Sur, and then Omar would turn the conversation to the expedition.

Miguel had been following the news, both online and in the newspapers, about the helicopter crash in the Llanganatis last month, but there had been little detail after a follow-up story of mechanical trouble or possibly pilot error causing the crash. He had learned more about the crash from his associates in the antiquities trade than from the newspapers.

Omar called at two o'clock. After a few pleasantries and a quick update on Antigüedades Sur, Miguel asked, "What do you think of the unfortunate helicopter accident last month in the Llanganatis?"

"Yes, Miguel, a tragedy. That is one reason we will use a base camp to minimize the flying through the mountains, and our helicopter with no tail rotor is much safer. Do you have any more details about the crash?"

"A little. Luis Alvarez, a former partner of Andrés Fernández-Salvador, was leading an expedition. They were almost certainly looking for the Inca gold. Fernández made over sixty trips into the Llanganatis, many with Alvarez at his side. Only a fool would believe they were looking for Inca settlements.

"And this is just a guess, but there does not seem to be an urgency to recover the bodies, so I doubt they found any gold."

Then Miguel updated him on Dr. Westhoven. "Everything is still on track, but they are bumping up against the November timeline, according to Dr. Westhoven."

"Good, my friend. As long as we have the five lakes by November, we will be okay."

Miguel was relieved. He had not known how important the timeline was to Omar.

Omar continued, "I hope to make it to Bogotá next month to meet in person, but keep me posted in the meantime. And please let me know if you learn anything more about the unfortunate helicopter crash."

Omar seemed genuinely disturbed by the crash, thought Miguel.

Fish or Cut Bait

Monday, September 16, 2019
Bangor, Maine

All the images were now in the neural network. Tom had spent the last two weeks fiddling, adding GPUs, running, and rerunning the data. He was only able to get the accuracy up from sixty to sixty-five percent, still not good enough.

Today was his dad's surgery. His mom would call him this afternoon with an update, and he planned to head to Limerock tomorrow.

He had also neglected his classes. Today was the last day of add and drop. He'd only registered for four classes, but he was still falling behind. This project, with so little chance for success, was consuming so much of his time and might delay his master's degree.

Before heading to campus, he went for a quick run over to Brewer to clear his head and consider his options. He was back as Jenny was making coffee. "You're up early."

"I went for a run. Today is the last day to drop a class. I decided to stay the course and keep all the four classes. Once I finish with this neural network, I'll have some downtime. I just have to get through the next four to six weeks."

Then he would catch up—he hoped.

Wednesday, September 18, 2019
Bangor, Maine

Yesterday was a long day. His dad would sleep in a hospital bed in the showroom for the next few weeks until he could make the stairs to their bedroom. It would still be another six to eight weeks before he could kneel, and then maybe three months before he could get fully back to work. His mom was less and less reassuring that they would "get by."

On the ride home yesterday, he daydreamed about how different life would be if he found the gold. No more just getting by. His dad could focus on getting better instead of getting back to work.

This morning, the results of his last tweaks to the algorithm would be ready. He had waited for Jenny to leave for school. Now at his desk, alone in the apartment, he opened his laptop, confident the last set of changes to the hyperparameters would make a difference.

He could not believe his eyes.

The accuracy had dropped from sixty-five to fifty-two percent.

Until now, every change he had made over the summer had improved the learning, even if only a little. And Dr. Westhoven had made it clear on the last Zoom call he was out of time. He needed a functioning neural network to meet the deadline.

Anger welled up in his chest. How foolish he was to think a pile of yellow plastic could really train a VGG-16 to find gold? And there was no do-over after the plastic dissolved. What was he thinking when he'd agreed to this last March?

There were so many variables and assumptions. Was the problem with the training data set, the control images, the hyperparameters, the number of images, the representational space, the quality of the Depth Cam images, or something else? There were too many unknowns.

All he could do was stare at the results. The anger dissipated. He finally had some clarity.

It was time to give up.

He did not have enough data or time, and he was tired of tweaking hyperparameters. Maybe a one-meter grid was too small, or too large. It didn't matter. He was done.

If he dropped this project now, he would be able to catch up. He thought he had saved enough to help his parents for a few months, and he could start tutoring again.

Jenny would be disappointed, but this project was also coming between them. She had started calling him Eeyore. And Tom knew she was right.

He felt a glimmer of relief. Hopefully, Jenny would be supportive. He would tell her tonight and Dr. Westhoven on the Zoom call on Saturday. Tom spent the rest of the day attempting to get back on track with his classes.

Instead of their usual Wednesday night takeout, he decided to make tacos for dinner, Jenny's favorite. The taco serving plate had been their first purchase together for the apartment. He even added mushrooms as a special ingredient.

Just as he was setting the table, he heard Jenny climbing the stairs. Tom opened the apartment door for her and greeted her with a kiss.

"I thought I smelled something good. What's the occasion?"

"I just felt like tacos...."

She dumped her knapsack in the corner and pulled up her chair to the kitchen table. She was crunching a taco in no time.

In between bites, she said, "I have a big test tomorrow. This is just what I needed. What did you do today?"

"The results of the latest change to the VGG-16 came back this morning."

"Great. And?"

"The accuracy dropped to fifty-two percent."

The only sound was Jenny crunching.

"That's discouraging," she finally muttered.

"Yeah."

After another bite and a deep breath, he continued in a low voice. "Yeah, I'm done. There just isn't enough data, and I'm out of time. I'm not sure the neural network would ever learn, even with enough time and data."

"What do you mean, you're done?"

Tom thought she sounded annoyed.

"I can't do this anymore. I'm telling Dr. Westhoven this weekend that I quit."

Jenny slowly lowered her half-eaten taco to her plate as she studied the diced tomatoes he had so carefully placed in the taco tray. He thought she started to flush, like a mini-beet head.

"Look, Tom, I can't fix your program, and I know your dad's surgery is weighing upon you, but all I ask is you do the right thing. If you're quitting because this is completely hopeless and a waste of everyone's time and money, I get it. Put all of us out of <u>your</u> misery.

"But if you're quitting because this is hard, and you hit a bump in the road, and you're afraid of failing, well, just be sure you're quitting for the right reason."

Tom dropped his taco on his plate, which cracked the shell. "I had hoped you'd be a little more supportive."

Jenny slowly looked up from the diced tomatoes and directly into his eyes.

"You still have a couple of days until the Zoom call. Clear your mind. Look at the process. Be creative. This is a setback for sure, but have you really exhausted all your ideas?"

He turned his gaze down, rubbing his chin methodically with his left hand. "I feel like this project is affecting our relationship. I don't want that to happen."

"Me neither, but I don't think it's the project. I think this is more about you than you realize. You seem to base your self-worth, your self-image, on your latest success or failure. You're more than that.

"You—we have put too much into this to throw in the towel at this point. Look, we both knew this was a long shot. I know you have a lot on your mind. Your dad will get better, but you'll always have to live with this decision. Just be sure you're doing the right thing for the right reason. But no matter what, you better get rid of the Eeyore attitude. It's not helping anything or anyone."

Jenny picked up her plate and headed to the sink. "I've got to get to work. I'll do the dishes later."

Tom sat at the kitchen table for a while until he realized Jenny was waiting for him to move so she could study for her test tomorrow.

There was still some sunlight left, so he went for another run. He didn't bother to ask Jenny if she wanted to go.

As he ran across the Penobscot Bridge to Brewer, his mind wandered. He remembered how excited he and Jenny were less than three weeks ago when they moved into their new apartment. The clarity that he had felt earlier today when he had decided to give up was now replaced by a muddle. He was on an emotional roller coaster.

The sun was setting as he turned right onto the Chamberlain Bridge back to Bangor. He was struggling with what Jenny had said. He knew most of what she said was true. It amazed him at how well she knew him, sometimes better than he knew himself. All he wanted to do was move on, but she knew he would likely regret that decision.

And what if he actually found the gold? All the money issues that had burdened him and his family would disappear.

As he chugged up the State Street hill, he wondered about the hyperparameters. What am I missing?

When he returned to the apartment, Jenny was immersed in her studies. He had received an email from Dr. Westhoven this afternoon. Normally, he would have opened it immediately, but not today. What was the point?

After his shower, he finally opened the email. Dr. Westhoven had all the Depth Cam images of the twenty-four lakes in the Llanganatis. He was "delighted to report" he had twenty-five million one-meter images ready to go. Tom had forgotten how much Dr. Westhoven had invested in this project.

❧◈❧

Thursday, September 19, 2019
Bangor, Maine

The next morning, Tom was up early. It had been a restless night. He remembered a phrase he read or heard somewhere, "Anything worth doing is worth doing to excess." Tom wasn't sure if this project was really worth doing, but he decided to take one more look at the data. He needed to convince himself that he had given it his all, and he was not there yet. He had two days until the Zoom call with Dr. Westhoven.

While tossing and turning last night, he had remembered that some of the original one-meter Depth Cam images at Pushaw were quite distinct from their neighboring images. One grid did not predict the appearance of the adjacent images. Each grid was unique, unlike a fractal that looks the same regardless of scale.

Jenny was still sleeping, so he went for a quick run. If nothing else, he was getting in great shape.

Tom wondered if there was another way to manipulate the data, like a frame shift. He was already rotating, shrinking, and enlarging the one-meter grids, but what if he carved up the grids differently by shifting the frame by half a meter? Perhaps he would pick up enough new variation to enhance the training.

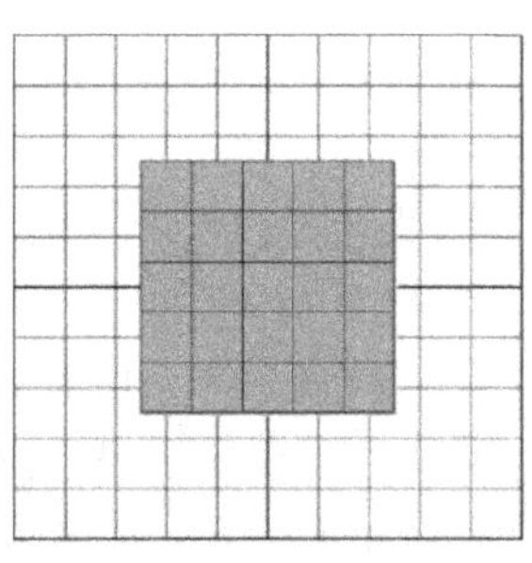

He didn't have the time to rerun tens of thousands of images, even with more GPUs, so he focused on the center, or the yolk, of the pile. He envisioned a five-by-five-meter grid over the existing dispersion grids supplied by Depth Cam and offset the grid by half a meter. A quick calculation revealed he could add about 24,000 high quality images.

Jenny was up when he returned, and they needed to hustle to make their classes. She was more subdued than usual, and he did not tell her about his idea. He also had a busy day, so he would have to wait until this evening to create the new grids.

That evening, rejiggering the frames was easier than he expected. He would add the 24,000 extra images to the training data set in the morning and reset the hyperparameters back to Monday, when the accuracy had been sixty-five percent. The final results would be ready just in time for the Zoom call on Saturday. He still wasn't sure what he would do if the additional images did not help.

❧

Saturday, September 21, 2019
Bangor, Maine

Jenny had been quiet, perfunctory, since Wednesday. Tom had decided to stick with the project, even if the results this morning didn't improve, but he wanted to wait until the results were back this morning before he broached this again with Jenny. Worst case, he could return the hyperparameters to Monday's values and have at least sixty-five percent accuracy.

He still wasn't sure why she was so upset with his decision to quit. Was she fed up with him, or his Eeyore attitude? What did it say about their relationship? That bothered him more than the failed neural network.

After a cup of coffee, and Jenny in the shower, he finally opened Google CoLab. He remembered how disappointed he was on Wednesday when the accuracy dropped to fifty-two percent.

He couldn't believe it.

The accuracy reached seventy-nine percent. He typically expected a mature neural network to be at least in the mid to high eighties, but this was still a significant improvement. The extra data made a difference. But he tempered the good news, remembering that all the other pieces also needed to fall into place to actually find the gold. But the neural network was done.

Jenny was getting ready to head to campus to work on a group project. She finally broke the silence. "What did you decide to tell Dr. Westhoven this morning?"

"I reran the data with some additional images. I got the accuracy up to seventy-nine percent."

Still no expression on her face. "Does this mean you're back on board?"

"For the time being."

"No Tom. Either do it or don't. We've all invested too much into this project to have you back out the next time something doesn't go your way."

"I get it Jenny. I'm in, but I can't guarantee the neural network will find anything in the lakes from the Llanganatis, even with a VGG-16 that identifies yellow plastic gold seventy-nine percent of the time. But I'll see it through."

He still couldn't get "garbage in-garbage out" out of his head.

"Tell Dr. Westhoven I'm sorry I'm missing the call, but this was the only time everyone in the group could meet. I'll be back by lunch." Jenny then gave him a long hug and whispered in his ear. "I'm glad both you and your program finally smartened up. Let's celebrate tonight."

It would still take another four to six weeks to run the images of the twenty-four lakes from the Llanganatis through the convolutional neural network. Only then would he know if seventy-nine percent was smart enough. But more important to Tom, they were talking again.

Saturday, September 21, 2019
Zoom Call
New Haven, Connecticut - Bangor, Maine

This was the first Zoom call since late August. Dr. Westhoven started the call promptly at eleven. Tom was at his unfinished pine desk in the living room. He noticed in his self-view he hadn't made the bed in the bedroom off the living room.

"Good morning, Tom. Where's Jenny? And your room looks different."

"Morning. Jenny and I have an apartment in Bangor. Jenny's at school working on a group project. She couldn't get out of it, but I'll fill her in."

Dr. Westhoven had a cup of coffee. Now that Tom was taking the calls at his desk instead of his bed at the Pizza Palace, he'd grab a coffee next time, too.

"Looks nice. So, where are you with the neural network?"

Tom took a deep breath and cleared his throat. "Seventy-nine percent. It took a while to tweak the hyperparameters, and I added about 24,000 additional images, but I think the current settings are as good as it gets with the time and data limitations we have."

"How many images in all did you use to train?"

"After I pulled out 19,000 images to test the neural network, about 74,000 training images."

"I thought you had over 100,000?"

"That included the infrared images, which did not add a lot, so I pulled them out. The red washes out too quickly underwater."

"Where did you get the extra 24,000?"

Dr. Westhoven's speech seemed pressured. He rarely asked one question after the other.

"I noticed early on that the images weren't fractal. I thought if I rejiggered the one-meter grid by offsetting them by one-half a meter, I might come up with unique, additional high-quality images. It worked. This risks overfitting the data, but we're out of time and data."

"What did you end up using for controls?"

"I re-imaged all the piles a month later after they dissolved and added another 100,000 images outside the dispersion field."

After an uncomfortable pause, Dr. Westhoven finally said, "Seventy-nine percent of finding an anomaly isn't great, but are you familiar with the expression 'fish or cut bait?'"

Tom nodded yes. "I grew up on the coast."

"Good. It's time to fish. Tom, we're done. We're out of time. Good enough will have to do. I know you wanted better accuracy, but remember, the enemy of good is better. Let's run the twenty-four lakes through the neural network and see what we get."

Dr. Westhoven leaned forward for a sip of coffee. The sun reflecting off a window across the street washed out his image for a moment. He took a deep breath and straightened up. His image stabilized.

"Take a moment, Tom, to consider what you've done. You created a training data set for gold out of plastic. You then trained a convolutional neural network to find the plastic thirty feet underwater that's seventy-nine percent accurate. That's incredible. I think we have a chance at finding the gold, if it exists, and a chance is all I expected. Whether or not we find the gold, this is an amazing achievement."

Tom needed this. He cleared his throat again. "Thanks, Dr. Westhoven, but there's still a lot of work to do." Then he remembered he was trying not to be an Eeyore.

"Agreed, but the heavy lifting is over."

After a brief pause, Dr. Westhoven continued, "Okay, let's talk about the next steps. You said it would take about four to six weeks to run the twenty-four lakes through the neural network and then we'll pick the top five possibilities. Is four to six weeks still a reasonable time frame?"

"I think so. I eliminated about six million images from the lakes in the Llanganatis that were too deep for Depth Cam, which helps."

"Okay, so by early-November at the latest, we should have five lakes to present to Miguel."

Dr. Westhoven took another sip of coffee, then asked, "How are you going to pinpoint where the gold is in each lake?"

Tom had put a lot of thought into this. "Each lake is hundreds of thousands of one-meter quadrants. Each quadrant will have a value assigned by the neural network of the probability of finding gold. I assumed a pile of gold will be dispersed over several contiguous meters, and I'll use an algorithm to track these hot spots. The five hottest spots will be our gold."

"Sounds good. Let's talk about the actual expedition. If we do go, I'm still counting on you joining me in the Llanganatis, right?"

"After all this, I want to be there to see this through." Although, he thought, perhaps I don't want to be there to see this fail.

"Great Tom. Miguel confirmed again, if we go ahead, the expedition will be in mid-March to coincide with our spring breaks. Neither of us will miss any classes. He has set aside seven days for the expedition, which includes two rain dates. That's why Miguel asked us to limit the number of lakes to five. The weather in the Llanganatis is so unpredictable. Even two rain dates may not be enough.

"Also, Miguel asked me to provide him with the list of lakes, in order of the highest probability lake first, and then in decreasing order. That way, if we run out of time, we'll at least have visited the lakes with the highest probability of finding the gold.

"Miguel has retrofitted the helicopter with pontoons and attachments for a Zodiac. The Tritons also attach to the pontoons. Deploying the Triton and setting up the satellite uplink will be your responsibility. Miguel ended up buying six Tritons, one for each lake and a backup."

That's over a quarter of a million dollars, thought Tom.

"By the way, thank Jenny again for tracking down the Triton. It's perfect for the job."

"Sure. It would've been a challenge to get all this done without her," said Tom.

"Understood. I know the importance of an extra set of hands. Now, if we find any gold, we're done. A separate team will extract the gold from the lake. The artifacts will be easy to recover, but any gold grains or nuggets might require some dredging after all these years."

He continued, "I know you just started, but how is your graduate program going?"

"It's going okay. I was worried I was falling behind, but I think I can catch up."

They planned to connect the first Saturday in November, when they both hoped the neural network would be done with the survey of the Llanganatis.

This week had been a blur, full of ups and downs. Tom finally realized finishing the neural network was another milestone. He wished Jenny could have been on the call. While waiting for her to return from campus, he did something mindless. He picked names for the five lakes in the Llanganatis.

Lake Alpha
Lake Bravo
Lake Charlie
Lake Delta
Lake Echo

❧

Thursday, October 10, 2019
Bangor, Maine

Jenny was twenty-one today. They celebrated at Novio's, which was a small, intimate restaurant downtown. Tom ordered a bottle of chardonnay. The server carded Tom, but not Jenny, which annoyed her a little after waiting twenty-one years for the experience.

After dinner, they stopped at the nearby Bangor Wine and Cheese and splurged again on some blue cheese to have with the Cold Duck waiting for them at the apartment.

Jenny was still looking for wall hangings, so, for her birthday, Tom had framed a large topographical map of Maine with a red circle around each lake they had visited this summer, with a star on Nahmakanta. He considered it a thoughtful gift.

Just in case, he also got her a green tourmaline necklace from the Rock & Art Shop downtown.

Five Lakes

Saturday, November 9, 2019
Zoom Call
New Haven, Connecticut - Orono, Maine

Tom was still processing the images from the Llanganatis and had asked Dr. Westhoven to reschedule the Zoom call from last weekend to today. It had taken almost seven weeks, but the neural network finished Wednesday. It had found and ranked twenty-five sites in the twenty-four lakes provided by Dr. Westhoven. One lake had two separate sites detected by the neural network, one ranked fourth and the other eighth. After double-checking the results, Tom sent the top five lakes along to Dr. Westhoven on Thursday.

He was done, but he hoped it wasn't too late. Dr. Westhoven had not replied to his email on Thursday, which was unusual.

Earlier, Jenny had found the Indiana Jones hat that Dr. Westhoven had sent Tom last March. While they were getting settled for the call, she asked, "Why don't you wear the Indiana Jones hat to celebrate?"

"I'm not sure we'll be celebrating. He didn't reply to my email. I might have missed the deadline."

Dr. Westhoven joined the call at eleven o'clock with a big smile. Jenny handed Tom the hat.

"Nice hat, Indiana Tom. I think you might get a chance to use it." After a few pleasantries, he presented his screen, another PowerPoint, with the lakes organized by probability labeled Lake Alpha to Lake Echo.

"It's all coming together. As you can see, I elevated the lake with the two anomalies to Lake Alpha, but otherwise, the lakes are in the order of your neural network."

Lakes of the Llanganatis

	Elevation (m)	Latitude, Longitude	Width (m)	Length (m)
Alpha	3415	-1.015109, -78.246597 -1.016225, -78.245956	323	512
Bravo	3709	-1.243702, -78.302048	375	378
Charlie	3184	-1.316935, -78.269218	229	591
Delta	3660	-0.905070, -78.194054	250	722
Echo	3789	-1.146835, -78.233406	171	780

Dr. Westhoven continued, "I also noticed all the lakes are on a declivity or slope, as mentioned in the Derrotero. I hope this is a good sign."

Tom took a moment to study the PowerPoint. "That all makes sense. By the way, I had noticed all the lakes were over three thousand meters or ten thousand feet high. Do we need to worry about high-altitude illness?"

"I don't think so. High-altitude illness is more related to the location of the base camp. A few hours at these altitudes is low risk. I know Miguel has been holding off on siting a base camp until we selected the five lakes as he was thinking of using one of these lakes, but they're all too high for a base camp. I'll be sure to ask Miguel to site the base camp as low as possible.

"And there's a medication called acetazolamide we can take to prevent high-altitude illness. I remember taking it on my trip ten years ago."

Dr. Westhoven continued, "I guess my other concern about the altitude is how the helicopter will perform. I know the thin air affects air speed and the ability to hover. And the wind at these altitudes is also a consideration. There's a website at Windy.com. Check it out and you'll see what I mean."

"We used Windy.com last summer. It was pretty accurate, but it underestimated the wind when local factors came into play." Tom remembered the effect of Bigelow Mountain and Hurricane Island on Flagstaff.

Dr. Westhoven chuckled. "It's hard to believe we're talking about the wind and helicopter, but we'll know soon enough if we're heading to the Llanganatis. I'll keep you posted."

Tom would not be disappointed if they were too late for this March.

"By the way, Jenny and I did some calculations. Based on the size of the lakes, the Triton will require about eight to twelve hours to scan each one and then another four to five to process the images."

Jenny added, "I'm glad we have enough Tritons."

"Me too. I've said it before, but excellent work, guys. I hope Miguel is as impressed as I am with what you've accomplished, and hopefully," looking at Tom, "you and I'll be spending our spring break in the Llanganatis. Miguel needs to decide soon. Let's connect after Thanksgiving, but I'll let you know as soon as I hear from Miguel."

Tom saw the beginning of a smile creep across Dr. Westhoven. "And now, maybe Tom, you can start working on the two articles you owe me."

Tom laughed. The two articles were the last thing on his mind. Although Tom knew Dr. Westhoven was ribbing him a little, he would eventually have to write the articles.

After the call, Dr. Westhoven copied Tom and Jenny on the email he sent to Miguel.

> *To: Miguel Titere*
> *Date: Saturday, November 9, 2019*
> *From: Jerome Westhoven, PhD*
>
> *Subject: Phase Two*
>
> *Dear Miguel,*
>
> *I met with my team earlier today to review the results. Phase One is complete.*
>
> *We have found six hot spots in five lakes, which appear worthy of further investigation with an estimated chance of 79% of finding an anomaly in each of these lakes.*
>
> *Attached is a PowerPoint of the Llanganatis of the five lakes. Small lakes in the Llanganatis are not named, so we have labeled them starting with Lake Alpha, the highest probability lake, down to Lake Echo.*
>
> *Lake Alpha had a hot spot ranked fourth, and another ranked eighth, so with two separate sites in the same lake, I elevated this lake to Lake Alpha.*
>
> *I've attached a summary of our findings. I'd like to review the results at your convenience.*
>
> *Sincerely,*
>
> *Jerome Westhoven, PhD*
> *Council on Archaeological Studies*
> *Yale University*

∾∾

Miguel reviewed the documents in some detail, although he understood little of the jargon. All he wanted to know was if there was a better than even chance of finding gold. He thought seventy-nine percent was good, but he did not understand finding an anomaly versus finding gold. The real question is, would Omar?

Miguel sent Dr. Westhoven an invitation for a phone call for that evening.

He then forwarded the email and documents to Omar, who replied with plans to meet with Miguel in Bogotá on Tuesday.

Miguel and Dr. Westhoven always talked on the phone, never a Zoom call. At six p.m. local time, Dr. Westhoven answered the call.

"Thank you, Dr. Westhoven, for all your work. This sounds very encouraging, do you not think? Please explain what is a hot spot and the seventy-nine percent of finding the term anomaly, if you please."

"Certainly Miguel. Seventy-nine percent is the best the neural network could do in finding the test gold in the training data set.

"To actually find the gold, we assumed it was spread over several meters on the bottom. We partitioned or divided up the lakes into one-meter quadrants. The neural network then assigned each quadrant a probability.

"When we found a grouping of quadrants with high probabilities close together, we called it a hot spot. The six hottest spots are in the five lakes I sent you.

"We call the hot spots anomalies because there are other things that might mimic a pile of gold and silver, like a pile of rocks, which might have fooled the neural network."

"I see. Still, this looks promising. Do you agree?" Not waiting again for Dr. Westhoven to reply, Miguel continued, "I will need a few days to consider and I will get back to you with my decision. If we do proceed to the Llanganatis, I am still looking at March to coincide with your school break of spring."

"Thanks Miguel. My team is ready, and we look forward to hearing from you."

Dr. Westhoven continued, "By the way, you'll notice the five lakes are at 10,000 feet or higher. You'll want the base camp as low as possible, ideally 5,000 feet, or 1,500 meters, or lower, to minimize the risk of high-altitude illness. There is also a medication we can take for a couple of days to prevent high-altitude illness called acetazolamide. Finally, you may want to double-check how the helicopter will perform at high altitudes."

"Yes, Dr. Westhoven. All important considerations. Thank you again."

Dr. Westhoven thought it was a quick call, considering the magnitude of the decision Miguel needed to make. He was not so sure Miguel understood the difference between an anomaly and gold.

He wasn't sure he did either.

Then, just as he was about to say goodbye, Miguel asked, "By the way, professor, did you read about the helicopter crash in the Llanganatis last summer?"

"No, Miguel. What happened?"

"Evidently, a small expedition crashed in the eastern mountains on their way back to Quito. The authorities have not released a lot of information, but Luis Alvarez, a former partner of Andrés Fernández-Salvador, was leading the expedition. They were almost assuredly looking for gold. Perhaps it is the curse."

Dr. Westhoven was well aware of the curse of the Inca gold. Although many explorers had lost their lives in pursuit of the gold, typically, the best explanation was either incompetence or greed, not the curse.

"Were there any survivors?"

"No, unfortunately not. They were flying back and forth each day from Quito. This is another reason I have chosen a base camp in the Llanganatis, to minimize the flight time."

Dr. Westhoven decided not to share this with Tom.

Tuesday, November 12, 2019
Bogotá, Colombia

Lake Delta was Ground Zero. The program had found the fake gold. Omar was on the Gulfstream, en route to Bogotá to meet Miguel. When Omar saw the elevations of the five lakes, he knew the base camp would need to be an independent central location at a lower altitude. He could not afford one of the team developing high-altitude illness.

Tarek, who had been in Quito, would also arrive in Bogotá today. He would fly back with Omar to Cartagena to help with the decision of where to locate the base camp.

Omar arrived for lunch, as usual, in his limousine after the lunch hour rush. The maître d' knew he was here to meet with Miguel and directed him to the table by the front window. He made a mental note to change restaurants.

"It is good to see you, my friend." Omar greeted Miguel with his usual hearty handshake.

After a few pleasantries, Omar became quiet and listened as Miguel updated him. Omar asked no questions. He wanted Miguel to think he was still contemplating a decision, but he had already decided to proceed when Dr. Westhoven named Ground Zero as Lake Delta.

Today, his real purpose was to rearrange the sequencing of the lakes. Omar needed Ground Zero or Lake Delta to be the last lake the team would survey.

"Are the professor and his graduate student still available in March?"

"Yes, they are both committed."

Omar surveyed the sun-bleached street as a dark cloud passed overhead. It was quiet this time of day. He wanted to appear contemplative.

Miguel waited.

"Good work Miguel." The cloud passed, and Omar returned his gaze to his business partner. "We will proceed. I will release the funds necessary for Phase Two. Please let Dr. Westhoven know.

"Now, let's review the next phase. The expedition team will be you, a pilot, a diver, Tarek who will manage the base camp, Dr. Westhoven, and his graduate student. I already have Tarek working on a suitable location for the base camp, which we need as low as possible to avoid mountain sickness. I also have hired a pilot and diver. They are all experienced."

The final loose end Omar needed to tie up was Ground Zero or Lake Delta.

"I have looked at the data submitted by Dr. Westhoven. I feel Lake Delta has a lower probability and is far enough from the others that it should be the last to survey."

"That makes sense," replied Miguel.

"Also, I want you on the helicopter with the team as you survey each lake. I need your eyes. Tarek will stay back at the base camp."

"I agree, señor."

"I also noticed that Lake Bravo and Lake Charlie are close together," said Omar. "Perhaps we could survey these two lakes in one day, weather permitting."

"That would certainly help our timetable. As a note on the side, Dr. Westhoven mentioned helicopters lose performance at these altitudes. Is that a concern?"

"The MD600N is lightweight and designed to operate in these altitudes. The HIGE is 3,400 meters, well above the altitude of the base camp."

"Sorry, señor—HIGE?"

"Hover In Ground Effect. This is the highest altitude a helicopter can still hover. Fortunately, we will not need to hover, just take-off and land."

"Sí," said Miguel. "The helicopter appears uniquely suited to our needs."

The helicopter crash from last summer did not come up in conversation.

That night, Miguel replied to Dr. Westhoven's email.

To: Dr. Jerome Westhoven
Date: Tuesday, November 12, 2019
From: Miguel Titere

Subject: Re: Phase Two

Dear Dr. Westhoven,

Good news!

After careful consideration, we will proceed with Phase Two.

I have changed the order of lakes because of their location to base camp. We will visit Lake Echo fourth and then Lake Delta last.

I will pick you up in New Haven and then your graduate student in Bangor, and fly you both directly to Quito, where I will meet you. Then, we all helicopter to the base camp in the Llanganatis.

The dates will be Saturday, March 14 to Sunday, March 22, 2020, to coincide with your break of spring.

Perhaps a brief phone call tomorrow evening at 7p.m. your time is in order. If that is convenient, I will call you.

Sincerely,

Miguel Titere
Antigüedades Sur

Wednesday, November 13, 2019
Phone Call
Bogotá, Colombia - New Haven, Connecticut

"That's great news, Miguel. We're ready to go."

"Wonderful. By the way, after reviewing the map, I'm hoping we can survey Lake Bravo and Lake Charlie in one day, weather permitting. That will give us an extra day if we need it."

Dr. Westhoven already knew how suddenly the weather could turn in the Llanganatis. An extra day might be important.

Miguel checked one last time, "Are there any unique or unusual requests we need for the expedition?"

"How about a bottle of Dom Perignon?" This was the first time Dr. Westhoven had heard Miguel chuckle in a long time.

After the phone call, Dr. Westhoven sent Tom a quick text message.

< You'll need your hat. We're headed to
the Llanganatis. I'll email later. >

Later that evening, he emailed Tom with the details, including the private jet. He also mentioned he had shipped one of the Tritons to Bangor so Tom could become familiar with its operation.

The private jet is a nice touch, thought Tom. Commercial flights to Ecuador were long and miserable. Mr. Titere must be even wealthier than he thought.

When Jenny came back later from her class, he shared the news. They would wait until the weekend to celebrate, as Jenny had a test tomorrow.

And Tom was not sure a trip into the Llanganatis was something to celebrate.

A Hallmark Movie

Friday, December 20, 2019
Bangor Maine

The time between Thanksgiving and Christmas flew by, with the search for gold on autopilot. Tom caught up in his four classes. A Zoom call with Dr. Westhoven last Saturday was the shortest yet, and he confirmed everything was on track.

According to Dr. Westhoven, Mr. Titere had picked a central location in the Llanganatis for the base camp and construction had already begun, by someone. Dr. Westhoven did not know who. Also, because Lake Delta was the farthest from the base camp, Mr. Titere planned to visit it last, flipping it with Lake Echo.

His dad's recovery was also ahead of schedule, and he hired a helper, something his mom had suggested for years. He was busier than ever.

With less than three months to go, there really was nothing for Tom or Jenny to do at this point. He expected his passport any day now. Tom had even started working on the articles for *Modern Archaeology.*

Jenny had her last final this morning and then they were on the road to Amherst for Christmas. This was the first time they'd been back since summer, and her friend Jackie would be home over the holidays, too.

They rolled in about six o'clock. Her mom and dad were waiting with dinner. During dinner, Jenny spent some time updating her parents on her classes, her major and minor, and Tom's master's program, in that order. She left out Tom's trip to the Llanganatis for now.

As Tom unpacked, he felt oddly settled, calm. His mind was quiet for once. The future wasn't so far away anymore. By next summer, they would be millionaires, he dreamed, and both looking forward to the last year of their respective degrees with their whole life ahead together. He wondered if this was what Mr. Gartley meant by staying out of the way of his future. Whatever it was, he liked the feeling, for a change.

Christmas in Vermont—this was a Hallmark movie.

Saturday, December 21, 2019
Amherst, Vermont

They slept in the next morning. Jenny had finished her last final less than twenty-four hours ago and she was exhausted. And no skiing on a Saturday before Christmas—too crowded. Today they planned to focus on Christmas with a little shopping in Ludlow in the morning, baking gingerbread cookies in the afternoon, and enjoying an egg nog before dinner with her parents and Jackie at the Echo Lake Inn. Jenny also stopped in the Tyson Store to say hi to Jeff and Tina, and buy some beer, the first time since she'd turned twenty-one. Jeff added a four-pack of Heady Topper as a late birthday present.

At the Echo Lake Inn, Jenny casually mentioned that Tom was heading to Ecuador in March on an expedition. They both wanted her parents to know, just not the details.

Jenny's dad, as expected, was quite interested. "Where in Ecuador?"

"The Llanganatis National Park." Tom thought using national park sounded more official. "A professor at Yale invited me to join him on an expedition. I feel like I'm earning a merit badge at scout camp. It's for one week during March break. We'll use a helicopter to move about the Llanganatis."

Her dad's eyebrows elevated.

"Interesting. Did you happen to hear about the helicopter crash last summer in the Llanganates? I still follow the on-line newspaper in Colombia, *El Tiempo*. I think it was around August. The helicopter was part of an expedition and crashed on the way back to Quito. There were not many details, but the authorities attributed the crash to pilot error."

Jenny needed to change the subject. The less Tom knew about helicopter crashes, the better. She asked her dad, "That's too bad. What was it like living in Colombia for you and mom? I don't remember too much."

"It was a turbulent time, but we felt safe in the embassy. It's better now. We still have some good friends in Bogotá." He then pivoted back to the expedition. Yale was his alma mater. He wanted to know more about the professor.

"His name is Jerome Westhoven. He was also an undergraduate at Yale and has been on faculty for the last fifteen years or so. I think he's in his early forties."

With a grin, her dad said, "I was there a few years earlier. What's the expedition about?"

"Apparently, Dr. Westhoven has found something interesting on satellite and wants to check it out. I'm helping with the technology part."

The topic of gold never came up, but Tom knew from his past visits to Amherst that her dad was well aware of the Inca legends. Tom also wondered if the helicopter crash was related to the treasure. He would ask Dr. Westhoven on their next Zoom call.

Tom cleared his throat, and Jenny gracefully changed the subject, again. "Hey Jackie, are you back again next summer?"

"That's my plan. What about you guys? You seemed really busy last summer."

"Yeah, we were. We canoed a lot but only camped once on a lake called Nahmakanta." She looked at Tom. "Maybe we could camp again at Nahmakanta next summer. Do you think you'd be up for it?"

He knew exactly what she meant.

❧❦

Christmas
Wednesday, December 25, 2019
Amherst, Vermont

Before Christmas, they were busy with Christmas stuff, so they only skied once at Okemo. They wanted to relax anyway. There would be plenty of skiing after the holidays.

Tom had kept in touch with his mom and dad every day by phone and text messages. His mother lived for Christmas. This was his first Christmas away from home. At Thanksgiving, he showed them how to Zoom call, but it was too much for them. For Christmas, he bought them an Echo Show, but he would need to set it up for them after Christmas.

On Christmas morning, Tom and Jenny gave each other snowshoes and cross-country skis. When downhill skiing was not a good choice, they still enjoyed getting outside but, they had to rent equipment to cross-country or snowshoe.

Even before hearing about the trip to the Llanganatis, Jenny's parents had picked out a Garmin EarthMate satellite device for Tom.

"The EarthMate works anywhere in the world to send an SOS signal with GPS coordinates," said her dad. "There's no cell coverage in the Llanganatis, so this might come in handy."

Tom set it up to text Jenny's dad to try it out. The SOS sent the exact coordinates of their home at Amherst to her dad's phone.

Her mom got Jenny a large non-stick frying pan. "Think of this as Maine humor," she explained. "A good dinner, along with a good whack beside the head every now and then, does wonders for a relationship." She smiled at her husband while pointing to the spot on his temple to whack.

Jenny and Tom gave her parents the *Maine Gazetteer* with a gift certificate to the Phenix Inn in downtown Bangor, along with a list of activities to do together. They hadn't visited Maine since Parent's Weekend her freshman year, and Jenny also wanted them to meet Tom's parents.

⌘

New Year's Eve
Tuesday, December 31, 2019
Amherst, Vermont

Jenny's dad was catching up on some online journals when he noticed a reference to a novel illness in Wuhan, China. Although a new virus in China was a world away, he understood the potential impact of a highly contagious virus like MERS or SARS.

It had been a busy week for Jenny and Tom in between Christmas and New Year's, and they were looking forward to a quiet New Year's Eve. They had traveled to Rutland earlier in the week to buy scallops for dinner and Cold Duck for midnight.

As they watched the ball drop in Times Square, Tom whispered to Jenny, "2019 was the most special year, and I know 2020 will be even specialer."

"Specialer is not a wor..." Tom cut her off with their first kiss of 2020.

⌘

Wednesday, January 8, 2020
Amherst, Vermont

By now, Jenny's parents realized Tom was uncomfortable talking about the expedition. Jenny explained to her mother that he was just anxious about the trip, so her parents only touched on it tangentially.

At dinner that evening, her dad asked how many were going on the expedition. Tom said he wasn't sure, but he continued to describe it as a Boy Scout camp.

"So," Jenny asked, looking directly at Tom, "a trip into the mountains to one of the most remote regions in the world to earn a merit badge?"

"Probably more than one. I may make Eagle Scout yet." Tom cleared his throat with an awkward smile.

Time to change the subject. Jenny knew her dad was a *New York Times* junkie. "Hey Daddy, anything interesting in the *Times* today? What's going on in Iran?"

"The usual Trump mess. The Dunning-Kruger effect strikes again," he said, shaking his head from side to side.

Neither Tom nor Jenny knew what the Dunning-Kruger effect was, but they were not going to disagree with her dad. They would google it later.

"Anything new with the virus in China?" Jenny asked.

"Not a lot. There are still no reported deaths, but it keeps on spreading. There's another case in South Korea. Certainly something to monitor."

No one at the table imagined the impact that COVID would have all over the world, except perhaps Jenny's dad.

Just before bed, Tom and Jenny googled "Donny Kruger." On Wikipedia they found…

The Dunning–Kruger effect is a hypothetical cognitive bias stating that people with low ability at a task overestimate their ability.

All he could do was mumble, "Ayuh."
"Ayuh, indeed," she replied.

They were heading back to Bangor tomorrow, and Jackie was already on her way back to Occidental. The expedition was now only nine weeks away, with the next Zoom call with Dr. Westhoven in a few weeks.

School didn't start for another couple of weeks, and they looked forward to celebrating Christmas again with Tom's parents in Limerock, seeing Joe and Lynda, spending some quiet time in Bangor, and a couple of days at Sugarloaf with Dave and Amanda.

After a year of hustle and bustle, it was eerily relaxing.

Triton

Friday, January 10, 2020
Bangor, Maine

Yesterday, on the way back to Bangor, Tom received a text message from the storage unit that a large package had arrived.

"Do you want to check out the Triton before we head to Limerock?" he asked Jenny.

"Sure. I'd love to see what a $55,000 torpedo looks like."

"It's only $50,000 with the discount. Remember, Mr. Titere bought six."

Tom was careful to preserve the packing material and container as they needed to ship the Triton to Miguel Titere at Antigüedades Sur in Bogotá when they were done.

Once Tom had it out on the floor of the storage container, it looked bigger than Jenny expected, weighing about thirty-five pounds. Tom thumbed through the documentation and handed it to her.

"This looks like fun reading," she said. Tom knew she meant it.

The satellite uplink, which arrived in a separate, well-padded container, was a deep blue cube about one foot on a side with a white wave logo. A separate fifteen-inch diameter satellite mesh antenna plugged into the top of the cube. Together, the cube and satellite dish weighed about fifteen pounds.

Tom said, "It looks like another trip to the Wave Tank to try it out. So much for a mental break."

"You still have a couple of months before scout camp. I'll read up on the satellite uplink and you focus on the Triton. You'll have to wait for Dave to come back anyway to access the Wave Tank. We can still enjoy the next couple of weeks."

They made the trip to Limerock for a late Christmas. The Echo Show might actually work. They didn't make it out to the CBI, but they did take in a dinner and a movie with Joe and Lynda.

Back at the apartment in Bangor, Tom, not so innocently, said to Jenny, "Lynda looks like a 'keepah.'"

"More Maine humor?"

"It a reference to lobst..."

"I know what it means. It's just a little demeaning. What if I said you're a keeper?"

"But I am...."

Jenny, wearing a smile, started opening kitchen cabinet doors and asked, "Where's my new frying pan from Christmas?"

They rarely argued. The only standing disagreement between them now was what to do with the millions if they found the gold. He still didn't think they'd find any. Jenny found his Eeyore attitude tiresome, but even she acknowledged it was a long shot.

But if they did find the gold, Tom wanted to spend it while Jenny wanted to save it for a rainy day. He kept reminding her, "It does rain a lot in Maine."

While Jenny was still looking for the frying pan, Tom stood up, held his head high, cleared his throat, and puffed out his chest. "You know, sometimes I feel like Valverde. After all, I fell in love with a princess, and I will almost certainly find the Inca gold, just like Valverde."

By now, Jenny had found the frying pan, and Tom was on the run. He needed to hide the pan, which Jenny had yet to use for its actual purpose.

೩⊷೯

Thursday, January 23, 2020
Bangor Maine

The spring semester had started on Monday, and Tom had his monthly meeting with Dr. Wade today. Even though they often ran into each other coming and going from the apartment, they'd agreed to keep academics separate.

Tom reaffirmed to Dr. Wade he was on the expedition to the Llanganatis during the March break with Dr. Westhoven but wouldn't miss any classes.

COVID was still a distant problem. The president continued to reassure the public, although Dr. Fauci, a grandfatherly fixture at press conferences who was director of the National Institute of Allergy and Infectious Diseases, seemed more concerned. Regardless, Tom didn't think COVID would affect the expedition.

೩⊷೯

Saturday, January 25, 2020
Wave Tank
The University of Maine
Orono, Maine

On the first Saturday of the new semester, they met Dave and Amanda outside the Wave Tank. The satellite dish needed a clear line of sight to the satellite for a stable broadband connection. It took Jenny about thirty minutes to establish a stable connection, but once set up, she could view real-time video and sonar from the Triton in the Wave Tank. They also tried the Triton with waves, and it worked perfectly.

Dave, of course, brought his bodyboard. The waves were his cue. Amanda had given him a wet suit for Christmas, so he lasted a little longer this time.

೩⊷೯

Saturday, February 1, 2020
Zoom Call
New Haven, Connecticut - Bangor, Maine

This was the first Zoom call since December and it was now only six weeks until the expedition. Dr. Westhoven reaffirmed the travel plans. They would meet Miguel in Quito and then they would all helicopter to the base camp in the Llanganatis. They would be at base camp by late afternoon.

"Miguel has selected the team. Besides you and me, there will be a pilot, a diver, and Miguel, along with a base camp manager who has been getting everything set up for the expedition," explained Dr. Westhoven.

"Do you know the location of the base camp?" asked Tom.

"Yes, Miguel shared that with me last week. I'll send along the coordinates." He tapped a few keys. "It's only about 3,000 feet long, but still larger than the five lakes we will visit. It's in the eastern part of the park at about 8,500 feet. The risk of high-altitude illness is low, but I'm going to take the acetazolamide for a couple of days to be on the safe side. Miguel will have some for you too on the Gulfstream."

"Do you think I should take it?"

"Yeah. Even a headache and malaise might affect our performance. Acetazolamide is safe."

"Makes sense. By the way, professor, did you hear about a helicopter crash last summer in the Llanganatis?"

He had been expecting Tom to ask some questions about the helicopter, but he did not realize that Tom was aware of the crash.

"Yes, I did. Miguel mentioned it to me. Luis Alvarez was leading the expedition, a former partner of Andrés Fernández-Salvador. The article I read online attributed the crash to pilot error. Remember, we've an experienced pilot, and our helicopter does not have a tail rotor."

"What was the purpose of the expedition?" asked Jenny.

"Although the article didn't say so, I suspect they were also looking for the Inca gold."

Everyone was quiet for a moment. This was the first time they had directly confronted the dangers of the expedition.

Tom finally asked, "I remember we talked about our helicopter. Do you have any more details?"

Dr. Westhoven then started his prepared narrative to reassure Tom. "It's an MD600N made by MD Helicopters. It vents the exhaust out of the tail instead of using a tail rotor, which gives it a better safety record. It also makes sense not to have a tail rotor bobbing up and down on the waves.

"It performs well at high altitude and is quieter without a tail rotor. Miguel retrofitted it specifically for the expedition."

Dr. Westhoven turned to look at Jenny. He wanted to move on from helicopters. "I'm sure we'll talk again before the expedition, but Jenny, I want to thank you again for all your help. You've been instrumental in moving the project forward."

"Thank you, Dr. Westhoven. This has been exhilarating. I only wish I could go with you to the Llanganatis."

Dr. Westhoven just smiled. "Okay, I think everything's on track. Let's connect one more time in a couple of weeks, and as always, if you run into any bumps, let me know. And keep an eye on COVID. We don't want anything derailing the expedition at the last moment."

"Where's the rest of the team coming from?" asked Tom, knowing that COVID was spreading rapidly in certain parts of the world.

"I'm not sure, but I'll mention to Miguel to keep COVID in mind. Perhaps he needs a contingency plan in case someone gets sick."

Tom felt a little reassured that Dr. Westhoven did not seem too rattled by the helicopter crash last summer. He googled the MD600N and found its technical specifications. Two odd acronyms caught his eye, the HIGE or Hover In Ground Effect, and HOGE or Hover Off Ground Effect. He didn't realize there were limits to a helicopter hovering. The HIGE is 11,100 feet above sea level for the MD600N. Above that altitude, the helicopter could not hover. Most of the mountain lakes they would explore were higher than the HIGE, but Tom assumed it would not be an issue as they would not be hovering, only landing and taking off.

He opened the map Dr. Westhoven had sent. The base camp was sited on the eastern shore of a small lake. Like most of the remote lakes in the Llanganatis, it had no name on the map.

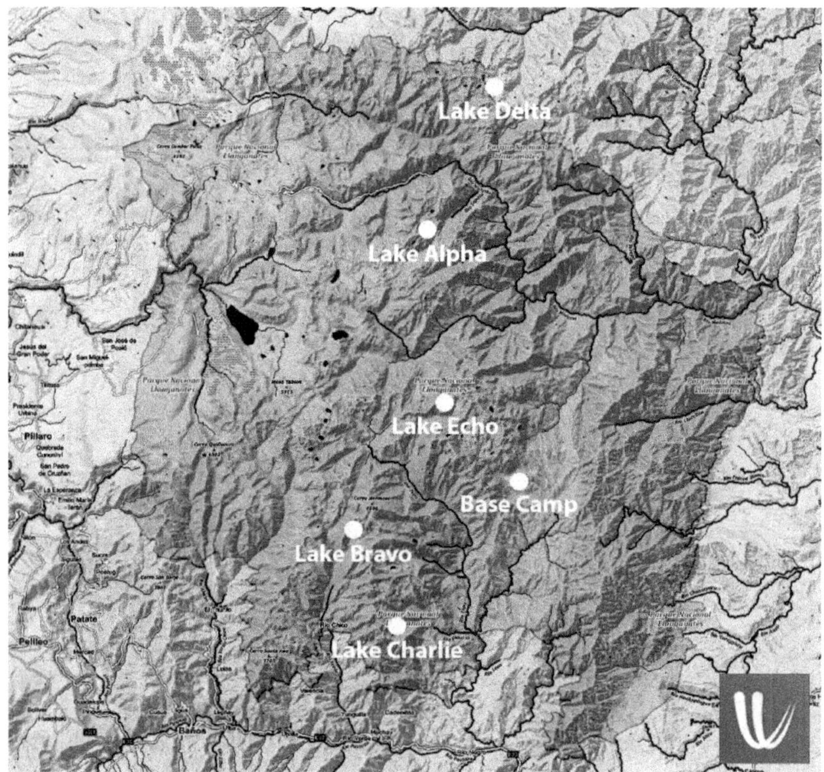

© www.windy.com

President's Day
Monday, February 17, 2020
Bangor, Maine

Two weeks later, COVID was having a significant impact in certain spots around the country, particularly in Washington state and New York. Despite warnings from the World Health Organization and the CDC, the president still appeared confident that COVID was under control.

The Zoom call with Dr. Westhoven on Saturday was uneventful. Everything was on track.

Four weeks until the Llanganatis.

❧❦

Saturday, March 7, 2020
Bangor, Maine

It was one week before Tom would board the Gulfstream to Ecuador. Jenny noticed he was quieter than usual. She suggested they go for a run. It was chilly but no wind. About ten minutes into the run, crossing the Penobscot Bridge over to Brewer, she finally asked, "Hey Roomy, what's up? Why so quiet?" She wondered if his fear of flying was catching up with him.

"Oh, I'm just thinking about my merit badges. It's weird heading into one of the most remote regions in the world without knowing more about the expedition. And I'm concerned about COVID. It seems out of control. I could tell from your dad's tone of voice on your FaceTime with them last week."

"Yeah, I know. But Dr. Westhoven will be there. He's been to the Llanganatis before. He knows what he's doing. Think about a new F-150 when you find the gold."

"Or maybe a Corvette."

"Yeah, a Corvette would be a fun ride on the Jo-Mary Road into Nahmakanta. I don't think it would make it out of some of those potholes."

COVID

Wednesday, March 11, 2020
Fogler Library
The University of Maine
Orono, Maine

Tom's watch buzzed. It was 9:15 a.m. He had a text message from Dr. Westhoven.

< I have COVID. Call ASAP. >

Dr. Westhoven was the seventh confirmed case of COVID-19 in Connecticut. It was three days before he and Tom were to fly to Quito.

Tom was in Fogler Library. He closed his laptop and quickly found an empty room and closed the door. He sat down at an oak table beneath the window and composed himself. It was supposed to snow this afternoon and then turn to freezing rain. The overcast sky darkened the room. A draft by the window gave him a chill.

Dr. Westhoven's voice was raspy, and he sounded short of breath. He was coughing.

"Tom—I'm so sorry. I've let you and the team down. I should have been more careful. I was probably exposed at an event in New York City last week." He coughed again. "My symptoms started yesterday. I just received my test results a few minutes ago. I can't smell, and this cough won't stop."

Tom could hear him take a deep breath.

"I don't know what will happen with the expedition, but I wanted you to know first. I'm calling Miguel as soon as we hang up. He's invested so much time and money."

"You sound sick. Have you seen a doctor?"

"I have an appointment later this morning. Let me call Miguel, and I'll get back to you. Sorry Tom...."

Tom placed his iPhone on the table and opened his laptop. He did not want to deal with this right now. He finished reading the article he'd started when Dr. Westhoven texted. The University of Maine System had announced all classes after spring break would be online due to COVID.

He needed to let Jenny know. She was on the other side of campus, waiting for her ten o'clock class, when Tom sent her a text.

< Dr. Westhoven has COVID. He is talking with Miguel now. Not sure what will happen.>

< You're going to need help. You can't go alone. >

< I know. >

Tom wasn't expecting a reply, so when his watch buzzed, he assumed it was Dr. Westhoven. Then he heard Don Campbell.

< Why don't I go? >

< That is not a good idea. >

His iPhone buzzed. It was Jenny.

"Why not? I know the routine. I'm in shape. Anything I don't know, you can teach me. I want a merit badge, too."

"No Jenny. This entire project has been a waste of time. We will not find any gold. And I don't know what to expect in the Llanganatis. I don't want to put you at risk, too."

"What are you talking about? You told me this is scout camp. You're getting a merit badge. What's going on?"

"I'm going into one of the most remote regions in the world with a group of people I've never met except for Dr. Westhoven, and now he's not going. This was already weird, and now that Dr. Westhoven is sick, I really don't know what to expect. Mr. Titere needs to postpone the expedition."

His chair squeaked as he turned about to see the storm clouds gathering in the distance.

After a moment, Jenny replied, "You said March was a golden window. That this is about the only time of year you might get a few days of decent weather to fly a helicopter."

She must be in an empty classroom, as she echoed on speakerphone.

"Jenny, it's not my call. I appreciate you wanting to help, but it's not worth it."

The echo emphasized her hardening voice. "You and I have both put too much into this to let it slip away." Tom heard her voice getting louder. "This is not about the Llanganatis. You're worried about failing, that your stupid program doesn't work. Get over it!"

All her frustrations with Tom and his Eeyore attitude spilled out. "You need to see this through. <u>We</u> need to see this through."

She took a deep breath. "Please tell Dr. Westhoven I'm willing and able to join the team, and then he and Mr. Titere can make the call."

She took Tom off speakerphone and slowed down. "And I do <u>not</u> like being patronized. I'm as capable as you. We have both worked too hard to let this fall apart. Do the right thing for once. Grow up!"

Tom hung up.

He had never done that before. He would have slammed the phone down, but you can't slam an iPhone.

And he felt the start of his beet head.

Sitting in the cold musty room staring at the dark clouds didn't help. It started to spit snow. He gathered his stuff and started walking to the Pizza Palace. He still had a key.

⁂ᾷ⁖

Phone Call

New Haven, Connecticut - Bogotá, Colombia

"Disturbing, yes, disturbing, señor. Please tell me, what are our options do you think?" asked Miguel.

"Tom can pilot the Zodiac. But he can't go alone." Dr. Westhoven coughed and took a moment to catch his breath. "He needs an extra set of hands to handle the GPS and deploy the Triton."

"What if we have Mr. Tom focus on getting the diver to the target and forget scanning the lake? Would that work?"

Before he could answer, Dr. Westhoven received a text message.

"Hang on, Miguel. I just received a text from the woman who has been helping Tom. She was his extra set of hands."

Dr. Westhoven coughed again while he read the text.

"Miguel, she's willing to go, and I can vouch for her competency. Her name is Jenny, and she also lives in Bangor."

"So, how would this work?"

"Tom would replace me and pilot the Zodiac. Jenny would manage the Triton and be the extra set of hands."

"Is this the woman who signed the NDA? Do you think Mr. Tom can get her ready by Saturday?"

"Yes, I'm sure he can." More coughing.

"Okay. Let me think. You say she lives in Bangor, so we can pick her up with Mr. Tom. Please confirm she has a passport and have Mr. Tom and the woman stand by. I will decide quickly.

"By the way, you do not sound well, Professor. Please take care of yourself."

This was obviously not his call, but Miguel wanted all the information and options before talking with Omar. He had already texted him that Dr. Westhoven had COVID, and that he would call him in a few minutes.

Dr. Westhoven sent Tom and Jenny a quick text message.

< Jenny, thanks for stepping up. Miguel contemplating options. Jenny do you have a passport? >

< Yes. >

She must have texted Dr. Westhoven directly. Tom sent Jenny a text.

< I'm staying at the Pizza Palace tonight. >

< Enjoy your pizza. >

❧✦

Phone Call
Bogotá, Colombia - Cartagena, Colombia

Omar was unnervingly quiet when Miguel explained the situation and that Dr. Westhoven had recommended a woman as the extra set of hands.

"I think she is our best option. She has been involved from the beginning. She signed the NDA with the graduate student, and Dr. Westhoven thought she would be a capable replacement."

After what felt like an eternity, Omar finally spoke. "Proceed with the girl." He knew if they did not move forward this weekend, it could be months before they had another opportunity with the weather. Omar was also concerned about the spread of COVID around the world, which might impact their ability to mount an expedition later.

Noon time
Pizza Palace
Orono, Maine

Pat's was busy with the lunchtime crowd. A storm warning was in effect for this afternoon and the University had canceled classes. Word was also spreading. The University was going remote after the spring break due to COVID.

Tom headed up the stairs to the Pizza Palace. He brushed off the snow. Even though he had a key, he knocked. Both Dave and Amanda answered.

"Hey Tom, what's up?" asked Dave.

"Can I crash here tonight?"

"Let me guess. Jenny wants to do something either fun or spontaneous, and you don't."

"It's not that simple, Dave."

"Sometimes it is, Tom."

1:00 p.m.
Bangor, Maine

Jenny was angry, but more disappointed—disappointed in Tom. It was a miserable day, and the weather predicted freezing rain this afternoon, which would make driving difficult, so she headed back to Bangor after her class in the F-150 without him.

She thought he was dealing better with his control issues.

"There's no reason I shouldn't go," she said to herself on the way back to the apartment. "He needs to grow up."

As soon as she dumped her gear on the kitchen table, she felt the need to get out of the apartment. She didn't feel like a run, so she went for a walk. The streetlights flickered on and off, trying to make up their mind, as she crossed the park to Broadway.

They rarely fought, but this was a fight worth having.

She was walking down State Street hill when she received a group text from an unidentified phone number that included Tom and Dr. Westhoven.

> < Miss Jenny. This is Miguel Titere. Nice to meet you by text. Thank you for helping. I look forward to meeting you. We will pick you up with Tom. Please contact him for instructions. Let me know if you have questions. >

> < Thank you Mr. Titere. I have already been in contact with Tom. See you Saturday. >

> < Please call me Miguel. >

Dr. Westhoven then sent a text to Jenny and Tom.

> < Thanks again Jenny. Miguel does not know you are a couple. I will let you two decide how to handle that. I know you can do this. I'm headed to the hospital as a precaution. It may be hard to reach me but please keep me posted. >

> < Thanks - take care of yourself. >

It started to snow, so she turned back to the apartment.

❧

1:00 p.m.
Pizza Palace
Orono, Maine

Tom finished a slice of pizza with Dave and Amanda. He wasn't hungry. He was quiet. It was weird to be back at the Pizza Palace.

Dave or Amanda didn't comment on his flushed face. Usually, his beet head lasted a half-hour or so, but it had been a few hours since the phone call.

Dave winced as Amanda asked, "What happened? Does this have anything to do with the project you guys have been working on for the last year?"

It took Tom a moment to respond. He couldn't share much about the actual project. "Yeah, the leader of the expedition has COVID and can't make the trip. Jenny volunteered to go."

"That sounds great."

"I said no."

"Why?"

"This entire project has been a waste of time. I can't get into the details, but this was the last straw."

The only sound was Dave chewing.

Amanda started to speak again. Dave, looking directly at her, slowly shook his head from side to side, but it didn't matter. Jenny was her friend.

"I don't know what this is about, but this feels stupid. Jenny is a very capable person. You should be delighted she wants to join you. But, like I said, I don't know what this is really about."

Dave stopped chewing and stared at a pepperoni.

"This isn't about Jenny being capable."

Dave started chewing again.

"I'm going for a walk. Thanks for letting me crash here tonight." Tom grabbed his coat and headed down the stairs.

He was upset with Jenny. But he was also upset with himself, and he wasn't sure why.

Heavy snowflakes covered the sidewalk. The freezing rain was supposed to start by midafternoon. Tom liked the snow, but nobody liked freezing rain. All it took was a quarter inch of ice and driving became impossible. Hopefully, Jenny was already back at the apartment.

As he walked, he realized most of his reservations about the project stemmed from his control issues. He was a capable programmer, but how was he supposed to train a neural network with yellow plastic gold? Even with all the mystery of the black box of the VGG-16, his neural networks had always learned, until now. This was a mess.

From the beginning, this was a slow spiral out of control, but Dr. Westhoven was always so upbeat, so supportive. Without him along, Tom lost whatever enthusiasm he had left for the trip.

He had walked about half an hour when the rain started, just a little, but it would get worse and eventually turn to freezing rain. He headed back to the Pizza Palace. By the time he made it back, he was soaked.

"You look like a wet rat. Jump in the shower to warm up and put on some of my clothes. And don't drip all over the place," said Dave. The Pizza Palace was clean, much cleaner than when he lived there.

His old bedroom was barren except for an exercise bike. Tom grabbed some of Dave's stuff and headed into the shower. He always loved that shower. It had a hot forceful flow, and he always felt squeaky clean afterwards. It was a perfect place to reflect and unwind.

But not today—the shower had the same good flow, and he warmed up quickly, squeaky clean, but with no pleasant reflective thoughts. He was consumed by his insecurities, the futility of the expedition, and losing control, and maybe Jenny. Hanging up on her was childish. He knew that, but he felt trapped. She did not always make it easy.

Drying off in his old bedroom was even weirder. He hadn't slept here in months. He didn't belong here. He was not one for epiphanies. He usually needed to think everything through, but he knew what he had to do.

❧

1:45 p.m.
Bangor, Maine

She made it back to the apartment just before the rain started, but she was still a little wet from the light snow. She had some tea to warm up, but she didn't feel any better.

Tom is so damn stubborn. Everything has to be his way. It was frustrating.

But this is his project.

What was I thinking? Sure, Tom needs to take a few chances now and then, but I really don't know what I'm getting into. Only Tom does. I was not always part of the conversation about the actual expedition.

But if this is risky, I want to go more than ever.

But—this is his project.

❧

2:00 p.m.
Orono, Maine

Tom didn't even bother to check. The Community Connector, the bus from Orono to Bangor, always ran, even in freezing rain. He borrowed a slicker from Dave and headed to Main Street to the bus stop. This was the first time Tom had ridden the Connector.

Dave's slicker wasn't warm enough, but fortunately, the bus was on schedule. On the ride down Route 2 to Bangor, he received a text from Dr. Westhoven.

< Hey Tom I'm in the hospital on oxygen. It
makes it hard to talk so I sent you an email
you should read today. >

< Are you okay? >

< I think so. The oxygen helps my breathing
but it is loud. Let me know if you have any
questions after you read the email. >

Tom opened the email on his iPhone. The bumpy ride made it a little difficult to read.

To: Tom Kirkpatrick
Date: Wednesday, March 11, 2020
From: Dr. Jerome Westhoven

Subject: Llanganatis

Dear Tom,

Here are some last-minute thoughts before you leave for the Llanganatis.

You are replacing me, and Jenny is replacing you. You are now the lead on the water.

Pay particular attention to the weather. You cannot always see the micro weather on the radar. It can change quickly, and it is different throughout the Llanganatis. Altitude matters. It can be a clear day in the forest but foggy in a mountain valley.

I know there will be no cell signal, but I'll be thinking of you.

*I'm so fortunate to have shared this journey with you
and Jenny over the last year, and I'm sorry I won't be
there with you. I am confident you will be perfectly
capable of leading the expedition on the water.*

Good luck.

Sincerely,

*Jerome Westhoven, PhD
Council on Archaeological Studies
Yale University*

☙❧

2:45 p.m.
Bangor, Maine

When Jenny opened the door to the apartment, Tom grabbed
her for a kiss before she could say anything. Then they both
started to apologize.

"Jenny, I'm sorry. I don't know what we're heading into,
but if this is happening, I want to do this with you. It just felt so
out of control with Dr. Westhoven getting COVID."

"I'm sorry too. Jumping on the expedition was wrong. We
should have talked this through first. I'm glad you came home.
Let's get you out of these clothes. Are these Dave's? How did
you get here?"

"The bus."

"Wow. By the way, I don't think your program is stupid."
Another quick hug and a kiss before Tom could respond. She
gently bit her lower lip. "Now, let's get you warmed up."

He was chilled again, but this time, he had company in
the shower. He took his time warming up.

Afterwards, when Jenny wasn't looking, he hid the frying
pan, just in case.

☙❧

Friday, March 13, 2020
Bangor, Maine

President Trump started daily press conferences about COVID. Dr. Fauci, standing behind him, seemed to be trying his best not to cringe. President Trump was still confident things would turn around quickly.

    Donny Kruger, thought Tom.

Quito

Friday, March 13, 2020
Bangor, Maine

The last couple of days had been a blur, getting Jenny up to speed. She was already familiar with the Triton—she'd taught Tom—so they spent most of the time reviewing how to interpret sonar images from the Triton.

Tom had also created a simple neural network he called SonarSeer to detect anomalies in the sonar images to reduce the time to review all the Triton images in the Llanganatis.

By Friday, she was ready. Tom was amazed how quickly she picked up reading the sonar. He, on the other hand, was still not comfortable in his new role. He had a lot to learn, and quickly.

Yesterday, Jenny had notified her parents she was a replacement on the expedition, and she would not be home for spring break. Tonight, they were going to FaceTime with them.

Also yesterday, the first COVID-19 case in Maine was diagnosed.

Earlier in the week, Miguel had sent Tom a list of essentials to bring. Miguel highlighted the rain gear. He suggested two pairs of boots, two jackets and two pairs of pants, all with Gortex. Gloves, again two pairs, should also be waterproof.

As they finished packing, Jenny said, "This is way easier than packing for Nahmakanta. And no dirt road. By the way, have you seen my frying pan?"

Tom had forgotten he'd hidden it. "I don't think you'll need it in the Llanganatis."

"No, but I keep it by the batteries in the kitchen."

"It'll turn up."

❧❧

7:30 p.m.

FaceTime

Bangor, Maine - Amherst, Vermont

They were at the kitchen table for the FaceTime call with her parents. Before the call, Jenny had spent half an hour arranging and rearranging everything in the kitchen to spruce up the background image.

Jenny started the call. Her mom and dad were in the living room. She could hear the crackling fire.

"What happened?" asked her dad. In the self-view, Tom noticed Jenny was wide-eyed.

"Hey, Daddy. Dr. Westhoven, the professor from Yale, developed COVID. I've been helping Tom from the beginning, so I volunteered to go. This'll be the experience of a lifetime."

Tom added, "We're looking for the lost Inca gold in a man-made lake described in the first sentence of the Derrotero. Jenny and I signed nondisclosure agreements, which is why we couldn't tell you before.

"I developed a neural network to look for gold underwater using satellite images. It took months to train, but eventually, it did detect some anomalies. The neural network chose the top five lakes in the Llanganatis, and the expedition is to survey these lakes. There'll be no trekking. We'll travel by helicopter, specially outfitted for the expedition. Jenny and I'll be working closely together."

Her dad leaned forward. "Who is financing the expedition?"

Jenny answered this time. "His name is Miguel Titere, an antiquities dealer in Bogotá. He calls his business Antiquities South."

Her parents looked concerned, something Tom hadn't seen before.

After a moment, her mom spoke. "Why doesn't Mr. Titere postpone the expedition until Dr. Westhoven is healthy?"

Tom replied, "March is the optimal month for weather, particularly the wind, in the Llanganatis."

Her father was quiet. He had been slowly rubbing his chin. He leaned back and looked up past the video camera to the frozen lake.

Her mom finally said, "Well, Jenny, it's clear you want to go."

Jenny nodded.

Her dad's gaze returned. "Take care of yourselves. Although the Llanganatis is a national park, there are still places where people don't come out unscathed. The weather is so fickle. Just be careful and keep us posted."

"We will, Daddy, but there's no cell signal in the Llanganatis. The whole expedition is only a week. We'll be in and out before you know it."

Tom also reassured them that the base camp had been set up and was managed by a professional guide.

Her dad then added, "There's a medication called acetazolamide or Diamox that prevents high altitude illness. I can get you both a prescription."

"Thanks Daddy, but we're all set. We start the medication in the morning."

Another awkward silence. Then her mother said, "Your kitchen looks nice. Maybe when you get back, you can give us a virtual tour of your apartment."

"Sure thing Mom."

"Okay, Jenny. Love you," said her mom with a wave goodbye.

Her dad added, again, "Please be careful, both of you."

"We will. I'll let you guys know when we're done as soon as I get a cell signal."

Fortunately, they did not ask for the location of the five lakes or base camp. Tom had decided before the call he could not, in good faith, share the coordinates, and Jenny agreed.

After the call, Tom felt a little guilty for not sharing the same information with his parents.

Tomorrow, the Gulfstream would pick them up at eight o'clock in the morning at the International Terminal in Bangor.

❦

Saturday, March 14, 2020
Bangor, Maine

Neither slept well that night. The sudden illness of Dr. Westhoven had cast a pall over the expedition. As much as he tried to suppress it, Tom was still worried that Jenny was coming along, and he had a leadership role he didn't want or deserve.

If he had tried to create a perfect storm, this was it. Heading into the Llanganatis with a group of people he did not know, looking for something underwater that probably did not exist, all based upon a neural network trained with yellow plastic that probably did not work—FUBAR.

They were both up early. It was a beautiful day. Tom pictured Dave and Amanda enjoying a day of spring skiing at Sugarloaf. They made it to the airport in plenty of time. Although both the domestic and international terminals were modest, the runway was over two miles long, a leftover from the former Dow Air Force Base. Neither of them had flown on a private jet or gone through the International Terminal. Mr. Titere had told them to pass through security and then head to the International Terminal to wait for a text message with further instructions.

At 7:47 a.m., Tom received a text from an unknown number.

< The Gulfstream will arrive in ten minutes.
Please meet me at Gate I-2. >

Tom thought a thumbs up emoji would
be too informal.

< Ok. >

In five minutes, they watched a small white jet land and taxi to the International Terminal. They watched the airstairs lower and the pilot disembark and quickly head for the terminal. He was not dressed for the cold in his crisp uniform. A few minutes later, he introduced himself at Gate I-2 and helped them with their gear.

They followed the pilot up the airstairs, and an attractive flight attendant greeted them in front of the galley and wood-paneled bar. She paid a little too much attention to Tom, that resulted in an elbow from Jenny when the attendant turned away.

They settled into reclining leather chairs in the aft cabin, which had a little more room to stretch out for the six-hour flight. The flight attendant mentioned once they were airborne, there would be a light breakfast and lunch later as they neared South America. Beverages would also be available soon after takeoff.

For the first time, Tom and Jenny understood the full extent of the wealth behind the expedition.

Once airborne, the attendant provided some coffee and offered a white round pill stamped with T53 to each of them. "I believe Mr. Titere mentioned this pill. It is *acetazolamida* or acetazolamide. I believe that is how you pronounce it in English, to prevent sickness in the mountains. If you choose, you will need to take it for two days." She seemed to ignore Jenny.

Tom looked at the small white pill and swallowed it.

After the attendant left, Jenny said, "That's the fastest I've ever seen you take a pill. And you seemed to have lost your fear of flying." She looked back at the flight attendant and then directly at Tom.

"I'm not afraid of flying." Tom left it at that.

"So, how does this pill work?" she finally asked.

"It causes a mild metabolic acidosis, and you breathe a little faster. The pill has a couple of weird side effects. It can cause some tingling in your fingertips and carbonated beverages taste flat. When we stop the pill, the side effects will go away quickly. Otherwise, nothing serious."

"What's a metabolic acidosis?"

Tom laughed. "I don't have a clue. I thought you'd be impressed I even knew that."

Jenny popped the pill.

For the first time since Jenny joined the expedition, he felt relaxed in the posh leather seat, almost sleepy. He wondered if it was the pill.

On the flight, he explained to her the connection between Dr. Westhoven and Miguel Titere. Jenny knew Mr. Titere was a dealer in pre-Colombian artifacts, but she didn't know the prior connection with Dr. Westhoven to authenticate pieces for museums or private buyers.

Tom then returned to the expedition. He needed Jenny to be as prepared as possible. "Let's review the on-lake protocol. There are still details I don't know, but Mr. Titere will brief the entire team tonight.

"The helicopter will land about a hundred feet away from the target to avoid stirring up the lake bottom. I'll disengage the Zodiac from the helicopter and navigate it to the precise location using the GPS/GLONASS. You'll drop the guideline over the exact spot, which will also anchor the Zodiac. The diver follows the guideline down and finds the gold." Tom tried to suppress a grin.

"A smirk is not becoming on you," she said.

"Whether or not we find gold, we'll still scan each lake with the Triton. You'll be responsible for setting up the satellite uplink and launching the Triton. The antenna needs to be on the southern shore for line of sight to the geosynchronous Zheng satellite. I'll take you there in the Zodiac. The first uplink on Lake Alpha will probably take more time, but once you find the azimuth and altitude to the satellite, the other four lakes should be quicker."

Back in Bangor, Jenny had already identified the best location on the southern shore for each lake using Peakfinder.org. She would still have to establish the actual satellite uplink on each lake, something she had only done once before in January at the Wave Tank.

Tom continued, "The Triton scan will take about eight to twelve hours for each lake, depending on the size of the lake, and another four to five hours to process the images. We won't get a good look at the data until the following evening, unless there is a day off because of the weather."

The flight passed quickly. There was not much to see out the windows except the ocean. The flight attendant served them a light lunch as they crossed the Caribbean. She mentioned Ecuador was one hour earlier with daylight savings time and suggested now would be a good time to set their watches back if they did not automatically adjust.

An hour and a half later, as they landed in Quito, overcast skies prevented them from seeing much of the city on approach. Jenny sent her parents a quick text that they had landed and she would let them know as soon as the expedition was over.

It was a busy airport, and the Gulfstream quickly taxied to a small hangar near the end of the runway where Mr. Titere met them. Tom had never met or talked with him. Everything had always been through Dr. Westhoven.

Miguel introduced himself and thanked them for all they had done to get to this point. He was a bit effusive, particularly thanking Jenny for stepping up at the last moment. He insisted they call him Miguel.

He was smaller and rounder than Tom had pictured. He did not look at all like the outdoors type. His khaki outfit looked directly from the pages of an L.L. Bean catalog, including his Tilley hat. Jenny whispered to Tom that the base camp must be "luxurious" if Mr. Titere was going to survive.

Miguel gave them a quick update on Dr. Westhoven. "As you know, he was hospitalized Wednesday afternoon, but he said it is more of a precaution. I talked with him yesterday. He could take off his oxygen for a few minutes. He was in good spirits and wants to be informed during the expedition."

Tom's phone call with Dr. Westhoven on Wednesday had sounded more dire. Perhaps he was on the mend.

"The only communication, however, will be through satellite phone, but I will inform the professor when we find something."

Miguel helped them with their gear and then through customs, which was perfunctory.

The last leg to base camp was by helicopter. Outside the hangar, a helicopter balanced on oversized pontoons was waiting for them. There was no tail rotor, as Dr. Westhoven had described. There was also no pilot.

As Miguel helped them stow their gear into the rear of the helicopter, he explained, "This is a MD600N. Originally, it was built for eight passengers, but I had it retrofitted for six. It has a payload capacity of 1,000 kilograms, more than enough for the expedition."

Tom asked him about the lack of a tail rotor.

"It is called NOTAR—NO TAil Rotor. Vented exhaust replaces the tail rotor. This was the one feature that sold me on this helicopter. In rough water, a tail rotor could bob up and down, causing an injury. It is also quieter."

The helicopter was a green-blue camouflage, including on top of the pontoons, which Tom thought odd. Perhaps this had been a military helicopter in a prior service. Standing beside the camouflage helicopter with a pontoon up to his waist, Miguel looked like a caricature of Indiana Jones in his khaki outfit.

Miguel continued, pointing to a pontoon. "Each pontoon has attachments for the Zodiac here and here, and attachments for the Tritons here and here. We will always bring two Tritons to each lake to have a backup, one on each pontoon."

Tom could tell he was proud of the enhancements to the helicopter.

"The MD600N has enough room to move the entire team in and out of the Llanganatis."

Tom also noticed a shiny attachment on the rear of the cockpit on the starboard side. It was clearly an add-on, with hinges that allowed it to swing out past the pontoon. Tom went over to get a closer look.

"Miguel, is this a hoist?"

"Yes. I installed it in case we need to pull something up, like gold. It can lift about one hundred kilograms."

Tom did the math, a little over two hundred pounds.

As they finished stowing their gear, a younger man approached. He looked a little scruffy, but in a reassuring way. Miguel briefly introduced Paikea, the pilot, but said there would be more formal introductions that evening once they settled into base camp. "The diver and base camp manager are already in the Llanganatis," said Miguel.

Paikea adroitly climbed into the pilot seat on the right side. "Good day, mate. Welcome aboard and buckle up," he said with a Kiwi accent.

Miguel continued. "It will be about one hour of flight time to base camp. Jenny, if you please, will you sit up front? I need to talk to Señor Tom on the way to base camp."

Tom and Jenny found the hand and footholds to climb onto the pontoon and into the helicopter. Miguel used a step stool. As Tom climbed into the second-row seat, he noticed a couple of green tanks in the back labeled O2 with a face mask attached to each one. Miguel was prepared. Tom had read that the best immediate treatment for high-altitude illness was oxygen.

The helicopter was loud, even without a tail rotor. Everyone needed headphones to talk. Tom noticed his cell phone lost its signal about ten minutes out of Quito.

Paikea headed east until he met the foothills of the Andes, and then south. He flew lower than Tom expected, which did not help his apprehension, moving up and down the cordilleras and valleys over a dozen lakes, and eventually up into the Andes. As they headed into the interior, the roads disappeared. About a half-hour into the flight, a gentle rain started, but visibility was still adequate.

As they gained altitude in the mountains, páramo, or scrub brush, replaced the trees. And then, as they dropped in altitude, trees again. By the end of the week, they would see all the flora of the Llanganatis as the five lakes were scattered over the park and at various altitudes.

During the flight, Miguel explained to Tom the challenges they might face this week. "The weather in the Llanganatis is a significant factor. March has the best rain and winds, but it can still be unpredictable. I have access to real-time radar data over the satellite phone, and I understand from Dr. Westhoven you can read weather maps?"

Talking helped distract Tom from the helicopter. "The mountains in New England have a similar radar signature, but my biggest concern is the micro weather patterns. The lakes nestled in valleys behind mountains are difficult to see on radar. We'll want current satellite images, if available, but satellite still can't see wind."

Tom looked out of the cockpit as the pilot banked to the east and pulled up on the collective pitch. He spotted a few small ponds surrounded by scrub and smaller pine trees. The mist let up again. The trees were thinning.

Miguel went on to discuss the schedule for the week. "We have seven days to survey the five lakes. Also, Lake Bravo and Lake Charlie are close enough to do in one day, if the weather permits.

"Tarek will stay in base camp, but the rest of the team will helicopter to each lake. Paikea and I will stay in the helicopter while you, Miss Jenny, and the diver find the gold."

Jenny heard him over the headset and turned back to Miguel. "Please call me Jenny."

"Certainly, Jenny. After you both have a COVID test, I'll give you a quick tour of the base camp. Everyone has a tent. The kitchen area is where we will meet around breakfast and dinner. Here is a diagram."

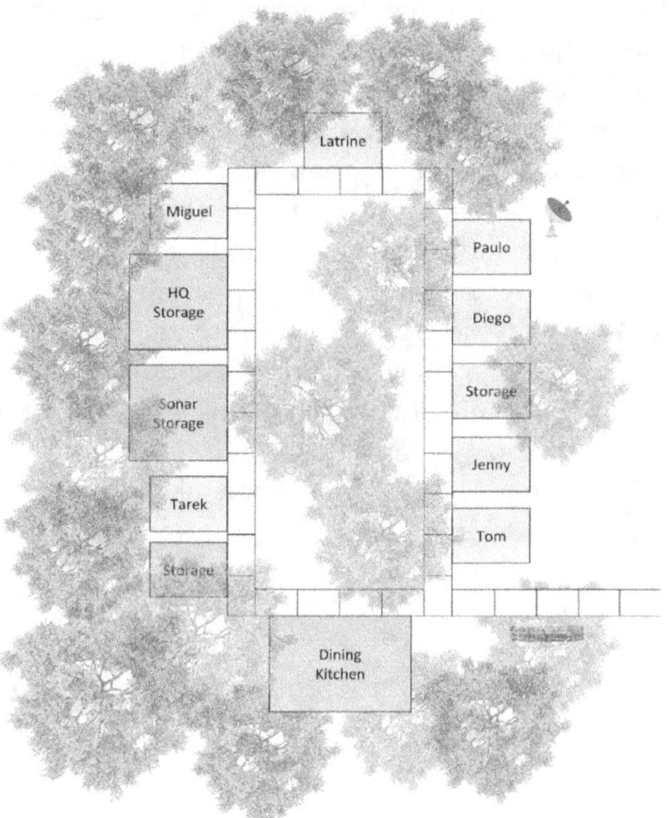

"COVID test? I didn't realize a rapid COVID test existed," said Tom.

"Oh yes, sorry. Tarek, the base camp manager, will test everyone on arrival and first thing every morning. We have test kits directly from China. I do not believe they are available in the

U.S." Miguel did not say how he got the tests or what would happen if anyone tested positive.

"Generators supply the power. Tarek has been preparing the base camp for the last couple of months. He started as soon as you picked the five lakes, Señor Tom."

Paikea turned and told them they would be at base camp in five minutes.

Miguel continued, "To keep everything dry, all the tents are on platforms around a walkway. If it rains, the walkway floats on the mud and can be a little unstable, so take care to walk in the middle. The mud can be deep in places."

Tom suspected Miguel was speaking from experience.

They flew so low it was hard to get a perspective, but as they approached, Tom recognized the oval lake from the topo map. It was a little over a half-mile long. The base camp was on the eastern shore and difficult to see under the trees. Tom could just make out a rectangular pathway peeking out beneath the canopy like a giant Monopoly board. Through the trees, he also noticed the hint of a shiny interior of the board with a trench system slithering and draining into the lake, resembling the veins on the back of his hand.

Although the last three days had taken their toll on Tom preparing Jenny for the Llanganatis, she remained wide-eyed since landing in Quito. "Where does she get her energy?" he wondered.

Base Camp

Saturday, March 14, 2020
Base Camp
Llanganatis, Ecuador

The water boiled beneath them as the helicopter gently settled on the lake just north of the base camp. A thin mist had settled upon the lake. Tom instinctively grabbed his iPhone for a weather update before he remembered—no cell signal. He would have to depend on Miguel for access to weather data.

After Paikea docked, he powered down the helicopter and asked everyone to wait for the rotors to stop completely. "No haircuts this week, mates. The water is an unstable platform. We will follow the same protocol on the lakes, always waiting for the rotors to stop before leaving the helicopter."

As they stepped onto the wobbly dock, Tom looked back at the helicopter. It looked like a weird party boat with its oversized pontoons. Tom noticed the Zodiac bobbing by the shore, covered with a camouflage tarp with a Honda outboard sticking out. It would be a snug fit under the helicopter, but it looked like it could accommodate Tom and Jenny, the diver, and even Miguel if he decided to come along.

It was quieter once the helicopter powered down, with the hum of a generator mixing with the waves breaking on the beach. Even though it was about 60 degrees Fahrenheit, the gentle breeze with the mist had a chilling effect. A screeching bird sounding like a Blue Jay seemed upset with their arrival.

The Monopoly board he had seen on approach was dozens of four-by-six-foot sections of green composite decking material all bolted together into a giant rectangle with a spur to the helicopter dock. Tom knew constructing this walkway was a significant achievement. He had helped convert the Orono Bog Walk from wood to composite material a few years ago. Each section probably weighed over a hundred pounds. This was at least a two-person job.

They grabbed their gear from the rear of the helicopter and followed Miguel in single file the ten yards to the Monopoly board.

On the spur, as they approached the main path, they saw a wall of red plastic gas tanks on the left covered by a green tarp and, on the right, large green leafy plants with bright red flowers and smaller red berries. Tom vaguely remembered his experience as a kid with red nightshade berries. Did the Llanganatis have its own unique poisonous plants? He had not studied the flora or fauna of the Llanganatis. He had been counting on Dr. Westhoven to keep him safe.

Behind the gas tanks sat two 10,000-watt generators. Each one could power a small house. One hummed. It was remarkably quiet for a generator. The exhaust floating by in the breeze, mixed in with another smell that Tom recognized but couldn't place.

The six Tritons were stacked by the Zodiac. Jenny saw the one she trained on. She had signed the tail. Tom was glad the Tritons were by the helicopter as each weighed about thirty-five pounds.

As they stepped onto the walkway, the shiny surface Tom had noticed on approach was smooth, almost iridescent, black mud. It was surreal. The base camp was already dark, but the trees growing from the mud with their broad canopies made it even more shadowy. The only dry area was at the base of the trees. Even without the mist, the trees would hide the base camp from above.

Tom chuckled.

"What?" asked Jenny.

"I figured out the smell. This muck stinks like clam flats."

"Yeah. You're right. It reminds me of Limerock Harbor at low tide."

On the actual pathway, the base camp resembled a small, dank, pea-green floating village. A dozen tents of various sizes were pitched on platforms extending off the walkway. Everything was covered with camouflage tarps. The trees were limbed up to about eight feet, but the canopy above was intact. The entire base camp was about fifty by one hundred feet. Tom tried to use metric, but feet was still his default.

The same large red leafy plants surrounded the perimeter, with taller coniferous trees behind in the forest. The ersatz Blue Jay was still going at it.

The rotten egg odor of clam flats permeated the base camp. But there was no tide here to cover up the stink twice a day. The exhaust from the generator masked it only a little.

Tom found the place unsettling. "Are you as creeped out by this place as me?"

"This is definitely not Nahmakanta," replied Jenny.

The base camp manager met them on the walkway and introduced himself as Tarek. He looked familiar to Tom.

"Welcome Tom. It is nice to see you again. We met about a year ago at the conference last February in Boston."

"Now I remember. This is Jenny. You asked a great question about training data sets."

"Ah yes, and you gave a great answer, and here we are."

At the conference, Tarek had presented himself as a professor or someone official. Tom could not remember. Odd that Miguel would hire him as the base camp manager and not as part of the actual expedition.

"What a wonderful coincidence," said Miguel.

Tarek then asked them to follow him to the kitchen area for COVID testing. The walkway was more stable than Tom expected, but he and Jenny still walked in single file, following Tarek.

Neither had been COVID tested before. The test box was covered with Chinese symbols. Tom wondered if Tarek could read the instructions. It was a little unpleasant, but the results would be available in fifteen minutes.

Tarek did the COVID testing in the combined kitchen and dining area in a large open tent about fourteen by twenty feet. The rectangular platform for the dining area was also remarkably stable. A large folding table for six people centered the dining area. Several LED lights lit the tent. An upright outdoor heater, like in an alfresco café, stood ready and the sides of the tent could drop depending on the weather.

Miguel continued, "This is where the daily briefings will happen each morning."

While they waited for the test results, he explained, "I wanted the base camp at a low altitude, central to all the lakes. Tarek also needed line of sight to the communication satellite for radio and the data stream from the Tritons. Finally, I needed a flat area close to the shore. It took Tarek a few months to find this spot and construct the camp, but here we are, ready to find some gold."

Miguel mentioned again every day would start with COVID testing for the team before they came together for breakfast and the morning briefing. Miguel assigned a specific time separated by fifteen-minutes for each member of the team starting at 5:30 a.m. He did mention to Tom and Jenny that since they arrived together, Tarek could test them at the same time.

As the setting sun across the lake peeked between the hills and cloud bank, the mist gradually lifted.

Once their rapid antigen tests returned negative, Miguel walked them around the Monopoly board counterclockwise for a quick tour before dinner.

By the shore, there were five tents, each on their own platform, for Tom, Jenny, Paikea, and the diver, who also had a separate storage tent for his gear. The tents were bigger than their Nahmakanta tent and Tom could almost stand up in his. Camouflage tarps covered all the tents. It was clear that rain was a significant concern.

Miguel discreetly mentioned to Tom that he and Jenny could share a tent, if desired. And they did. They put their gear in one tent and sleeping bags in the other.

As they continued the tour, the diver was reading a book in the door of his tent and introduced himself as Diego. No last name, just Diego.

Miguel shuffled Tom and Jenny along. "We will all gather in about a half of an hour for dinner when there will be more formal introductions," said Miguel.

Tom noticed an eighteen-inch green satellite dish by the shore pointing to the northern horizon, with a thick coaxial cable running through the muck.

They took a left-hand turn and walked past the latrine. Miguel mentioned a solar shower was available, "But it requires sunshine, which may be in short supply."

The walkway turned again to the left. Miguel's tent was next, which was the same size as the others.

The next two tents were much larger. The first one was well lit on the inside by the clean white light of an LED. "This is my headquarters," he said. Tom noticed a thick black coaxial cable and another large cable, probably power, entering the tent through a carefully sealed opening on the side.

The other large tent was dark, also with cables entering from the side. "This is for equipment like the GPS device, depth finder, cameras, batteries, and the six Triton satellite uplinks," said Miguel. "This tent also has power, with a computer connected to the satellite to download images from the Triton. This is where you will review the sonar images."

They passed two other tents for Tarek and supplies, and another left-hand turn brought them back to the dining area.

"Why don't you stow your gear, and we'll meet back here in about twenty minutes," suggested Miguel.

Tom followed Jenny back to their tents. She asked, "Do you have any idea where we are?"

"We're on the eastern part of the park, which hasn't been well mapped."

"That was weird you met Tarek at the conference a year ago. And Miguel didn't seem to know about it. Do you think it was just a coincidence?"

"I'm not sure. I wonder if Dr. Westhoven knew Tarek was the base camp manager. He always said he didn't know the rest of the team. I wonder if someone else is involved."

❧❦

As the sun set over the lake, Miguel gathered everyone to the dining area for their first meal together. Tarek was also the cook. The smell of clam flats had dampened Tom's appetite.

The generator humming in the distance powered the overhead harsh LED lighting, which cast odd shadows on everyone. At least they didn't look pea green. Tarek had fired up the heater, which took some of the dampness out of the air.

During dinner, Miguel started introductions. He spoke in English, the default language for the expedition. He introduced everyone by their first name.

Paikea was the pilot that brought them into the Llanganatis. He was also a diver as a backup. He had dark, closely cropped hair like a military cut. On the flight over, Tom had noticed a scar on the left side of his neck, which he'd tried to hide with a tattoo of a serpent. He was slightly taller than Tom, trim and fit. He looked like he was about thirty years old.

"Good day mates. Nice to formally make your acquaintance."

Diego was next. He was the one who had been reading by his tent when Tom and Jenny first arrived. His job would be to dive to the target and put eyes, and hopefully, hands-on the gold. Miguel mentioned Diego could also fly the MD600N, again as back-up. He was smaller than Paikea, with longer black hair and also a little unkempt. Perhaps that was from being in the water. He looked about the same age as Paikea.

"Good evening, señores, and señorita. I am pleased to be part of this adventure."

Tom noticed both Paikea and Diego had sidearms. Were there other weapons in the base camp? He had brought his hunting knife, but he was not sure why.

Miguel then introduced Tarek. He was also in good shape and evidently a jack of all trades. In battle fatigues, Tarek did not look like the official Tom had met at the conference a year ago. He would stay in base camp while the rest of the team surveyed each lake. Miguel mentioned Tarek was a veteran of many expeditions, although this was his first in the Llanganatis. He looked about the same age as Miguel.

Finally, he introduced Tom and Jenny as graduate students of Dr. Westhoven. Tom did not bother to correct him. The team knew Dr. Westhoven had contracted COVID, but no one other than Miguel actually knew Dr. Westhoven. Miguel acknowledged the groundwork laid by them. "We are here today in the Llanganatis because of the hard work of Dr. Westhoven, Tom, and Jenny. Thank you again."

Miguel then filled everyone in about himself and his interest in the lost Inca gold. He reiterated their goal this week was to find, but not extract, the gold. "If we are fortunate to find gold, a separate team with a larger helicopter will follow up. Also, we will not recover the Triton torpedoes and satellite uplinks. Our focus is on the gold."

He continued, "Dr. Westhoven has ordered the lakes in the likelihood of our finding the gold. We will start with Lake Alpha, the highest probability lake. We have two sites to check in Lake Alpha, so tomorrow will be a busy day.

"The following day we will try to visit the next two lakes, Lake Bravo and Lake Charlie. They are close, only fifteen minutes apart, but about 500 meters difference in altitude. That leaves Lake Echo and Lake Delta for the last two days.

"The weather in the Llanganatis is, how you say, fickle, but with some luck, we should be able to visit each lake. With a little more luck, we will find some gold."

Miguel explained he flipped Lake Echo and Lake Delta because of logistics.

By now, the sun had set. With the cooling temperature, the mist returned to the lake and base camp. This wasn't a fog you would see back in Maine. It penetrated. Everything was cold and damp. And the stink lingered. Tarek fired up another heater.

Miguel then brought out from under the table a bottle of Dom Pérignon. "This was a suggestion of Dr. Westhoven."

Under the harsh lights, he poured everyone a glass. "To the success of the mission and a speedy recovery of Dr. Westhoven."

His cheerfulness was at odds with a team focused on the task at hand, in the depths of the Llanganatis.

This was only the second time Tom had tasted champagne. It was flat, and terrible. Jenny noticed it, too. "It must be the pill," she said.

Everyone else seemed to enjoy the champagne. "We must be the only ones taking the acetazolamide," whispered Tom.

At eight o'clock, Tarek shut down the generator and issued everyone an LED headlight and flashlight. The team scattered for last-minute preparations.

On the walkway back to their tent, Jenny mentioned to Tom, "The team seems well prepared, but we still don't know a lot about them. Miguel did all the talking."

"We'll probably get to know them better over the week," replied Tom.

Miguel, however, had already shared as much as he knew about Diego, Paikea, and Tarek.

Before retiring, Jenny wandered over to the supply tent to look at the satellite uplinks, and Tom returned to the helicopter to check out the attachments for the Zodiac and Tritons on the pontoons.

The LED headlights were remarkably bright, but Tom still was not entirely sure how to deploy the Zodiac. He planned a closer look in the morning.

In the supply tent, Jenny's LED headlight revealed a computer and monitor on a folding table in the back. The six satellite uplinks were stacked to the left and other supplies on the right. It was too dark to see much else.

Back at their tent, although tired from a long day of travel, they reviewed the protocols one more time. They had so much to do and think about. The reality of being in the Llanganatis had not yet sunk in.

As they crawled into their sleeping bags, Tom said, "Are you having any tingling from the pill?"

"Yeah. My fingers are tingling a little. How about you?"

"Yeah, fingers and another appendage, too." replied Tom, looking down.

"Oh my, I better check it out," as she reached down, much like she had at Nahmakanta. "We need everything fully functional."

Camping with Jenny was fun....

Back in his tent, Miguel thought it odd that Tarek would know Tom from a conference a year ago. This was about the time Omar had first approached him about the expedition and when he had first met Tarek in Cartagena. Omar must have been laying the groundwork for well over a year.

Miguel realized it should come as no surprise. He knew Omar was methodical. Although he was glad he had, Miguel still wondered why Omar had reached out to him for this adventure.

Lake Alpha

Sunday, March 15, 2020
Base Camp
Llanganatis, Ecuador

It was still dark at 5:30 a.m. when Tom and Jenny woke up. They took their third acetazolamide. One more tonight would complete the two-day course. Tom noticed the tingling was still there despite Jenny's best efforts.

Everyone wandered over to the well-lit dining area for their COVID test at their assigned times. Breakfast followed. They all ate well despite the smell, as there would be no lunch today when they were on the water.

The radar suggested the fog would burn off in about ninety minutes and then they would have partly cloudy skies. Although the temperature was about 55 degrees, it felt cooler with the mist and steady breeze. Miguel, the only one with internet access, had Windy.com up. The wind at Lake Alpha would be about twelve knots from the southwest throughout the day.

Tom and Jenny charged their phones during breakfast, although they were essentially useless without cellular or Wi-Fi. Miguel had made it clear no photos, either. Only Diego had an underwater camera to photograph the pile of gold.

The sun was streaming through the trees behind the base camp by 6:30 a.m., highlighting the western shore across the lake. Everyone scattered for last-minute preparations.

Tom headed for the helicopter. Paikea had already secured the Zodiac and two Tritons, one on each pontoon, attached on the outside waterline for easier deployment. There was about two feet of clearance between the helicopter and the gunwales of the Zodiac, just enough for Tom to slip in.

Paikea followed shortly thereafter for his preflight check. He showed Tom how to disengage the Zodiac and the Tritons.

The Honda outboard started easily. Tom confirmed the gas tank under his seat was full. He noticed a locker under the bow seat. He would check that out later.

Tom released the Zodiac and backed out slowly from beneath the helicopter, ducking his head. He was glad the helicopter had no tail rotor as he passed under it.

While he was on the water, Jenny came down the trail with one satellite uplink under her arm. Paikea showed her where to store it and waved for Tom to come back in. Miguel was ready for the morning briefing. Jenny would get the second backup satellite uplink after the briefing.

Tom carefully guided the Zodiac back under the helicopter in between the pontoons. This might be tricky if the water was rough, like on Flagstaff. He secured the Zodiac to the pontoons.

The rest of the team had already gathered in the kitchen. Last night, Miguel had not gone into a lot of detail, but this morning, he did. He reviewed everyone's responsibilities, both preflight and on the lake. Any mishaps could be costly.

He started with preflight preparations.

"Tarek will charge the electronic devices, including the Tritons and satellite uplinks, and the GPS.

"Paikea, besides your usual pre-flight routine, you will secure the Zodiac and two Tritons, one to each pontoon."

He continued, "Jenny will stow the satellite uplinks in the helicopter and Tom will handle the GPS device and fueling the Zodiac.

"In the helicopter, I will sit in the front on the left side. Tom will be behind me, Jenny behind Paikea, and Diego in the third-row seats with his gear." With a subtle grin, Miguel continued, "I have also removed the fourth row for the gold."

"Any questions?"

He then turned to Tom to review the on-lake protocols. "Okay, Señor Tom, once we are on the water, you will take over."

He motioned for Tom to stand up and continue the briefing. Tom had not expected to say anything this morning. Fortunately, he had just been reviewing the data about Lake Alpha.

"Certainly Miguel. Remember, Lake Alpha is the only lake with two sites. It's twenty-three kilometers from base camp at an elevation of 3,400 meters. Lake Alpha, like all the lakes, is small, about 300 by 500 meters." He was becoming comfortable with metric. Converting feet and yards to meters was easy, but kilometers to miles, not so much.

Tom continued, looking at Paikea. "As we approach the lake, I'll point out the landing area. Normally, we'll be about one hundred meters downwind to avoid stirring up any bottom silt, so today, with the southwesterly wind, we will land near the northeast shore.

"Once Paikea secures the anchor, he will power-down the rotor. No one leaves the helicopter until Paikea gives the signal.

"I'll then swing over the port side and into the Zodiac. Once I start the Honda, I'll release the Zodiac from the pontoons and bring it around the starboard side to pick up Jenny and Diego. We will then load the GPS unit and satellite uplink.

"I'll follow the GPS to the northern coordinates. Once there, Jenny will drop the guideline for Diego, who will then enter the water, following the guideline down.

"If Diego finds gold, he will photograph the pile and collect a sample of the pieces. We will then head to the southern site and repeat the process. The last step is to deploy the Triton. Diego will board the Zodiac and we will all head to the southern shore, where Jenny will set up the antenna and establish a connection for the satellite uplink.

"Once we return to the helicopter, Jenny deploys the Triton, and we wait to confirm real-time data is streaming from the Triton.

"Finally, with everyone on board, we head back to base camp."

It took Tom about five minutes to work through the above. It was a little after seven.

"Thank you, Señor Tom. Let's gather at 7:30 a.m. by the helicopter. Any questions?"

The sun was creeping higher in the sky but still behind the trees, so there was a chill in the air. The breeze had picked up, coming in off the water. It helped with the smell, but Paikea preferred less wind for take-off.

With everyone and everything secured, Paikea taxied out about twenty meters and ascended. The last of the mist was burning off, but it looked like rain on the cockpit window beating down from the rotors. Even with the communication sets on, it was loud. And this machine is supposed to be quieter without a tail rotor, thought Tom. Once it was off the water, it was less noisy, but there was not much to say, anyway. Everybody knew by now what they had to do.

Tom looked over at Jenny. She was looking out the starboard side as the terrain blurred by. He noticed her white knuckles gripping the armrest. He caressed her left hand. She turned and returned a smile. An anxious Jenny was unusual. Normally, it would have unnerved Tom, but after a year of preparation, he felt an odd calm in the beat of the deafening helicopter.

One way or the other, this would be over in one week.

They flew low like yesterday, northwest to Lake Alpha. As Paikea approached the lake, he rose above the lingering mist as the lake was about 1,000 meters higher than base camp. It was windier up here, but this was their first clear view of the Llanganatis.

As Paikea gained altitude, the connecting tops of the serrated Andes looked like a huge highway that went on forever. But this mountain highway had no actual roads or trails. Some lakes they would visit this week were not even on the tourist maps.

He let go of Jenny's hand to point to a vicuña drinking by a small stream.

As Paikea followed the terrain up, the trees became shorter and shorter until it was only prairie grass.

Lake Alpha was nestled in between two smaller hills that hopefully would block the wind. As they descended onto the lake, Tom could tell the helicopter was working harder in the thin air. He noticed the vegetation at the south end of the lake was slightly different. Was this an old riverbed that Dr. Westhoven had detected?

Tom directed Paikea to the landing spot in the northeast part of the lake. Diego geared up. Paikea gently brought the helicopter down and Tom didn't realize they were on the water until the helicopter started rolling on the waves. Paikea dropped anchor, and the helicopter drifted downwind about ten meters. The rotors seemed to take forever to wind down, while the waves bounced the helicopter around.

Finally, Paikea gave the thumbs up, and Tom swung out the port side, over the pontoon, and into the Zodiac. The waves made it more challenging. He pictured Miguel trying this maneuver.

The Honda started up on the first pull. Tom could go forward this time, but he needed to stay even lower with the waves. Watching his head, he swung the Zodiac around to the starboard side, where Jenny passed him the GPS unit and then the satellite uplink package. Tom helped her into the boat.

Diego passed down his oxygen tank and flippers and climbed into the Zodiac. Miguel had provided him with a video camera that he attached to his diving mask for real-time imaging, although of relatively poor quality. The satellite connection in the helicopter did not support significant bandwidth like the Triton. Miguel in the helicopter and Tarek at base camp could monitor Diego's video feed, but they would not see the finer details.

As Tom approached the northern target coordinates in the Zodiac, the water was remarkably clear. The polarizing sunglasses helped with the glare.

Even though the depth was only about four meters, the waves obscured a good view of the bottom. All Tom could see was what looked like a pile of rocks.

"They look like erratics," said Jenny. "But they're not. I bet they're volcanic, even though there hasn't been any volcanic activity here in a long time."

There was no need for a guideline for Diego in this shallow water, but it also served as the anchor for the Zodiac, so Jenny dropped it onto the pile of rocks. Tom shut down the Honda, and the Zodiac drifted downwind.

The sun was poking around large cumulus clouds. For the first time since they'd arrived in the Llanganatis, everything was quiet. Just the sound of wind and waves on the gunwales of the Zodiac.

"Maybe they hid the gold and silver under rocks," said Jenny.

Diego adjusted his oxygen and flipped backwards over the gunwale.

After dismantling the pile of rocks, it was clear this was not hiding gold, but he carefully surveyed the surrounding area to be sure.

Diego, by now, was way outside the edges of the satellite images. He brought up a couple rocks and Jenny confirmed they were igneous. "This was a geologically active area in the distant past."

Tom had a sinking feeling his neural network had detected piles of volcanic rock across the Llanganatis instead of gold. The pile of rocks didn't look like a pile of plastic gold, but no one really knows what's under the hood of a convolutional neural network.

With all his gear, Diego needed Tom's help to climb over the gunwale into the Zodiac. With everyone on board, Tom started the Honda. Jenny pulled the anchor, and they headed south to the second site, about one hundred and fifty meters away. Tom did not turn to look back at Paikea or Miguel in the helicopter, pretending to focus on the GPS. Even though he hadn't expected to find any gold, he was still disappointed. The calmness he felt in the helicopter was gone, replaced by an emptiness.

The lake was deeper here and, even with the polarizing sunglasses, Tom could not see the bottom, but Diego confirmed his concerns when he brought up another igneous rock the size of a grapefruit.

Diego decided to swim back to the helicopter rather than go with Tom and Jenny in the Zodiac to the southern shore, where Jenny would set up the satellite uplink. He said it would give him an opportunity to look around more. It made sense, but Tom still felt a little snubbed.

Tom used an oar to push as close as possible to the shore, but Jenny still got a little wet carrying the satellite uplink to the beach. The southern shore was relatively flat, with only scrub brush. Tom had noticed a few lakes on the way to Lake Alpha had steeper shorelines. One looked like a cliff or quarry wall, like those in Limerock. Hopefully, the other four lakes would also have a stable base for the uplink.

After about fifteen minutes of fiddling by Jenny, Tom was starting to worry the uplink was broken. But she didn't look concerned. She was focusing intently on the signal indicator while gently adjusting the twelve-inch antenna ever so slightly, trying to maximize the signal.

After twenty minutes, satisfied she had the best coordinates, Jenny waded back out to the Zodiac. "I have the azimuth and altitude now. Tomorrow will be quicker," she said, climbing back over the gunwales into the Zodiac.

By the time they were back at the helicopter, Miguel confirmed Tarek was receiving a signal from the Triton. Jenny released the starboard side Triton, and it slid into the water. This was the first time Tom and Jenny had seen a Triton in action in an actual lake. Jenny had already programmed the search grid. The Triton headed to the north shore.

They were done with Lake Alpha, with only igneous rocks to show for it. As the helicopter ascended, they could see the Triton circumnavigating the lake, following the shoreline as programmed.

Tom wanted to tell someone Lake Alpha was actually lower on the probability list, but with two sites in the same lake, Dr. Westhoven arbitrarily elevated it to Lake Alpha. Also, his neural network had detected something. It had found an anomaly. Hopefully, however, they would not spend all week collecting volcanic rock.

It was about one o'clock when Paikea turned the helicopter back to base camp. They needed to be quicker tomorrow, as they planned to visit both Lake Bravo and Lake Charlie.

Back at base camp, balancing on the walkway, Tom and Jenny headed to the storage tent to review the raw images coming in from the Triton. Based upon the size of the lake, it would take about ten hours to scan the entire lake, and then another four hours to finish processing the images through SonarSeer.

If SonarSeer found any anomalies, they would then look at the corresponding video images, but details washed out quickly after ten meters. So far, the Triton had found nothing of interest other than piles of rocks scattered on the bottom.

Although Depth Cam and the Triton could see up to ten meters deep, the sonar on the Triton could go down to one hundred meters. He doubted Lake Alpha, however, was over thirty meters deep based upon the Depth Cam images from last fall.

"Do volcanic rocks usually end up in piles like this?" Tom asked Jenny, pointing to an image on the monitor.

"Not that I know of. Maybe the ancients collected rocks like New England farmers, using them for walls or borders."

They would take a closer look at the images after dinner, but it would not be until tomorrow they would have the entire lake scanned and processed. He wasn't looking forward to reviewing piles of volcanic rocks.

Before everyone gathered for dinner, Tom and Miguel met in the kitchen to review the updated weather data for the next day. It looked like another good day, two decent days in a row. This expedition might be over quicker than Tom thought.

Tom found Lake Bravo and Lake Charlie on the weather map. Lake Bravo was about fourteen kilometers from base camp at 3,700 meters high, and Lake Charlie was about nine kilometers at 3,200 meters. Both lakes were small. Lake Bravo was a square, while Lake Charlie was more elongated and shaped like an hourglass.

By dinner, it had clouded up again. The breeze had remained steady throughout the day and was still coming off the lake, which helped with the smell, but it was chilling. So far, no fog or mist.

Everyone gathered around the kitchen table. Even though Miguel had warned them this morning not to get discouraged, disappointment etched their faces. All they found today were a couple of piles of volcanic rocks. And everyone thought Lake Alpha was the highest probability lake to find gold.

Tom was also disappointed. A pile of rocks fooled his neural network.

After dinner, Miguel made a few brief remarks and then turned to Tom for the weather update.

This time, he was prepared. "After some heavy rain overnight, tomorrow looks like a windy but otherwise decent day. To take advantage of the good weather and survey two lakes, everyone needs to be ready to fly by seven."

Miguel handed out the COVID testing schedule for the morning. Everybody needed to be up by five o'clock to get their test and breakfast. No one had questions.

Tom and Jenny took one last look at the Triton images from Lake Alpha before retiring. SonarSeer was picking up anomalies, a lot of them. Toward the center of the lake, what looked like smaller piles of rocks were scattered everywhere on the lakebed. They had a jagged appearance on sonar but were too deep to be seen by Depth Cam. It would require a careful review of the video, but neither Tom nor Jenny had any unrealistic expectations.

It was odd the rocks were in piles. Perhaps Dr. Westhoven would have an explanation.

That evening, on his satellite call with Miguel, Omar was also disappointed, but he did not share that with Miguel. He knew Tom's program worked. It had detected his fool's gold at Ground Zero.

Lake Bravo

Monday, March 16, 2020
Base Camp
Llanganatis, Ecuador

Heavy rain pattering on the green camouflage tarp woke her. Tom was still sleeping. Everything in the tent was dry but damp. In fact, everything was damp from the moment they arrived. Green used to be her favorite color. The miasma greeted her when she opened the tent flaps. The lack of a breeze along with the steady rain must have stirred something up.

They took their last acetazolamide last night, and her tingling had subsided.

Tom had mentioned that it would rain overnight, then clear up today with some winds higher up. Now it was so calm, but she knew the weather could change unpredictably.

The rain already was lightening to a drizzle as Tom stirred. After a good stretch and donning some warmer clothes, she gave him a nudge. Hopefully, he'd slept better than she had. This was so different from Nahmakanta in so many ways.

While she waited for him to wake up, she knocked off the dried mud and slid on her boots. Remarkably, the composite walkway was not slippery, even in the rain. She was eager to get going, away from the mud and smell.

During the morning briefing, Tom mentioned the weather would be clear in the region of the target lakes, but windy. "Although it's difficult to predict micro weather in the Llanganatis, we'll still try for the two lakes today."

After a closer look at the weather patterns this morning, he worried about the wind at Lake Charlie. Windy.com predicted steady winds from the southeast, about the same orientation as the hourglass lake, at fifteen knots with gusts of twenty to twenty-five knots. He also noticed the winds gusting to forty to forty-five knots about 500 meters off the lake. He hoped this would not affect them on the surface of the lake.

On the topo map, Lake Charlie was nestled in a horseshoe of mountain peaks. In addition, the actual target coordinates were in the middle of the hourglass, the narrowest part, which could further intensify the wind. Tom shared this with Paikea, who did not seem too concerned.

Just as predicted, the rain stopped while the team was having breakfast. The dampness and mud and stink, however, persisted.

Tom hoped the two target lakes being so close together was a good sign. If General Rumiñahui hid the gold in more than one lake, it made sense they would be close together, probably near a lost Inca trail.

He was impatient to find out. The calmness he felt yesterday on the ride to Lake Alpha was gone. Finding piles of rocks from yesterday still stung.

Last night, Paikea had attached another Triton to the helicopter. They would use both Tritons and satellite uplinks with no backup today.

They were in the air by seven. Again, Paikea followed the cordilleras and valleys up and down. They arrived at Lake Bravo twenty-five minutes later. Although Lake Bravo and Lake Charlie were close together, they were at different altitudes. At 3,700 meters, Lake Bravo was about 1,100 meters higher than base camp, with páramo surrounding the lake.

As they approached, Tom recognized the lake from the satellite images. It looked like a flattened diamond. They could not waste valuable time on the satellite uplink, and he noticed the southern shore where Jenny would set up the uplink looked clear.

Everything, starting with the water landing, was smoother today, even with the wind. Paikea set the helicopter down about one hundred meters north, downwind from the target, and powered down the rotor. The exhaust from the tail dissipated with the breeze, but the waves seemed calmer than yesterday.

It took about four to five minutes for the rotors to stop completely. It was still overcast, but no rain, with the sun peeking out now and then.

Diego suggested something different. He found it cumbersome to climb into the Zodiac with all his gear, so he suggested he deploy directly from the helicopter. "This also gives me a look around on the way to the target."

Miguel agreed. "Anything that improves the odds of finding the gold."

Tom disengaged the Zodiac and brought it around to the starboard side. Jenny didn't want any help into the Zodiac today. Jumping in, she created a few waves. From the third row seats, Diego slid into the water on the port side and his bubble trail headed to the site. He would still need the guideline, however, to find the exact spot.

Miguel stayed in the helicopter again with Paikea, watching Diego's live video feed.

Tom piloted the Zodiac to the target. Diego stayed deep under the water to avoid the outboard.

They were in about four meters of water when Tom idled the Honda. The sun was out. Tom could see something on the bottom, but the gentle waves obscured the view. Please don't be another pile of rocks, thought Tom.

As Jenny lowered the guideline, a dark cloud obscured the sun. Only the outline of Diego was now visible. As the guideline hit bottom, Diego's air bubbles came faster and bigger. He was surfacing.

His right hand broke the surface first, holding a small golden llama about ten centimeters long. Tom's eyes widened.

Then his left hand breached the surface, holding a small human skull. He dropped both into the Zodiac. Jenny recoiled as the small skull bounced on the floor and rolled toward her feet.

Tom knew what Diego had found.

Diego removed his mouthpiece. "It's a pile of bones and a few scattered artifacts. The pile is about four to five meters in diameter. Hand me the camera and collection bag and I'll bring up some samples."

After Diego descended again, Tom looked over at the helicopter. Miguel was focused intently on the video feed. Uncertainty lined his face.

Diego brought up the collection bag. It held a ragtag collection of bones and small golden and silver artifacts, including a cup, a three-centimeter medallion of the sun, and small camelids. Mostly, however, it was bones, and they looked like small ones, including another couple of skulls.

Tom said into his headset, "These are the bones of children. This is an Inca sacrificial site."

Jenny added, "They're often found in the higher altitudes, perhaps to be closer to the sun. The Incas included gold and silver trinkets as part of the ritual."

With frustration in his voice, Miguel replied, "I doubt this has any... to do with... gold."

The radio static surprised Tom, but he got the gist of Miguel's message. This was not the lost Inca gold.

But if there was an ancient Inca village and road network nearby, maybe General Rumiñahui would have also used this lake to hide the gold. The Triton scans would be important to review.

The trinkets were still worth something. Tom asked Diego to finish photographing the pile and then pick through to find as much gold and silver as he could. He handed Diego another collection bag.

"But leave the bones," he told Diego.

Miguel could sell the artifacts, but it would not come close to covering the costs of the expedition.

Diego brought up a bag full of trinkets. It was time to move on.

Tom caught something shiny on Diego's weight belt, but he quickly pushed it back into a pocket as he said, "I'm headed back to the helicopter. I'll look around to see if there are any other sites on the way back."

Jenny had picked a clearing on the southwest shore for the satellite uplink. With the azimuth and altitude from yesterday, she established the uplink in less than ten minutes.

Back at the helicopter, she deployed the starboard Triton. Again, Miguel in the helicopter and Tarek back at base camp confirmed receiving real-time images. With the Zodiac secured to the helicopter, it was still only eleven o'clock, plenty of time to head to Lake Charlie.

Lake Charlie

Lake Charlie
Llanganatis, Ecuador

Paikea continued to stay close to the terrain, going up and down over cordilleras and valleys.

"Hey Paikea, why do you follow the contours of the land so closely?" asked Tom, wondering if it had to do with the performance of the helicopter at these altitudes.

"Orders, mate," he replied.

Orders from whom, Tom wondered.

Lake Charlie was southeast, about a fifteen-minute ride from Lake Bravo, but longer today, heading into the wind. Lake Charlie was the lowest lake they would survey this week at 3,200 meters. The landscape changed when they descended, with the páramo giving way to stunted trees on the border of the montane forest.

When they took off from Lake Bravo, the cloud cover thinned, but the wind picked up. Tom noticed Paikea had both hands on the stick. Tom remembered the wind, according to the prediction, was gusting higher off the lake.

So far, the weather data was accurate. Although it was still cold and damp, an occasional ray of sunshine lifted Tom's spirits, but watching Paikea struggle with the stick still concerned him.

They met some turbulence as they crested the last peak. Lake Charlie was aligned in a northwest to southeast direction, the same direction as the wind today. The lake was on a declivity nestled in a horseshoe-shaped mountain ridge, with the toe to the northwest and a dramatic drop in the slope to the east.

There were short trees on the mountain slopes but stunted brush around the lake, almost like páramo, which was unusual at this lower altitude. Setting up the satellite uplink should be easy.

The weather data from this morning predicted winds from the southeast at about fifteen knots, with gusts of twenty to twenty-five knots on the lake. Higher up, about 500 meters off the lake, the winds gusted from forty to forty-five knots, but Paikea had said he was comfortable flying in these conditions. "I'll just slide under the winds higher up."

As Paikea descended toward Lake Charlie, however, the gusts worsened. The horseshoe shape created a wind tunnel. Paikea estimated the wind gusted forty to fifty knots on the lake. Diego agreed based upon the whitecaps on the lake.

Tom now realized why there were no trees around Lake Charlie. The constant wind, like on the top of Sugarloaf, stunted their growth. This was a micro weather pattern.

Tom remembered the HIGE effect for the MD600N was about 3,400 meters, even if he couldn't remember the actual acronym. Lake Charlie was about 3,200 meters, so the MD600N could hover, but only about ten meters or less off the water.

The wind howled and buffeted the helicopter the lower they dropped. Paikea, even with both hands on the stick, was struggling.

"Hey mate, I can't land on the water. A sudden gust and we crash. And I have to approach directly into the wind. With those waves, the tail could dip underwater and get water into the engine."

"What about on the páramo?" asked Tom.

"Only in an emergency. As I land, a gust could easily topple us over. We'd be stuck here."

As the wind wailed around the cockpit, Tom wondered what had happened to Andrés Fernández-Salvador years ago, and to the team last summer, when their helicopters crashed.

Tom turned back. "Diego, how high can you safely drop into the water?"

"Four meters."

This was within the HIGE. "Okay, Paikea, let's do this. I'll take us directly over the target site and then you lower us to four meters off the waves.

"Diego, there will be no guideline, but we'll be directly over the target. You then drop into the water. We'll ascend to wherever it is less windy, while you look. If you find anything of interest, we won't retrieve it today, but it will save us a trip back if we know the lake is clear.

"This is a small lake. When you're done with your scan, swim to the southern shore and we'll meet you there. Jenny will lower the satellite uplink and walk you through the set-up. Be sure to keep your video uplink on so she can watch."

Tom continued, "We'll then use the hoist to bring you back on board. We may need to lift your gear separately. Paikea, the hoist was rated for one hundred kilograms, right?"

"Correct, mate, but it will swing like a wallaby in heat in this wind."

"Is it easier to do the lift from the páramo or water?"

"Yeah, nah—the páramo—no waves up and down, mate. But you'll have to handle the hoist controls while I steady the helicopter. They're here over my head."

"Got it, good. Diego, stay on land and we'll get you up. Once you're on board, Jenny will activate the Triton and we head back to base camp."

Tom then turned to Paikea. "We're using more gas by staying in the air. Do we have enough?"

Paikea answered quickly. He must have been considering this as well. "Eh, just barely. We have about forty minutes of extra fuel. To be on the safe side, we need to be done in thirty, maybe thirty-five minutes."

"That's enough time. Does anyone have questions?"

Miguel was the only one. "Señor Tom, this sounds risky. Perhaps another day?"

"We can do this. We have the right people with the right equipment. Miguel, I need you to count out every five minutes. When we hit twenty-five minutes, we need to wrap this up."

No one said anything. Apart from Miguel, everyone looked ready.

"All right. Let's move. Paikea, head sixty degrees for about one hundred meters. Once we get closer, I'll direct you to the site. When Diego is ready, we'll drop to four meters."

Tom's biggest concern was the hoist. "Diego, what does your equipment weigh?"

"About fifteen kilograms."

"And how much do you weigh?"

"Ninety kilograms."

"That means two trips up the hoist, one for your equipment and one for you." And an extra three or four minutes, thought Tom. The hoist otherwise looked straight-forward with the controls over Paikea's head. It was a lever, up or down.

Everyone had already been through the protocols on Lake Alpha and Lake Bravo and dozens of times in their heads. The howling wind and turbulence, however, were a significant distraction. But everyone was focused, except Miguel.

He was pale and rocking. They would have had more gas to spare if Miguel had stayed back at base camp, but perhaps he was useful as ballast to stabilize the helicopter, thought Tom.

"Time?"

"Two minutes and fifteen seconds," replied Miguel.

Tom followed the GPS coordinates to the target. Today it was too deep and wavy with white caps to visualize anything on the lake bottom. But Depth Cam must have seen something here.

"Jenny, after Diego drops into the water, Paikea will take us twenty-five meters to the north. Before we ascend, I'll release the port side Triton, but don't activate it until Diego is back on board."

"Diego, can you hear me? Are you ready?"

Diego had his mouthpiece in. He gave a thumbs up.

"Good. All set Paikea."

Paikea dropped quickly to four meters off the water and Diego stepped off the starboard pontoon, splashing feet first over the target. Paikea took the helicopter up ten meters and then north twenty-five meters. It was a bumpy ride.

"Paikea, bring us down to about four meters again. I'm going to release the Triton."

The turbulence worsened closer to the lake.

Tom wrapped a rope around his waist, which he secured to his seat, and stepped out onto the port side pontoon. The wind and downdraft from the rotors buffeted him in unpredictable gusts. He released the Triton with a splash as it entered the water nose first. Tom scrambled back into the cockpit.

"Five minutes," yelled Miguel.

Tom watched Diego's video feed while Miguel monitored the clock. Initially, his video had a lot of bubbles, but when they cleared, it was still too dark to see anything. Then Diego turned on the LED.

Tangled delimbed trees about fifteen to twenty feet long lined a steep drop-off that was probably an old river. Tom took this to be a good sign.

But where did the trees come from? Even though they were only at 3,200 meters, páramo surrounded the lake with no large trees. As Diego swam in ever-widening circles, Tom noticed half of a shattered canoe. He wondered if the Incas brought the trees here by an old river to construct or repair their boats. Hopefully, Diego would find something more interesting than delimbed trees and a wrecked canoe.

"Ten minutes."

After another few minutes, Diego shook his head from side to side and crossed his arms in front of the video, and then pointed south as he headed to the shoreline. His video did not show much detail, but Tom knew Diego had not found any gold. The Triton scan would still be important, however, if this was a man-made lake with an underwater river running down the middle.

Tom shouted into the headset. "Be careful, Diego. Stay away from the trees. Don't get ensnarled."

Tom tapped Paikea on the shoulder, who headed slowly to the southern shore with both of his hands still on the stick, the wind battering the helicopter all the way.

Again, the neural network found anomalies, but trees do not look like gold. Possibly, the combination of curves from the canoe and tangled trees confused it. Whatever the reason, another deep disappointment.

The helicopter was lurching. Miguel, still gently rocking, stared at the watch.

"Fifteen minutes."

As they descended over the páramo, the turbulence worsened. The gusts became more frequent. Paikea was still white knuckling the stick.

Jenny pointed to a clear spot on the shore for the satellite uplink. Diego slowly climbed out of the water, leaning into the wind. The gusts pushed him around. Although Tom gently lowered the equipment with the hoist, the satellite uplink swung wildly in the wind with a high-pitched, piercing whine from the cable. He wasn't sure what a wallaby in heat looked like, but it must be an impressive sight.

"Diego, step back. I'll try to swing cable and time the drop at the end of a swing."

Each swing of the pendulum was erratic with the gusts, but after a few swings, Tom timed the drop at the end of a particularly long arc and quickly released about five meters of cable. The box landed on some grass with a thud. Hopefully, it still worked. Diego quickly disengaged the cable, and Tom brought it back up to avoid any tangles.

Jenny had already dialed in the azimuth and altitude, but Diego would still have to fine tune the satellite settings. Normally, this took her about five to seven minutes, but these were not normal conditions.

Jenny was leaning out the starboard side of the helicopter, straining against her seatbelt, pointing and yelling to Diego over the headset where she wanted the uplink. She grabbed her flying hair with her free hand. Diego looked like a fish out of water with all his gear. She walked him through the process, yelling into the headset and pointing a lot.

The fussiest part was positioning the mesh antenna. The wind did not affect it as much as a typical dish antenna, but Diego still needed to secure it with guy wires. He inserted the dish into the top of the cube and then started securing the antenna with guy wires and stakes.

Jenny yelled. Her voice crackled. "As you secure the antenna, verify the azimuth and altitude."

Diego struggled to adjust the antenna.

"Twenty minutes."

"Miguel, please count every minute from now on," asked Tom.

"Twenty-one minutes."

"Twenty-two minutes."

Diego continued to adjust the guy wires.

"Twenty-three minutes."

Done. Diego gave Jenny the thumbs up.

"Okay, press the green power button on the side. The signal should read at least thirty-five. Perfect," said Jenny.

It had only taken ten minutes at Lake Alpha and five minutes at Lake Bravo to confirm a signal from the Triton. They only had ten minutes of fuel left before they needed to head back. Tom kept Diego on the ground in case some final adjustments were necessary. Once Diego was back on board, they would not have time to drop him again.

"Diego, let's get your gear up while we wait to verify the signal," said Tom.

Diego had already shed all his gear and tied it together in a heap.

Tom lowered the cable. It took a few tries, but Diego finally corralled the cable and attached the heap.

"Twenty-four minutes."

Tom and Jenny quickly stashed his gear in the back and lowered the cable again. Diego deftly clipped in. Tom let out some slack. Paikea still struggled with the stick but was doing a remarkable job of keeping the helicopter steady.

"Twenty-five minutes."

Tom shouted above the din, "Jenny, can you verify the satellite uplink is functioning? Maybe the drop damaged it."

"I can, but it will take ten minutes to redirect the signal. I set it up to communicate through the Triton."

"Twenty-six minutes."

The noise was deafening. Tom yelled into the headset. "Diego, double check the azimuth and altitude readings." Tom let out some more of the cable already attached to Diego.

"Twenty-seven minutes." Tom sensed the urgency in Miguel's voice.

The gusts and downdraft buffeted Diego. He had positioned the antenna correctly. He gave Tom the thumbs up.

"Twenty-eight minutes."

Still no signal.

"Twenty-nine minutes. Señor Tom, we need to finish this up now."

Still no signal.

"Diego, we can't wait any longer. Let's get you back on board."

Tom activated the hoist. Diego was about three meters off the ground, swinging wildly around, when a gust suddenly rolled the helicopter to the port side, the opposite side of the hoist. With a screeching sound audible above all the other noise, the hoist buckled. Diego dropped about a meter, but he did not appear to be hurt. The hoist and cable were still attached, but the motor was not functioning. The cable was snarled in the mangled hoist.

"Thirty minutes."

"Paikea, take us down as low as you can. Jenny and I'll pull Diego up with a rope."

"Thirty-one minutes."

Tom knotted the end of the rope while Paikea slowly brought the craft down another couple of meters. They were about four meters off the ground. The rope was swinging wildly, but Diego grabbed it with his left hand, and then, letting go of the cable, his right. Paikea then slowly climbed a few meters while Diego, still attached to the cable, wrapped and tied the rope around his torso. Tom and Jenny pulled. Miguel in the port front seat was not positioned to help.

"Thirty-two minutes."

They still had two meters to pull. They needed Diego safely on board before they could head back to base camp.

"Thirty-three minutes."

With one last effort, Diego was close enough to grab a handle on the pontoon. He pulled himself up and slid over the pontoon into the Zodiac. He was much more agile without his diving gear.

"I'm in the Zodiac. I'll climb in the cabin once we get out of this wind," yelled Diego.

Tom secured the other end of the rope to a leg of the second row seat.

"Thirty-five minutes." Miguel had missed the last minute.

Paikea quickly brought the helicopter up above the peaks shouldering Lake Charlie. The gusting subsided at this altitude, but the wind was still blowing.

Diego said he was okay, but tired. "I'll stay in the Zodiac. Time for a siesta, Señor Tom."

Tom turned to Paikea. "How are we doing with gas?"

"We'll have a crosswind back to base camp. We should be okay, but no detours."

Like getting Diego back into the cockpit, thought Tom.

"Thirty-six minutes."

"Thanks Miguel. You can stop counting."

"We have a signal from the Triton," yelled Jenny, who had been monitoring the uplink. "That was quite a show, Indiana Tom. So much for your fear of flying. That should be worth a couple of merit badges."

Tom managed a smile. "I'm not afraid of flying." He was not sure what had happened, either. Normally, he would have thought this through, considering all the contingencies. This was so out of character for him.

When he was a kid, his mom talked about the Finnish word *susi,* but she couldn't easily explain it. Apparently, there is no equivalent word in English. Was this susi?

Miguel looked at them, puzzled and haggard. At least he had stopped rocking.

Three lakes down, two to go, a pile of rocks, a bunch of skulls and trinkets, a shattered canoe, and a broken hoist—but no gold.

The neural network was picking up anomalies, but as Tom had cautioned back in September, anomalies were not necessarily gold. The neural network was not smart enough with its limited training data set to discern the anomalies on the lake bottom from a pile of Inca gold and silver.

Once they got above the wind, it was a quieter ride back to base camp. Miguel's color returned. Paikea flew in a direct line, no longer following the contours. He needed to be sure he had enough gas to get back.

On the flight back, Tom reflected on what they found at Lake Bravo. It might be a significant find from an archaeological point of view. He looked forward to sharing this with Dr. Westhoven. Other sites of human sacrifice scattered across the Inca empire were near villages in the higher altitudes. There had to be a village nearby, consumed by the forest. The satellite imaging techniques refined by Dr. Parcak in Peru might find some clues of a nearby village. Perhaps another Machu Picchu. Lake Bravo was definitely worth a return visit at some point.

Finding a village in the forest was always a challenge, but he remembered *Congo* by Michael Crichton, where the expedition team used the albedo or reflectivity on satellite imagery to find the lost city of Zinj in the Congo. It was like the bands now used by Dr. Parcak.

Tom then turned his thoughts to Dr. Westhoven. Hopefully, he was on the mend and out of the hospital. Miguel had not provided an update since the first day.

He surveyed the landscape. The views were expansive, with the plains below and majestic peaks not too far away.

"That's Cotopaxi," said Jenny, pointing off to the left. She had told Tom on the Gulfstream that it was one of the highest active volcanoes in the world, with the last eruption in 2015.

They were higher than usual when they approached the base camp. Tarek had sited it well. It was well hidden from the helicopter.

Only two lakes to go, but their luck with the weather was turning. When Tom reviewed the data this morning with Miguel, tomorrow's weather looked uncertain at best. At least they were ahead of schedule.

The wind was significantly less at base camp. After Paikea landed and taxied to the dock, Diego popped his head up over the gunwale of the Zodiac.

"How was the ride, Diego?" Tom asked.

"It is good to be on the ground, Señor Tom. Good work."

Paikea was quiet as he secured the helicopter. The wind at Lake Charlie had tested his abilities.

Miguel took Tom aside by the gas tanks on the walkway. "I am not sure what to say, Señor Tom. I do not want to do that again, but quick thinking."

Tom was eager to look at the sonar for Lake Bravo, even though they would only have limited images so far. If tomorrow was a no-fly day, they should be able to review all the images from all the lakes by tomorrow afternoon.

Before dinner, Miguel disappeared into his headquarters tent for about thirty minutes. Tom wanted to connect with him to review the radar and satellites images for tomorrow's weather, for what they were worth, but he would wait.

Just before everyone gathered for dinner, Miguel wandered over to Tom and Jenny's tent. Discouraged, he showed Tom the weather data.

"Tomorrow is almost certainly a bad day, Señor Tom. After today, unless there is a big change overnight, I suggest we do not fly tomorrow. We are already ahead of schedule. Are you okay with my reasoning?"

Even if the weather was perfect tomorrow, Miguel looked like he could use a break.

"Makes sense. Jenny and I'll catch up on the Triton images. Do we make the call tonight or wait until morning?"

"The weather is such a mystery here. Let's wait until morning to make the final call."

At dinner time, Miguel confirmed the weather tomorrow was not promising, but he still needed everyone to be prepared to fly if the weather broke. "Señor Tom and I will make the final call in the morning. We completed Lake Bravo and Lake Charlie, so we are still on schedule, even if we cannot fly tomorrow. Unfortunately, still no gold but we have two lakes left."

After a pause, Miguel asked, "Any questions?"

"Yeah mate. How much gold was in the boneyard?" asked Paikea.

"Not much," replied Diego. "I brought up everything I could find in the pile."

Miguel added, "This is clearly not the lost Inca gold. Perhaps Lake Delta...."

Tom felt all eyes, except Jenny's, were on him. Everyone thought the first three lakes were the highest probability lakes. At least that's what Miguel told them on day one. And everyone was damp and discouraged, except Jenny. Although not showing it outwardly to the team, Tom could tell she was still basking in the whole experience—mud, stink, and all. She always seemed to handle any new challenge with aplomb. The white knuckles from Lake Alpha had not recurred. He knew she really didn't expect to find gold either, but she was still enjoying the adventure.

After dinner, Tom and Jenny huddled to review the Triton images and stay warm. He wanted to start with Lake Bravo, which was about half done. SonarSeer worked better on Lake Bravo without a lot of debris on the bottom.

He was glad to have something else to focus upon other than his failure to find gold.

Grounded

Tuesday, March 17, 2020
Base Camp
Llanganatis, Ecuador

Tom woke up to pelting rain. Tarek had done a decent job siting the base camp, but mud was everywhere, clogging the delicate trench work. The walkway was now crucial to getting around the site. Everything was damper this morning, if that was possible, and colder and darker. He let Jenny sleep.

The treetops swayed in the steady wind coming in off the lake. It wasn't promising. The wind blew the miasma into the surrounding woods, but Tom would trade the smell to be drier.

He took the pathway over to the kitchen, dodging raindrops on the way. Miguel was already there, studying the radar image on his computer screen in the harsh lighting. When Miguel looked up, he shook his head slowly from side to side and slid his laptop over to Tom.

"We're not flying today?" asked Tom.

"No, Señor Tom. There might be a break later in the afternoon, but it is difficult to predict in these mountains, and that does not give us enough time to do Lake Echo. I also had enough, how you say, excitement yesterday."

"It's okay. This gives Jenny and me a chance to look at Lake Bravo. Maybe we'll find other sites worth exploring."

"We will need more gold than bones in Lake Bravo, my friend, to justify the expense of this expedition." Miguel's upbeat demeanor had faded since Lake Charlie. He was out of his element.

Everyone was in slow motion this morning. Miguel confirmed to the group at breakfast, "No flying today, amigos. Lake Echo will wait until tomorrow. This is of no concern. We are ahead of schedule."

The mood was so different from the first night. The actual concern that no one mentioned was not the weather—but no gold.

৯৩৬

Mid-morning
Amherst, Vermont

Jenny's dad was struggling. John Kellogg had holed himself up in his cramped study across from his bedroom all morning trying to find something on the internet to reassure him. How could Jenny, at the last moment, replace a tenured Yale University archaeology professor on an expedition planned for over a year into the middle of nowhere?

And why all the secrecy?

And who was Miguel Titere?

And, most importantly, were they safe?

Over the weekend, he found a copy of the Derrotero online. Just as Tom had said, the first sentence referenced "a lake, made by hand, into which the ancients threw the gold."

He knew he would not hear from the kids until the expedition was over. Still, he was struggling—two college kids in the middle of nowhere, looking for the lost Inca gold, underwater. It just did not add up.

John was a retired physician in the Foreign Service. He wasn't a spy. But anyone posted to a hostile location received some training in spy craft. He had absorbed perhaps more than necessary. With his civilian credentials, he had also helped with a few operations in Colombia.

This morning, he used what he had learned in the Foreign Service to research Antiquities South. There was a fair amount of background information about Miguel Titere. He appeared to run a reputable business in pre-Colombian artifacts.

But there was no other information about any prior expeditions that either he or his company had sponsored. This appeared to be a new venture for Mr. Titere and Antiquities South, unless he shrouded his prior expeditions in secrecy, too. This didn't help his uneasiness.

The entire venture must have cost a fortune. A private jet picked up Jenny and Tom, and then they flew into the Llanganatis by helicopter. It did not seem like Antiquities South had the capital to fund an expedition on this scale.

With COVID engulfing the world, he also thought it odd Ecuador would allow the expedition to go forward.

He had called Dr. Westhoven at his Yale office yesterday, but his office said he was on spring break and indisposed. The administrative assistant shared nothing about COVID. John even pretended to be an old friend, and that he knew "Jerome" had COVID, and he just wanted to check in on him. That didn't work either. She didn't know how to contact him. He wondered if Dr. Westhoven had taken a turn for the worse.

He found a home phone for Dr. Westhoven, but only reached his voice mail, which was full.

From his time in Colombia, John understood how dangerous the Llanganatis could be, even for an experienced explorer. Every couple of months, the newspapers would have a story of a tourist who needed rescue. Even with helicopters, the mountain weather was treacherous, as evidenced by the crash last summer.

Today, on day three of the expedition, he needed some reassurance that they were okay. He decided to reach out to Antiquities South.

He waited until noon to call, to allow for the one-hour time difference. When the office answered, before he could say hello, a recorded voice message started…

"Antigüedades Sur está de vacaciones hasta el 31 de marzo. Por favor, deje su nombre y número, y le devolveremos su llamada lo antes posible. Gracias."

(Antiquities South is on holiday until March 31. Please leave your name and number, and we will return your call as soon as possible. Thank you.)

I guess that makes sense, he thought. An expedition like this requires all hands on deck. Even though he probably wouldn't get a return call until next week, he still left his name and number and a brief explanation, in Spanish, that he was looking for an update on the expedition.

He did not mention he was Jenny's dad or the Llanganatis.

As soon as he hung up, he worried he'd overstepped. But at least he was doing something. He returned to the Derrotero.

His iPhone vibrated a few minutes later, which startled him. It was an out-of-country call. When he answered, a woman with a soft voice in Spanish explained Antiquities South was on holiday and closed for the next couple of weeks. Mr. Titere checks in periodically and she would pass along any message.

"Gracias. Solo estaba buscando una actualización sobre los Llanganatis. ¿Tienes alguna noticia?"

(Thank you. I was just looking for an update about the Llanganatis. Do you have any news?)

The voice hesitated and then spoke with a distinct edge.

"El señor Titere está de vacaciones, fuera del país y es inalcanzable. No tenía conocimiento de ninguna expedición. Envió un breve correo electrónico esta mañana diciendo que estaba bien."

(Mr. Titere is on vacation, out of the country and unreachable. He was not aware of any expedition. He sent a short email this morning saying he was fine.)

John was persistent. He thanked her for returning his call so quickly and asked how he could connect with Señor Titere directly, even if by email. He said he had some information about Dr. Westhoven that he wanted to share with Señor Titere, which was not true.

She converted to English. "That would not be possible, señor," she said. "But if you give me the information, I will update Mr. Titere when he next contacts me. Sorry, I cannot be of more help."

The call itself was of no particular concern. He understood the confidentiality surrounding the expedition. What bothered him was how her soft voice hardened when he mentioned the Llanganatis.

It was now lunchtime, but he had no appetite. He was even more unsettled.

Ingrid could tell he was up to something. No matter what he was doing in his office, John would usually sweep around the house every hour or so to get a cup of coffee, check the mail, look at the lake, or whatever. He was not one to sit still for too long.

He had been upstairs, however, most of the morning. She heard him on the phone, but she couldn't make out the conversation. Did this have something to do with the expedition?

She was concerned, too.

With the vacuum cleaner as a prop, she wandered upstairs to see what he was doing.

"Do you mind if I vacuum?" She could tell something was bothering him. "What are you up to?"

"Hey. No, vacuum away. I need a break. I've been trying to track down any information about Jenny and Tom and the expedition, and I'm not having much luck."

He reviewed his phone calls from yesterday, trying to reach Dr. Westhoven. Then he described his phone calls from this morning to Antiquities South.

They both trusted Tom, and they had faith in Jenny, but her circumspect answers sometimes left them with more questions. John always suspected the project was about the lost Inca gold, but there was still much they did not know about the expedition.

"There's an undue amount of secrecy surrounding the expedition, but I guess it makes sense. The last thing the Ecuadorian government wants is a gold rush into the Llanganatis National Park," said John. "But I have to admit, the secrecy just adds to my concern."

He didn't say this to Ingrid, but if something about this project was illicit, that would also explain the secrecy.

Ingrid put down the vacuum cleaner. "Why don't you call Lucille and ask her to do some checking?"

Lucille Escot was a spook from John's past. She had taken over as Chief of Station of the CIA field office in Bogotá when John was wrapping up his service in Colombia. John worked with her on a couple "diplomatic" issues. Also, Lucille's husband was from Vermont. They'd all became good friends in their brief time together in Colombia, and had spent a 4th of July weekend together in Vermont years ago.

"To be honest, I can't stop thinking about Jenny, either. All I remember about the Llanganatis is how dangerous they could be," she added.

John rubbed his chin. He hadn't shaved this morning. "I haven't connected with Lucille in over a year. This would be a great time to say hi."

The last time they talked, Lucille had been thinking about retirement. He wasn't sure she was still in Colombia, but he'd find out soon enough.

< Hey Lucille - do you have a few
minutes to catch up and I have a
favor to ask. >

Mid-morning
Base Camp
Llanganatis, Ecuador

Tom and Jenny were still holed up in the storage tent, reviewing sonar images. By mid-morning, Tom needed a break. "I'm going to check the weather maps for tomorrow and see if Miguel has an update on Dr. Westhoven."

A few minutes later, he returned. As he opened the flaps of the tent, Jenny asked, "What's the weather for tomorrow?"

"I don't know," he replied in a low voice, staring at the tent floor.

She turned. "What's the matter? Is Dr. Westhoven okay?"

"I don't know. I didn't mean to eavesdrop, but Miguel was talking to somebody in a low voice about yesterday and the weather today. I thought this was supposed to be a supersecret mission? There must be somebody else involved. Somebody important enough that Miguel disappears for a half-hour every day to update."

"Was it Dr. Westhoven?"

"But why whisper?"

"He was probably just talking to his wife." Jenny always had a positive spin.

Tom continued, "It also seems weird that Tarek attended the conference a year ago and Miguel doesn't appear to know him that well. If Miguel didn't send our base camp manager to the conference, then who did?"

They spent the rest of the morning carefully reviewing the Triton images from Lake Bravo. Tom was not just looking for Inca gold, which they did not find, but for other sacrificial sites.

After a few hours of staring at green blips, they found a half-dozen other smaller sites, all within 250 meters of the target coordinates, with the same sonar signature as the sacrificial site they had found. They were all too deep to see on Depth Cam or the video from the Triton.

"There must be an Inca village nearby. I noticed a trail on the map called *Ruta Cerro Hermoso* about two kilometers north at the same elevation as Lake Bravo. The satellite images of the area surrounding the lake might provide some clues. This may be a worthwhile expedition with Dr. Westhoven once COVID quiets down."

"I'm coming, too," said Jenny.

"Of course." Tom had learned his lesson.

Ideally, he should leave the sacrificial remains untouched until a formal expedition, but Tom needed to tell Miguel about the other potential sites. Perhaps he would fund another trip to search for the lost Inca village that might harbor a stash of gold.

With the downtime today, the foul weather, and the lack of internet, the isolation in the Llanganatis was even more pressing.

As a break from green blips, Tom took a closer look at the Chromebook presenting the Triton images. Whoever set it up had locked down the BIOS from accessing the internet. Tom did not want to risk corrupting the BIOS. If he ever came back to the Llanganatis, he would bring his own satellite phone.

By late morning, the rain was diminishing a little, but the humidity was stifling. And the constant rain fueled the smell.

The winds had also picked up. Even if it cleared, it was not safe to fly. Although the MD600N was ideal for this mission with its range, capacity, and payload, it was no match for the winds and weather of the Llanganatis. Was any helicopter, wondered Tom.

Today was the first day the team gathered for lunch, and Tom and Jenny headed over to join them. The walkway, now floating on mud, was more unsteady, and the hinges connecting the sections of the walkway squeaked when they walked.

The dark sky and rain made it feel colder than it was. The LED lights were on in the dining area. With no sunlight, there was no pea-green hue from the tarp. But the tarp amplified the rain drops. The wind coming off the lake also moved the rain about, so Tarek had dropped the side facing the wind. The kitchen and dining area stayed remarkably dry.

Miguel was next to arrive with his laptop. He wiped off the rain and opened the laptop on the table to review tomorrow's weather with Tom.

The rest of the team arrived shortly thereafter, looking glum. Was it the rain or mud or no gold? Other than Miguel, this was an experienced team. So, it was probably not the weather.

After a light lunch, Miguel asked for everyone's attention. "Tom and I have reviewed the weather data. This wind and rain will pass through this evening and the winds will die down overnight. It may still be raining in the morning, but the weather should be good after breakfast. We will fly tomorrow a little later, about nine in the morning."

Miguel then asked Tom and Jenny for an update on the Triton scans. Tom had not had a chance to tell him about the other sites in Lake Bravo. He was not sure if Miguel wanted to share this with the entire team, but he'd asked for an update.

"We didn't find anything that looked like a pile of gold, but in Lake Bravo we found six other smaller potential sites of human sacrifice on sonar within 250 meters of the target coordinates. The sites are deeper than what we found yesterday, and I can't separate trinkets from bones on sonar. Otherwise, no gold."

Everyone was quiet. So far, the expedition had been a failure. Tom did not bother to mention the archaeological value of possibly finding an Inca village by Lake Bravo. No one would be interested.

Tom rubbed his neck. It was stiff from hunching over the sonar display for hours. The constant dampness didn't help.

Miguel was the first to speak. "If we have some additional time in the next few days, and the weather cooperates, we can return to Lake Bravo, but our focus tomorrow and the next day will be on Lake Echo and Lake Delta."

Then he continued, "It has been a busy couple of days. Try to rest this afternoon. We will leave later than usual tomorrow morning, so we may be hurried once we reach Lake Echo."

As the meeting broke up, Tom approached Miguel. "Hey Miguel, any updates on Dr. Westhoven?"

"No, Señor Tom. I think he is still in the hospital, but I'm having difficulty tracking him down. I'll try again this afternoon."

Then who was he talking to on the satellite phone this morning if it wasn't Dr. Westhoven?

Most everyone drifted into and out of the kitchen area throughout the afternoon, but with little conversation. The kitchen was the driest part of base camp and Tarek had the LEDs fully lit, along with a pot of coffee. Paikea had a book. Diego fiddled with a regulator he had dented yesterday at Lake Charlie. Tarek was preparing dinner. Tom and Jenny spent most of the afternoon staring at Triton scans but swung by the kitchen for some coffee to warm up. Miguel, on the other hand, spent most of the afternoon in his headquarters tent.

The weather was miserable. The treetops gently swayed, and branches dripped from the constant rain. Tom was looking forward to dinner just to do something else than listen to raindrops and blips.

By afternoon, even with the trenches and tarps, the base camp was a swamp. The walkway was increasingly essential to getting around the camp. Tom wished he'd brought his Sou'Wester hat. He noticed some stumps already had small shoots growing out of the mud. Tarek must have cut these trees a while back. He wondered if any squirrels lived in the remaining trees. He had seen no wildlife in base camp, and the ersatz Blue Jay had been quiet.

He and Jenny wandered around as much as they could on the walkway. The large green leaves near the ground had a blackish mold growing on them. Little red berries grew everywhere. A few had fallen on the walkway and then squished, leaving a red splotch with a tiny pit in the middle. There was so much about this place he did not know or understand. He wished Dr. Westhoven were here, but then Jenny wouldn't be here, balancing with him around the floating walkway. This would be a totally different experience without her.

"How are you doing?" she asked.

"Okay, I guess. I didn't really expect to find any gold, but the sacrificial sites are interesting. I was worried this might happen with the dataset shift."

"What's that?"

"Dataset shift happens when you shift from the training data to the real world. The difference between training data, or plastic gold, and the actual gold, may be so significant that the neural network doesn't work."

"Well, we still have two lakes to go," she said half-heartedly.

It was a quiet walk the rest of the way around the Monopoly board.

Jenny went back to the tent to lie down, but Tom wasn't tired. He returned to reviewing sonar images from Lake Charlie. A steep drop off ran through the middle of the lake that was too deep for video. This was almost certainly an ancient river. But Tom couldn't tell from sonar if Lake Charlie was man made. He still held out some hope that the sonar would find gold, but he was nearly finished with the Triton images from Lake Charlie.

By late afternoon, he needed another break, so he strolled around the walkway, the hinges squeaking with each step. He stopped by their tent. When he opened the flap, Jenny was still napping. He looked out over the lake. The rain had died down. He wondered what the Incas called this lake.

It reminded him of Lake Amherst. He reminisced back to a year ago when he had finished his capstone and Dr. Westhoven thought it was good enough for publication. Dr. Wade had accepted him into the master's program for computer science. His presentation in Boston had gone well. Life was good back then.

Then, last February after the conference, Dr. Westhoven dumped this virtual expedition in his lap to find Inca gold, which changed everything. He remembered wondering at the time if his future was out of control.

And now, here he was in the middle of nowhere. He had been discouraged all last summer, ready to give up several times, but he fed off the energy of Dr. Westhoven and Jenny. When Dr. Westhoven contracted COVID, however, he was done. He had not wanted to come here.

But because of Jenny, here he was, wiping the constant mist off his upper lip. And Lake Bravo was a significant, albeit unexpected, find. Despite the miserable weather and failing to find gold, Tom surprisingly felt an easiness watching the wind dance on the water. He was not sure why. Maybe because it was almost over.

Watching the sun desperately trying to break through, he realized that without the support of others, all throughout his life, he would also not be here. He remembered a poem from high school English that no man is an island. It was true. He did not always fully appreciate the others in his life.

But here in the rain, mire, and stench, overlooking an unnamed lake in the Llanganatis, Tom reflected on what Mr. Gartley had told him over a year ago—don't get in the way of your future, and take opportunities as they happen. He also remembered his meeting with Dr. Wade when Tom had wanted his advisor to convince him not to do this, but Dr. Wade did not. Now, with only two lakes to go, it would be over soon.

Tom thought he now understood Mr. Gartley's advice better. Over the last year, he had done things he never would have even tried a year ago. Yesterday at Lake Charlie felt so natural. He didn't have time to think—he just did.

Even with no Inca gold, he felt oddly content.

Of course, he still wanted to find the gold, but Lake Delta and Lake Echo were low probabilities. For perhaps the first time in his life, he would finish a project, it would fail miserably, and he was okay with that.

Early Afternoon
Amherst, Vermont

A half hour later, Lucille replied.

> < Hey John. Nice to hear from you. Today is
> crazy. How about if we connect tomorrow
> first thing about 8 a.m. EDT? >

> < Sounds great. Please call me at this
> number AYC. >

John would have a restless night. Lucille must still be in Colombia to name the time zone. Bogotá was now one hour earlier since daylight savings had started in the U.S.

Lake Echo

Wednesday, March 18, 2020
Base Camp
Llanganatis, Ecuador

Day Four started out dark, but with streaks of sun shining through the trees behind the base camp. There was color in the clouds. In Maine, this would suggest "red sky at dawn, sailors be warned," but the radar looked promising. As the team had learned the hard way on Lake Charlie, however, the radar was not great at predicting micro weather or wind. Nevertheless, the rain stopped earlier than expected.

There was a gentle breeze coming in off the lake. Everything was still wet, but the base camp was no longer a swamp. Still, Tom felt wetter after four days in the Llanganatis.

The stink that enveloped the camp yesterday was also better. Either the breeze off the lake helped or his nose had given up.

Hopefully, the breaking weather was a good omen. Today, they would visit Lake Echo, the least likely of the five lakes to harbor the hidden gold.

As the team made their way to the kitchen area for COVID testing, everyone, including Jenny a bit, looked discouraged except Miguel, the one with the most to lose. He was in remarkably good spirits, but by now, everyone ignored his mood swings.

After briefly consulting with Tom, Miguel confirmed that the weather looked good throughout the day. "Today, my friends, is a rare day in these mountains. Let's take full advantage of our good fortune and find some gold."

Lake Echo was the closest to base camp, only nine kilometers and about a twenty-minute flight. It was also the highest. Lake Delta was too far away to try for two lakes today.

It was also the longest lake at about 800 meters, oriented southwest to northeast, and the narrowest at about 170 meters, nestled on a declivity. Fortunately, the wind was mild, blowing from the northwest across the lake, so no wind tunnel effect today.

Everyone was at the helicopter, ready to fly at nine o'clock.

"Day four, fingers crossed," said Jenny to Tom.

He thought Jenny seemed a little uneasy. He felt it, too.

"Yeah." He was still worried about the "red sky at dawn."

With everyone secure, Paikea started the engine. "No acrobatics today, eh, mate?" The noise of the helicopter continued to be jarring.

As much as Tom had always believed the likelihood of finding gold was negligible, he was still a little disappointed as they headed northwest to Lake Echo. Whether or not they found any gold, he was glad Jenny was here.

His mind wandered during the brief trip. Could the additional images from the Triton somehow further train the neural network for a future expedition, if Miguel wanted to waste another million or two?

∂∘∾

Early Morning
Amherst, Vermont

While John was waiting for the call from Lucille, he reminisced. The Foreign Service is a lot like the military. You make a lot of friends in a brief period of time, and you stay in touch, perhaps infrequently, but you stay in touch.

Although his involvement with the CIA was peripheral, he'd learned Lucille was no nonsense, and she got things done. His time in Colombia was during some significant turmoil and strained relationships between the United States and Colombia, primarily over the drug trade and the paramilitary.

The embassy personnel in Bogotá had developed a hunkered down mentality and supported each other in ways beyond the call of duty. He always felt his family was safe with Lucille as Chief of Station.

Another connection was through the spouses. Ingrid and Lucille's husband, Rob, were both from Vermont. Ingrid grew up in Proctor and Rob in Burlington.

Lucille called as scheduled. "Hey, John. It's nice to hear from you. How are you?"

They spent a few minutes catching up on family news and the whereabouts of their kids. Lucille had a daughter Jenny's age, about ten years old when they were in Colombia.

Lucille continued, "I'm following in your footsteps. We're moving to D.C. this summer to finish out my service and then retire back to New England, hopefully also in the Green Mountains."

"That's wonderful Lucille. There's a camp for sale on the lake. I'll put a deposit on it for you."

Lucille laughed. "Don't tell Rob. It will be another two to three years. So, John, what's up? I know you didn't text me to sell real estate."

"Yeah, well, I'm probably overreacting but—"

"John, I've never seen you overreact. What's up?"

"Jenny was a last-minute replacement on an expedition into the Llanganatis. She replaced a Yale archaeology professor who contracted COVID last week. She joined her boyfriend, who's a computer whiz. Apparently, he developed a computer program that used satellite images to search for the lost Inca gold underwater. They left on Saturday and are due back this Sunday.

"The expedition is well financed. Jenny and Tom, her boyfriend, flew in a private jet from Bangor directly to Quito. They get around the Llanganatis by helicopter. But the guy financing the expedition doesn't look like he has that kind of money.

"I'm also surprised the Ecuadorian government allowed the expedition. The last I remember, they were tired of rescue missions into the Llanganatis and limited all expeditions. Has that changed? I guess I also expected them to pull the plug with COVID."

"I'm not sure, John, but I'll do some checking."

"Sorry to dump this on you. I know you're busy, but this happened all so suddenly. There's been no communication from the kids, which is expected. But when I called the company sponsoring the expedition, they acted like they had never heard of the Llanganatis. Also, I can't track down the Yale professor. He was hospitalized, so maybe he's home recovering, but who knows?"

"I can tell you're concerned. Text me the name of the sponsor and the Yale professor. Let's connect this evening."

"Thanks Lucille. I'll also send along some photos of the camp for sale to Rob."

"Don't you dare."

Lake Echo
Llanganatis, Ecuador

Paikea was back to following the contours of the mountains. During the flight, fog hung low in the valleys. Tom hoped they would not encounter poor conditions at Lake Echo. As they ascended, the trees shrank until they looked like bonsai and eventually gave way to páramo.

As they approached Lake Echo, Tom asked Miguel, "Any news on Dr. Westhoven?"

"Yes, Señor Tom. Sorry, I forgot to mention at breakfast. I believe he is still in the hospital, but I have been unable to talk with him directly. I'll try again this afternoon. Do you have any way to contact him other than his phone?"

"Only email."

Tom wondered if an eight-day hospitalization was typical for COVID.

At 3,800 meters, Lake Echo was the highest lake, about 1,200 meters higher than base camp. Tom worried about the wind at this altitude. In Maine, the higher you went, the faster the winds, but Windy.com predicted only a breeze.

On the satellite, páramo surrounded the lake with a flat shoreline. The elongated shape suggested an old river. He also noticed a small pond to the southwest, possibly a remnant of a river. On satellite, there were no significant issues on the southern shore to affect the setup of the satellite uplink.

The target coordinates suggested the anomaly was off the northwest shore. Tom peered down as they passed over the target area. It was deeper here, and he could not make out anything on the bottom.

On approach to the lake, Tom noticed a subtle mound highlighting the southwest end of the lake. Was this man-made? The mound reminded him of a beaver dam, but much bigger. A stream entered on the opposite, northeast end of the lake.

Paikea set the helicopter down near the northern shore. After Lake Charlie, the gentle bobbing on the waves felt almost relaxing.

Tom sat in the Zodiac for a moment before starting the Honda. The weather was holding. It was a remarkably calm day with scattered clouds. The sun darted in and out, mostly out.

Tom took off his headset for a moment. It was so quiet. This was the first time since their arrival that he'd felt the full warmth of the sun.

He replaced his headset and started the Honda, then maneuvered the Zodiac to the starboard side to pick up Jenny. Diego deployed from the port side. Diego had already turned on the video feed and LED.

The bubble trail showed Diego on the way to the target. Tom followed in the Zodiac. Diego went deep to avoid the Honda. With his polarizing sunglasses, Tom could follow his outline against the darker bottom.

As they approached the target coordinates, something on the bottom caught Tom's eye. Then he remembered the volcanic rocks in Lake Alpha.

As Tom arrived over the target, he said, "Okay, Jenny, drop the guideli...."

Before he could finish, Diego surfaced.

"Oh no, now what?" thought Tom.

Diego's eyes were wide open, bulging, as though his oxygen supply was compromised. He ripped his mouthpiece off with his left hand and held up a dirty vessel with his right. It sparkled in the sunlight where he had rubbed off the silt.

"GOLD! There's a pile of gold and silver down there, Señor Tom!"

Tom and Jenny hugged each other and high-fived Diego's free hand.

"Tom—you did it—you did it! Your program worked. It actually worked," she yelled, echoing off the surrounding hills, as she bounced up and down on the gunwale.

Over in the helicopter about one hundred meters away, Miguel, focusing on the computer screen, tried to fist bump Paikea, almost hitting him in the jaw.

Diego passed the gold jar to Jenny.

The gold was cold from the water. "It's a lot heavier than the plastic gold," she said as she rubbed off more of the silt and handed it to Tom. She blew into her cupped hands to warm them up, which momentarily hid her bright smile.

Tom stared at the jar. It was about thirty centimeters tall, only slightly larger than the plastic jars they had dumped all summer. Dr. Westhoven had guessed the size and shape correctly.

He had worked so hard for so long on the neural network, never really expecting to find any gold. He had already accepted his failure. As he turned the jar over in his hands, he was not prepared for this affirmation.

"Yeah, a lot heavier," he replied.

Jenny hugged him again, this time with a big kiss, which helped convince Tom that this was really happening.

Tom was still examining the jar when Diego came back up with a couple of large gold plates. Tom yelled, "How much?"

"A pile. It looks like there are dozens and dozens of jars and plates of different sizes, and cups, and figurines like llamas and people. It is mostly gold, but some silver, too."

Then Tom remembered they had broken protocol. The plan was to photograph any find before disturbing it. He could understand Diego's excitement, but before the diver went down under again, Tom passed him the underwater camera, with the measurement tape to photograph the pile. This would help estimate the value of the gold in the pile. Jenny handed Diego the mesh collection bag to bring up a sampling after he finished photographing the pile.

In the helicopter, Paikea and Miguel huddled around the computer screen watching Diego's video feed. Miguel was animated and yelling, but he'd taken off his headset in the celebration.

With the sun out now between clouds, Tom and Jenny could see Diego lay out the measurement tape. He was careful to avoid stirring up the silt. It took a few minutes to photograph the pile, and then he got back to the gold.

Tom and Jenny watched his silhouette while Diego filled the mesh collection bag. He tugged on the guideline to signal Jenny to pull it up. It was already heavy, but when the bag broke the surface of the water, she needed Tom's help to lift it over the gunwale. Tom could see plates, tiles, jars, and cups with scattered figurines, just like Dr. Westhoven had predicted.

The collection bag landed on the floor of the Zodiac and slid to the center. The water was calm. If it had been at all rough, stabilizing the boat with gold and silver sliding around might have been a challenge.

"You did it, Señor Tom!" exclaimed Diego as he climbed back into the Zodiac with Tom's help for a ride back to the helicopter.

Diego took one large cup and, while rotating it, gently rubbed off all the silt. It gleamed in the sun. Tom wondered how much the cup was worth.

After collecting the gold and some silver ingots, Diego looked tired. It had been a long week for everyone, but he had been the most physically active of the team, especially two days earlier at Lake Charlie.

Even though the plastic jars were bulky, Tom was glad he had included them in the training data set. Rocks, bones, and even trees had fooled his neural network, but possibly it was the larger jars that made the difference. It was hard to know with machine learning.

"You know, Señor Tom, there are actually two piles close together down there. It looks like a *mancuerna*, a dumbbell, like a number eight," said Diego as they motored back to the helicopter. "I also see small gold nuggets on the bottom, but it is hard to see how much with all the silt."

That makes sense, thought Tom, if the Incas dumped multiple boatloads here. Although it was hard to tell after Diego had stirred up the bottom silt, Tom estimated the pile was about six-by-twelve meters. He could not tell the height of the pile from the boat, but based upon the dispersion experiments in the Wave Tank, Tom thought the two piles could contain thousands of items. The photographs Diego took would give a more precise estimate.

He realized he was using metric without having to convert from feet.

If the legend was true, this was only a fraction of the gold headed for Cajamarca. Hopefully, the Triton would find evidence of other piles in Lake Echo.

But at least part of the legend was true. General Rumiñahui had hidden Inca gold in a man-made lake in the Llanganatis, and they had found some of it.

Back at the helicopter, with the broken hoist, Tom and Diego in the Zodiac, and Paikea in the helicopter, lifted the collection bag into the rear of the cockpit. Miguel helped Paikea place it into a specially constructed box. With his biggest smile yet, Miguel's hands were shaking as he closed the lid on the box.

Diego climbed into the helicopter.

Now it was Jenny's turn. The helicopter was anchored near the northern shore, so it took Tom a few minutes to pilot the Zodiac to the southern shoreline. He was heading directly into the sun.

Tom easily found a flat area for Jenny. While she set up the satellite uplink, he took the Zodiac over to the mound nearby on the southwest shore. It had looked smooth from the air, but up close, it was covered with scrub brush. This must be manmade, he thought.

He beached the Zodiac and climbed the subtle slope. On top of the mound, he estimated it was about fifty meters in diameter, but only about five meters high off the lake. The mound blended into the landscape.

When he looked to the south, he couldn't see any obvious old riverbed, but he saw the small pond he'd noticed on the satellite, maybe a remnant of a river. He would take another look with the infrared bands. This might be the key to finding other man-made lakes.

He picked up Jenny, and Tom turned the Zodiac back to the helicopter. She looked content with a gentle smile. "That's another merit badge. Excellent work, Scout Kirkpatrick."

Back at the helicopter, Jenny released the Triton. As programmed, it headed to the north shore and started its scan. Miguel and Tarek confirmed that the real-time images were uploading. It would take about eight hours for a complete scan of the lake, and another four hours to run the sonar through SonarSeer. It would be a long twelve hours, but this was the best chance so far to find more gold.

The mood in the helicopter ride back to base camp was distinctly different. The serious demeanor was gone. Nobody talked about the money or what they would do with it, but everybody was probably thinking about it.

He and Jenny were the youngest on the team, and he wanted to be perceived as professional, but he also wanted to scream and shout and jump up and down. He didn't know how to celebrate something like this.

But Jenny was otherwise quiet on the ride back to base camp. She was thinking about something. Tom would ask her what, back at base camp.

That night was a celebration. Miguel brought out more of bottles of Dom Perignon.

"How many bottles did he bring?" Tom whispered to Jenny. "We should have brought some Cold Duck."

"Dom will have to do."

Miguel led the first toast. "To my American amigo, Señor Tom, the best programmer of whatever you do. You found the hidden gold after five hundred years."

The champagne tasted a lot better without the acetazolamide. Maybe even better than Cold Duck.

Besides the gold, Tom was also pleased his neural network could support archaeology. His capstone was theoretical. This was real-life.

He was also grateful Jenny was there to share the experience. He wouldn't be here without her patiently, and sometimes not so patiently, nudging him along.

Tom looked forward to sharing this moment with Dr. Westhoven. He was not sure if Miguel had let him know yet. Tom wasn't even sure how he was doing.

After five days in the Llanganatis and all the toasts and celebration tonight, Tom still knew little about the team, especially Tarek, who rarely spoke. Regardless, the team performed well together, and they still had one more lake tomorrow.

Before bedtime, with a slight champagne buzz, Tom and Jenny took a quick look at the Triton images. SonarSeer found an interesting sonar image more toward the center of the lake. Lake Echo was about twenty meters deep there, too deep for quality video images or Depth Cam.

"Jenny, this may be another pile of gold. It must have been a lot of work to create the man-made lake. It makes sense the Incas would have placed more than one pile in the lake."

He continued, "Maybe we can go back after Lake Delta tomorrow, or we skip Lake Delta tomorrow and go back to Lake Echo. But that's Miguel's call."

They passed Miguel's tent on the walkway back to their tent, but it was dark. Tom let him sleep.

As Jenny bent down to unzip the flap on their tent, Tom looked up at the stars over the western horizon. As his eyes adjusted to the darkness, more and more stars appeared, but he couldn't recognize any constellations. He took some solace in seeing a sliver of the moon, something familiar.

Back in their own tent, he finally had a chance to ask Jenny, "What were you thinking about on the helicopter ride back to base camp? You had something on your mind, and it wasn't my merit badge."

She blinked a couple of times. "As happy as I am we found gold, I'm even more happy I'm here with you, that I met you, and we're going to be together the rest of our lives, gold or not. I was wondering what my life would be like if I hadn't enrolled in COS 140 on a whim."

Then she started to cry, trying to hide it with a firm embrace that lasted a while, as she composed herself. Tom wiped a tear from her eye. Then he gave her a soft kiss.

Noon
Amherst, Vermont

John received a text message a little after noontime from Lucille. He wasn't expecting a call until tonight. It was short and to the point.

> < Ecuador has issued no permits for any
> expeditions since the helicopter crash in
> August. In addition, there's some unusual
> activity on satellite in the eastern Llanganatis.
> Are you available to talk? >

He dialed at once. Lucille's tone of voice concerned him. She was a seasoned spook, but he sensed something was amiss. She explained she had connected with her counterpart in Ecuador, but the name did not ring a bell for John.

"It's possible someone higher up sanctioned this expedition and kept it quiet to avoid a gold rush into the Llanganatis, but I doubt it," she said. "My contact in Ecuador likely would have known.

"As you know, Miguel Titere is the sole proprietor of Antiquities South. Although his business doesn't seem to have the revenue to fund the expedition, he received a deposit of $2,500,000 about a year ago into a separate bank account in Bogotá. I'm still tracking this down.

"There's also something going on in the Llanganatis to the east. It's hard to tell from the current satellite images, but I'll have another satellite in position in about three or four hours. It will be dusk at that point, but we still can pick up infrared activity."

"Thanks, Lucille. If Titere sold an artifact worth $2,500,000, you'd think it would have made the news, but maybe not. Miguel Titere seems to be in the middle of this. Will you check him out? I'm wondering if someone else, someone who doesn't want to be identified, is behind the expedition."

"Sure, John. That's more up my alley."

They did not schedule a follow-up phone call. Lucille would reach out as soon as she had some information. "I should have something by tomorrow. Have a good evening, John."

❧⚬❦

Early Evening
Cartagena, Colombia

Omar was pleased, but he'd expected success. Otherwise, he would not have invested close to a million dollars into the operation. Some, if not most, would view this as arrogance, but he understood how to calculate risk.

Miguel called him on schedule.

"Congratulations, Miguel. I knew you were the one for the job. You and your team have accomplished what many have tried for over five hundred years. Good work."

"Thank you, Omar. It is still hard to believe, but the gold is really there."

"Tomorrow, ask Diego to turn on his video camera when you approach Lake Delta. I want to see everything."

Omar was already thinking ahead to Ground Zero tomorrow.

Lake Delta

Thursday, March 19, 2020
Base Camp
Llanganatis, Ecuador

Day Five felt different, besides being the last lake. Miguel had planned a later start so, for the first time in the Llanganatis, sunshine, albeit muted pea-green by the camouflage, greeted Tom and Jenny when they woke. A gentle breeze carried the smell away. The generators were off. The only sound was the lapping of waves on the shore and some sizzling from the kitchen. Even the screeching, ersatz Blue Jay wasn't as annoying.

Jenny stirred. Tom gave her a gentle kiss as she opened her eyes and smiled.

He didn't feel damp, or not as damp, for the first time in the Llanganatis. The morning sunshine helped. Even the mud seemed less muddy.

After putting on his boots, he followed the walkway, which was no longer squeaking, to Miguel's tent, where he heard rustling inside. Through the tent flaps, he said, "Miguel, I need to update you on the Triton scan of Lake Echo."

Miguel had enjoyed as much champagne as anyone had last night. When he popped his head out, he was still in pajamas, rubbing his left temple, squinting his eyelids against the sunlight, and quickly closing them.

"We reviewed the initial Triton scan from Lake Echo late last evening. There may be another pile toward the center of the lake that has a similar sonar footprint as the pile of gold and silver we found. It's too deep to get any video, but I wanted to let you know in case you wanted to change plans and go back to Lake Echo today.

"Also, the pile we found yesterday is thicker on sonar than I thought. I bet it holds well over a thousand pieces."

"I see," said Miguel, who was now in the door of his tent, rubbing both temples with his eyes still closed. His flannel pajamas were also from L.L. Bean.

He finally opened his eyes. "Let's stick with our original plan. We'll review the weather at breakfast, but the rest of the week does not look good. We may want to think about heading back to Quito later today. Also, I need to come back anyway to Lake Echo to extract the gold. I can check the other site then. I don't want to lose the opportunity to check Lake Delta.

"Señor Tom, let's not share the other pile with the team. Let's stay focused on Lake Delta."

Before breakfast, Miguel inspected the photographs taken by Diego in his headquarters tent. His head still throbbed. He wondered how a sudden influx of this many artifacts into the antiquities market would affect their value. Hopefully, Omar was not a modern-day conquistador who would melt everything down like the Spanish did five hundred years ago. The Ecuadorian government would not permit that, anyway.

Although Miguel wanted to tell Omar about the other pile that Tom had found on sonar, he decided to wait until his scheduled afternoon phone call. By then, he would know if the team was returning to Quito later today, and he also wanted to start packing.

Tom and Miguel arrived early to the kitchen to review the weather data. Today was the best day so far in the Llanganatis, but they both remembered the micro weather at Lake Charlie.

Miguel reiterated to Tom, "The rest of the week does not look promising. We may be stuck here if the weather turns as bad as predicted. Let's check the weather again when we return from Lake Delta. We may want to head back to Quito later this afternoon. We shall see."

After all the champagne last night, the rest of the team was also slow moving this morning. By eight o'clock, everyone had had a negative COVID test and gathered for breakfast. Miguel started their last briefing. He was subdued. Tom was glad he and Jenny only had a few glasses last night.

"We are down to our last lake today. Excellent work again everyone. Tom and I reviewed the weather data for the rest of the week. Today looks like the best day so far, even better than yesterday, but it does not look promising for the rest of the week. We need to finish today.

"We will check again this afternoon. If the weather prediction does not improve, please be prepared to return to Quito later today. The helicopter can easily handle the six of us and the gold.

"Tom, why don't you fill in the team on the initial scans from the Triton?"

Tom was puzzled. Miguel had told him not to share anything about the second pile. Then he realized Miguel meant the original one.

But before he started, Tarek asked, "Any idea of the size of the pile?"

"Based upon the sonar footprint, it is over a meter deep, with possibly over a thousand pieces."

This was the first question Tarek had asked all week. It reminded Tom of his question at the conference a year ago. How did Tarek fit into all of this?

Miguel continued. "Good news, good news indeed, Señor Tom. Okay, everyone, let's meet at the dock at 9:30 as planned. This gives everyone a few minutes to start packing if we need to leave later today."

They dispersed quickly. Everyone is probably eager to head back to Quito today, thought Tom. He certainly was.

At 9:30, the team headed down to the dock. With everyone buckled in, Paikea headed north to Lake Delta, the farthest away at thirty-four kilometers. It would take about thirty-five minutes. There was little conversation on the way. Everyone was deep in their own thoughts, and hungover.

On the way, Tom wondered how Dr. Westhoven was doing. Miguel still had not provided any meaningful update. Besides the gold, Tom also looked forward to telling Dr. Westhoven about the sacrificial sites at Lake Bravo.

As they approached Lake Delta, everyone brightened up. The lake was just outside the park boundaries. Dr. Westhoven had included all the lakes within the Llanganatis range, whether or not they were in the park. This was the second highest lake at about 3,700 meters and was surrounded by stubby trees and páramo, like Lake Echo. The weather was still holding. This was the best day so far. But Tom still hoped they would return to Quito later today.

"Diego, please turn on your video. I want to record everything," instructed Miguel.

Amherst, Vermont

Lucille sent John a brief but cryptic text.

> < Text me a current photo of each ASAP. I'll
> connect when it is over. >

Connect when what is over? He texted her a photo of Jenny and Tom from Christmas. He desperately wanted to reach out to Lucille, but he understood when an operation is in play, you need complete focus on the task at hand. Something was happening, and he trusted Lucille. He did not immediately share the text with Ingrid.

Cartagena, Colombia

In his office, Omar was setting up the video uplink of Diego's camera. Only Omar and Tarek knew about the fake gold they had planted at Lake Delta. He had two reasons for planting it.

The first was to ensure the program worked—it had.

The second was to have the team at the remote Lake Delta on the last day—they were.

He never intended to share the gold with anyone except Tarek. If the team found the actual gold, Omar had other plans for Lake Delta. That is why he'd hired Tarek to be base camp manager, why he needed Miguel on board the helicopter, and why Lake Delta was the most remote and final lake to visit.

Last night, with a proprietary satellite phone, Omar had instructed Tarek to proceed with the plan. Tarek then molded enough EPX-1 plastic explosive into the tail section to blow up the helicopter three times over. The EPX-1 would even explode underwater if needed. The detonator, controlled by Tarek, was a separate, dedicated satellite link with the antenna mounted inconspicuously on top of the tail.

Tarek, back at base camp, monitored Diego's video feed as the helicopter approached Lake Delta. Tarek would use the video and the communication channels to time the detonation.

On the proprietary communication channel with Omar, Tarek asked, "Do you have visual?"

"Yes," replied Omar.

Omar knew there would be repercussions. Paikea and Diego had no family, but there would be an investigation into the whereabouts of Miguel and the two young Americans. It would take a while for the authorities to figure out what happened, but the investigation would ultimately lead back to him. The team was expected back Sunday, so he would need to act quickly to recover the gold and then disappear.

Lake Delta
Llanganatis, Ecuador

The weather remained sunny, with scattered clouds and a gentle breeze from the northwest, by far the best day for flying of the week.

As the helicopter started its descent onto the lake, it always sounded louder. Paikea had explained it was the reflection off the lake.

But today, Tom thought he heard an unfamiliar sound coming from the tail. Perhaps it had something to do with the humidity or the mirror surface of the lake.

Tom pointed to a landing area about one hundred meters northwest of the target.

The images from Diego were choppy because of the limited bandwidth of the video uplink, but Tarek recognized Ground Zero. He needed the helicopter on the water to minimize the blast dispersion. He had his finger on the trigger, waiting for Omar's signal.

Paikea landed and powered down the engine.

For the first time this week, with the rotors still slowing down, Paikea turned around with a thumbs up and said, "Hey mates, the water is as smooth as a baby wallaby. You can leave the chopper anytime, eh." Diego was already sliding into the water.

"The diver is in the water! He's in the water," shouted Tarek to Omar. "He's not supposed to be in the water. They changed protocol."

He fingered the trigger.

"Wait, Tarek," ordered Omar. "I want them all in the helicopter." Tarek released the trigger. "We will do it just before take-off. This should not take long. We know there is no gold here."

Back at the helicopter, as the rotors finally stopped, Paikea removed his headphones and motioned for Miguel to do the same.

"Something doesn't sound right back in the tail. I don't trust these NOTAR choppers without a tail rotor. I'm going to take a quick look back there," he said to Miguel.

"Are you sure you know what you are doing?" asked Miguel.

"Not really, but I want to be sure nothing is loose."

Paikea pulled a tool set out from under his seat and climbed out on the starboard pontoon, working his way back to the service panel on the tail.

Tom and Jenny were over the site in a couple of minutes. Before she could even lower the guideline, Diego broke the surface holding a brick.

He spit out his mouthpiece. "There is a pile of debris down there, bricks, jars, plates. I will look around some more, but I do not see any gold."

Diego was underwater again.

"This doesn't make sense," said Tom as he turned the wet red brick over in his hands. "This place is so remote. How did bricks get out here?"

"It wasn't the Incas," replied Jenny. "They didn't use bricks. This place is starting to give me the creeps."

Diego surfaced again. "It's just debris. I'm heading back to the chopper."

As Diego went under again, Tom, still shaking his head, turned the Zodiac toward the southern shore for the last satellite uplink.

As he revved the Honda, he yelled at Jenny. "Let's get this over with so we can head back to Quito today. Those clouds to the east look ominous."

Jenny turned back to Tom to hear him better. Then she cocked her head.

"What's Paikea doing?" she yelled, pointing back to the helicopter.

Tom turned around just as Paikea dove into the lake, almost hitting Diego, who was surfacing. Miguel was screaming something at Paikea, but Tom couldn't make it out.

Tarek was monitoring Diego's video feed. As Diego broke the surface, Tarek saw Paikea dive from the pontoon into the lake, just missing him. Tarek saw the service panel was removed from the tail where he had packed the EPX-1.

Omar was watching all this as well.

"NOW!" Omar yelled to Tarek.

Tarek detonated the plastic explosive.

They immediately lost the video feed from Diego.

"Good work, Tarek. We will deal with those kids later. Contact the salvage helicopter to start the recovery process of the gold."

Tom and Jenny saw and then heard the explosion, starting in the tail, that quickly engulfed the helicopter. Instinctively, Tom sprang at Jenny. As he lifted her up and over the bow, he felt a sting in his right calf and then a cracking sensation in his right arm, the one holding Jenny. His headset, along with Jenny's, came loose and sank.

Underwater, when he looked up, shrapnel rained down around them. Dozens of fragments sizzled when they hit the water, and then slowly sunk. It reminded him of fireworks. Jenny's hair floated in a surreal appearance. Her eyes were wide open as she clutched the left side of her chest.

The rain of shrapnel was over in about twenty seconds. Still holding Jenny tightly, he surfaced. Detritus was scattered everywhere.

She was shaking, and ghostly white. She tried to speak, but only a whisper came out of her blue lips. "I can't breathe. It hurts."

Tom knew what had happened. "I cracked your rib. Take a deep breath now."

"Arrrgh...."

"All right, Jenny. Now take shallow breaths. Let's get to shore. Shallow breaths."

Tom only had minutes to get them out of the frigid water. Then he noticed red in the water. "Are you okay? Did you get hit anywhere?" His left ear was ringing and he couldn't hear out of it.

She just stared at the sinking helicopter. Her pained eyes fixed on the wreckage. "I'm okay, except for my chest."

The two pontoons and what was left of the cabin were detached and sinking fast.

The Honda was still idling, but the Zodiac was taking on water rapidly, with a dozen or so small holes and one gaping hole by the bow where Jenny had been sitting.

Tom started swimming to the Zodiac, pulling Jenny along, who was still clutching her left chest. His right calf cramped.

The outboard was now underwater, and pulling the Zodiac down.

Everything floating in the water had some damage from the shrapnel. Life vests were scattered everywhere. Tom grabbed one for Jenny. He needed to get her to shore. He was feeling the cold, too. She felt even heavier now, with her jacket soaked through.

"Jenny, take a deep breath and get out of the jacket. I'll help you with the life vest. Hurry, we need to get out of the water."

When Tom turned to get another life vest for himself, the Zodiac was gone.

Suddenly, as Jenny was sliding the life vest on, something pulled her down.

As her head went underwater, Tom took a deep breath and dove. A bowline from the Zodiac was wrapped around her right ankle and was pulling her under. One powerful kick and he reached the line. The Honda had settled on the bottom with the Zodiac still attached, fluttering like a flame bleeding bubbles.

Jenny desperately kicked her left leg, but her right ankle was tightly bound to the line. Tom unsheathed his knife and frantically cut at the rope.

Time slowed down, just like in the movies, as he severed the last strands. Jenny was about one meter below the surface. She surfaced first, followed by Tom. The pain hampered her cough as she gulped for air.

The lake was frigid. She was struggling. He grabbed onto another life vest for himself. They were both buoyant, but they were about seventy-five meters from the southern shore.

The seat locker from the Zodiac floated nearby.

"Jenny, grab the locker and hold on. Kick as much as you can. We've got to get out of the water."

Jenny grabbed it with her right arm. Her muscles were stiffening, but she could still kick.

Tom muckled onto a line attached to the seat locker and wrapped it around his shoulder. He could swim while pulling Jenny along. His right leg hurt and his muscles were stiffening, too.

Still fifty meters to shore. It seemed insurmountable.

Then he remembered. On the Depth Cam images near the shore, the lake was relatively shallow. Another twenty-five meters and he might be able to touch the bottom.

"Just a little more, Jenny. You're doing great."

Tom finally touched the bottom, but walking on the slippery bottom was slow going with his muscles seizing.

As he pulled Jenny the last ten meters, he searched in the deep pocket of his cargo pants. He pressed the triangular SOS button of the Garmin EarthMate that her parents had given him at Christmas. There was no beep or buzz. He could have missed it with the constant ringing in his left ear. Maybe it wasn't waterproof.

They collapsed on the narrow beach. Jenny was still holding onto the seat locker and started shivering. Tom flung open the seat locker and found a small emergency kit. His hands and fingers were stiff and numb. He rummaged through the bandages, tapes, and ointments and found what he was looking for at the bottom, thermal blankets and waterproof matches.

While he clumsily unfolded the mylar blanket, he told her, "Get out of those wet clothes."

Jenny struggled, but he quickly wrapped her up and started rubbing her arms and legs. She was ghostly white, but her shivering improved.

"Keep moving, Jenny. I'll get a fire started. We've got to warm you up. Keep moving."

Tom knew he also had to keep moving. Although there were no trees on the páramo, the beach was littered with stunted driftwood and he was able to get a small fire crackling. He then stripped down and wrapped himself in another thermal blanket, and huddled next to Jenny. Only her face poked out of her shiny cocoon. She had stopped shaking and Tom could see color returning to her cheeks.

She leaned gently on Tom. "What happened?" she asked softly.

"I don't know. Maybe a gasoline explosion. I don't think anyone else survived. How's your chest?"

"It aches a little, but I'm numb all over. I'm just so tired."

"Let's warm up a little more and then we'll build some shelter. We only have one box of matches, so we need to keep this fire going. We may be here a while until Tarek realizes what has happened."

❧

Amherst, Vermont

John received a text message. He thought it was Lucille with an update, but it was from Garmin. Tom had sent an SOS. The message included GPS coordinates.

John texted the coordinates at once to Lucille. She replied quickly.

< On it. >

৯৩

Lake Delta
Llanganatis, Ecuador

Tom woke up. He wasn't sure how long he had dozed off, but the sun was now overhead, and the sand was warm on their crescent of a beach. Jenny was still sleeping. He tried to be quiet as he unrolled from the thermal blanket. He wondered how long it would take Tarek to figure out they were in trouble and get another helicopter to rescue them. It had to be today, or they could be here awhile. Tomorrow's weather would ground most aircraft.

The ringing in his left ear was still there, and his right calf was sore. He must have pulled a muscle swimming to shore.

He added a couple of sticks to the fire and gathered the rest of the driftwood from the beach.

Although the sun felt warm and their clothes were drying out, that would all change when the sun went down. The temperature would drop quickly after sunset.

Some of the detritus from the explosion was drifting to shore, but nothing much useful, other than some rope. He collected everything into a neat pile by the shore. Tom started planning a lean-to with the extra thermal blankets.

Jenny stirred, rubbing her eyes. "What's that?" she asked as she unwrapped from the thermal blanket. She looked to the north. Then Tom heard it too, the thumping of a helicopter.

"Over there, Tom." She pointed to a speck on the horizon. "Tarek came through."

Tom added sticks to the fire for more smoke. A helicopter, camouflaged like the MD600N, but much larger, was rapidly approaching. They quickly donned their shirts and pants and then started waving the shiny thermal blankets.

Within two minutes, the chopper was hovering over them. The downdraft scattered all the driftwood Tom had collected and extinguished the fire. They both shielded their eyes from the flying sand.

Tom could see an airman in the large open door, who quickly attached his harness to a guy wire. He then descended on a winch controlled by another airman in the chopper. Once on the ground, the airman opened his collar and pointed to a patch of an American flag. Otherwise, he had no other identifying patches. It was too loud to try any meaningful conversation.

As the airman helped Jenny into the rescue harness, Tom yelled as loud as he could, pointing to her left chest. "She has a broken rib!"

After a thumbs up, the airman secured her and up she went, clutching her left chest. Tom followed.

Once they were onboard, the rescue door closed, and then the helicopter turned and left as quickly as it had arrived, heading northwest.

When Tom looked back at Lake Delta, the MD600N was gone, with debris floating everywhere.

The airman placed a headset on Jenny and then on Tom. He unfolded a large wool blanket and said, "This will keep you warm." He started to wrap one around Jenny first, but she grabbed Tom, and she wrapped them both in the same blanket. Tom hugged her gently.

The five crew members in the helicopter were clearly military.

"Who are you?" Tom yelled at the airman through the communication set. "Did Tarek send you?"

The airman yelled, "You're safe now. We're United States Navy. We are on our way back to Quito where a medic will check you over," he said to Jenny. Tom turned his head to hear with his right ear, his good ear.

The airman continued, "You'll then transfer to a military jet to transport you to Tolemaida Air Base in Melgar, near Bogotá. I'm not authorized to tell you more. Here's some coffee. It will help you both warm up."

The helicopter was much bigger and louder than the MD600N and also much faster. The pilot flew higher and did not follow the contours of the land like Paikea.

Jenny's breathing seemed more normal, but she was still rubbing the left side of her chest as she huddled next to Tom.

"How did Tarek contact you?" Tom finally asked into the headset.

Shaking his head from side to side, the airman who rescued them simply said, "I don't know who Tarek is."

The landscape changed as they left the páramo behind and descended from the mountains. The grass turned into scrub and then trees.

Tom noticed the airman had a video camera like Diego. Who was watching?

"Tom, you're bleeding," said Jenny, pointing to blood on the floor of the helicopter that she had traced back to his right leg.

He had forgotten about the pulled calf muscle.

The airman pulled up his cargo pants. "You'll be okay. A piece of shrapnel went through your calf. We will also get you some medical attention on the ground."

The airman touched his headset and nodded. He then handed the headset to Jenny. "Here, put these on. Someone wants to talk to you."

"Hey Jenny. This is Lucille Escot from Colombia. Do you remember me?"

"Of course I do. I still stay in touch with Pammy." Jenny's eyes and smile widened, which provided a sense of relief to Tom.

"I don't have a lot of time to talk, but you're safe now. You're heading back to Quito. We'll get you both checked out, and then you'll board a plane to Tolemaida Air Base in Melgar. I'll meet you there. It's about a two-hour car ride to Bogotá from Melgar. We can talk on the ride. You'll be in Bogotá a couple of days, and then we'll get you both home."

"It's good to hear a familiar voice. Did Tarek contact you? Will you let my parents know we're okay?"

"They already know. See you soon."

Once they landed in Quito, everything went quickly. A medic confirmed she likely had bruised, but not broken, her rib, and gave her some pain medicine. He also cleaned and bandaged Tom's wound.

The medic also tested them for COVID—still negative.

Before they could thank the rescue team, they were shuttled to an old, stubby looking jet with U.S. Navy markings. The pilot told them it was about a 90-minute flight to Tolemaida Air Base.

Tom wanted desperately to talk with Jenny, but they were on an open channel. He also still had a ringing in his left ear, but it might be improving. It was hard to tell with the jet engines.

Once in the air, he chuckled.

"What's so funny?" asked Jenny.

"I was just remembering our flight on the Gulfstream—and the flight attendant. Do you think this flight has beverage service?"

Jenny elbowed him in the ribs. She grunted too, as her pain medication had not yet kicked in. Tom thought he saw the pilot grin a little.

They both fell asleep and woke up on the approach to Tolemaida.

By the time they landed, Jenny's pain was much better. Everyone on the ground wore surgical masks. Had COVID worsened that much in one week?

∽∾

12:30 p.m. COT
Phone Call
Melgar, Colombia - Amherst, Vermont

Lucille had texted John as soon as Jenny and Tom were safe on the military helicopter. Now she had a moment to talk.

"It's over. They're safe and on the way to Tolemaida Air Base, where I'll meet them. I'll keep them in Bogotá for a couple of days for debriefing, but you'll be able to talk with Jenny in a few hours. I'm sorry I couldn't connect with you earlier, but things unfolded quickly when you sent the SOS from Tom.

"Here's what I uncovered. Miguel Titere was the CEO of a few corporations out of Nevis that listed some interesting people on their boards. He was the front for another individual, Omar Al Tajir, from the Middle East, who funded the expedition. Al Tajir recently moved to Colombia, where he likely connected with Titere. He has the resources, and we know him well in the intelligence community. He's ruthless.

"John, when you forwarded the SOS message, I scrambled a rescue helicopter from Quito. When the chopper arrived at the lake, the expedition helicopter was gone. The debris field suggested an explosion. We believe everyone on board perished."

Lucille waited a moment, but the line was quiet. "John, Ingrid, are you still there?"

John spoke first. "Sorry, Lucille, we don't know how to thank you. What would have happened if I hadn't texted you? This is a lot to process. Please let us know when we can talk to Jenny."

"Thank you, Lucille," said Ingrid. "Thank you...."

Debriefing

Thursday, March 19, 2020
Tolemaida Air Base
Melgar, Colombia

Lucille met Tom and Jenny at the air base. She was wearing a mask, but Jenny recognized her at once. After a gentle hug, being careful not to hurt Jenny's rib, Lucille ushered them to a waiting black limousine.

Before entering the limo, Jenny pulled Tom down for a gentle kiss and then whispered, "I love you" into his good ear, followed by a long embrace. For the first time since the explosion, Tom felt safe in Jenny's arms and hoped she felt the same.

"Jenny, what did I get you into? I'm so sorry."

"It's what did <u>we</u> get into—we. And I don't know, but hopefully, Lucille will fill us in."

Once everyone settled, Lucille signaled the driver and removed her mask.

"Nice to see you again, Jenny, and nice to meet you, Tom. I've heard so much about you from Dr. Westhoven. We'll cover a lot of ground over the next couple of days. On our ride to Bogotá, I'll ask some questions and then give you an overview of what we know. We'll have you home by the weekend.

"First question, did you find the gold?" asked Lucille, looking at Tom.

"How did you know we were looking for gold?" asked Tom.

"Dr. Westhoven. I connected with him this morning. He's much better, by the way, resting at home. He said to say hi. His wife took away his phone when he was in the hospital."

"Yes, we did find some Inca gold and silver, mostly gold, yesterday. We called it Lake Echo. I have the coordinates. Jenny and I found another smaller pile on sonar that may also be gold, but it was too deep for video confirmation."

"Thanks, Tom. Dr. Westhoven already sent us all the documents, but we didn't know about the smaller pile from Lake Echo."

Lucille opened the middle console. "Can I get either of you something to drink?"

"I'd love a Diet Coke," replied Jenny.

"Me, too," said Tom, although a Hipster Apocalypse would also go down nicely, he thought.

"So Tom, how did you get involved with the expedition?"

Tom explained he'd met Dr. Westhoven through his advisor at the University of Maine, Dr. Gordon Wade, who had forwarded his capstone to Dr. Westhoven for review.

"I first met him on a Zoom call around Thanksgiving in 2018. He is the editor of *Modern Archaeology*, and he asked me to condense my capstone into a commentary piece for the journal. Then he invited me to present the paper at a conference in Boston about a year ago last February. At the conference, he approached me about joining him on a project. He explained that an associate in South America had the idea of looking for the lost Inca gold underwater using satellites and artificial intelligence. That was Miguel Titere. My role was to program a convolutional neural network, a type of artificial intelligence, to find the gold. That was partly what my capstone and conference presentation were about."

Tom continued, "I don't know how long Dr. Westhoven or Miguel had been hatching this idea. It didn't seem too long to me at the time, but I did incidentally meet Tarek, the base camp manager, at the conference as well. I don't remember his last name. He asked me a question about training data sets. At base camp, Miguel did not seem to know him that well, or know that Tarek was at the conference. That seemed odd. I don't know how to put this together.

"It took me a while to commit. I wasn't convinced there was gold to find in the Llanganatis, but once we did commit," he said, looking at Jenny, "it was a full-time job. There was no training data set, so we created one out of plastic. I never thought we had a shot at finding the lost Inca gold with plastic."

"What did you find on the other lakes? Dr. Westhoven wasn't sure," asked Lucille.

"We did find anomalies. Lake Alpha, the first lake, was a pile of rocks. At Lake Bravo, we found an Inca sacrificial site. In the third lake, Lake Charlie, we found a shattered canoe with limbed trees in the middle of the lake. It looked like the Incas were building or repairing boats. All three lakes fooled the neural network."

"Are the lakes named in order of the visits?"

"That was the intent, but Miguel changed the order of Lake Delta and Lake Echo. We found the gold at Lake Echo yesterday. Today was Lake Delta. I asked him why he flipped the order of the last two lakes. He said it had to do with logistics."

Lucille then turned to Jenny. "Tell me about today."

"Today was like the first four days, except we slept in after celebrating last night," said Jenny. "And the weather today was the best all week. After our COVID testing and morning briefing, we headed to Lake Delta. It was about a thirty-minute ride."

Jenny took a slow sip of her drink. "All we found today was a pile of bricks and other debris. The Incas didn't use bricks. It didn't make any sense. Then, on our way to shore to set up the satellite uplink, the helicopter exploded."

Jenny became silent as she reflected on the events of the day. She squeezed Tom's hand. After a deep breath, she asked, "Lucille, what really happened today? How did you find us?"

"I still have a lot of questions, but you deserve an explanation. Briefly, your dad reached out to me Tuesday to check into the expedition. I found out that the Ecuadorian government had not issued permits. That was the first red flag.

"Then I checked into Miguel Titere. He ran a reputable business, but Antiquities South did not have the revenue to fund the expedition. That was the second red flag.

"So, I started looking at his business associations. I found several connections to a person we call Omar Al Tajir, a known arms dealer, who is on every watchlist we have. He's cold-blooded.

"Al Tajir had recently moved to Cartagena, Colombia. He has the resources and the finances. That was the final red flag."

Tom interjected, "We never heard about an arms dealer. In fact, we only met Miguel for the first time this week. Dr. Westhoven had done all the talking with Miguel."

"I know," said Lucille. "Dr. Westhoven said the same thing. This is typical. Al Tajir always has a front man, or middleman, at least one person between him and his dirty deeds. For this expedition, he had two. Titere was the front man, and Tarek Sharif was the henchman.

"I contacted my counterpart in Quito to let them know the situation. The plan was to monitor the situation and only intervene if necessary. What we didn't know is that Al Tajir had booby-trapped the helicopter."

"What?!" exclaimed Tom and Jenny in unison.

"We recovered evidence of EPX-1, a plastic explosive, from the tail in the debris field. Al Tajir wanted you all dead.

"And your meeting Sharif a year ago at the conference was not a coincidence. He was involved from the beginning. He's gone missing in the Llanganatis."

By now, they were entering a suburb of Bogotá.

"We recovered the body of the diver and pilot but not Miguel, but we presume him to be dead, as well.

"You know, Tom, your quick action saved Jenny's life. Our divers recovered the Zodiac. The explosion shredded it. A large piece of shrapnel hit the bow where you were sitting," said Lucille, as she looked directly at Jenny, who was inadvertently rubbing her bruised rib.

"Tom prevented a direct hit. Also, the SOS signal saved a lot of reconnaissance. We knew exactly where you were."

Lucille let the events of the day settle. There would be plenty of time over the next couple of days to fill in the details.

"When we get to the Embassy, I'll show you to your room. Jenny, I've set up a video call with your parents. Tom, I can do the same with your parents."

"That's okay," replied Tom. "They think this was a routine expedition. I'll pop them a quick text message that the expedition is over, and we'll be home this weekend. Thank you, though."

"When you talk to your family and friends, remember that what happened in the Llanganatis is classified. Jenny, your dad still has high-level clearance, but please don't get into any details and do not tell anyone else you found gold. Understood?"

They both solemnly nodded their heads.

When they arrived at the Embassy, Jenny remembered a lot about the compound. She would show Tom around later.

Lucille showed them to their room. There was a computer already set up for a Zoom call, but she knew her parents preferred FaceTime.

"I'm going to take a quick shower. I still feel a little chilled," said Tom. He also wanted to give her some privacy during the FaceTime.

"Sounds good. I'll call my parents and get that out of the way." She was expecting them, especially her father, to be upset. She texted them she would FaceTime in about five minutes.

She waited until she heard the shower start and then plugged in her Air Pods to place the call. As the FaceTime image stabilized, she could see her parents were huddled around the computer in her father's upstairs study. They looked distraught. Her dad was the first to speak.

"Jenny, are you okay? I can't believe Tom dragged you along on this disaster." He was angry and not hiding it well.

She was glad Tom was in the shower, and she had her Air Pods in. "Yeah. I'm fine. Tom is okay too. He saved my life."

"He wouldn't have had to save your life if he hadn't taken you on this ridiculous adventure."

Jenny took as deep a breath as she could muster, with the pain in her rib.

"Let's be clear, Dad." Her voice wavered a little. "Tom did not ask me to go. In fact, he was adamant that I not go. We got into a huge fight, and I went behind his back and forced my way onto the expedition. It is not his fault."

After an uncomfortable silence, her mother spoke. "We can talk more about this later. The important thing is that you and Tom are okay, other than a bruised rib and Tom's cut."

Thankfully, Lucille had not exaggerated their injuries.

Her mom continued, "Lucille didn't tell us much, except there was an explosion. We're just grateful you're okay, and Tom, too."

Another uncomfortable silence.

"When are you headed back?" her mother finally asked.

"I'm not sure, but I think this weekend. We're obviously not flying back on the private jet."

Her dad finally spoke in his usual calmer, more reassuring voice. "Let us know when you find out. Lucille will help, I'm sure."

Her mom followed. "Do you know your schedule for the next day or two?"

"Lucille is debriefing us tomorrow, whatever that means. I'd like to show Tom around Bogotá a little, but it's been so long, I'd probably get lost."

Her dad shifted in his seat, visibly uncomfortable. "Lucille mentioned the Arab character is still at large. He doesn't sound like someone who gives up easily. Don't leave the compound unless it's okay with Lucille."

"We won't. Let's talk tomorrow afternoon. I should know better by then when we'll be back in Bangor. And don't be angry with Tom. This guy fooled everyone, including Dr. Westhoven and Miguel, who lost his life. Tom was never gung-ho about this expedition. I pushed him along. If you need to be angry with someone, be angry with me."

Jenny wanted to end the call on a positive note. "What do you think of using your Christmas gift certificate to come visit next week? School will be back in session, but all the classes are online. We'd love to see you."

Her mom was the first to respond. "We'd love to. I think we both need to see that you're all right. Let's talk tomorrow. Say hi to Tom."

Tom came out of the shower as Jenny signed off. She'd expected her parents to be upset, but she was still a little surprised at how angry her dad was. Hopefully, she cleared things up.

"How did the call go?"

"About as well as I expected. It's all good and I think my parents are coming over next week to visit."

"Great, I think. I just assumed they would be upset with me for taking you along on this expedition."

With a sigh, "You didn't <u>take</u> me along. I volunteered and I'm glad I did. This would have ended differently if I hadn't gone along with you, and my father hadn't called Lucille. And, well, you get the picture.

"And yes, they were pissed off, but it's all good, and they said to say hi."

After his shower, Tom sent his mom and dad a simple text that the expedition went well, and they'd be back in Bangor by the weekend. He didn't mention anything about the gold, the explosion, the rescue, or that he was in Bogotá. He told them that Jenny's parents may visit next week and suggested this might be a good chance to meet them. His parents still did not know how to Zoom call, and they were not yet comfortable with their Echo Show. They typically left it unplugged to save electricity. He said he would call them tomorrow.

Tom and Jenny were both exhausted. After a quick dinner in the room, they went to bed, which they appreciated after a week in sleeping bags.

"How's your rib?" asked Tom.

"Better. How's your leg?"

"Not too bad either. Are you thinking what I'm thinking?"

Evidently, she was, as she gingerly rolled over onto Tom.

❧❦

Friday, March 20, 2020
American Embassy
Bogotá, Colombia

Lucille let them sleep in the next morning. They spent most of Friday morning reviewing what they had talked about the day before, but in more detail. Lucille asked a lot of questions.

By early afternoon, she was wrapping up. "One more thing, Al Tajir and Sharif are still at large." She looked somber. "Until we track them down, you may still be at risk. Now that he's tasted gold," she said, looking directly at Tom and then Jenny, "he may need you more than ever. Please be careful. Report anything unusual when you get back home. Until we know his whereabouts, we'll monitor your communications, but he will expect that."

Surprised, Jenny said, "This sounds serious. I thought this was over."

"He's ruthless, and we need to play this game at his level. I doubt he'll leave hundreds of millions of dollars of gold in the Llanganatis."

Lucille paused a moment.

"Let me change gears. Tom, I had some people from NSA, sorry, the National Security Agency, look at your neural network."

"How did you get it? I encrypted it."

She just smiled. "They tell me what you accomplished without a defined training data set was brilliant. I can see why Dr. Westhoven sought you out. They were impressed."

Lucille folded her hands together and took a breath. "Well, things are pretty much wrapped up here. Rob and I are hoping we can take you two out to dinner tonight, no business, just pleasure. Jenny, we'd love to hear about Vermont and just catch up."

"That would be great, Lucille. By the way, do you know when we leave tomorrow?"

"The jet leaves about ten. It'll be military and fly direct to the Mainiac Air National Guard Base in Bangor. It won't be as nice as the Gulfstream, but it'll get you home. You'll be in Bangor by four o'clock local time, and you won't need to go through customs.

"And Tom, Dr. Westhoven hoped to connect with you this afternoon. He's eager to hear about what you found in Lake Bravo. I've set up a video call in your room. He said to text him when you're ready. Apparently, his wife gave him back his phone, which I take to be a good sign.

"And remember, you're not allowed to talk about the expedition or what you found with anyone other than Dr. Westhoven and Jenny's dad. Understood?"

Again, they both nodded.

"Good. We'll swing by and pick you up around five."

When Jenny spoke to her parents in the afternoon, they were more back to normal, discussing their visit for the coming week. Her dad was a little subdued, but finally spoke. "Look Jenny, I want to apologize for yesterday. I was upset. The thought of losing you was too much. I'm sorry."

"That means a lot, Daddy. Thank you." She saw her mom give him a big hug and a kiss on the cheek.

Tom also phoned his parents. They were excited about meeting Jenny's parents. He casually mentioned that he had pulled a calf muscle so they wouldn't ask about his limp.

While Jenny showered, he called Dr. Westhoven, who looked gaunt on the video call, with a lingering dry cough, but he was in good spirits. He still couldn't smell.

"Thank God you and Jenny are okay. What a disaster. I'm so sorry, Tom. I had no idea. I still can't believe Miguel is dead. Are you two really okay?"

"I'm sorry about Miguel. I know he was a friend and a reputable man. We're okay, other than some bumps and bruises."

Dr. Westhoven looked down at his desk as he tried to stifle a cough. "I hope they catch Al Tajir and Sharif quickly."

After another cough, Dr. Westhoven returned his gaze to the monitor. "You did it, Tom. You did it. You actually found the gold. Unbelievable."

"We did it," replied Tom.

"Let's be honest, Tom. I handed you some lakes and a kick in the ass every once in a while. I know Jenny was important, too, but this was essentially all you. When I read your capstone, I knew you were the one I needed for this project."

"Thanks, Dr. Westhoven. It's too bad we can't publish."

"It's also too bad we don't get to share any of the gold." Dr. Westhoven looked contemplative. "I wonder if once the Ecuadorian government recovers the gold, we might be able to publish. From their perspective, this might be a wonderful tourist attraction to the Llanganatis."

Dr. Westhoven leaned into the camera, which distorted his face. "Regardless, I expect a lot of interesting articles from you, including the two you already owe me." He leaned back with a slight smile.

"Now tell me what you found at Lake Bravo. We definitely need a return visit, but this time, we'll do it by the book," said Dr. Westhoven. "I'll make sure we cross all the t's with proper funding."

"I'm not sure, but it looked like a half a dozen sacrificial sites are scattered throughout the lake. There must have been a significant Inca settlement nearby."

"I agree, Tom. I've already reached out to Dr. Parcak to see if she could look at the region around the lake for any evidence of an old Inca settlement."

Dr. Westhoven then looked contemplative again. "One last thing, Tom. I'm going to be a little philosophical. One of my mentors told me this when I was a graduate student. The secret to success is to get used to it. Don't let the fear of failure ever get in your way. I know you struggled from the beginning, but this is what happens when you persevere. Expect success, but accept failure. They're part of the same continuum."

All Tom could do was nod his head. "Thanks, Dr. Westhoven."

∾

Saturday, March 21, 2020
Bogotá, Colombia to Mainiac ANG Base, Bangor, Maine

The flight back was on a transport jet. They sat behind the pilot and co-pilot, and it was comfortable but still loud, which was good, thought Tom. His hearing was mostly back to normal. About halfway home, over the eastern seaboard, he realized his fear of flying was gone. All it had taken was a week in a helicopter, topped off by an explosion.

They were back in their apartment by five o'clock with a bottle of Andes Cold Duck.

"I can't believe the algorithm worked," said Tom, staring blankly at the topographical map of Maine he had given Jenny for her birthday.

His eyes settled on the star at Nahmakanta.

Jenny noticed. "You want to play Nahmakanta?"

Camping with Jenny was fun…

Nevis

Saturday, April 18, 2020
Bangor, Maine

The expedition seemed like a distant memory, even though preparing for it had consumed the better part of a year. It took a week or two for both Tom and Jenny to dry out from the constant dampness of the Llanganatis, and it would also be a while before they could eat steamers again, with the stink of clam flats still imprinted.

By now, COVID was taking off across the country. President Trump's declaration that life would be back to normal by Easter, which had sounded silly at the time, was now simply foolish.

Earlier this week, Lucille had reached out to Tom and Jenny for a final meeting this morning. She didn't give any reason other than she wanted to clean up some loose ends. She sent Tom an application yesterday to install on his laptop to encrypt the call. Lucille started the video at eleven o'clock.

"Good morning, guys. How are you doing?"

"All the classes are now virtual, so we're together all day long, and we're not driving each other crazy—yet," said Tom. Jenny just rolled her eyes.

"That's great." Lucille matched Tom's smile. "Enjoy this weird time. It will end eventually, and hopefully you'll have some pleasant memories amid all this craziness.

"I have a few things to follow-up. First, Jenny, how are your ribs? And Tom, your leg?"

Jenny lifted both arms over her head. "All better."

Tom replied, "A lot better. I even jogged a little last week."

"Great. Well, we finally have Al Tajir and Sharif in custody. Al Tajir is negotiating, but he doesn't have much to negotiate with at this point."

Tom and Jenny had forgotten Al Tajir and Tarek had still been on the loose.

"That's great news. Thanks, Lucille," said Jenny.

Lucille looked down at some notes.

"Tom, remember when I told you in Bogotá that you impressed the folks at NSA with your work? I was serious. They asked me to explore some type of relationship with you, formal or otherwise. I know you're planning a doctoral program at Yale, or at least that's what Dr. Westhoven tells me. There are ways we can structure this around your studies and help pay for your degree. You have a remarkable talent. Your skills would be put to practical use."

This was a surprise for Tom. He imagined what he could do with access to government supercomputers. And graduate school cost a fortune.

"I'll definitely give it some thought. How do I learn more?" asked Tom.

"Great. I'll set up a phone call next week."

Lucille checked her notes again.

"I also wanted to let you know the divers found a pile of bricks and old plates and jars in Lake Delta at the target coordinates. Al Tajir had placed a fake pile of gold in Lake Delta to test your neural network. So, you actually found two piles of gold, the real one in Lake Echo and his fake one in Lake Delta.

"Finally, the Ecuadorian government also wanted to thank you both, in a more tangible way. They are even calling it *Lago Echo,* and they're pleased, very pleased indeed. And the other, smaller pile you found on sonar was also gold. They suspect even more is still hidden in the lakes of the Llanganatis.

"To show their appreciation, the government set up a joint account for you two in Nevis. Ecuador doesn't give away money, so don't be surprised if they ask for your help to find more of the gold."

"Where's Nevis?" Tom asked.

Lucille smiled again. "Nevis is a haven for offshore accounts, accounts that are difficult to trace. I'll send each of you a secure email, which will have a link to your joint account with a unique account number for each of you. You'll also each receive another secure email directly from the bank with a unique password for each of you. To access the account, you'll need both account numbers and the corresponding passwords.

"And please don't lose the passwords. The nature of an offshore account is that it's difficult to recover your account if you lose the password.

"That's it. Do you guys have any questions for me?"

"Thank you, Lucille, for taking such good care of Tom and me. If you hadn't been so thorough, this would have had a different ending. Thanks."

"You're welcome. Maybe we can all connect in Vermont at some point when COVID quiets down. Your dad is still trying to sell Rob the camp a couple of lots down from your parent's house."

After the call, Jenny said, "No Such Agency."

"What?" asked Tom.

"NSA—No Such Agency. That's what it's called in intelligence circles. I can't believe this fell into your lap. This is a big deal. You need to give this some careful consideration. Think through the ramifications."

Tom was still planning on a doctoral degree in archaeology, but he also enjoyed the simple pleasures of programming. Perhaps there was a way to integrate everything. He imagined being a student with a side gig with the NSA and another looking for hidden treasure in the Llanganatis.

"What are you smiling about?" asked Jenny.

"I always wanted to be a spy. Will I get a sports car?"

"Tom, it feels like you're rushing into this. Don't you think you should think this through? Remember, if you go with your gut..."

"It comes out crap," answered Tom with a big grin. "Nope, you were right. I spend too much time deliberating about this stuff. This feels right."

"Okay, but you'll need a new 'crappy' cliché."

When they checked, each had an email from Lucille with a unique account number. The two other emails from the National Bank of Nevis were in their spam folders. If Lucille hadn't given them a heads up, they never would have seen them.

"Maybe it's an all-expense paid trip to the Llanganatis," joked Jenny.

Tom chuckled and then did not. "It better not be. Whatever it is, it has a lot of security."

The emails from the bank were identical, except for the hyperlink to a secure file server to retrieve their individual passwords. Each unique password was twenty-one characters long.

Tom then clicked on the hyperlink to the National Bank of Nevis. The log-in screen appeared. He entered his account number and his password, and then Jenny entered hers. No other form of identification was required. No callback numbers, no dual authentication, no CAPCHA, nothing.

The log-in button was now highlighted, and Tom clicked it.

Nothing happened for a few seconds, but Tom could tell the connection was active.

Finally, the screen presented the dashboard for their account, displaying their names with the account balance at the top.

Without saying a word, Tom got up, headed to the fridge, pulled out a bottle of André Cold Duck, popped the plastic cork, and grabbed a couple of paper cups. Jenny was counting the zeros over and over again while he poured.

"Four, five, six zeros, Tom—five million dollars!"

COVID or not, life was good....

Valverde's Derrotero

English Translation of Valverde's Derrotero's Notes by Richard Spruce

Placed in the town of Pillaro, ask for the farm of Moya, and sleep (the first night) a good distance above it; and ask there for the mountain of Guapa, from whose top, if the day be fine, look to the east, so that thy back be towards the town of Ambato, and from thence thou shalt perceive the three Cerros Llanganati, in the form of a triangle, on whose declivity there is a lake, made by hand, into which the ancients threw the gold they had prepared for the ransom of the Inca when they heard of his death. From the same Cerro Guapa thou mayest see also the forest, and in it a clump of *Sangurimas* standing out of the said forest, and another clump which they call *Flechas* (arrows), and these clumps are the principal mark for the which thou shalt aim, leaving them a little on the left hand. Go forward from Guapa in the direction and with the signals indicated, and a good way ahead, having passed some cattle-farms, thou shalt come on a wide morass, over which thou must cross, and coming out on the other side thou shalt see on the left-hand a short way off a *jucál* on a hill-side, through which thou must pass. Having got through the *jucál*, thou wilt see two small lakes called "Los Anteojos" (the spectacles), from having between them a point of land like to a nose.

From this place thou mayest again descry the Cerros Llanganati, the same as thou sawest them from the top of Guapa, and I warn thee to leave the said lakes on the left, and that in front of the point or "nose" there is a plain, which is the sleeping-place. There thou must leave thy horses, for they can go no farther. Following now on foot in the same direction, thou shalt come on a great black lake, the which leave on thy left-hand, and beyond it seek to descend along the hill-side in such a way that thou mayest reach a ravine, down which comes a waterfall: and here thou shalt find a bridge of three poles, or if it do not still exist thou shalt put another in the most convenient place and pass over it. And having gone on a little way in the forest, seek out the hut which served to sleep in or the remains of it. Having passed the night there, go on thy way the following day through the forest in the same direction, till thou reach another deep dry ravine, across which thou must throw a bridge and pass over it slowly and cautiously, for the ravine is very deep; that is if thou succeed not in finding the pass which exists. Go forward and look for the signs of another sleeping-place, which, I assure thee, thou canst not fail to see in the fragments of pottery and other marks, because the Indians are continually passing along there. Go on thy way, and thou shalt see a mountain which is all of *margasitas* (pyrites), the which leave on the left-hand, and I warn thee that thou must go round it in this fashion *(The Valverde mark)*. On this side thou wilt find a *pajonál* (pasture) in a small plain, which having crossed thou wilt come on a *cañon* between two hills, which is the way of the Inca. From thence as thou goest along thou shalt see the entrance of the *socabón* (tunnel), which is in the form of a church-porch. Having come through the cañon, and gone a good distance beyond, thou wilt perceive a cascade which descends from an offshoot of the Cerro Llanganati, and runs into a quaking-bog on the right hand; and without passing the stream in the said bog there is much gold, so that putting in thy hand what thou shalt gather at the bottom is grains of gold. To ascend the mountain, leave the bog and go along to the right, and pass above the cascade, going round the offshoot of the mountain. And if by chance the mouth of the socabón be closed with certain herbs which they call "salvaje," remove them, and thou wilt find the entrance. And on the left-hand side of the mountain thou mayest see the "Guayra" (for thus the ancients called the furnace where they founded metals), which is nailed with golden nails. And to reach the third mountain, if thou canst not pass in front of the socabón, it is the same thing to pass behind it, for the water of the lake falls into it.

If thou lose thyself in the forest, seek the river, follow it on the right bank; lower down take to the beach, and thou wilt reach the cañon in such sort that, although thou seek to pass it, thou wilt not find where; climb, therefore, the mountain on the right-hand, and in this manner thou canst by no means miss thy way.

SPRUCE, Richard On the Mountains of Llanganati in the Eastern Cordillera of the Quitonian Andes Illustrated by a Map Constructed by the Late Don Atansio Guzman, Vol. 31, Isha Books, 1861, pp. 177-178.

Bibliography

Adams, Mark. *Turn Right at Machu Picchu.* Dunton, 2011.

Bingham, Hiram. *The Lost City of the Incas.* London: Weidenfeld & Nicholson, 1952.

Charbonneau, Steven. *Lust for Inca Gold: The Llanganati Treasure Story & Maps.* CreateSpace Independent Publishing Platform, 2012.

Crichton, Michael. *Congo.* New York, New York: Alfred A. Knopf, Inc., 1980.

"The Dunning-Kruger Effect" https://en.wikipedia.org/wiki/Dunning%E2%80%93Kruger_effect (Accessed May 1, 2024).

Faux, Jennifer L. "Hail the Conquering Gods: Ritual Sacrifice of Children in Inca Society." *Journal of Contemporary Anthropology,* Volume III, Issue 1 (2012). https://www.google.com/url?sa=t&source=web&rct=j&opi=89978449&url=https://docs.lib.purdue.edu/cgi/viewcontent.cgi%3Farticle%3D1017%26context%3Djca&ved=2ahUKEwjZmLPf8f6FAxVGEFkFHeM2BKwQFnoECA4QAQ&usg=AOvVaw0JUqRmmd7sl32-k415Sbz2. (Accessed October 15, 2023).

Finkel, Michael. *The Stranger in the Woods: The Extraordinary Story of the Last True Hermit.* Deckle Edge, 2017.

Grann, David. *The Lost City of Z.* Vintage Books, 2005.

Hemming, John. *The Conquest of the Incas.* Mariner Books, 2003.

Honigsbaum, Mark. *Valverde's Gold: In Search of the Last Great Inca Treasure.* New York, New York: Farrar, Straus, and Giroux, 2004.

IBM. "What is deep learning." https://www.ibm.com/cloud/learn/deep-learning (Accessed October 1, 2023).

Lourie, Peter. *Sweat of the Sun, Tears of the Moon.* Bison Books, 1998.

MacQuarrie, Kim. *The Last Days of the Incas.* Simon & Schuster, 2008.

McCarthy, John, Marvin L. Minsky, Nathaniel Rochester, and Claude E. Shannon. 2006. "A Proposal for the Dartmouth Summer Research Project on Artificial Intelligence, August 31, 1955." http://jmc.stanford.edu/articles/dartmouth/dartmouth.pdf. (Accessed October 1, 2023).

McEwan, Gordon F. *The Incas: New Perspectives.* New York, New York: W. W. Norton, 2006.

MetroBlue. "Simulated historical climate & weather data for Cordillera de los Llanganates." https://www.meteoblue.com/en/weather/historyclimate/climatemodelled/cordillera-de-los-llanganates_ecuador_3654710. (Accessed October 1, 2023).

Parcak, Sarah H. *Archaeology from Space: How the Future Shapes Our Past.* New York, New York: Henry Holt and Co, 2019.

———. *Satellite Remote Sensing for Archaeology.* Routledge, 2009.

Spruce, Richard. *On the Mountains of Llanganati in the Eastern Cordillera of the Quitonian Andes Illustrated by a Map Constructed by the Late Don Atansio Guzman* vol-31. Isha Books, 1861.

Thubron, Colin. *To the Lost City.* London: Chatto & Windus, 2002.

About the Author

 The author grew up in Rockland, Maine and practiced internal medicine in Bangor, Maine at St. Joseph Hospital.

His interest in programming dates back to the 1980s when he developed an electronic medical record for primary care, and was an early adopter of predictive analytics, a type of artificial intelligence.

Dr. Wood attended the University of Maine, where he was inducted into Phi Beta Kappa and Phi Kappa Phi.

His medical degree was from Dartmouth Medical School (now called Geisel School of Medicine) and he completed his residency at the Mount Auburn Hospital in Cambridge, Massachusetts, an affiliate of Harvard Medical School.

He and his wife still live in Bangor, where they raised their two boys, who are now scattered.

Thank you!

I truly hope you enjoyed *The Lost Inca Gold.*

If you have a moment, I'd be grateful if you could leave a short review on Amazon or your favorite platform, even if it's only a few words. Your review helps authors like me connect with new readers.

And don't forget to check out www.TheLostIncaGold.com for more fun stuff and behind-the-scenes information.

With warmest regards,

Bill